PACIFIC REDWOOD MYSTERY

DO YOU BELIEVE IN THE LITTLE PEOPLE YET?

d.l. Brooks

Pacific Redwood Mystery
Copyright © 2023 by d.l. Brooks

ISBN:
Paperback: 978-1-63945-620-8
e-book: 978-1-63945-621-5

All rights reserved. No part of this publication may be reproduced, distributed, or transmitted in any form or by any means, including photocopying, recording, or other electronic or mechanical methods, without the prior written permission of the publisher, except in the case brief quotations embodied in critical reviews and other noncommercial uses permitted by copyright law.

The views expressed in this book are solely those of the author and do not necessarily reflect the views of the publisher, and the publisher hereby disclaims any responsibility for them.

Writers' Branding
1-877-608-6550
www.writersbranding.com
media@writersbranding.com

Contents

DEDICATION v
ACKNOWLEDGMENT vi
INTRODUCTION vii
CHAPTER ONE 1
CHAPTER TWO 6
CHAPTER THREE.. 13
CHAPTER FOUR 20
CHAPTER FIVE.. 35
CHAPTER SIX 40
CHAPTER SEVEN.. 48
CHAPTER EIGHT 56
CHAPTER NINE... 63
CHAPTER TEN.. 84
CHAPTER ELEVEN 94
CHAPTER TWELVE 106
CHAPTER THIRTEEN 124
CHAPTER FOURTEEN 140
CHAPTER FIFTEEN 154
CHAPTER SIXTEEN.. 168
CHAPTER SEVENTEEN 176
CHAPTER EIGHTEEN... 185
CHAPTER NINETEEN... 204

CHAPTER TWENTY	221
CHAPTER TWENTY-ONE	234
CHAPTER TWENTY-TWO	241
CHAPTER TWENTY-THREE	253
CHAPTER TWENTY-FOUR	264
CHAPTER TWENTY-FIVE	276

DEDICATION

To a family that loved deeply, suspended in time by two small figures hardly old enough to remember. For Mary and Peter that demanded justice for them only to be struck by an angel of the devil. Their spirits were felt strongly in re-living this story. They will be seen again when the sun shines through those Redwoods where the meadow lies.

For her two precious little children where ever they may be, but find them she will as Peter stands watch until they meet once again for eternity.

ACKNOWLEDGMENT

Most grateful to My Lord and Savior. My family for their support and belief in me. There is always someone that is forgotten and feelings get so hurt, so to avoid that, I will not name anyone except three people that are extremely responsible for helping me get to this point and beyond.

Nancy Edwards, from the beginning, her unconditional friendship and support in every step of this journey. For Russell Means, our amazing talented actor and speaker for All Native American Heritage. To Leonard Peltier, A Native American activist and militant member of the American Indian Movement. Please see the Web. For further information, an innocent man with proof beyond your normal investigation, but a spirit taken for freedom just to serve justice to close a case that would have rocked the world of our government justice system. My prayer for you Russell, be at peace across the veil with all those you cared for and those you were destined to meet.

I do remember all those that have been part of my life. My only son and three daughters, always in my heart and on my mind. The heart rules emotions while the mind makes choices and decisions. When put together and used wisely you can conquer your dreams. Make sure you do that Johndavid & Kinda Flores, Harold Rile Jr., Savannah, Sweet Ilene Niccole Martinez, Rebeka & Jisung,, Ryden, Tyler, and Madison. I can not forget my Hero's that brought such beauty into my life, "Sonia and Anthony."

Thank you **Art Hai Tuan**, for completing my life with all the blessings, strength, endurance and unconditional love to achieve our Destiny.

INTRODUCTION

What is so amazing is the fact that even with today's forensic knowledge, some seem to still walk away, but we must remember no matter how long it takes, "You can run but you cannot hide." That phrase should always hold true to those that have the power to solve crimes or know facts they keep hidden inside about any crime.

It is only time and long over due like so many stories untold, this murder is exactly that; still unsolved with someone knowing what happened. The truth is actually in print from the beginning, but no one took the time to notice or bring everything full circle. Why? A good question. It is hard to accept when you might be a mother, wife, co worker, friend or family member. Yes, that is hard and I acknowledge any family or friend that has had to endure such a nightmare.

I tell this story with tears in my eyes, not just for me emotionally telling the story, but also for all those that carry the burden. Can we forgive? I do not know, all I know is that after forty-five years I believe along with this family there is a God and we look for justice. Sometimes justice is not for the hands that commit the act itself but your voice has to count, theirs didn't. So I acknowledge the person herself. For the life one led, although short it was, she truly lived and loved before she was abruptly taken from this earth. I miss you Ellen Marie, but I know you are playing among the redwoods near the ocean.

CHAPTER ONE

Katie Lee stopped playing as she heard her little spotted puppy jumping wildly barking continuously near the woodpile. Her mother shouted from the porch while hanging clothes as the wind whipped in the winder breeze. "Katie Lee, shut that pup up or I am going to give her away." Katie Lee was trying to quiet the little pup as her mother's were exactly to the point and she knew they would be carried out if she got mad enough. Patting her hands across her knees she kept called to the little fella. "Penny get over here, stop barking, stop it." She tried pulling the mutt away from the woodpile but without luck. "It is probably old man Steven's car, Mom." She looked at her mother with hope of understanding. The small pet was the only thing that kept Katie Lee content, without her there would be no one distracting her intolerable life.

Turning with hands on her hips and leaning forward in the direction of her daughter, her mother yelled. "Katie Lee, get over there and get that dog away from that pile, right now!" Her mother was standing firm, Katie Lee noticed her other siblings coming to see what the commotion was all about. She saw her stepbrother coming on the porch as he began making his usual faces. "Let me get dad's gun and just shoot the darn thing." Charles David spoke out laughing towards Katie Lee knowing it hurt her. With fear racing through her she struggles with Penny to get her away from the woodpile but she continued returning with her aggressive bark for such a small pup.

Surprisingly, her oldest stepsister came from the barn smiling while motioning for Katie Lee to wait. As she approached Katie Lee she said nothing but the look of assurance on her face was the only peaceful feeling Katie Lee connected with. As her stepsister bent down to pick up the pup she wiggled fiercely making the task harder. Seeing Katie Lee almost in a panic of what her mother would do, she had mercy on the little girl. "Let's move some of the wood from the pile and I will take the cat back to Mr. Stevens, you take Penny into the barn until dinner." Patting her little stepsisters on the shoulder she saw a sigh of relief as Katie Lee held the pup firmly with one hand. "Hurry up you two, there is work to be done. Neither of you have time for that stupid dog." Both girls glanced at Mina as she continued hanging clothes on the line.

Looking up from where she was standing with her little stepsister Vera could see dark clouds forming in a circular motion across the sky. "Come on sweetie, let's get this done we can take your pup to the barn when we are done. I think we are about ready to have rain and maybe some lightening." She thought to herself that if that happened even though her father had made a clothes line on the porch for her stepmother, she would be angry complaining all day about how much longer it would take for the clothes to dry. Vera motioned for the little girl to just move the top row of the wood pile. Katie Lee started to throw the wood to one side, then without any warning something came flying out from the pile where they stood. Vera yelled staggering backwards landing on the ground. The pup jumped to the ground as Katie Lee looked in utter astonishment, throwing her arms up in front of her face. Everyone turned and they saw the little creature cut across the woodpile down the path to the barn and out of sight. Suddenly Vera pulled herself up off he ground as the pup began wiping her little paws across her eyes and rubbing them at the same time.

"Mina, Mina come quick." Vera was yelling as her stepmother jumped off the porch getting closer.. She was instantly struck by the scent. "Oh my God, Katie Lee you stink horrible. He sprayed you good little girl." Vera was walking backwards as far as she could to avoid the smell, the other kids came running but quickly retreated back on the porch. Skunk, everyone yelled laughing while pointing at Katie Lee. Taking her youngest daughter by the hand leading her to the middle of the front yard. Her stepmother demanded Charles David to bring the washtubs. "Stop rubbing your eyes, you will only make it worse, now take your clothes off and give everything to me right now." Katie Lee began to plea with her mother that she couldn't take her clothes off there, could she go to her room and change? But no was the answer, she was firmly told she would not enter the house until that smell was totally gone. Vera watched as her stepmother was just being her abusive self, she tried to come close but the smell was over powering. Vera rushed into the house grabbing a large towel while hitting her brother in the ribs on the way in. Hearing him grunt knowing she got a good hit, that was meant for his laughing, made her feel good as she rushed back out past him.

As Charles David came carrying the tub around holding his side he began to laugh harder making fun of his little stepsister that was standing there without one strip of clothing on her little body. Trying to cover what she could by folding her arms in front of her, her stepmother slapped her hand pushing them to her side. "Bring the water hose over here Charles David." His stepmother's firm voice bellowed out, motioning for him to fill the rub as she went into the house. When she was out of sight Charles David deliberately turned the cold water from the hose on his little stepsister. Mocking and taunting her a she started crying begging him to stop but the other children on the porch were egging him on making their own jokes poking fun. Katie Lee noticed her only blood sister coming from the neighbors just over the hill. "What have you done now Katie Lee?" Returning with a towel Vera started down the steps intervening between the two girls. "Just get into the house Ellen she got sprayed by a skunk, it was not her fault." Ellen gave her little sister a dirty look as she leaned over pulling her hair as she passed. Vera stood there but not very long due to the horrible scent that was so strong. Feeling terrible sorry for Katie Lee it was just too much for anyone to stand that close. She was on her own, it was not worth getting into any situation with her stepmother.

As her mother came back out giving orders like a drill sergeant, she had a pan of red liquid. Katie Lee asked what it was and what she was going to do. "Well, since you decided to ruin everyone's afternoon with you silly nonsense with that dog of yours; it is the only thing that will take the smell off you." Katie Lee was shivering so bad from the cold water being sprayed by Charles David and no clothes. "What is it Mommy?" Before she could answer they were all looking in disgust, "What is that?" Charles David spouted out turning the hose off. "Tomato sauce" Smacking Katie Lee's hands again leaving her hand print on the upper part of the little girls back. Trying not to cry for fear of making it worse, she asked about her dog. Smacking her the third time in the same place she demanded Charles David take the pup to the barn, tie him up until his father got home. He knew better than to argue seeing the marks on his stepsisters back. He snatched up the small dog that was close to the porch, still rolling and trying to rub her eyes with her little paws. "She stinks as bad as Katie Lee does, man." Carrying the pup by her collar for fear of the stench getting on him, he headed for the barn shooting devilish looks at his little stepsister. Katie Lee looked haunted as she watched from the cold tub, her little puppy dangling by her collar.

Katie Lee bit her lip to hold the tears, pleading with her mother to make all the kids get in the house and stop making fun of her. Yanking Katie Lee's hair she motioned for the kids to get in the house. As they lingered on the porch she continued to tell Katie Lee she had no sense at all nor worth anything except trouble otherwise this would never have happened. Katie Lee tried to cry only within herself but it was cold and her little body was beginning to shiver. This mid afternoon breeze was turning crisp with a light mist beginning to fall over her.

After about fifteen minutes irritated by the weather her mother jerked her out of the tub and threw a large towel around her. As Katie Lee started for the porch her mother motioned for her to stop. "You are not going into the house until you're completely dry, especially your hair. I need to make sure you don't smell that horrid scent any longer. Until you do, sit right here on the porch little girl." Passing her daughter with not even a look or care she closed the front door behind her leaving her daughter standing all alone. Katie Lee sat in silence watching the little rain drops hit the tub still full of water and tomato sauce. "Dear Lord, please let me dry fast, I am so cold and let my hair not smell. Please Lord" she begged. Trying to wrap the towel closer and more around her body she felt so alone and humiliated as she talked to herself trying to understand. "I am so cold sir, I want to go to my room, please Lord can you at least try and hear me." Thanks to her stepfather Katie Lee had learned to talk to the Lord sincerely. She wished he was home, but it may be hours before he arrived. He was good to Katie Lee always treating her with fatherly love. Always asking her to tell her side of the story he would listen. He was also very strict, did not hesitate to use the paddle when needed or time out to think before you speak. Katie Lee knew she hardly ever gave him cause, why couldn't her own mother see her like he did? Why wasn't she treated the same as the others and especially her own blood sister. Was the story true about her real father giving his life for her, was that why they hated her so? Could it really be that bad to justify their verbal and physical abuse?

It was getting colder. she was so tired, her hair was still wet. She wondered how her puppy was. Had Charles David taken care of her or just tied her, thrown and scared? She curled up in the chair near the corner of the porch while waiting for permission to enter the house.

CHAPTER TWO

What a spring day this turned out to be, Katie Lee was so excited. It was her graduation day, the biggest day of her life. How she got there was another question but she did. Her aunt and uncle had already gone to work but not before leaving her a note on the kitchen table with instructions for the evening. She was to meet them back home at exactly 6:00pm dressed and ready to go. She was not too excited about the dinner but it seemed so important to her uncle Jack, she couldn't refuse him.

Her aunt Loie was head cashier at the local grocery store with enough spunk and love for everyone. It had only been three years since she had come to live with them, three years of utter heaven. Her life had been turned around, she would forever be grateful. They wanted her to attend college of course, but she was not certain if that was best for her. That summer before her senior year, Katie Lee had gotten herself a small job filing in the only doctor's clinic in town. The office manager repeated daily how Katie Lee was such a natural she could learn it all. In time with the right opportunity the doctor could give her a good future. She would be trained well, benefits, chance to move up into manager some day. Mrs. Owens had told her several times they would need someone like her, she wasn't going to keep working till she dropped.

Katie Lee constantly talked about the job at home, she loved working there. Her coworkers were great and the patents were friendly and open to her. The doctor always heard comments and thankfulness they were having such a bright friendly girl to greet them. The doctor himself was always smiling nodding his head when they passed in the hall. She never shirked a task and never found time for idle play. She was impressed with herself and learning ability, it was something that came very easy to her. With little knowledge in this field, it seemed to hold her interest wanting to learn more. The question was, how was she going to approach her aunt and try to explain that this was where she really wanted to stay? Besides, there was no money for college. There would be so much to learn and she felt this was a place she could subdue her memories – even managing a life of happiness rather than endless memories, pictures in her mind of her taunted past. No, college was out, not even a junior college. A personal loan or grant, that would be good but she convinced herself she wasn't in that league either. Without wanting to hear herself use the correct words "wrong side of the tracks" she was not as optimistic as her aunt and uncle were.

If she could make it through another summer showing them how good she was, the fulfillment she felt, maybe they would agree to the full time job. Since she had arrive at her aunt and uncle's the neighbor girl made herself known right away. It was decided before she arrived she'd be riding to school with Nancy and her mother; that way she had a new friend immediately. Plus her aunt was assured she did not have difficulty in the goings and comings of school. Nancy was a smaller girl with a huge smile and pearly white teeth. Her eyes were pale blue, her hair almost a shabby medium brown. She was not up with all the latest hair styles but she dressed appropriately and her personality was likable. Nancy was the youngest of two other daughters that Mrs. Hansen had but the older sister's were already married settled down with their careers. Katie Lee was amazed how Nancy and her mother always seemed to be happy no matter what happened. So it turned out to be a good friendship, not a real close one but one that worked for them both.

That morning, they didn't have to be at school until 10:00am for rehearsal, she was feeling butterflies tickling her stomach. She had done it, she made it through these last three years with her head held high receiving her diploma, just like all the other kids in her class. She wondered what would happen if any of them knew where she had really come from and what she had really gone through. Would they look at her any different and would they think of her differently? She had been very careful not to participate in too many activities those three years, nor run for any office keeping a subdue profile. She had popular opportunities her second year, but veered away on purpose.

One of the most popular boys in her homeroom tried to get her involved, he seemed to like Katie Lee very much. What was there not to like? Katie Lee was a pretty girl, a natural beauty. Her thick auburn hair was always in a long shimmering ponytail, or in one single braid swirling from side to side as she walked. She was a modest girl with a smaller figure than most of her classmates and most pleasant to be around. Her mouth was thin for her face and her nose was small, but cute. Her stepfather used to call her pug nose, always trying to pinch it but never seemed to be able to get enough in his big hand. He would just laugh and walk away. Her hazel eyes that sat perfectly above her high cheekbones showed a natural manner of another nationality, but don't guess most were not quite sure what it might be. Her smile was faint but attractive, she seemed to light up a room when she walked in with or without knowing it. She was not a real conversationalist but she did knew when to put in her two cents. Her reputation around campus intrigued everyone, she was not afraid to tease and get the better of you in a good way.

Even though Katie Lee refused to join all the activities the upper crowd continually tried to include her. She still became their most liked classmate. From the most domineering kids to the nerds, they all liked the times she could joke and play around in the hall with anyone. They also learned that she was a good listener which made it easier to share with her, it was learned very quickly that Katie Lee never gossiped or gave advice, her respect was admired. She did not feel she was capable of telling anyone what to do or not to do, especially girlfriend-boyfriend issues. She always had someone walking her to class and carrying her books but she was very careful not to give the wrong impression. Dating was something Katie Lee dreamed about but the fear she held inside did not allow her to do so; she just joked each time and gave feeble excuses while holding her disappointments and pain inside.

She was in the drill team, continually being placed in lead position, first girl out. She ate lunch with so many friend, she just didn't allow herself the extra activities that most teenagers were privileged to have. It was behind her now and in just another month she would be of age and would never fear again. She would be free to work and earn her own money, plan for her own place, move on with her life and bury the past. It has been long enough since she had last seen her mother, she felt she could do it. Yes, she had to, these three years had proven she could do it. So now was the time for her to again take another step into something even better.

Pushing all her thoughts back she grabbed her toast and headed for the bathroom; the phone began to ring as she passed through the hall. "Hello, Wayne's resident." There was giggling on the other end, she could tell it was her neighbor Nancy, "Hey girl, are you ready for the big day?" Katie Lee always seemed to greet most of her friends with the phrase "hey girl" she never knew why but it just seemed natural. "You will never guess what my mother has done." Katie Lee could hear the excitement in Nancy's voice. "What has your mother done my friend?" "Wait and I will be right over, just need to put on some shorts and shoes." Katie Lee heard the click of the phone and held it in her hand for a second, thinking that was odd even for Nancy.

Laughing to herself she put her clothes on and headed for the front door when the phone rang a second time. Picking it up she heard her sweet aunt that she had grown extremely fond of. Katie Lee wanted to please her aunt in every way. "Hey, what's up?" Katie Lee liked the way her aunt would try to talk to her in a jive sort of way. She explained Nancy's excitement and after finding out what the big deal was she'd be heading for the shower then school. Her aunt reminded her of the time schedule but before hanging up she asked Katie Lee the same question for the hundredth time that week. "Did anyone call Katie Lee that I should know about?" She assumed her aunt was talking about some boy trying to get her to go to one of the parties or something. That answer was always the same in a kind way. "No, but thank you so much for asking me."

Picking up her dried piece of toast she headed for her friend next door. Barley knocking she could hear Nancy squealing like a little pig. She was jumping and bouncing all over the place. "Come on, hurry." Nancy's mother was just standing there with a large grin looking at her daughter in pure delight. Mrs. Hanson motioned for Katie Lee to follow her daughter through the entrance way to the living room. Once she got to the living room, it did not take long to see what all the commotion was about. There in the modest furnished home stood a shiny black grand piano, taking her own breath away. "Come on Katie Lee, play with me." In her mind all she knew was chopsticks, something she thought all kids knew. As she began to put her fingers down from Nancy's and plunk the keys to what the tune was suppose to sound like, they all broke out in laughter.

Mrs. Hanson broke up the fun and insisted the girls put this on hold there was little time that morning and lots to be done. Katie Lee hugged her friend tight expressing her warm approval of a gift well deserved. "What did you get Katie Lee?" Seeing the surprised look on her face Mrs. Hanson quickly distracted her daughter. "Now Nancy, that is not a question to ask, maybe her surprise has not arrived yet." As quickly as she could she took charge and ushered the girls back toward the entrance hall, Nancy going to her room and Katie Lee out the door to her own home for preparations at hand.

As Katie Lee walked back to her home she wondered if she misunderstood. Was she possibly going to get something? She had not asked for anything nor expected it. Just giving her a home and a life was really all Katie Lee needed. It was at that moment that she pictured her stepfather, a gift in hand coming through that door. She remembered the many times he praised her for even little things. Unfortunately, the praise had to remain quiet because of her mother's temper. She wondered now after all this time if he was ever aware how she cherished those moments. Surely he did, but the words never crossed between them. It was like something forbidden to speak about.

Shaking off her feelings, she had no idea why she had even thought of him She needed to stop this and get her mind back to where it belonged. It was something she couldn't do to herself. Rushing into the house, she took off down the hall and into the bathroom. Hearing the phone ring again, she made little sounds and let it ring. It could not be her aunt and it was not Nancy, so whoever it was could leave a message on the machine. As quickly as she bathed she dressed and hurried back next door. She did not have to worry about books today, Nancy was so excited she was more interested in returning home to play her piano than the school events or rehearsal. Katie Lee laughed as they arrived at school with the students rushing here and there. Nancy and Katie Lee parted ways at their locker heading for their homeroom. As Katie Lee entered most of the kids in her homeroom were all over the place. Music was playing, some were dancing and others were involved in conversation. It was a great day! As she approached her desk, one of the girls pulled out a set of keys for everyone to see. "Look out the window by the bus and eat your hearts out." She shouted for everyone to hear and beamed. Before Katie Lee could move, other classmates were all around the window's; of course it had to be a new 1963 T-Bird. They continued to talk about their plans after graduation, some leaving right away to visit the college they hoped to attend come fall. Others off to visit family and friends, it went on and on.

She smiled, pleased for her friend and her jokes amused them deeply. "Wait until you see what I have." Not understanding she was joking they all laughed with eagerness to hear her but before she could think of anymore to say, the teacher arrived and took charge of the class. Being interrupted was a god sent she gladly accepted. What was she thinking, what had she said? Pushing herself into her seat, she softly grinned and sat silent the rest of the period. In fact, the rest of the day was the same for her. She made sure she kept pretty much to herself and stayed from all the turmoil going on around her. Suddenly she wanted this day to be over, get the diploma and head back to her little job. Again she shivered at her stupid remark. She did not have to play big shot to anyone, she never had. But deep down in her heart feelings were hurt, she could not envy their happiness or rewards. Her reward was just the fact that she was allowed to finish school in a home with food to eat and someone caring enough to clothe her and give her peace rather than constant turmoil. She was with people that loved her, not abusing her. No one was taking things from her anymore, making her stay out in the cold, or putting her to bed without something to eat for things she did not understand.

But most of all, she was thankful there was no drinking in the home or drunks to worry about coming home late at night and having to listen to the horrid fights which usually ended up with them having to leave the home and seek shelter. No matter the love and respect, the free ride was over. The more she thought about the doctor's office the better it sounded. She would never be sorry for the last three years but in all reality she needed to face facts. Do what she needed to do, learn to make a living in her own way while supporting herself.

CHAPTER THREE

Katie Lee could hear the excitement from the barn, the last couple of days since sprayed by the skunk, she pretty much kept to herself and as always her stepfather's kind words gave her the courage she needed. He usually knew what really happened but Mina's story was always different and this made two different stories. There was little he could do, it was useless to try and it would only lead to another hostile incident. She often worried why such a wonderful man stayed with her mother. Yes, Mina was a beauty but so mean and unpredictable. Katie Lee's heart ached as she watched her mother that morning after the facts were twisted, talking to her stepfather over the breakfast table. So many lies, so many stories, could he not see through all this? Did he really believe her, sometimes he acted like he didn't but other times she was not sure. This time apparently not. Mina's beauty even in the early morning was striking. Her tall lean body seemed to float across the room rather than a walk. Those long sable locks midway down her back seemed to flow with every step. Mina was aware of her beauty and unique features, using them to her advantage whenever possible. Her skin tome was almost olive but there was a shadow of peach that made her emerald green eyes jump out at you with that hypnotic fashion. Little or no makeup was ever needed but when applied she would turn heads like she was some celebrity or exotic model from afar.

Katie Lee watched as her mother played her magic that morning on her stepfather, but amid the defeat something deep within Katie Lee told her that she would learn the truth one day. Peter worked long hours, sometimes into the evening and many weekends. It left little time for the family but Katie Lee knew material items her mother possessed was more important than any family. Katie Lee's mind wondered back to that moment when she first remembered seeing her mother. Why didn't she just leave her alone? Why didn't she just take her sister whom her mother favored. It made no matter to her step siblings that lived with them, they made their own way.

They had learned early to stay out of Mina's way, her injustice would prey down upon anybody unless she got to do and get what she wanted. As long as Peter's children could get in and out of the house as they liked and be free to live the way they choose without given too much attention, they were cool with her mother's deception. Many times Katie Lee went to bed at night in tears wondering why he couldn't be her father too. But he was not and she knew that if she tried to express her thoughts she would suffer more than just a slap or kick. She liked to fantasize that her father would have been exactly like Peter.

Peter always seemed to know her pain especially when something was truly wrong with her. She loved those memories when Peter would place her on his knee and tell her stories, silly stories that used to make her feel better. He was the only one that ever asked her how she was, what she was doing or what she wanted to be when she grew up Her only reply was "To go far, far away." Peter would joke with her and say "If you go far far away, I may never see you again and I will be so sad." She never had to say a word just wrap her small arms around his neck and squeeze tightly. "No, daddy Peter, you can come with me and we will live in Herpy Turtle Land forever.." Herpy turtle Land was a make believe fair tail she often placed in her mind when things got too rough or when situations that she had no control over happened. It helped when she was punished and didn't understand why. It was just a better make believe place to be. All her favorite cartoon charters lived there, especially Micky Mouse and Donald Duck, she loved to play make believe with Goofy. Peter's bass tone laughter always brought a smile to her face and eased that inner turmoil but never the full pain, never enough to go completely away. The times he was at home were memories she delighted in. He always had time to throw a ball with her or let her watch while he worked on his old Mack logging truck. Katie Lee loved to ride in that truck and sometimes he would start it up and go down the hill just so she could blow the horn and have a ride. He gave her the job of keeping the emblem of the silver bulldog shinning. He even gave her a special rag for it which she kept hidden in her room. She was forever asking him to take her with him on his jobs when she was not in school but her mother would throw him the most horrid look. He would just say that the woods was no place for young kids. She knew that wasn't true, Charles David had gone with his father plenty of times as well as the others. But not Ellen, she never even thought about it. So, for what ever reason she was rarely permitted to go. She even thought about sneaking in the truck then when they were so far from home she would jump out and say surprise, they would be too far from home for him to turn back. Just the thought of what her mother might do shot her back to reality. That thought quickly went to the back of her mind, the farthest part she could bury it.

  The other kids had been long gone before her that morning after breakfast as her mother continued her conversation with Peter. She realized that her little pup was the topic. The conversation was not going well, her mother wanted the dog gone and Katie Lee be punished for the woodpile incident. As her mother glared at her every time she walked close to the kitchen she wondered if she was going to be forced to give up her little pup. Her only hope was that she knew Peter was also attached to Penny and loved having her around. She could not understand why she should be punished for the woodpile incident but her mother needed no reasons for anything. Katie Lee felt that sometimes Peter knew her mother's schemes but still she was not sure. Suddenly she heard a slap, running to the entrance of the kitchen she saw her mother rubbing one side of her face. Peter turned to see his young stepdaughter staring at them. Katie Lee hated it when Peter would slap her mother but she knew sometimes he was backed into a corner deliberately by her mother. She would never let Peter walk away. Time and time again Peter would try to get away from Mina but she seemed to like the abuse. She would stand right in front of Peter and physically hold on to him while her screams penetrated into his space. It would go on and on until he would either hit the wall, a cupboard, throw a chair or something. But that never seemed to justify Mina, she continued until he ended up slapping her or pushing her aside so he could get away from her. By that time his shirt was usually torn to pieces from her grip refusing to let go. She always fell or pretended to fall if he would get away from her, this always seemed to please her. Katie Lee felt she did it to punish him in someway but she could not understand why. Why would she hang on to him and not let him leave and why did she have to push it so far? This seemed to be happening more and more. Each time he returned home seemed to lead to more fights than usual. Still Katie Lee missed him terribly when he was gone, the others she could not tell if they missed their father except Vera but Katie Lee's own mother seemed to resent it when he return unless it was payday time.

    The time he was gone usually consisted of shopping, spending money, buying everything they think they could not live without. Mina made sure his children always went with her, even if it ended up in a fight right in public. Ellen of course never left her mother's side especially when the word "shopping" was mentioned. The only one that never went was Vera, she was satisfied at home wanting nothing especially from Mina. That was another thing Katie Lee noticed that her mother enjoyed, a public scene. Mina also seemed to take pleasure in putting Peter on the spot in that way when she insisted he tag along. She was always making sure everyone saw and heard the abuse, in public. She always played the little shy feeble housewife but at home she would win the Academy Award for her performance of anger and obnoxious behavior. Mina also loved to entertain lots of friends in her home. Little did Peter know her party habits did not stop when his work kept him away a few days at a time. To party meant to drink, in Mina's eyes anyway. Knowing Peter did not like to drink hard liquor, she usually managed to manipulate the situation and win her way. She was never satisfied with just beer, it had to be the hard stuff and she always insisted on making them which ever way she wanted. Oh yes Mina was the life of the party, she was the party. Beautiful, stylish, cleaver and extremely revengeful.

Katie Lee stood in the doorway watching as her mother stood in Peter's way as he tried to move past her and out of the kitchen. Tearing his new shirt she had just purchased he grabbed her hands together in his and moved her forcefully. Katie Lee could see he was straining to keep control. Seeing her daughter so close Mina said "See how he is, you think he is so great." Peter stormed past the two of them feeling as low as any man seeing the look on Katie Lee's face. Her mother flung the mop bucket through the back door after Peter, dirty water still in the bucket from mopping that morning. Slamming her own bedroom door behind her, Katie Lee felt sorry for her stepfather She knew it was not right, Peter hitting her mother; when this happened she wished he would leave and never come back. Then fear would rise in her mind, what about her? He could not take her, she was not his blood.

Peter would stay out of the house most of the day now, returning later and apologize to Mina asking her what she would like to do. Go to town, shop more or did she need something that he was not aware of. Maybe she wanted to go to town that night to a club to go dancing. In Katie Lee's heart, she felt that was probably it, Mina loved the clubs and to dance. What was happening in town or who was out and about, Well that Mina could not stand, she had to be the grand Bella. There would be a fight for sure when they came home because Mina was always dancing with everyone except Peter. The alcohol would be talking by the time they returned home. It was getting more out of control. For now the day would be quiet, the other siblings would know something was up so they would be scheming to have their own friends over for a get together. Especially Vera with her boyfriend Davie. They would stay in Davie's car as long as possible or until Allie signaled with the porch lights three times. Katie Lee would spend the night in her room, knowing well enough to keep her mouth shut – or else. She had made the mistake one time and found out what the "or else" was. Her own sister beat the crap out of her with a toilet plunger. You would not think it hurt that much but when you were getting full blows over and over again it can put the hurt on you and bruised just as easily.

Again and again she thought, was it ever going to be over? It had never been over since her mother came for her and Ellen in the middle of the night like a thief. Katie Lee has no idea who this woman was but Ellen sure did. She remembered being woken by this strange woman, Ellen all excited telling her it was their mother as they hushed her out the back door, through the yard to the front gate, into a dark car and off they went. That was when it all started, that was when all the different fathers started. Well, she couldn't really call any of them her father. Peter had been the only one her mother married that she knew about anyway. Until her mother showed up that night she had lived with the Paddocks somewhere near a creek. Peter's property was similar and when that memory came to mind Katie Lee tried desperately to remember but she was no more than five when her mother came for her and Ellen, All she remembered was she came in the night, they were gone before daylight. Prior to that Katie Lee could not remember anything, all she knew was the Paddocks, more like grandparents, reminded her of what Santa Claus and Mrs. Santa would be like. How she got there she had no idea, why she was taken was the same mystery, a mystery she had learned to hate. If she could find her way back she would leave, except Peter protected her like his own. It was Mina, her own mother that saw to it that she would never see the elderly couple that she missed so much. She pondered these things in her mind more and more if she only knew more.

Did that couple miss her, did they ever think of her? When did they realize she was missing, did they know who had her? Little good

Pacific Redwood Mystery: Do you believe in the little people yet?

all these questions were going to do so she quickly cleaned the kitchen putting all the stuff back on the stove. The chairs were back at the table and she picked up her mother's apron that lay on the floor near the kitchen door. Mopping up all the water in the hallway took most of her time but if she wouldn't do any cleanup, no one else would do it. It would only start another fight if her mother came out of her room and there was water still all over. Little did it matter than it was her mother who was the one that created the mess. Did anyone really think she would do the mopping? Wrong? Turning to look towards her mother's room she closed her eyes and felt no comfort or compassion. She felt little emotion as she lowered her head and walked out of the kitchen towards the barn.

CHAPTER FOUR

Beginning to skip Katie Lee headed towards the barn as she approached she could hear her siblings laughing and enjoying themselves. It was fairly warm with just enough breeze to make the winter day pleasant. Seeing her coming her little puppy came rushing to her side. Penny was such an adorable pup, to her she was her security blanket and lifeline. Her barking and jumping brought attention to her as she entered the barn.

    Surprisingly her siblings were in good spirits and were offering her to join in the fun, except her own sister. She had a way of making Katie Lee feel inferior to her, enjoying it immensely. Sometimes her stepbrother, Charles David would intervene and make her stop, but he had to be in a pretty good mood. Vera was always friendly to her, but she was the oldest and had a boyfriend she spent most of her time with. So she was home little especially on weekends. Allie was the worst besides her own sister, aside from being a bully she loved to pull pranks on everyone. Allie had her own way of making sure she did less than anyone else, covering her domineering demands. Allie was more of a tom boy which caused her lots of trouble in school. It never seemed to matter whether it was a girl or boy. She wanted to be sure everyone knew how tough she was. Katie Lee tried not to make her mad because when she got to beating you up, none of the others would come to your aid even if they wanted to. She was tough and she knew it. Even Charles David would run away so if you were in her path, there was no mercy.

Pacific Redwood Mystery: Do you believe in the little people yet?

Allie was smart she always went for the back, if she could get you down your face would be smashed into the dirt, you felt like a truck ran over you. It did no good to try and get away from her. She knew every wrestling hold imaginable. It was easier to lay still and repeat how sorry you were or start screaming "UNCLE" especially the minute she started punching. Allie was between Vera and Charles David in age, making her in her second year of high school. Mary was the youngest and the most quiet, missing her own mother terribly. She was smart in school, but she kept her feelings to herself, minding her own business. Sometimes she would let Katie Lee come into her room when Allie was nowhere to be found. Not a whole lot of words were ever exchanged between them but it was just the way Mary treated her; the smiles, the pat around her shoulder or wanting to brush Katie Lee's hair. Mary loved brush Katie Lee's hair, it was very much like what hers used to be, the same texture. Katie Lee had never had her hair cut, it hung almost past her waistline, Mary envied that. Mina made her and the others wear their hair short, it did not help that she also gave those permanents that made Shirley Temple popular. Mary was always writing in a little pink book with lace and flower prints, it even had a lock so no one could open it.

Being brave, one afternoon Katie Lee asked her what it was for. Smiling, Mary told her. "All my secrets and dreams." She told Katie Lee that when she got a little older maybe she would let her read it. She wanted more than anything to read Mary's book. Mary even told her that when she was a little older if she wanted she could help her start her own journal. Journal, that sounded so important, Katie Lee could not wait. Mary never joined in much of the playing with any of her own sisters or brother. There seemed to be an understanding between them about it and even Allie never tried her bully attitude on Mary. Mina totally ignored the girl, which suited Mary just fine. You could tell that the young girl detested her stepmother but she was respectful and never made her feeling known, not out loud anyway. Katie Lee was not sure how Mary felt about her own father, it was questionable. When Katie Lee would cry and feel sorry for Peter,

Mary would rub her back and just remark it was his own stupidity; she didn't feel sorry either. Mary spent her free time on long walks by herself, especially near the creeks or paths no one seemed to know about except her.

    Katie Lee knew very little about their real mother, it was a forbidden subject in the house. Even her stepsisters and stepbrother dare not go there. That was established when they first came together as a family. It seemed that as long as they all had their own life, being strangers in the same house was okay. There were days like today playing in harmony could be good, it was like a real family. Did that make everything alright? Getting involved in the day's play soon Katie Lee forgot what the night may bring. Charles David had rigged up a rope over the top of the rafters in the barn. It hung midway down as they proceeded taking turns riding his go-cart to a designated point where they would meet the swinging rope. Standing on top of the bales of hay that were stacked ceiling high in the barn for the winter, one would start to swing the rope. They had two people on the go-cart, one to drive, one to jump. As they rode, the rider would get ready to stand on the mental rail behind the driver's seat, lift up, leap and grab for the rope. Hoping one made it, the driver was not going to stop and wait to see if they made it. It was one man show. The driver was next in line for the rope and the one swinging the rope had to come back down from nearly the rafters and drive the go-cart. If one made the leap successfully the next task was swinging madly from side to side, seeing how far out one could go. Then they had to maintain enough momentum to swing high enough to land as close as possible to the top of the hay bales. One would get ten points if one reached the top but if you didn't it depended on where you landed as to how many points was taken away. The one with the most points at the end of the game got to pick everyone's booby prize. This usually involved everyone's allowance or chores. Or it ended with a lot of band-aides under your jeans and scraped knees but heck who was talking. I never entered their mind how much of a risk they were taking, or how dangerous it was.

Pacific Redwood Mystery: Do you believe in the little people yet?

There was always enough things to do, games to play – swimming at the pond or river, horseback riding, horseshoes, pitching, good old fashioned baseball or just free time with plenty of room to run wild. The best prize was to win time riding Charles David's bike or go-cart for a whole week. Chasing the animals with his bike or go-cart was fun, especially the geese. The goats were not so much fun, they fought back. If one caught any of them just right, he could plant their rear end clear across the fence. The go-cart was Charles David's favorite, so you had to really be in his favor to ride it. He built that himself with his father, so it was his; it was a male thing. Mina did not care to have animals around but Peter's kids were used to having lots. So he paid Mina no mind when she complained about them; he just made sure everyone took their own responsibility regarding their choice of pets seriously.

Rabbits, they had plenty multiplying often but they made the best pets. Their funny noses and warm fluffy fur made anyone enjoy the pleasure. The horses were also everyone's favorite, they liked to ride them but did not care like pulling saddle, blanket, bridle off and rubbing them down after a ride, except Vera and Mary. Vera was very good, in fact before her parent's marriage split she rode in the State Fair taking two first place ribbons. One for barrel racing and the other for calf roping, Allie was the best when it came to breaking a horse and she took no shame in flying off one several times before they submitted defeat to her She had a unique was of working with the horses and she didn't like anyone around when she worked with them. She sometimes used water but mostly she used the good old fashioned Native American method of "touch and breath." She went through more handkerchiefs than any man from binding one across the nostrils for over a week if necessary. Katie Lee would often see her take sweat from her face and forehead wiping over the horses face and nostrils but Katie Lee stayed her distance never asking questions.

Vera was too involved with her boyfriend now that she lived with her father and Mina, she had no time for any animals. In fact, Davie never believed she could get near a horse for the way she acted. It was very different to see how all she did now was prance around as if she was part of some royal family. The closet she ever got to any animal was Mina's blue and white parakeet. Even at that, she tormented it when she could. The bird went from swinging and singing to squawking and flopping. Then he turned his head around it was almost to keep an eye on her of what she might do; she claimed the bird was possessed just like her stepmother. That may be true but Katie Lee felt like the poor bird had to keep his head going around just to avoid Vera's constant attacks. Everyone seemed to have the same feelings for Mina, but no one was going to be the first to speak up. Why should they? There was nowhere else to go.

When it came time for Katie Lee to ride Charles David's go-cart to catch the swing she was just too small to obtain the speed needed to reach or leap far enough to catch the rope. If she missed or any one of them missed the concrete floor beneath them was their fate. Do you think any of them took the time to think of that visual? I doubt it, especially Katie Lee, not until she actually was in motion. All the yelling and screaming of encouragement did not seem to help. She was part of the group tying so hard to please them. Each time she would hear "Stretch Katie Lee, stretch." It was a delight to her ears, her little heart pounding. How hard could it be? She was beginning her fourth run when Charles David took pity on her. Stopping her and trading places with her own sister, he helped her onto his shoulders. It was not until she actually got on his shoulders did she realize how high she was that she had a sudden change of heart. Her stepbrother did not ask if she was ready or not as he hit the gas on his go-cart, it was nothing like the others had done. The go-cart lunged forward as he hit the gas and gained speed the closer the rope came swinging in her direction. The fear that ran through her was like a bolt of lightening. But it was to late, the swing was almost directly above them. As she put her hands up to get it, Charles David lifted his body up off the go-cart seat pushing her upward into the swinging rope. Feeling the rope in her hands she did not dare to let go, as she looked down she

Pacific Redwood Mystery: Do you believe in the little people yet?

realized just how high she was. "Don't look down stupid" her own sister shouted and Katie Lee was sure she was going to die at any moment.

Thanks to her stepbrother he had given her enough power to swing hard enough to head right towards Allie who was standing at the very top of the haystack. With her eyes shut she could only think to hold on while the air sucked her breath in and out of her mouth, If Allie had not caught her on the first swing, it may have ended very differently. She did not know is she was exited because her stepsister had caught her or that she had actually done it. Laughing and cheering her on, she felt as if she was really part of the group, but she remained silent until she made sure she was still in one piece. She could hear her little dog barking while trying to climb on the hay to get where she was. The only animals that made it that far were the cats, now Katie Lee understood why. Next was Charles David himself to see how high he could go. So Allie threw him the rope as hard as she could then jumped heading for the bottom. Katie Lee was to wait for Charles David and come down with him. Looking down from where she was she decided she would do better watching Fright Night at the movies. It was so far, she did not know how far but it was real far. The barn was old but still had it's purpose at about twenty feet high. To young kids that was fun, to adults that was unthinkable if they knew what was going on It did not take Charles David long to reach exactly where Katie Lee was standing. Ellen had been the driver on the go-cart. As he sung high and wide towards Katie Lee she grabbed for the end of his pants wanting to help him make his mark. If he fell, there was no doubt as to what the outcome would be. For young kids it did not seem to be a problem, how many would have thought it could happen to them." None! But to this nine year old there was no question and the fear was overwhelming. Smiling he said, "Thanks kiddo." If she had not been so scared, his new nickname for her would have been the high light of her life. All she wanted to do was get to the bathroom so bad, she knew if she didn't go now she was going to wet her pants. Maybe that would save her because right at that moment she had her legs crossed. What a day it was turning out to be, something Katie

Lee was not so sure if she ever wanted to be part of their little carnival again. Telling her brother she had to go to the bathroom he just looked at her, but he must have taken her to be serious after looking at her legs crossed. Heaven must have smiled upon her just as Allie started to pull the cord to start the go-cart she started whispering to Ellen. Then without warning Charles David was on his feet, grabbing for the rope and trying to tie it to a beam. Whispering in a firm tone at Katie Lee to help him, she rushed to accommodate him. He fastened it as fast as he could, he dare not waste time. Charles David told her, "Shut up, you are going to get us into trouble." The look on his face was very serious but she was not sure what he was talking about. Allie and Ellen had taken off through the back of the barn, down the creek and toward the orchard. Katie Lee lay there as still as possible, then heard a ruffle of noise below her. She saw Charles David peek out over the hay, not wanting anyone to notice him. As she turned her head to look at him he placed his hand to his mouth like to say, "Shh.." She waited until he peeked up again, lifting her little head saw what he was staring at, her stepfather.

Again Charles David looked over at her and quickly pushed her head back down the second time making a look as if saying "You better keep your head down." She huddled into a curled position trying to hold herself. Charles David gently put his arm over her back. Was he trying to help her or was he going to slam her if she did not do what he wanted? They lay so still if angels were real or spirits lured close by they might question their whereabouts. Hearing shuffling here and there, it seemed endless before Peter finally left the barn. Just as quickly as he had pushed her down, he drew her up right into his face. They were so close Katie Lee could not imagine what was coming, "Little girl, you better keep your mouth shut and I am not joking." Letting her go with force she landed on her back. Without even helping her he was making his way down the haystack without using the rope. Katie Lee just lay there for a moment and then called her stepbrother "Charles David, I am scared please wait for me. I really have to go to the bathroom." Her voice must have sounded desperate as he turned in frustration putting one hand on his hip with the other hand pointing towards the rope. Looking shocked she was not sure what he meant. "I am not crawling all the way back up there Katie Lee, just untie the rope and I'll catch you." Without another word he turned jumping the remaining distance to the barn floor. Making his way to the middle of the barn he looked up toward her with further frustration. "Well?" was his only remark. Katie Lee took the rope from where he had tied it loosely on to a huge beam. She knew this was her only way down, she had no choice. Wrapping her small hand around it and closing her eyes she pushed herself with as much force as any nine year old could manage. Her small body lunged out from the hay as she looked down at her stepbrother, she was silent and weary looking. In her mind she could not believe that such a good day could end so bad, but that was the story of her life.

She swung across once and Charles David missed her feet as he almost lost his balance standing on his father's long worktable surrounded with tools, grease rags, all kinds of mechanic stuff. He didn't dare start his go-cart for fear of his father returning and no one to help him. As she came back around the second time he took hold of her shoe. Trying to stop her she began to twist a little. Looking her stepbrother directly in the face she felt something in her gut quench. She was not sure what was happening, but it was like a voice out of nowhere was telling her to jump, jump to her stepbrother. She knew better that would have caught him off balance and the distance was too far. If she got injured or hurt her stepbrother, there was no idea what that would arouse. If she jumped and he missed her she may miss the table and fall to the cement floor. Then instantly she saw her stepbrother's eyes widen, without hesitation Charles David put both arms out and demanded her to jump, "Jump Katie Lee, NOW!" His piercing voice caught her off guard and then she felt some kind of release. Landing towards the table she realized her stepbrother had a hold of her and was gripping with all his might just to hold on to her. As he struggled to get her beside him she had the look of confusion. "Lord Jesus, Katie Lee, are you alright? Oh Lord, Lord,

Lord." She could hear him repeat those words over and over again. They lay there for what seemed longer than their earlier venture on top of the hay hiding from Peter, Charles David's legs and lower body were hanging over the table with Katie Lee hanging onto him for dear life. As gently as possible he was helping her without loosing his own balance and falling to the cement floor. Getting them both to their feet he was inspecting them both. Still confused and dazed he was assuring himself she was okay. Shaking his head, they seemed fine until he leaned down bending to the side of her feet, he picked up the rope she had just swung on. Her first impression was what was the rope doing hanging from the worktable to the barn floor. As she watched her stepbrother look upward she realized the rope had come loose and came down from the top rafters..

Her legs began to wobble and her small hands began to shake as her stepbrother turned to wrap the rope around his forearm. He noticed the tears coming down her cheeks but he also noticed she no longer needed the bathroom. Her soaked jeans told him enough. Without her stepbrother's quick thinking Katie Lee could have been sprawling now across the concrete floor. Charles David had scared himself trying to cuddle his little stepsister but wanting to have a little distance from her wet jeans. He began patting her back, still shaking. Allie and her real blood sister Ellen came rushing back into the barn with weird looks on their faces. After helping his little stepsister off the workbench Charles David showed them all what had occurred. Allie gasped and put her hand over her mouth. Ellen began to laugh out loud. That was the first time she ever saw Allie turn on Ellen, belting her between her rib cage and stomach area. She brought the girl almost down to her knees. "What was that for, stupid? Allie, are you crazy?" The girl shouted as she looked harshly at both Charles David and Katie Lee. Grabbing Katie Lee by the arm, Allie blurted out "Are you okay, are you hurt anywhere?" All she could do was shake her head no, but her stepsister wanted to make sure they both did not have any marks on them that were noticeable. Then Ellen realized her little sister had wet her pants, she began to roar with laughter. Allie quickly reminded her of how much trouble they would be in if either parents found out what they had been doing. The look they all three gave one another was a fear they all felt down to their toes. Assuring each other this surely would stay only between them, they all swore to secrecy. As Ellen turned to exit the barn she stuck her tongue out at her little sister pinching her nose shut. "Elk, you stink and you can't blame it on a skunk this time, ha ha." It hurt deep within her to know her own sister had no warmth in her soul for her. Charles David turned telling Ellen to knock it off and head for home, he would bring Katie Lee with him.

 She wondered what was going to happen to her, what was her stepbrother going to do. He threw the rope behind some hay that was lying over to the side of the barn where no one could see it. Taking his little stepsister by the hand he led her out through the back of the barn. As he began to walk he started telling her how sorry he was but if she told they would all get in so much trouble from their father. He would have to tell Mina which could result in harsher punishment for Charles David, which was something he tried very much to avoid. Katie Lee was surprised not only on his gentleness but also his revealing to her his thoughts. "I thought you hated it here Charles David, and me too?" Shaking his head, he stated kicking a few rocks that lay on the edge of the creek bed behind the barn. "No, who said I hated you? It isn't a piece of cake here but it is the only home we have." He added an ugly remark about her mother, that is was her fault their being in this mess. Charles David sensed her uncomfortable feeling, she looked so sad. He kicked some more rocks and told her many things that took her by surprise. For the first time she believed Charles David did not dislike her. He just had to play the part with her, he could not take sides against his own sisters. He confessed his sisters were not the best in the world but they were all one another had. He wished she could have met his mother, he told her she would have liked her. She was a lot like Mary but more of the southern charm side. Here he had the opportunity to still have his father. If he stayed with his mother he would be in foster care somewhere. Foster care sounded good to her, but then she did not have a mother like Charles David was describing. NO wonder they despised her mother, who wouldn't? And Mina was an artist at ruining people's lives. No one knew that better than Katie Lee herself. She had her own few years of agony locked away concerning Mina prior to that, it was blank.

Charles David became restless and needed to be alone, before she could say anything which she tried he cut her off, not wanting to discuss it any further. He just dropped her hand and motioned for her to head to the house. He started to walk on down the path farther towards the creek as Katie Lee stared to go back around the barn to sneak through the back door. Suddenly she remembered that feeling she had, that voice she thought she heard. Had it been possible Charles David heard it too? Either way he had saved her life. She turned running after him just a few feet from the creek she wrapped her little hands around his waist with a quick hug from behind and then took off again before he could respond. She ran as fast as she could through the back door straight to her room. Dinner was being prepared as everyone heard Katie Lee's abrupt entrance into the house. Mina yelled down the hall in a scolding manner. Rushing to her room and grabbing some dry clothes she went to the bathroom ignoring her mother's demand to get in the kitchen. This time it did not matter how rude and unloving her mother's words were, she had understood that her stepbrother did not hate her. He actually like her and liked playing with her but he could not let his guard down nor was he going to lose his father over some woman that had stolen him from his mother. He was not going to live any less than he had before the affair with Mina had begun. She understood how he felt more than he could imagine.

"Affair," that word stuck in Katie Lee's mind but she guessed he was right. What else would you call it before Peter's divorce? Even being married did not take the ugly taste out of everyone's mouth, certainly not Peter's children; her mother had taken Peter away from their mother. I had been the talk of the whole town when it first happened. A marriage of nineteen years ending because this woman decided she wanted to get her hooks into him. Why not? She would not have to work any longer, she would not have to pay any bills. She could shop, party, have a new home, new car. Why, it was exactly what she wanted. The only thing that stood in her way was their mother. Mina had been smart and convinced Peter that she adored children and always wanted more herself but due to an accident some years back before she lost the girl's father there would be no more children. Her scheming, plotting, always planning, flirting and whatever else she had to do finally won Peter over. When the children first started coming to the house they just lived together. Mina made sure the children got whatever they wanted and they had the best time. Unfortunately for Peter her acting convinced everyone. Katie Lee thought it might even be better for her mother, she could change but no, her mother never changed. In time her old ways resurfaced even towards her. The cold, hostile emotions came too soon and her lies began just as well. When Peter began to question her new behavior, Katie Lee heard her mother tell Peter one night that she needed him, her girls needed him. She heard her mother tell Peter that the accident of her late husband had taken such a toll on her and Katie Lee was so little. Her husband had given his life for their little daughter to live. Katie Lee never knew what she meant by that but it made her feel worse. She would sob dragging Peter into her web, Katie Lee watch as her new stepfather assured his new bride all would be well. It left Katy Le with the tormented mystery had she been the cause of her father's death? Is that why her mother hated her? Was that why Peter felt sorry for her? Not because he wanted to be her father but it was for her mother?

Well, having Peter feel sorry for her was better than nothing but she lay awake several nights wondering what she had done that her father had to give his life for her. She even wondered what he looked like, there was never any pictures of him. Mina said it was too painful, so that subject stayed where her mother wanted it, never discussed. She was sure that maybe that was the reason her only sister hated her too. There would never be any forgiveness. Maybe if it had been her, it would have been better. But her daddy must have really loved her and maybe at one time her mother too? Maybe in time with Peter and his children in their lives her mother would come around. Standing in front of the mirror she looked at herself and realized how close she came to death. Picturing how much space between the end of the rope, the table and the cement floor made her shake all over again. She at least knew she could handle things a little better now. At least as far as her stepbrother Charles David was concerned. She made a vow right there in front of the mirror that no matter what Charles David did or how rude and unfriendly he was, she would never feel anything bad about him again.

 She would keep their secret only for him. Not her other siblings, but for Charles David. Then the thought again of what voice, or had she heard a voice at all. Yes, she had, she was certain of that. Was it the angels that she heard about on TV and in the movies or was it a ghost? She wished she had someone she could talk to about it. Maybe in a day or two she could bring it up to her stepbrother but she would have to wait until no one was around. Hearing her mother gathering everyone around the dinner table, she belted out of the bathroom as fast as she had entered. Everyone was looking at her as if asking what was happening. This was not Katie Lee's personality and they all noticed. "Katie Lee, what is wrong with you?" Mina asked. She shrugged her shoulders and said she was just hungry and thought she was late for dinner. Seeing her mother's ugly look Peter reminded her that he had not seen her all afternoon, in fact he had not seen any of the them while he was working on the his truck. Before anyone could speak Charles David took the lead, "Hey dad those peaches in the orchard are getting pretty ripe, we got to playing over there and forgot about time. You know how we like to roll down the hill." Looking one to the other he felt this was a con job but Mina distracted his conversation immediately. "Well, make sure you don't bring any home, but you can tell the neighbors, especially Mrs. Stevens. She loves to can fruit and do all that nonsense."

 The look on Peter's face was obvious disappointment and Allie made the worst mistake with her innocent remark. "Remember daddy when we used to go berry picking and mom always canned

Pacific Redwood Mystery: Do you believe in the little people yet?

jam and all kinds of good stuff?" She immediately realized her input was not acceptable and that very subject was not allowed at Mina's table. A quietness swept across the table as Peter tried to change the conversation but Mina was not going to have it. "Well Allie, if you like your mother's way so much why don't you go back home and enjoy them. Especially since she is crazy in the head." Without another word Peter slammed his fist down on the table and defended his daughter. Mina stood her ground and continued with the argument, then without warning she faked her tears turning to Allie. "Just look what you have done, the very few times that your father is home and going to take me somewhere you have to ruin it." Allie looked at her in utter surprise, she tried to explain herself but blurted out at Mina that she had no right disrespecting her mother. Setting an angry stage, she was not going to back down either not where her mother was concerned. Mina went on and on about how Peter had spent the whole day outside near the children and she had spent the whole day cleaning and taking care of them. Making sure they all had fine things, wonderful things, a better life and this was the way she was repaid. She insisted Allie had said it on purpose, when Peter tried to defuse the situation he was overpowered by Mina's hysterical outburst. Rushing off to her room, she was so distraught for their selfishness, they just didn't want her and Peter to have any fun or be together. She left the whole table in silence.

Allie looked over to her father, she apologized for her outburst but refused to apologize for her mother's disrespect. She desperately assured her father the remark was innocent. Peter only nodded his head at her as he got up. Walking away from the table towards the closed door everyone just looked down but Ellen blurted out they always try to ruin her mother's good mood. As they all looked at one another, Mary started to laugh out loud. To their surprise Mary just shook her head taking her plate to the kitchen sink and laughing all the way. Not another word was said as each one left the table going off by themselves. Katie Lee knew exactly what would happen, her mother would cry and pretend to be crying until Peter insisted they go out and have a good time. Her mother would get all decked out, Peter's face would show how disapproval of her outfit but not mentioning a word for fear of another fight.

    She would be acting all poised kissing and begging Peter and telling him how she was so sorry too. She probably misunderstood poor Allie. She would brag how much she adored all her babies, yes her babies as she put it. Katie Lee knew too well she was not considered in the phrase. There were a good looking couple but unfortunately they were not good together.

CHAPTER FIVE

Nancy came barging down the hall, spotting Katie Lee at her locker. Being pushed aside by a large group in the hall she noticed her friend was dabbing her eyes with a tissue. "What on earth?" Trying to push her way through the active group, she called to her friend, "Katie Lee." But the girl turned from her locker in the opposite direction That was strange, Nancy thought all seniors were suppose to be in the assembly hall before the other grades. Shrugging it off, she figured her friend was just going to get something, she would save her a seat. But she could not shake off the feeling in all the time she had known Katie Lee, never had she seen her cry or show any emotional discomfort to cause her to cry. The gym was getting full, so Nancy made her way to the very top where the seniors had decided to sit during the assembly. The reason behind this was they were seniors and when things were said or any of them had to be recognized they could make a great commotion from the top and everyone would notice. By the time she climbed the bleachers she was tired and remarked to one of her fellow classmates. "Man, I guess I need more exercise I am out of breath." Laughing they all reminded Nancy that she did not do much in the way of exercise, including physical education or sports period. "I do too, I did PE just yesterday. I dressed down and walked the whole basketball court." Again laughing they poked fun at her until they heard the mike squawk, making too loud of a noise.

The Vice Principal was trying to get everything under control but the more noise it made the louder the seniors whopped and hollered. Finally, he made his voice sound reasonable enough to get some attention. But before he could get very far the seniors were on their feet yelling, shouting, some stamping their feet. Turning the Vice President saw the coach had just entered. With a smile he kindly bowed, handing the mike to the couch standing back. As the seniors finally began to settle down, without hesitation the couch leaned forward and asked. "Seniors are you ready?" loud shouts and deep hoots rang all through the building. It sounded like the Roman Army was coming through the school gym. Nancy was on her feet looking everywhere for Katie Lee. Turning to those near her she asked if they had seen her. Many shrugged their shoulders and others shook their heads no. One of Katie Lee's classmates leaned down to Nancy and told her she had seen Katie Lee leaving out the front door just before she came into the gym. That was even more of a shock to her, what on earth would she be doing leaving the school. But Nancy got caught up in the excitement just like her other classmates, with the thought of Katie Lee pushed back in her mind only to get answers later. Awards were given, students and teachers were acknowledged, students were talked about not only by the principal and some counselors but some of the teachers put on a cute skit about the seniors and their flamboyant days during the year. It was a time when teachers and students came together to make a day of memory that would never be forgotten. As in the past years, the freshmen class was made to bow down to the seniors and carry their books for the rest of the day, the sophomores and juniors were given praise and goals by many of the seniors. Even though the student speakers made fun, they kept the crowd in hysteria, especially about the freshmen They never left the gym until everyone was aware that those seniors were serious about their education and passed a lot of goodwill and advice. As the assembly came to an end, their were tears and excitement.

Then shouts of joy overcame the sadness. Trying to make sure the seniors understood, the coach was yelling through the mike for all

Pacific Redwood Mystery: Do you believe in the little people yet?

seniors to be back at the school by 7:00pm for lineup. As the seniors demanded to be first, they weaved and made their way through the bleachers shaking hand, joking and just doing what seniors do best, have the final word. It was a great sight and Nancy was at her best. As she went through the final door into the hall, she ran into Jacob Williams, landing a huge hug on her. "Where is Katie Lee?" "I tried to see where she was sitting, do you know if she is coming to the party tonight?" Nancy was shaking her head as if she did not know, there was so much noise in the hall you could not hear yourself think. "She was not in there. One of the girls said they saw her going out the front door just before the assembly started." Looking like she had to be joking Jacob kind of pushed his head back as if saying no way. "What, we need to get a picture of her tonight and the coach wants to talk to her right now." Nancy in return looked as surprised at Jacob's remark. "Why?" she asked. Smiling just as wildly with pride swelling in his chest, Jacob answered. "She is going to be asked to speak at gradation tonight. She won the most outstanding student award by the teaching staff." Nancy's eyes widened and she placed her hand over her chest. "Wow, that is awesome Jacob. Picked by the teachers and staff, man she is going to be ecstatic." Several students came around to see what the conversation was all about Nancy's overwhelming excitement. They both just started laughing. Jacob took Nancy's hand and they took off down the hall running, looking over their shoulder and not saying a word. The puzzled look on their classmates faces intrigues both Nancy and Jacob. Running into the drill team director, they slowed down to a fast walk. Smiling with all their teeth showing, they walked past her like two kids just getting caught in a candy store eating more than what they paid for.

Ducking around the corner they ran into more students who were looking at them confused but delighted in their playful manner. Jacob came to a sudden stop in front of the coach's office, seeing the coach at his desk and talking to some football players. Seeing Jacob he immediately excused himself coming to escort them into his inner office. Motioning for Nancy to sit, Jacob jumped into the chair before her as the coach gave him a look of "oh no" you did not do that. "Where is our girl?" The coach had a twinkle in his eye that even Nancy could see. "Well, that is why I brought Nan. She said that one of the girls saw her go out the front door just before the assembly." Sitting back In his chair, the coach asked, "Was she sick, did she have to go somewhere, what's up?" Both students looked at each other and then back at the coach at the same time. Both shrugged their shoulders. "Do you have a number for her Nancy or do you know if she is returning before graduation?" Pulling out her little address book Nancy turned to the R's. "She was real excited this morning when she came to see my piano and we talked about school and the fun for today. She never said anything about leaving, she rides with me." The coached picked up the phone while Nancy was still holding her address book. He dialed a number on his phone and waited for an answer. "Hello, this is Coach Miller, I need to talk to the senior counselor." As they waited the coach smiled at Jacob and noticed Nancy seemed a little nervous. She grinned at him and Jacob but she can't help thinking what could have happened. Katie Lee should be riding home with her, and she never let Nancy know of any different plan. She leaned into Jacob whispering. "Jacob, when I saw Katie Lee at her locker earlier she was crying but turned and went the opposite direction of the assembly." Jacob turned to Nancy as he became unsettled in the chair. The coach could see that there was something transpiring between the two of them and was wondering what they had not told him. But before he could question them, Mrs. Turner came on the line. "Yes Coach, what can I do for you?" Sitting up straighter and sliding his chair away from this desk, he started to respond to her question. "What do you know about Katie Lee Rossman leaving school this morning before the assembly?"

Not being able to hear what the counselor was saying Jacob and Nancy just stared back and forth. Not saying anything for a few minutes he held the phone in his hands twisting it around before placing it back on the receiver. "What?" Jacob finally ask. The coach learned forward looking directly at Nancy. "Seems like Katie Lee had some kind of family emergency this morning and her uncle came to pick her up. She won't be returning." "What?" came from both of them at the same time. Jacob kind of sunk back in his chair as Nancy looked at them both in disbelief. "What kind of emergency?" Came out of Nancy's mouth. Looking at her he paused then leaned over his desk towards the both of them. "I am not sure but the business office cannot give any information out." More confused, they did not seem to know what to do. "What about her award, how will we be able to give it to her?" Nancy was not thinking like Jacob and could not believe he asked the question, she was more concerned about what could possibly have happened to her neighbor and friend. The coach seeing Nancy's distraught suggested they get back thinking about their big night and things would fall into place.

Jacob was still shaking his head when they walked out of the office. Nancy was quiet and then turned to Jacob, "I have to go call my mom. I'll catch you later Jacob." Before he had the opportunity to answer her she took off in the direction of the main office. Jacob walked slowly towards the north end of the hall, out the side door to the students parking where his truck was. "What a bummer, man." He whispered to himself as he got in his truck and headed home for his own preparation for the graduation.

CHAPTER SIX

Vera was coming down the hall when she heard her boyfriend honking in the driveway. Her eyes suddenly moved around the room to see where her father was, that was one thing Peter never allowed. No one was allowed to come and just honk. He felt that if you could not come to the door and ask properly then you had no business coming at all. Especially if you are taking the young lady out for the evening. Respect for all children was very high on Peter's list. She thought it was okay, not seeing anyone except Allie sitting up the checkerboard to play a game. She grabbed her sweater headed for the door. Unfortunately she didn't get far, just off the first step when she noticed her father was right at the front door of Davie's car, motioning for him to get out. Her heart pounded fiercely as she hurried down the rest of the steps. "Daddy, hi" she said thinking she could get them out of this. "We are leaving to the movies but going to be late. Come on Davie." She jumped in his car as if all was well, hoping that her father would just let it go. Wrong! Peter did not even look at his daughter, he just made a finger motion for the young man to follow him into the house. Vera exited the car immediately. "Daddy, we are going to be late and I won't make my curfew back home." Ignoring her he continued up the steps and into the house. Davie looked at her motioning with his head for her to do something. Starting up the steps, she met her father, he opened the screen door. Vera, realizing her father was not kidding, stepping back and sat on the bottom of the steps. As Davie passed

Vera whispered "Don't say anything, just agree." She heard laughter from behind, turning she noticed Ellen coming towards her. "Trouble in paradise." Vera was not in the mood for this snipping little brat.

Vera tried real hard not to interfere with any of the siblings but Ellen made it impossible most of the time. She was the rudest, meanest, most cunning adolescent she had ever been around. Even her own brother and two sisters, although they could be a pain in the butt sometimes were not as devious as Ellen. She was not going to miss this place when she left. Only one more month and she hoped to be gone. She just needed to know how she was going to pull it off. Davie wanted her to apply for Chico State and come there, work, get an apartment and move on with their lives. When they both graduated and had their lives in order they could marry. Davie came from a good family with a thriving auto-parts business. His father had worked hard for Davie to attend a good college and get a better education. Vera got along with them wonderfully but they had talked with her one day about taking care of herself and getting an education first before any unexpected arrivals. She knew they were afraid she might get pregnant and ruin both their lives, ruin their lives, boy what did they know. She remembered Davie telling his parents there was no way neither were ready for marriage and they would not be foolish. They was something about that conversation that made her feel uncomfortable. Was it that she had thought about it on her own and not include Davie or was it that she was afraid that if she did not get him to marry her soon, she might lose him. He was a good catch and she wanted out of here, but she did not want to go to college at Chico State, it wasn't far enough away. Her mother had never worked a day in her life and she wasn't going to end up like her, with nothing. Her father had always made the living and they wanted for nothing, that was until Mina got involved then everything changed.

She knew that Ellen was hanging outside near the front porch just to irritate them both. Ellen loved to get the best of her and she continually made advances at Davie. He was not lacking in popularity in the girl department. She knew that when she came here she was fresh meat, so to speak. It was a small town and most of the girls had been here since birth. She was someone new, someone fresh, someone not from a little town and someone that cared about fashion and what she looked like. She took advantage of Davie's advances right away, mostly because she did not want to spend much time at the house with the woman that took her father away from them, but she was interested in his popularity and financial security for such a young man. His car, his clothes and his appetite for material things. Yes, she was not going to let him go easily and she would do what she had to do. She just needed to figure out a way that he would not hate her or lose him back to his parent's control. She was not a bad person but she was not above doing what she had to in order to get them away and together. Things were different now that she no longer lived with her mother she was taken from her friends, her surroundings. But it had turned out to be a good thing in away for her. She had met Davie and he had what she wanted in life. She just needed to be careful and make it work. Be it that she would make him always believe she was the best thing that ever happened to him. Interrupting her thoughts she heard Davie come down the steps. She looked back towards the direction of the door, he made a face at her that she had to laugh as she spotted her father inside the screen door. She could not see his face clearly but only his fingers as she hurried to the car with Davie. Making a small wave of her hand she saw Ellen jumped two steps at a time and laughed as she waved as if they both were friends. "Man, your dad was mad, Vera. What is his problem?" She threw her sweater into the backseat and scooted over right beside Davie. He put his arm around her with a quick kiss on the cheek. They increased their speed and he laughed harder. "Was he a prison guard or something in his other life, or what?" Finally Vera pushed hard against him smiling. All she wanted to do was be with Davie and not talk about her father. They sped down the hill onto the main road towards town.

Ellen went in the house passing her stepfather laughing, he just looked at her ignoring her disrespect. He was not in the mood to deal with her He knew he had to deal with her mother before the night was over and that was enough for him to handle for one evening. He thought about the lecture that he just gave to Davie. He had asked this young man more than one time to come to the door properly, not to speed up the hill and most especially not to sit out in the driveway and honk. He was not sure if he had gotten the message through to him, he just sat there and said nothing just, "Yes sir, yes sir." He hoped he did because he was about ready to stop this relationship if it continued. Vera was getting too serious anyway and they were too young He knew about the conversation his parents had with her, she came home crying and Mina took control. He remembered Mina wanted him to go over to that house and confront Davie's parents. Little did Mina understand that Peter agreed with them and voiced his opinion to both his wife and daughter. After that, Vera became more distant to Peter. He was surprised Mina had interfered in the situation at all but she did. He was grateful she had such love for his children. She stood up for Vera like a trooper, Peter just happened to agree with Davie's parents on this subject. Hearing an argument already in the dinning room, he moved away from the door to see what was going on. Allie was throwing checkers all over the table while Charles David was trying to retrieve them. Ellen was yelling at Allie about how stupid and what a baby she was. "What is going on here, stop throwing young lady, this minute." Charles David was on the floor trying to pick up the ones that flew under the table. "She is an idiot Dad, a real idiot." Allie reaching as far as she could started kicking Charles David in the legs, making it hard for him to get up. Ellen was not helping she was instigating the situation further by her insults to keep the argument going. "All of you, to your room right now and I better not hear another word for the rest of the night." Charles David hit his head as he tried to come out but Allie landed a good one below his knee cap; leaving him speechless. "I said to your room both of you, girls right now." Raising his hand up and pointing towards the hall, he was firm. His jaw was set, both girls pushing each other through the hall continuing to insult until they got to their separate rooms.

Charles David got to his feet holding his knee limping to the couch. "What was that all about Charles David?" Not paying any attention to his father he was pulling up his pant leg to see the damage his sister had done. Katie Lee's little voice came from behind the dinning room table. "Allie had set up the checkers to play when Ellen came by, she knocked all the checkers off the board and pulled Allie's hair. Then Charles David said he was not going to pick up any checkers and Allie bent his fingers until he agreed to pick them all up." Closing his eyes and looking totally disgusted he ran his hand gently across Katie Lee's little face and told her to go get ready for bed now. "Man, Katie Lee you are stupid. You told now you are really going to get it. When are you going to learn to keep your little mouth shut?" Peter stared at his son's outburst and ran his hands through his hair. Katie Lee kind of spurred back against the wall as if someone was going to hit her. "No one is going to do anything sweet girl, go on to bed now." As Peter stood looking at his son, he was concerned with those words Charles David was so focused on his knee and the throbbing he did not realize his father was still standing there. "Charles David," his father spoke rather firm "I am going to hold you responsible to making sure Katie Lee get no kickbacks on this." Charles David was not sure he heard his father correctly. "Why do I have to be the babysitter? She said it, let her lay in her own stew." It was very rare for Charles David to see anger directed towards him from his father. He was careful not to get caught in either of his childish pranks or deliberate outbreaks, but that look tonight while he was staring right into his son's face was something that told him he had gone too far with his own mouth. "Do I have to repeat myself or are you going to do what you know is right?" Realizing the age of Katie Lee and that she never did create problems, his father was right. But he also knew what he had to deal with regarding his own sister and then worse Ellen.

Bending his head down on his knee Charles David was quiet and never looked back up. Peter left the room to go speak with Ellen. As he reached her door he took a deep breath. Opening her door without knocking the lights were off. "Ellen, turn the night light on, please." No sound, no response. "Ellen, turn the night light on, please." Stepping farther into the room he realized there was no one there. Turning back to the door he turned the overhead light on, the room was empty. More anger filled his emotions to the point that he started talking to himself just to stay under control. He walked down the hall to Allie's room not stopping to knock on the door that she shared with Vera. She was sitting very quiet on the windowsill not even turning nor care who was entering her room. Peter walked slowly toward her, noticing she was alone. There on the bunk bed was Vera's clothes that she did not bother to put away before she left, in fact everything that as out of place in the room belonged to Vera. Taking a deep breath he touched the top of his daughter's head very gently. Hearing her sniffle he knew she had been crying. With guilt in his heart he sat down beside her, "I am so sorry, Katie Lee told me what happened." Again not even looking towards her father Allie sat in silence. Reaching over her curled up knees he slowly wiped away the tears coming down her cheeks. She only responded by resting her head on her father's shoulder. "I am sorry Allie, but it does not help for you to escalate a situation that has already exploded." Only shaking her head she wiped her nose and cheeks. "Where is Ellen?" Shrugging her shoulders she did not answer her father. Knowing they had a thing about telling on one another, he was insistent on knowing where she was. Standing up he rubbed her back and walked back to the door. "She is in your room with her mother." Peter tuned with a frown on his face, his thoughts were bothered as he studied the back of his daughter while she was almost lifeless against the window.

Standing in the hall for a few moment, he went back to Ellen's room to see if Katie Lee was there, she was just finishing putting her PJ's on when Peter opened the door. Surprised, Peter never entered any of the girls rooms unless he knocked first and called out. "Get your pillow and come with me." He did not wait for her to answer or question. He pulled the blanket off her bed and led her back into the dinning room. Charles David was just putting the checkers away when his father appeared with his little stepsister. Knowing exactly when his father's intentions were, he forced a smile at her and nodded to his father. Charles David's bedroom was just off the dinning room, which was suppose to be a library. It was not very big but it fit Charles David just fine. He was away from the girls and had his own things, did his own thing. He was close to the living room so late at night when everyone was asleep he could sneak in and watch TV or go outside. No one ever knew or he thought they didn't. "You stay in Charles David's room tonight, I will see you in the morning for breakfast and you stay with Charles David. You hear little girl?" Not used to Peter talking to her like that, she just agreed starring at her stepfather. She was not afraid of her stepbrother but she was not sure if he would start his verbal nonsense. So she just went into his little room and laid down on the floor covering up with the blanket her stepfather had handed her. She gently put her pillow under her head feeling warm tears in her eyes. "Get in the bed Katie Lee, I won't have dad finding you on the floor." Charles David was kind of kicking her with a gentle kick to the leg, not meaning any harm she refused to obey. "Come on, you are going to get me into more trouble." Still she did not move or open her mouth She heard him sign and sat down beside her. Trying to play her into a better mood, he started acting as if he was crying and then started making faces right in front of her. She tried to move away but he would not let her. Finally, she laughed and he helped her off the floor. She curled up on the bottom of the bed and he looked at her strangely. "I will sleep down here, you can sleep up there and we will both have plenty of room, okay, Charles David, please?" He was surprised but it worked for him she didn't take up that much room. If his father came to check, she was there with enough room. Putting his stuff away and taking his dirty clothes to the laundry room he heard loud voices in his father and stepmothers bedroom. He could tell it was Ellen and Mina with his father interrupting every word. He moved just as quickly as he could back to his room to tell Katie Lee. But when he came in she was fast asleep. Good thing, he thought. So he turned back out of his door and headed for Allie's room.

Pacific Redwood Mystery: Do you believe in the little people yet?

He did not have to knock she was coming out, "Charles David you need to knock on the door. It is getting real loud in there?" Allie was not the type to get scared or worry about anything so Charles David knew that for her to ask concerned, well that was reason to try. "What is going on?" he asked. "I am not sure, dad went in there and I heard him ask Ellen why she was in there instead of her own room. Mina yelled at him. She could be in there any time she wanted and the fight went down." They both just stood there in the hall listening as the voices would go up and down. It seemed as if it went on forever. Even Mary came into the hall every concerned. They were so involved they didn't hear little footsteps coming up behind them. "What is the yelling about?" Katie Lee was rubbing her eyes "Shush, we don't know? Ellen, your mom and dad are in there, been in there forever." Charles David remarked. They all stood there like robots not knowing what to do. Each time the voices would go down, Allie would move close to the door trying to hear. When they would hear Mina raise her voice she would jump back. Finally Charles David said he was going to bed. As he turned he saw the look in his little stepsisters face he just took her by the hand and pulled her down the hall leaving both sister's standing there. Charles David was very gentle telling his little stepsister not to worry, they would stop pretty soon and everyone would go to bed. Tomorrow no one would remember anything. He knew that was a lie just as big as the nose on his face but he was tired and he wanted to sleep. He could not afford to leave her for fear she might go back down the hall and be caught by his father. He did not want to be punished. So he rubbed her little back until he saw her eyes starting to close. Every once in awhile he could hear the loud yelling and see Katie Lee jump while her eyes would pop back open. He was getting mad himself, this was silly. That darn Ellen always had to cause trouble. Tomorrow would be worse. Mina didn't get to go out and party. So hell would hang over them all. As he looked down at Katie Lee he truly felt sorry for her. She never caused anyone any trouble but she was easy to blame things on and easy to manipulate. What a horrible thought, but he just pushed it to the back of his mind and drifted off himself.

CHAPTER SEVEN

Leaving both his daughters speechless, Allie ran to her room with sobbing tears. Mary did not bother to comfort her sister as she had always done. Mary just sat wondering why they had to endure all this. Allie on the other hand was in deeper more drastic thoughts. She was beginning to think it might be better if she ran away. She wanted desperately to go back to her mother, she could take are of her. Her mother was no longer capable of taking care of herself, let alone any children. But that was okay, she was going to do it. First, she would ask her father's permission, she would give him that respect. Mina would probably love to have one of them leave anyway. Mina was not fooling Allie, she was not really fooling any of them, only her father. They all detested Ellen, not Katie Lee but she was not her problem; she wanted to go home. Allie got out of bed and started writing all the things she wanted to say to her father on a piece of paper. When she finally realized what time it was, the clock read 3:34am. Getting back to bed she looked over at her sister. Vera was fast asleep, in fact she had cried herself to sleep. She was in no mood to baby her over her boyfriend issues. Verna had been warned several times to come home when told, so she didn't feel sorry for her when she got caught. Allie sat in the dark reading what she had written her father. Again, not being able to keep the tears back she read through her heart aches and what she felt. She even asked him to let her go for a trial period, if is did not work out she would come back and never ask again. She even appealed to him from the point that her mother had brought her into this world and she was alone, without anyone not even one of her children. Why could she not have at least one sibling to comfort her.

On and on she read until she felt it was perfect and held all that her heart wept for. This was extremely hard for her, she was all tomboy and emotions did not come freely for her like the others. She had learned young to be tough and domineering, her personality came from her father's side. Laying her writing down under her pillow she stared out her window, the sky was full of stars and she closed her eyes as she repeated The Lord' Prayer. With a heavy heart she offered her simple prayer whispering like her mother had taught her as a child, hoping with all her might that her mother's love and belief in God would be true because sleep would not come. Allie wondered if she dared take her letter out, leaving it where her father could find it first thing. Her biggest fear was Mina might find it first. If she did, her father may never see it and she would have to deal with her stepmother. Lying there and thinking she decided to risk it. What did she have to lose? Worst case was he would say no, if that occurred she had made up her mind to run away. Throwing her covers off she slipped across her room, not wanting to wake her sister. Slowly turning the knob she slipped into the hall. Yep, Vera was right there was her stepmother and Ellen fast asleep in the master bedroom. She wondered why the door was open, most likely Mina did it on purpose to make her father more upset.

Tiptoeing down the hall she heard soft music. The fear of her father still being awake made her stop and rethink what she was doing. Standing there with stillness all around, she listened to see if she could hear other than just the music. Allie felt the peace in the moments, she did not want to move. Is she did, all the hurt, memories and disappointment's would return. Then she thought of her own mother, this was something she had to do, so she took a deep breath continuing on down the hall. She noticed her father was asleep in the recliner. The music seemed to taunt her emotions a she looked at her father, he looked older, worn-out, almost broken. Then some anger surfaced within her as her heart pounded through her chest. She thought of her sweet mother alone and sick. She eased closer trying very hard not to make a sound. He had a glass in his hand that was empty. Allie smelled the faint aroma of the contents, relieved to smell only soda. Slipping the glass from his hand she put it on the table beside the chair. As she glazed around the room she felt her dislike of everything about this place. It was not a home, it was a house with a lot of people in it. People that did not want to be there. Folding the paper in half, she placed the letter directly in her father's lap, then she worried that if he moved it would fall. No, that would not be good either, he could take off his shirt and Mina could find it for sure. Where on earth could she put it? She even thought about his boot, laughing to herself. That could work but if Mina came out she would see it. Again she risked her father never knowing about it. Getting discouraged she noticed her stepmother had left her sewing basket by the fireplace, searching she found some safety pins. Attaching the letter to a safety pin she eased her father's shirt out just enough not to stick him accidentally.

    She held her breath as she carefully pushed the end of the pin through his shirt as his chest breathed in and out. She knew if anyone tried to take if off him, he would surely wake up. The trick was to pin it on him without waking him. She stuck herself trying to watch his breathing and make sure he didn't open his eyes. Trying not to touch his arms, she let the letter hang sideways as she fastened the pin and backed away. Sticking her finger in her mouth from the prick of the pin she was surprised she managed it so carefully. Satisfied, she walked backwards until she was in the hall, but her heart stopped when she heard the bathroom door shut. Crap she thought, please don't let it be Mina. She didn't care if it was her sister, but what about Ellen? It would be a scene but that would be okay too, at least her father would have the letter for sure. Trying to make it to the bedroom before the bathroom door opened she was sliding along the wall on her tiptoes as fast as she could. Almost at the entrance of her room, thinking she had made it, she reached to brace herself on the threshold. Mina came from the bathroom. "What are you doing standing there, are

Pacific Redwood Mystery: Do you believe in the little people yet?

you spying?" Allie looked at her as is she was crazy but answered bravely "No, I have to go to the bathroom, it was occupied." Mina just passed her slamming the bedroom door behind her. What a relief she thought, now she did not have to worry about the letter. It was safe until her father woke. She knew she better go into the bathroom just in case she was listening. She did not like to lie, not like this but she was not taking any chances. She stood in the bathroom for what seemed a good amount of time and then flushed the toilet. Washing her hands she quickly went into her room closing the door behind her. Her body was flat against the inside of her door and she got scared. Maybe Mina might get back up and go into the living room. She opened her door, making sure all was okay. She felt more at ease to leave her door open for it gave her the opportunity to hear any squeaks or movements the night could make. Her mind played the normal tricks on a young girl waiting in the night for daylight to come. She dozed off a couple of times but something woke her as she found herself listening carefully to make sure all was still the same. Each time she would look at the clock it did not seem to be moving very fast; it was as if time was standing still.

This was the mot agonizing night of her life but she needed to hold on. One way or the other she was going home. She made herself believe she could make her mother well, it might be a slow process but she could. Her mind started going back to the last time she saw her mother. It was too painful, making her more angry at her father. Remembering how Mina had always played the little innocent Susie homemaker against her own mother when they were first together, her diva side was waiting to come out and it did. How in the world did Katie Lee live like this? Where and who was her real father anyway? In all of Allie's years she had never see her father lay a hand on her own mother, or any woman for that matter. He never even came close, where did this domestic crap come from? It certainly was not something she or her siblings were use to. Poor Katie Lee, she needed to get out of here, but how at her age? She was too shy to complain, too dominated by her mother and sister. It was obvious Katie Lee was not her mother's delight. Unfortunately Ellen was aware of her mother's devotional scheme's, Mina played if for all it was worth. Allie wondered what would happen to Katie Lee if her father left, as if that was going to happen. Her father thought the sun rose and set in Mina's eyes. For all she knew both girls would end up just like their mother. Man, that was a horrible thought, Ellen was already headed that way but she hope Katie Lee turned out different.

With her father's temper surfacing so badly, Allie felt Mina and her father deserved each other. What was it going to take for her father to wake up, "after the fact situation?" When someone was already hurt or maybe even dead? What about Charles David? Oh, he would be fine, he was such a little spunk he would always be fine. He did not let anyone push him around he was busy with sports and all he cared about was getting a car and having fun, She wondered if he ever thought about their mother, yes she was sure he did. It was just easier not to talk about it. Vera would probably go off with Davie for sure, she knew she would try to find a way to marry him. Poor Davie was so into Vera she didn't even see what was coming. She thought, oh hell life goes on. His parents would be really upset but it had to work. If Davie turned her loose then she could always come home to help with their real mother. She would need the help because her father would insist she stay in school. That was fine, she did love school but not here. Again checking the time, finally she was getting there, twenty minutes to 6:00am. Her father should be waking up soon and starting the coffee. Allie's father always made the coffee, Mina tried but it tasted terrible. Peter never said anything just made it sound as if it was something he liked to do. It wasn't like the old days when her real mother did everything. Mina would never take the Susie Homemaker banner of the year, it would be more like "shop until you drop and show it off." Allie knew with her father having all the children now it made it easier on them financially but if he would have to pay child support like the judge ordered in the divorce, Mina would not be so quick to put people down.

Pacific Redwood Mystery: Do you believe in the little people yet?

    Peter had gone back to court when their real mother of his children had her breakdown. She had held on for as long as she could but the divorce was too much for her. Peter had been her life, her childhood sweetheart and she never worked. She thought they had a good life until her husband started to change and stay away from her and the children more. It had become such a nightmare overnight. It all happened so quickly, she and Allie saw him one day with Mina; he was suppose to be working. As Allie thought back to how it happened in her heart she knew it was her stepmother that planned for them to be seen together, it was too perfect, too planned out. Now that Allie had lived with them, she was sure of it. She remembered the day her father left, clothes and all. Charles David was furious and threw away what he did not take. All remembered watching their own mother go deeper and deeper into depression. It was the school nurse that finally came to the house and discovered the problem. She called not only the protective authorities but also Peter. He came immediately but worse Mina was with him. Oh, how she played the sweet concerned stepmother insisting on the children be released to their father. It only made matters worse when Carol Ann saw Peter had brought her along. She had such a negative reaction they called the ambulance and took her to the psychiatric ward. Allie thought back to the hearings, the constant questions from some case worker, then a meeting before the judge. Mina had made a marvelous performance for the judge, the children were placed in Peter's custody. Charles David was the worst, he did not want to go live in a house with Mina, but it was either that or foster care. She remembered them all begging their brother to come, they could not accept the idea of him going to foster care. That was when Mina did her next public masterpiece, telling them she was so sorry but how could they blame her for falling in love with their father.
    How she only wanted to comfort them "only" until their own mother was well and they could return home. Why she even promised to make sure she got the best care in the best facilities they could visit her often and she would drive them herself if Peter was working. Peter was so pleased as she leaned on his arm while she was wiping her eyes,

asking for a handkerchief. The amazing part was if you looked close enough there were no tears in her eyes, no wet cheeks, no red eyes. Another grand slam performance by Mina. That was over four years ago now since then her mother had been in and out of mental facilities. The first time her real mother had been released the children could not go home. Mina had told Peter that when she took the children to visit her for the first time she talked about taking her life. Mina was afraid one of the children would find her. That was all Peter needed to go back to court to gain full custody over his ex-wife, the mother of his children. Mina pretended she did not want to testify against Carol Ann for fear of hurting her stepchildren and making matters worse for their real mother. So again she played the part crying and getting all hysterical on the stand, begging Peter and his children to forgive her as the judged looked on. Mina's testimony was beyond question, especially when she looked Carol Ann straight in the face and pleaded with her to forgive her, she only wanted the children to be safe until Carol Ann could seek proper mental help. What a farce!!

Allie knew from rumors her mother was home now, but not able to care for herself. So Peter was giving full custody of the children and when they asked to see their mother it was always a fight. Mina ranted and raved to her stepchildren about how they might find their mother, never letting them forget all she had done for them and being Peter's children, not hers. She constantly asked how could they want to even be with such a nutcase as their real mother had turned out, There was always an excuse and when Peter tried to plan around Mina's ranting, she would find out and instantly come up with something or somewhere they had to go, always telling Peter they needed good strong family roots, good family outings that Carol Ann was not stable and the children could fall into that trap. He would be responsible if something terrible happened to his own children under the hands of their own mother. Allie knew she was in this alone, she was not going to get any help from any of them. Maybe Charles David would visit, but he would not leave his material things now. He was in so much denial about his mother's sickness that he could not handle being around her for any length of time. He had learned to use guilt to his advantage also. Vera was not going to give up Davie. Mary had gone into her own shell that no one understood. Mary was special, but she kept herself very silent most of the time she never stopped dreaming of their mother. Mary had a lot of their mother in her but she was stronger. That was why Mina stayed away from Mary and let her be, Mary was too much of a reminder of their real mother. Allie prayed again as she lay there, this time she asked for not only a dream come true but also for the Lord to send his angels around her father to bind him so he could not deny her request. Did she dare believe this fate, a fate her mother instilled in her a long long time ago?

CHAPTER EIGHT

All the halls were decorated in school colors, it was as if they were talking to you as you walked between the corridors where you had spent the last three years of your life. Jacob could not help but look down each hall as he made his way to the gym. This would be his last walk, the last time he would be in these facilities as a student. With butterflies in his stomach he turned the final corner towards the boys locker room. There was a lot of hustle and bustle, it would have been impossible to hear what anyone was saying. With the usual handshakes and well-known signs, they all exchanged emotions in different ways. They had just learned all the seniors were going to graduate, not a single one failed. With pride circling through the halls, a tight feeling fell among them. They were all going to walk across the stage, except Katie Lee.

As Jacob passed the coach he pulled him aside. "Have you heard anything Jacob?" He asked the young man as he leaned into him, not wanting anyone to listen. Jacob shook his head no and that made the mood change. Jacob had always had a crush on Katie Lee but it had not gone anywhere. Not because he didn't want it to, she kept everything simple pretending as if she wasn't aware of Jacob's feelings. So they remained good friends doing several things together, he liked that. She was the best, he thought in his mind. He tried to shake the sad fact she was not there, he may never see her again or worse may not know what had happened. Little was known about Katie Lee before she came there. When asked, she would always say she came from the stars, where else did they think she came from? She said little but her personality made up for her lack of information. She was a good student, studied hard and participated whenever possible; except she was adamant about not running for any offices or anything like that. But when asked for help she would be the first there, Jacob remembered when she was elected junior princess at the prom, he knew she was going to win, but he along with Nancy had to practically drag her up on the stage to get her crown. When the parade came she was sick, so the runner-up got to take the glory and had all the fun. Jacob questioned her illness but backed off when he realized it might cost him her friendship.

Placing his gown over his suit, he wondered if maybe she would be with the girls in their gym and everything was okay? He was having a problem with his hat, the tassel would not stay on the correct side. He was about ready to jerk it right off when he saw the couch motion for him to come to the door of the boys lockers. As he came forward he noticed Nancy standing outside. Moving a little faster and listening to his buddies making cracks about Nancy coming for him in the boys gym, he just laughed at them knowing they were jealous. He was trying to read her face but she only smiled, already dressed in her cap and gown she looked so grown up and all. He almost wished it wasn't graduation day yet; after this night he may not see many of his classmates again. Is some cases that could be good in others as with most schools, it was a bad thing. Life does go on. "Have you heard anything?" he immediately asked her before he reached her. She pulled him out into the hall and around the corner. "My mother went to her house before she came and got me but no one was home. She called her aunt's workplace but they said she had left for the day. I went over before we came back but the house is all dark." Jacob just wouldn't put anything negative in his mind. Standing in silence Jacob felt his spirits became challenged. Nancy waited for Jacob to say something, she felt out of place just standing their watching him fidget. Nancy broke the silence "Well, I better get back, Mrs. Sullivan will be looking for me.

See ya inside, okay?" Nancy moved away from Jacob in a backward motion keeping her eyes on him. She felt bad leaving him standing there, she almost wished she had not said anything at all. She did not have any right making him feel so bad on such a special occasion. She slowly turned the corner herself and disappeared into the girls gym. Mrs. Sullivan was hurrying the girls in single line formation getting ready to exit down the hall towards the boys lockers. There they would join the boys going in pairs to the assembly hall.

Nancy took her place in line smiling as the other girls were all gleams with excitement. As the door opened she began her own last walk through the hall. Coming back around the same corner she had just left Jacob she could hear the boys cutting up in the hall. They paired off in two's continuing on down the hall with Mrs. Sullivan in the lead. Nancy noticed the boy beside her tugged at her arm, as she looked over at him she noticed he was moving out of line ahead two rows. Then she watched as Jacob took his place, moving in beside her. Not a word was said between them, they just walked in silence holding hands, knowing each other had the same thought. She was so glad Jacob had done this, it made the moment easier and she knew how Jacob felt about Katie Lee. See knew he must be all torn up inside, worried and confused. Entering the assembly hall was breathtaking, it was packed. The lights were dim as the seniors entered, the roars excelled. There were shouts of different names from families and friends in the crowd. It was exciting as they marched up front taking their seats. They could see the principal and his staff. One the table to the far left were all the diplomas, she wondered what they would do with Katie Lee's, surely they would save it for her. Maybe it was not even there.

The band began to play the school song with everyone coming to their feet. They could see more seniors in that hall than any other time in the school year. As the pastor made his way to the pulpit for the opening prayer, it took some time for the crowd to settle down. It was a long prayer as many of the seniors grew restless. Nancy was accustomed to prayers, she never missed church and it was the day her mother always took her out to eat afterwards. They were a rowdy class extremely well known for their pranks and wild activities. She had great memories of her last year but she had not joined any social groups, Katie Lee could have but she chose not to, she just loved school and being Katie Lee.

The speeches seemed to go on forever, Nancy grew tired. Then the coach made his way to the stage. Jacob leaned over to Nancy, "I didn't know he was going to talk, it will be short, he hates to give speeches." They both giggled as they watched him take his place in front of the crowd. He had a little trouble getting started as it seemed strange to everyone what he was doing up there in the first place. Then he cleared his throat for about the third time. "Ladies and gentlemen, children, fellow students and seniors. I have been asked to give a special award tonight to one of our seniors that was voted outstanding student by the staff." He went on to explain this award was voted on by all teachers, office staff and anyone that worked within the school system. Anyone could be up for the award, they met three times one month prior to graduation to vote and pick only one student that they felt was deserving of this award. The student could only have three approved absences all year, never in trouble or kicked out of school, including suspension for any reason, a good example off campus as well as on. The student must be liked by their fellow students, not just seniors but also from freshman class and up. He or she had to have participated in many activities in school but not necessary hold any student office. The had to maintain at least a B average all year. Nancy was looking around to see the reaction of the classmates as the recipient of the award was never know until graduation night.

No matter how you tried to find out who it was, the teachers seemed to keep it a perfect secret even from the student that won. Nancy wondered who was going to be given the award, she knew that her sweet friend was not going to get it. Being present was expected, her heart was sad, and she was glad under the circumstances the other classmates did not know that the coach had confided with her and Jacob. But she knew that the award would have to go to someone else now. She looked over at Jacob as he had his head down, just playing with the band on his watch. If anyone deserved that award it was Katie Lee. She sighed and settled back in her seat, placing one hand over Jacob's but he never looked up. The coach paused one last time then continued to explain that the person who had won the award with a unanimous vote was unable to be present among them this evening. The rule was, if the chosen applicant did not come to graduation, the student could not possibly get the award. Then he went on to say the staff had met that afternoon and again unanimously voted that in this case the student awarded this great honor should still get it. The had made an exception and felt very strongly about it. Nancy's head turned straight towards Jacob. "Wow" came out of Jacob's mouth as he straightened his back looking around. Then the couch did something that surprised everyone, he asked Nancy Hanson and Jacob Williams to come forward. Looking at each other they just sat still The students around them were telling them to go get up there. With hesitation, Nancy stood then Jacob followed. Nancy moved in front of him taking his hand leading the way to the stage. There was little commotion through the crowd and Nancy felt they were surprised as her and Jacob but were also wondering what was really happening. Nancy was the first to stand in front of the coach as she pulled Jacob around where he stood directly beside Nancy, the class applauded as Jacob's faced turned red as a beet. "Seniors I have asked these two students to come forward to accept this aware on behalf of your fellow student due to family emergency." Shock went through the whole room with endless murmurs. Students were looking around trying to figure out who was not thee. You could see their faces wondering how they missed one of their own. The the coach leaned forward into the mike.

"Nancy and Jacob, the staff here at Westland Redwood High would like you both to accept this award on behalf of Katie Lee Rossman." He handed a frame toward them and stepped back. The seniors began to shout and yell and some stamped in approval then the students stated in rhythm shouting, "Katie Lee, Katie Lee" showing they were all very much in agreement. Nancy stepped forward first

Pacific Redwood Mystery: Do you believe in the little people yet?

as they settled down, she briefly said how proud she was to accept this for her neighbor and friend. She spoke just a little about their morning excitement of the day and she knew in Katie Lee's heart if at all possible she would not miss this night with her classmates. Then she pushed Jacob to the mike, he stood there just looking at the frame his mind going in all different directions. He never looked up as he spoke with a voice that everyone could tell was difficult while staying focused and keeping his composure. He assured his fellow students that if anyone deserved this award, it was Katie Lee and he would give anything if she was standing there receiving it herself. As they turned to walk away the coach embraced Jacob and Nancy following them off the stage. Walking back to their seats, several seniors yelled out, "Way to go Jacob, Yea Nancy." So halfway to his seat, Jacob held the frame award above his head and stood for a second in the aisle. The seniors stood and applauded. As Nancy and Jacob settled back in their seats she was teary eyed. She could tell Jacob was also trying to get himself under control.

    Neither one expected this but Nancy felt very proud to have been picked to hold this for her friend and she was very pleased that Jacob had been there with her. In her heart she knew no one could have taken the award with more pride than Jacob. The rest of the ceremony was exactly as expected, breathtaking and memorable. As each senior crossed the stage to receive their reward for the years completing their education, it erupted. It was a small senior class but a mighty one. Nancy was so pleased to be a part of it. She knew most of them would be going off to the senior party at the country club. There would be swimming, eating and all kinds of activities. She would attend for a little while but she knew there would be drinking so she would leave before things got out of hand, She knew it was the same for all senior classes but that was not her thing and she wanted to get home, not only to be with her mother but also to plan their trip that was in three days. She also wanted to know if there was anything new about Katie Lee. Jacob asked her to ride with him to the party, she hesitated wondering how she would get back, thinking it was not good for Jacob to be alone right then, she agreed to go as long as he would bring her home when she wanted, he could return. She was surprised when he remarked that he probably would not be staying long himself.

It turned out to be a wonderful night, living up to all their expectations, it also had a foggy feeling lingering over them all. They had no answer for any of their classmates at the graduation. Nancy could tell Katie Lee's absence did make a difference. So many seniors were feeling the loss of a good friend and fellow student, caring very much that she was not there. She was deeply missed, she was deeply cared for by her class and teachers.

CHAPTER NINE

Mr. Sunshine was beginning to beam through Allie's bedroom window waking her, she had forgotten to put the shade down. The stars had been so beautiful she had fallen asleep. Sitting up immediately, she flew out of her bed towards the living room. She could smell the aroma of coffee still in the morning air. She had failed to stay awake waiting for her father. Rushing to her brother's room it was empty. Leaving without shutting the door, she went down the hall, she was the only one in the house. Where was everyone? Even the door to her father's bedroom was open, all the beds were made. She went to Mary's room where she heard voices. Listening closely at the door she realized it was Mary talking to Katie Lee. Knocking lightly she opened the door with a slight smile, asking where everyone was. Looking sad, Mary motioned her in and to shut the door. As she entered Katie Lee started to leave but Mary stopped her. Katie Lee sat back down on the end of the bed as Mary motioned for her sister to join them. "Allie, dad said when you woke up stay here at home and he would talk to you later this afternoon, you would know what he meant." She breathed in real hard letting the breath out almost instantly. Both sister's sat looking at each other. Allie wondering how much her sister knew, if anything.

"What is going on, Allie? Mina is driving everyone crazy trying to find out what dad meant by that message for you." Allie knew she was in for a horrible day with her stepmother. If her stepmother did not know what she had written her father, then she knew darn well she would do whatever she felt like doing to find out. Definitely before her father got home. "Did she talk to dad before he left, do you know?" Mary shook her head no. "I know he didn't sat anything. In fact he refused to talk to her at all and when he left he slammed the door in her face." There was that feeling one got in their gut, yep she was going to be in for a bad afternoon. No, she decided she was not. Why should she have to go through anymore abuse from this woman? She hadn't done anything wrong, she was not going through any verbal or physical abuse for one more day. She got off her sister's bed looking at them for a second, then left the room.

She did not know how much time she had, but whatever it was she needed to use it. She started throwing as many clothes that would fit into an old suitcase of her father's, grabbing what she felt she needed and did not want to leave. She would not be able to come back for anything, that was a fact she knew for sure. She heard a noise behind her, turning quickly she saw Mary standing with her arms folded. "What do you think you are doing?" Turning back to pack even faster she just ignored her sister. Frustrated, Mary came over throwing things back out. "Stop Mary, I am leaving and you cannot stop me. I am going home to mom." Grabbing her sister by the hand, she smiled. "I know, and I am not going to stop you, but you are not thinking smart here." Mary left the room coming back with the truck from her room. "What is that for?" asked Allie. "Well you will not be able to come back for anything so lets get as much as you can. Start packing as fast as you can and pack tight. I'll be right back keep the door shut."

Allie wasn't sure to trust her own sister or not? Well, she did not have time to question. If it would have been anyone but Mary, she knew it could be fake. She was pretty well done with most of the things in her room that she wanted, there were things she did not want, it would be a memory of Mina and she wanted to leave all that behind. Mary knocked on Allie's bedroom door, Allie noticed her sister was not alone. Standing behind her was her oldest sister's boyfriend, Davie. Mary began to instruct Davie what to do and make haste. "Take this truck and get it in your truck real fast Davie. If Mina should come into the driveway just drive off and don't stop." He looked at Allie and just winked, then moaned as he lifted the trunk at Mary's instruction. "What do you have in here, the kitchen sink?"

Her oldest sister Vera joined Mary and Katie Lee back into the room as Davie headed out to his truck. Vera took some money out of her pocket handing it to Allie hugging her tightly for what seemed long and wonderful. Vera stood in front of Allie looking into her tattered face speaking only to her with firmness in her voice. "Don't look back Allie, even if dad and Mina come for you, don't come back. Stand your ground and take care of our mother." The reaction of both her sisters took Allie by surprise, she couldn't believe what she was hearing. Mary spoke next as she fought to keep calm for her sister Allie. "I got up last night to check on things, I don't trust Ellen. I saw you pin something on dad. I tried to take it off without waking him but, he woke up." Startled, Allie's eyes went wide as her hands went over her mouth. "It is okay, dad and I read it together. It is okay, he is going to let you go." Starting to quiver Allie just stood there with her feet frozen to the floor. "You better get out of here girl, daddy was trying to figure out a way to get around Mina, now he does not have to. We will stand in for you and protect dad, just get out of here and don't look back." Vera hope those words penetrated Allie's mind, she needed to move fast. Grabbing her purse and jacket she went into the hall, little Katie Lee was standing in the entrance of her door, she didn't know what to say or if she could say anything but she couldn't let her go without knowing how she really felt about her. "I really love you Allie and I will miss you, but I promise no matter what I won't tell." As Allie looked at her, that tug in her heart was real, she did care. Katie Lee's face looked so sad and broken. How Allie's heart went out to this brave little soul. Putting her arms out to her little stepsister, Katie Lee ran to her stepsister. They had never been close but only because of things put in their path that was far beyond their control. Holding her for only a stolen moment she put her hand under Katie Lee's chin holding it upward towards her. "You are special, I wish I could take you with me but you have my dad. He loves you Katie Lee, just like his own but if he ever leaves your mother get out yourself. Whatever means you have to get out, do you hear me?"

Katie Lee nodded her head as if she understood watching along with her two stepsister's as Allie rushed out the door. They all ran to the front porch as Davies pickup whizzed past the driveway disappearing out of sight. Just standing there the silence could be cut with a knife. Mary reached over and took Katie Lee's hand. Without looking at her, she spoke words that shocked Vera and Katie Lee. "You remember those words Katie Lee, if my father ever leaves your mother promise me that you will leave." Squeezing Katie Lee's hand in hers she asked the second time. "Promise me, Katie Lee." The little girl looked up at Mary she moved closer to her stepsister. "Yes, I promise, no matter what I promise." Mary let go of her hand walking back to her room and closing the door behind her to let everyone know she wanted to be alone. Vera took her little stepsisters over to the steps and sat her down, talking to her about how much trouble they would be in when Mina got home. She did not expect Katie Lee to stand up for them but try real hard for her own safety not to get involved. She left her stepsister sitting on the steps, she seemed frozen herself until her little puppy came for approval of her presence. Katie Lee gently put her pup on her lap and promised him nothing bad was ever going to happen to him again. She never went back into the house, she stayed on the porch with her pup hoping her stepfather would be home soon. She could hear the girls in the house coming and going from their room but she did not want to go in. If Katie Lee just didn't think about it, maybe the memory of Allie's face would fade away. She was the first to hear a car coming up the hill from the road below. She jumped to her feet running for Mary's room with Penny at her heels. She did not even know she had gotten that far until she had the door open with both girls staring at her abrupt entrance.

"Someone is coming up the hill," she shouted with her eyes wide open and such fear in her voice. Mary was the first to her feet, "Take your little puppy and go to the barn and stay Katie Lee. Do not return until you are called." She took off out the back door without a word.

Pacific Redwood Mystery: Do you believe in the little people yet?

Mary closed the door behind her as though nothing was wrong and continued pasting pictures with her sister into an album they had been working on. They heard the car come into the driveway and a door close. Was it their father or Mina? Sometimes Peter would use the spare car if he didn't have a job pending. That was the question on both their minds as they just looked at each other without a word. Hearing a noise in the kitchen, they came to the conclusion that it most likely was Mina but no other voices were heard. Where was Ellen? If fact, they had not heard nor seen her all morning. "What about Katie Lee in the barn, if Ellen was out there?" Vera tried looking out the window as far as she dared. "We cannot think about that right now, we have to just play dumb and act like everything is cool, I am sorry." Both girls looked sad over what they were having to do but felt they did not have a choice. Touching Mary's hand Vera whispered to her sister. "One of these days Mary, before I leave I swear I just want one swing at Ellen and her mother."

They heard the back door open again and close but no other noise. Then they heard it open and close. Footsteps in the hall told them someone was just standing outside their door. That was when they knew it was either Ellen or Mina. The girls started a conversation of nonsense for the purpose of whoever was listening. Both just talked and watching for the door to open, it didn't take long. Mina stood before them in a new outfit she obtained from shopping that morning, which was no surprise to anyone. "Where is Allie, I need to talk to her in the kitchen right away?" Mina barked at both girl as they continued to look at each other pondering an answer. Unexpectedly rushing into the room was Katie Lee, her eyes as big as saucers looking as if she had seen a ghost. "Hi mom, is that a new outfit? It looks real good on you." The girl was acting so strange. Her mother glanced over at her, not even saying a word. "Where is Allie? I will not ask again" Before either sister's could speak up their little stepsister jumped to the bottom of the bed and looked directly at her mother. "She left a long time ago mom, said she was going for a walk." The girls looked absolutely in a daze on what was Katie Lee trying to do. Her mother turned directly towards her daughter grabbing her hard by the shoulder and hauling her off the bed by force. "When did she go for this walk and with whom?" Mina's temper was already showing, the girls were getting concerned for their young step sister. "Just walking Mommy. She just went walking towards the orchard that's all." It was Mary who realized that her little stepsister was trying her best to protect them and Allie. She was no match for her mother and the girls knew it but they did not want to discredit her for fear of what may happen to her for lying to her mom. Vera needed to get the attention away from her stepsister before Mina really blew. "We saw her about close to 11:00am or so walking towards the orchard like Katie lee said, she looked like she might be going berry picking." Mina's eyes were furious and one could almost hear the anger rising within her. "Where is Charles David?" That, they honestly did not know. Shrugging their shoulders they didn't have a clue. Mina turned to Katie Lee "I have not see him, Mom. I really haven't." Mina was beyond anger, she jerked the little girl out of their room and down the hall. Mary and Vera immediately rushed after her. They knew something was going to happen but not sure what they could do. As they approached the kitchen, Mina was taking a spatula in her hand with Katie Lee held hard with the other. "What is this I heard you slept in Charles David's room last night?" Katie Lee was trying to circle her mother knowing she was going to get smacked. "Yes, daddy Peter told me to, honest, ask him." Before the words got out of her mouth, her mother spanked her several times over and over on her little bare legs. Katie Lee was begging her mother to stop, telling her Peter have given her permission. Mina kept yelling that she did not have permission, so she was a bad girl and bad girls needed to be punished.

    Mary had seen enough without warning she grabbed the spatula from Mina and told her that was enough. There was outrage on Mina's face. She lunged into the girls face, fists in the air. Katie Lee rushed in, thinking her stepsister was going to get hit. Pushing Mary back so she didn't get hit, she said. "No mommy, you cannot hit her. She didn't do anything wrong either." The whole kitchen became a battleground.

Pacific Redwood Mystery: Do you believe in the little people yet?

Mina grabbed the mop by the stove and started swinging it towards all three girls. She hit Mary so hard she cried out. Vera was trying to get the mop away from Mina as Katie Lee held on to the back of her mothers shirt screaming for her to please stop. With all the commotion going on no one saw Peter come through the door. Quickly shoving them all in different directions to keep them separated he could not believe his eyes. Katie Lee looked at her stepfather. "It was my fault daddy Peter, my fault, not the girls I slept in Charles David's room last night. I saw Allie go for a walk, and she is mad at me." Standing behind her mother, she was desperate pleading towards her stepfather in what seemed the most sincere plea any child could beg for. Mina threw her husband a horrifying angry look, pushing Katie Lee from her she shouted her demands towards Peter, "Living room this minute, including Allie. You better believe me, Peter, I am not joking, get them all in there."

    Charles David was standing in the door frame carrying two bags of ice as if he had just walked into the twilight zone. Peter was sure Mina was crazy, lost all her common sense. "Charles David, put the ice away and go outside and take everyone with you." Peter never looked at his wife. He did not have to, he knew what was coming. Watching his son move towards the freezer he pointed his finger outside with the look they knew he meant business. Mina took her stand and blocked the door, she was not letting any of them out. "In the living room Peter and I mean it, all of them." Peter shook his head in despair. Mina started to open her mouth again as Peter walked away from her towards the hall. "Fine Mina fine, but not until I check something then we will have this meeting. You may wish differently when I'm finished." Peter snapped back at her. Mina pointed her finger to the living room ignoring Peter and not bothering to pay attention to what he was doing. One by one they went single file into the living room. Mina stuck her head out the screen door and bellowed fiercely for Ellen to get in the house.

    Peter ignored Mina's looks as he stared down the hall alone, as he got to Allie's room he entered but his heart filled with grief to see her not anywhere. He opened the two drawers seeing only a few handful of items left behind. The closet was empty except for things left on the floor of the closet. No shoes, no pictures, no personal items. Standing helpless in the middle of the room, Peter felt betrayed. Not by his children but by the very beat of his own heart and selfish lust. There were no words for what he was feeling, there was no one to blame but Peter himself. How could he have taken such a wrong turn in life? It took awhile before he could compose himself enough to leave the room, he only could hope she was safe and had not made any decisions that would bring her harm. He needed answers, he needed answers to a lot of things.

Peter could hear all the commotion still in the living room. Mina's mouth was the main source of confusion. She was not listening to anyone, she was only yelling beyond the limits of a parent. As Peter entered the room Ellen was just coming through the door from outside. Everyone was on the couch together while Mina stood by the fireplace, waving her hands and running her mouth. Charles David was the only one sitting on the floor at the end of the couch near his sisters. As Ellen came close, she took Katie Lee by the arm trying to pull her off the couch. "I'm sitting here, go sit on the floor by your pal over there." Peter came behind his older stepdaughter taking her gently by the arm moving her to his recliner sitting her down firmly. "Stay right there Ellen," pointing his finger at her as he motioned for Katie Lee to stay where she was. "Sit down, Mina, stop your yelling and sit down." Mina stood firm by the fireplace refusing to budge. Ignoring her, he pulled up the small footstool sitting down in front of the children. This infuriated Mina even more. Peter was watching his wife out of the corner of his eye as he saw her bend to pick up the soot brush from the fireplace. "Don't do it Mina, please don't."

It became so quiet they could have heard a pin drop, even Ellen's facial expression changed. She did not look towards her mother, she kept her eyes to the floor. Turning the stool so everyone could see him, he acted as if Mina wasn't even in the room while being on guard for any verbal or physical outburst. Katie Lee put her hand up as if she was in school waiting for the teacher to recognize her so she could speak. "Put your hand down little girl or that smacking in the kitchen will be just the beginning." Mina snarled at her little daughter. Peter immediately noticed Katie Lee's legs begin to shake. He turned to make sure Ellen as well as his wife could see and hear him. He heard muttering from Mina but could not make it out. Peter looked up at her, then turned his face away, looking towards his son first. Charles David thought his father was going to address him but soon realized his remarks was directly for his stepmother but looking directly at his son. "Shut your mouth Mina, just shut your mouth." Peter had never been so forward with Mina in front of the kids. Everyone knew Mina would usually take this as a challenge to start a fight, this time the look on Peter's face was different, it was a look and feeling Mina had not experiences before. But Mary knew Mina would keep pushing his buttons to provoke his anger, hoping he would strike her. It was like Peter instantly read Mary's mind, her father turned towards Mary giving her that calm fatherly smile. "No kids, I am not going to hit her nor am I going to let her hit me. If it gets that far I expect all you kids to jump in, I promise, do you?" Not only were they shocked in their father words but also they were relieved. Thinking at first that it was a joke, Ellen giggled until Mina came forward and hit Peter on the top of the head with her open hand. "Who do you think you are? Get out of my house and take all your brats with you." Peter just sat there as everyone didn't know what to expect. Do they stay still or move?

Again, Mina came forward but Peter blocked her hands, stopping her next blow. Charles David was on his feet but the girls just sat in silence not daring to make a move. "This is my father's house, not yours." Peter put his hand up to his son and pointed for him to sit back down. Peter knew this was not good, it was going to play out but he was not going to let anyone get hurt. Had this been the first time she lost her temper like this with Katie Lee, something he was in denial about. Standing up Peter placed one hand in his pocket as he ran the other hand through this thick dark hair. "Who can tell me where Allie is?" "That is all I want to know, no one is in trouble. I just want to know she is safe." Twisting her hands, Mary felt she had nothing to lose at this point, her father was so disconnected with uncertainty. Clearing her throat leaning forward "She should be home with mom by now." Mina threw her hand up so fast she knocked all her knickknacks off the top shelf on the fireplace. Peter immediately sighed a breath of relief as his body seemed to relax in just knowing.

"Her mother, that nutcase, how did she get there?" Mina's shouting her remark regarding the children's mother hit hard to Peter's children, as Mina continued she whirled around looking Katie Lee right in the face as Peter stepped in front of Mina to block her attack that was coming, then bending down on one knee right in front of his little stepdaughter he placed his hands over hers shaking uncontrollable on her lap. "Katie Lee, I am not leaving you unless you want to stay." The little girl was afraid to look forward for fear of having eye contact with her mother. Utter fear ran through Katie Lee's body so she whispered to her stepfather, "I am scared daddy Peter." That was all Peter needed to hear as he helped his granddaughter off the couch towards Mary, "Take her and pack a few things right now." Turning to Ellen, he stayed distant. "You can stay with your mother, you need to." Ellen grinned like she was pleased in the whole matter turning her whole body away from her stepfather, looking down. Mina went into another rage, demanding he could not take Katie Lee anywhere, she was not his child and was not of age to make any decisions. She would call and have him picked up for kidnapping.

Peter continued to ignore his wife as he tapped his little stepdaughter on the nose, rising to walk down the hall he gave Charles David a nod to follow. Going into his bedroom he took a duffle bag from the top shelf of the closet. He was beginning to gather some items as Mina entered the bedroom. As the voices began to get louder Charles David ran to knock on Mary's door, as she opened the boy didn't explain. He just grabbed her wrist taking her with him back to the bedroom. Vera came out into the hall, she too could hear loud voices. Peter had decided he just was not going to listen anymore, it was not worth the agony to any of the kids, so he took a step away from Mina but

Mina moved in fast, shutting the door in his face and keeping him in the bedroom. Charles David acted fast, whether it was from fear or gut feeling he opened the door instantly. Peter grinned at his son with approval. Passing his wife he took hold of the duffle bag leaving her talking to herself. He did not bother to shut the door as he left, telling the children to hurry up.

Mina was standing firm, screaming obscenities out her bedroom door as Katie Lee started to pass with Mary. She reached grabbing Katie Lee without warning by the child's hair. Mary lost her hold on her little stepsister as she screamed for her dad. Peter raced back down the hall but Mina had managed to get Katie Lee into her bedroom, shutting and locking the door before Peter could make it in. Charles David looked at his father. "We cannot leave her dad." Peter moved his son away from the door with one huge hit, the bedroom door came flying open against the weight of his body. To Mina's surprise seeing Peter quickly turned forcing the little girl into the bathroom. Peter caught Mina by the arm whirling her onto the bed. Charles David was in the room to try to stop anything that may start to provoke his father further. Mary entered taking Katie Lee into her arms, she never looked at Mina just walked quickly and got them out of the room. "Come one dad, we need to go." Those were the only words that were heard as Mary calmly spoke, but the intensity of her words whispered a caution they all understood. As Charles David started for the door way with his father, Mina took her antique silver handed mirror from the dresser, slamming it across the cedar chest at the end of the bed. Glass flying everywhere, she flung the handle straight toward Peter's head as her eyes pierced Peter's soul.

"Calm down, Mina, get control of yourself." Peter could not believe her behavior as he spoke firm to her. With one hand he was trying to motion her to get under control, with the other hand he was reaching for a towel to thrown across the bottom of the bed to push the broken glass aside. He had seen her mad before but never like this. In his mind he kept repeating not to hit her not matter what she did. That would be exactly what she wanted, he had to keep his own control.

He kept motioning towards the glass, they needed to clean it up before someone got hurt. "Son, go get the broom and dustpan." Charles David took off to obey his father. The words coming out of his wife's mouth could teach any sailor a new vocabulary. He was struggling from within both physically and mentally to maintain his own composure as Mina's none stop screaming continued. He even thought that something had happened to her, maybe she finally snapped, no not her. This was just a plain temper tantrum, but one she was not going to win. This would probably be the first time in her life if the truth was known. When Mina realized she was getting nowhere, she started picking up whatever was within her reach, trying to bash Pete. It was easy to avoid, she was so angry she was just throwing rather than aiming. There was a sudden change in Mina's eyes that Peter began to see, like a wild animal when they decided to make that fatal decision. He tried to brace for what she might do next, trying to move away from her and get out of the room period. She let out a yell that sounded worse than some animal being wounded, she ran full force at him with her hands ached like claws.

"Mina" Peter shouted towards her, "What the hell is wrong with you?" She was trying to reach his chest, face, everywhere. She was so out of control her words were more spit than complete sentences. Mary came back to assist her father as Charles David sprang over her. Seeing the situations had escalated to a level her father and brother could not handle, her mind raced with fear as she ran for the phone. The cord had been jerked out, no dial tone, my God, what was she going to do? Racing back to her father's side, she found herself in danger as Mina lunged or her with a piece of glass in her hand. Peter threw his daughter in the opposite direction to avoid her getting cut. Mina did not even seem to notice her feet were slipping through cut glass herself, nor did she seem to care.

Ripping Peter's shirt as she tried to pull herself off the floor, he was trying to avoid her advances. Trying to distract her by bringing attentions to the cuts on her feet it seemed to anger her more. Mary knew her father was not going to be able to deal with this much longer. Mina wanted a physical conflict she wasn't stopping. Mina could see her husbands temper rising, he was losing control. The sweat dripping off Peter's forehead and cheeks seemed to increase as Mina kept coming and coming after him. The screaming, the ripping, the cut glass buried in the bottom of Mina's feet, still there was no end. Mary started screaming at her brother as the fierce fight continued. He had taken everyone's bags to the truck to hurry their departure. The more Peter tried to release Mina's fingers and hands from him, the more she would lunge, bite, kick and growl like a wild animal. It was almost as if she had became possessed. Peter took both his hands and pushed Mina backwards with a force that would make most people land in the next room. As she hit the floor, he thought for a moment he had knocked her out. He could hear his son somewhere behind him running down the hall as his own eyes were trying to focus on his daughter lying on the far left side of the bed, trying to understand what was happening as much as her father. Peter was exhausted with sweat now rolling down his back, he was leaning with hands on his knees looking towards Mary when the expression on her face gave him more alarm. Frozen and unable to move Peter could not believe his eyes as he looked into the barrel of his own hand gun. Where did she have time to get her hands on it, unless the short time she pulled Katie Lee into the bedroom she retrieved it from his nightstand. Oh Lord, his heart stopped.

Peter straightened his body, moving in slow motion towards his wife but she shot, missing Peter my inches. As she brought the gun up a second time they all watched as her fingers trembled on the trigger, another shot then another. Peter drove to the floor Mary crawled in terror to her father's side as he was coming off the floor like a buffalo. Mina lost her balance falling, as Peter turned his daughter gasped loud in a panic. Standing in the doorway of the room was his son with his father's 22 caliber rifle. Peter immediately knew what could happen. With sweat on his hands , his mouth dry, words would not come; Peter slid one foot forward in the direction of his son. "Jesus, Charles David, give me the gun." There was a white power still shifting from the ceiling where Mina' had just put two bullet holes. Peter had to dis fuse this situation before they had an after the fact incident.

Charles David's fingers were clenched tightly on the gun, Peter kept talking to his son as he manged to get him to point the barrel in a different direction "I only wanted to scare her dad, but if she tries to shoot you again, I swear." Fear was shuttering inside Peter, God help he whispered to himself, he did not underestimate anything at this point from his wife. She had tried to shoot him point blank, his son could have shot back and killed his stepmother. At this point Peter was sure that if Mina had not missed his son would have killed her. "We have to leave now dad, Right now." Mary was rubbing her hands across her father's shoulders as the room still echoed the sound of death. Ellen was the first to step through the doorway around her stepbrother, getting to her mother trying to assist her to a chair in the corner of the room. Katie Lee had her hands over her ear's, eyes closed as her head was bent into her chest. Vera could not believe her eyes as she huddled against the wall outside the doorway.

With Ellen's help Mina rose from the floor. Ellen slowly kicked the hand gun to her stepfather making her mother more angry. Peter was still trying to get his son to release the rifle. Mina's eyes began to burn like fire as her own daughter began to fear her mothers mood. Ellen could see and feel more trouble. She knew she had to warn her stepfather but she did not want to bring attention to her mother. "Peter, Peter" she was trying to restrain her mother but even Mina's jerk was stronger than Ellen expected. "How dare you try to kill me, Ill have you arrested." Mina was shouting towards Charles David as her body began to shake from the anger that began to mount once more. Ellen was scared out of her wits, she let her mother go, fearing for herself. There was no fear in this woman's soul. "I only shot at the ceiling you witch, to stop you from shooting my dad." Charles David snarled right back at her. Peter made two attempts to retrieve the rifle from his son, but he would only turn his body making it hard for his father. Peter was smart enough to realize the situation was far too tense for anyone demanding anything. Again, Ellen tried to get her mother's attention. "Mommy, come lay down, I'll get some tea or water or something but you need to rest." Ellen was the only one in the room to get her mother under control. They may all end up victims in this room if Peter did not get all the children out soon. Mary and Ellen together came close to Mina, guiding her again towards the chair in the far corner. "Oh look, we need to change your clothes. Let's put those new PJ's on we bought today that you said was something Lana Turner would probably buy." Ellen's voice was breaking, Mary knew this was not good. Mina seemed to be in some kind of trance all of a sudden so Perter stood perfectly still, letting the girls take control. Mary's soft voice spoke as she smiled towards Ellen it was like the presence of an angel, tender and soothing, If anyone could defuse the situation it would be Mary. Gently, she just kept talking to Mina, guiding her with Ellen's help towards the chair.

Vera returned and immediately began pulling Katie Lee back farther from the doorway, getting her closer to the back door. Charles David looked as if he had seen a ghost. The poor lad was dumbfounded, not only in what he had done but also for being a part of this dysfunctional situation for so long. Feeling a strong hand on his shoulder father and son stood looking eye to eye. Peter eased the rifle out of his son's grip. Turning, Peter took only one step towards the gun case to replace it under lock and key, stuffing the shells in this pant pocket as he motioned for his son to hand over the key to the gun case. His hands was reaching for the door of the gun case when he heard a commotion behind him again, "Mina, wait. No, wait, calm down." Ellen was trying to help but with fear, "Mom stop, mom wait please." Looking over his shoulder he could see Mary struggling to hang on to his wife. Ellen was already knocked to the floor by the chair. "Mom," please wait, mom." Ellen was shouting and grabbing for her mother's ankles knowing Mina was to much for Mary, she had become too much for anyone.

Did you ever hear the statement if someone snaps or loses all control, they are five times their strength? It's true!!

Mina raced towards her husband, barely turning from the gun cabinet he felt the weight of her body. He felt what was left of his shirt come off. Reacting quickly he kept trying to keep the gun above his head so she could not reach it. Mina began pounding her fists everywhere, biting again and pulling at Peter's arm. Charles David was begging his father to pass the rifle but Peter couldn't get Mina off him long enough to get the assistance and avoid her blows all at the same time. Mina managed to grab the butt of the rifle, yanking with all her might. Peter could not think with all the emotional screaming and his wife whirling out of control. The terror and anger through emotions was rising. "I hate you, I hate your kids." Mina's voice was bellowing like a banshee right out of some horror movie. She kept yanking harder and harder but as she reached higher to get a better grip on the barrel of the gun, she slipped and landed with her feet across the doorway of the bedroom. In her fierce anger, she could see Katie Lee hovering beside Vera closer to the back door with her little arms completely covering her head and shoulders. "What possibly could be going through such a young girls mind to witness such madness." Vera was so tensed up she couldn't hardly move herself let along try to move Katie Lee, if the door laying in the middle of the hall from Peter breaking it down, she could pull Katie Lee closer to the back door and out o there.

Mina, not completely coming to her feet, got to her knees crawling towards her younger daughter on all fours like an animal. The heavy breathing coming from her whole body alarmed Vera as she tried to jump over the door from Peter and Mina's room laying in the hall. Screaming for Katie Lee to move, the young little girl could not hear with her hands over her ears as her other was getting closer to her. Vera ran from the house stumbling all the way leaving the small girl to defend for herself. Katie Lee had no idea the danger she faced. Her head was bent totally into her knees and her ears were covered. Peter didn't waste time as he dove past Charles David, the rifle hit the floor near the threshold of the bedroom. Mina was already on top of the child. All Peter could see was his stepdaughter's hair flying with her head being hammered into the wall. Her painful cries put Peter into a rage. Screams from Ellen could be heard as she huddled near the chair, "Mom, stop stop." Her voice was as hysterical as the others but nothing seems to penetrate through Mina, nor her state of mind. She was beyond anything but her own means of destruction. "I'm going to kill you, do you hear me, Katie Lee, kill you." Blood was flowing from the little girl's nose, her hair was so long it became her worst nightmare against her mother. Mina was holding her daughter with her hand wrapped around the child's ponytail using it as a weapon to hold her down. Charles David stumbled trying to get out of his father's way, he didn't know whether to try and help or stay where he was. He could feel the barrel of the rifle against the bottom of his feet. He was too scared to move, he couldn't even help his little stepsister as her mother continuously hit her head into the wall.

Peter reached for the back of Mina's shirt and upper arms, with one huge force he threw her off the child. Her body flew backwards almost hitting Charles David as her body came down with a tremendous bounce. She began slapping Charles David swinging wildly towards him, he scrambles to his knees joining his father and little stepsister in the hall. Peter was holding the child in a cuddling position with his handkerchief over her little nose as the blood was dripping through his fingers. He knew her little nose was broken, as he looked towards his wife he wanted so much to break her neck and hear every bone break as he did it.

"Hold this tight now, we are going to get you and everyone out of her pumpkin." "Dad, I think her nose is broken." "Yes, son just get the truck started. We need to take her to the hospital." As Peter bent to retrieve the rifle off the floor, Charles David saw what seemed to be two broken teeth lying in the blood. Once again Mina rushed for the rifle in Peter's hand. He was quicker and ready for her attack. He managed to keep her far away enough to maintain height above her. He thought she was clear, but he underestimated the distance, as she lunged she sunk her teeth in his upper arm right under the arm pit. Unfortunately, the weight from her body and pain from her deep bite brought the butt of the rifle swiftly connecting a direct blow with Mina's forehead. Ellen's screams were piercing. "Oh my God, oh my God, Mommy mommy." Peter knew she was no longer near him, he could feel no weight. He was trying to focus what had happened, he had heard the sound. A sound he was too familiar with when something hits hard and the sound of broken bones. Ellen's screams were loud but dull to his ears. Snapping to reality he saw his wife's unconscious body before him. The rifle still in his hands, he threw it to the bed. He did not have to look at his figure in the mirror to know he was covered with sweat and blood.

Ellen crawled on all fours to reach her mother as Mary was gathering sheets from the bed around Mina's head. "Son, call 911, son, Charles David" Not realizing his son's vision was anything but normal. He staggered to where he thought the door was. "Mary the phone." Peter instructed, falling beside Mina Peter was holding a blood soaked towel as firmly as he could around his wife's head not knowing exactly how bad the wound was. He knew she was in danger for her life. Mary told Charles David the phone wires had been pulled out but maybe they could hold the wires together long enough to get a call out, that didn't work. "Jesus, help us, It's not working dad." Charles David looked to his dad shaking his head no, Peter swung Mina's unconscious body into his arms as he rushed out of the room down the hall towards his truck. Ellen was right on is heels, refusing to obey his orders to get back in the house. Mary stood at the back door assuring her father he needed help and who better than Mina's own favorite daughter. She felt cold with panic as she watched her father speeding off down the hill with Ellen holding her mother's head close to her chest.

Vera had disappeared earlier when she deserted Katie Lee, she could not stand the drama. As she heard the tires burn rubber from her father's truck, she ran back into the house. She saw Mary standing in the doorway and felt worse seeing the towels she held in her arms were soaked with blood. "What, oh God what happened?" What she really wanted to know was trapped somewhere between her thought process, as her mouth was unable to ask. Charles David and Katie Lee were in the bathroom running water in the bath tub as the little girl huddled against the bathroom door between severe pain and fear. "Oh God, did her mother do that?" Guilt spread through Vera, she had ran she had left her stepsister unable to defend herself against her mother. "What are you doing Charles David?" Seeing her brother's face in the mirror, she realized why he couldn't see for those few seconds. He had long nail marks down the left side of his eye and over his nose that continued down this throat. Mina had managed to take the skin clear off parts of his face. Mary was more than sure he had a cut or some kind of damage on the inside of his eye. It was real red, watery and he had problems keeping it open. The pain was unbearable he was having a terrible time withstanding the discomfort. Mary helped him put a patch made of a large band-aide over his eye to keep it shut. They taped it with white medical tape Vera found in the emergency kit. Vera told everyone just to go to Charles David's room. They looked at her as if she lost her mind. "I am sure the police will be here soon. We need to make sure nothing is disturbed. They need to find everything exactly as it was."

Everyone knew this was more for their father's protection, this was extremely important. Who knew what the story Mina would tell, but this time they were all witnesses and they had Katie Lee not to mention Charles David's injuries. Mary was looking forward to them coming, especially to see this child and what her own mother had done to her. As she thought of that, she knew if she cleaned her up there would be no evidence. She begged everyone to start looking for a camera. No luck, not that they were surprised either. As they sat there with Katie Lee they could not let her stay like that. They needed to clean her up and change her clothes. Charles David said there was enough evidence between his stepsister and his face. Mary was not sure, as she sat beside her little stepsister she asked her if she realized what they were talking about. Katie Lee was still in shock and her nose had to be terribly painful. Two of her front teeth had been knocked completely out. She still held the wash cloth in her mouth that Charles David had given her to bite on. Then Vera remembered something, she took off for the back porch. When she returned she had a large black bag. "Cool, where did that come from?" Vera was grinning, "David bought it for me for Christmas but I had to promise to hide it." As she carefully pulled out the camera she looked at her brother. "Well do we have time to read the instructions because I don't know how to use it." Her brother laughed "Can bears crap in the woods?" He took the camera filming his little stepsister, Mary began talking to Katie Lee gently turning her head, running her hands gently through her hair as she help up the hair that fell out and stayed within her fingers. The blood, the nose, the clothes and her mouth where the teeth were missing. She nodded her head and suggested to Charles David that was enough. They took turns taking pictures of their brother, hoping they had gotten what was needed. Charles David took more pictures of the bedroom and hall. It was difficult with just one eye but he was determined. "Hide it Charles David and don't say a word until we can talk to dad." Getting angry he replied, "Why not, if they come out accusing they need to see this?" "Yes, they do Mary replied, but we have the only copy and if it comes up missing, what do we have then?" With that her brother left the room giving his sister thumbs up not commenting further.

 Mary guided Katie Lee back to the bathroom. She sat on the side of the tub swishing her hands through the water and making sure it was not too hot but not too cold, she had to coach her little stepsister into the tub. She knew her father had not forgotten about her or the seriousness of her injury, but Mary would be surprised if Katie Lee's mother was even still alive. Each step the little girl took to reach the tub was painful and Mary had to hide her own anger. Vera came to help and brought Penny with her. Katie Lee's eyes lit up, they let her hold her puppy for a long time and just cry. Mary could not help but think the two might end up as orphans before this night would end. They probably would not let Peter keep her, especially after this night's ordeal. Petting her pup with such compassion and love, she looked at her stepsister, "Is my mommy dead?" It was difficult for her trying to talk with missing teeth. Vera immediately answers, "No, oh heavens, no darlin, she is not. She won't die and leave you. Come on, let's put

Pacific Redwood Mystery: Do you believe in the little people yet?

Penny out on the porch and clean you up." Katie Lee held on to her little pup and she looked at Vera with soft words through tears "Why can't she die?" Totally shocked in her stepsister's remark, Vera herself hated to admit long ago she wished the same thing. Mary motioned for Vera to take Penny outside, she smiled at Katie Lee stroking her back with the warm water, "I don't know, but I just know she will be okay, it is up to God." Mary told her. "Why?" Katie Lee asked as she looked to Mary. "Katie Lee you sound like you want her to die." The little girl put her face close to the water. "She wanted me to die, if God lets her live then I will die." Mary was stunned with Katie Lee's remark. "Where did you get that nonsense, Katie Lee. That is just not true." Katie Lee became upset and raised her voice as she tried to talk as plain as she could through her missing teeth. "She said she wanted to kill me, she tried to kill me. If she lives she will come back." Vera was standing at the bathroom door listening with as much astonishment as her sister to what they just heard.

What possibly could one say to a child at that point? How was ether girl going to answer such a question? Mary was praying that her father was not facing the death of her stepmother, in spite of how she felt about her, she didn't want her dead. She got up motioning for Vera to continue to help the child closing the door behind her. As she moved down the hall she closed all the doors, reaching her father's master bedroom she called Charles David to bring her a large sheet and some nails. Together they nailed the sheet over the bedroom door shielding their innocent eyes from the bloody scene.

CHAPTER TEN

As Peter paced restlessly up and down the hospital corridor, he had not been told anything since they took Mina from his arms. Ellen sat in the far corner looking at her stepfather for some kind of hope. He tried several times to assure her all would come out okay but within his heart, he did not believe his own words. Both covered with blood, it couldn't help but bring strange looks of those coming and going through the emergency room. Little information was requested which surprised Peter but then time was the essence. So much blood had been lost, he feared the worst everything was going through his brain like a fast video, the things he wished he had done, just grabbed all the kid's and took off; he could have bought them clothes and food for the day or weekend. Got legal advice and sent her and Ellen on their way with enough money until the next fool came along. There was little Peter knew about Mina's health history, she was extremely secretive about not only her past but also her life in general. He was beginning to understand why. He was also beginning to wonder just how many men had she been with. How many times had she actually been married and most of all how many marriages did she destroy along the way? He felt grief stricken as he looked over to his stepdaughter, no wonder Ellen was an angry teen. What an example her mother had been to her. Most of all, his mind could not help but wonder what this child had been through to be so hateful and already trying to be manipulative to those around her. Peter sank into a chair beside his stepdaughter as he thought of his own life before Mina.

Pacific Redwood Mystery: Do you believe in the little people yet?

Vile filled his whole system as he realized what he had done, how he too had been caught up in her mysterious life. But not without a price, his family, yes, he had his children at least, but not Allie. He had destroyed the mother of his children, his childhood sweetheart. The woman he believed he would spend the rest of his life with. Carol Ann had no life, she was almost a vegetable in her own home. He had done that, he had created this nightmare when he let his lustful emotions take control for his desire for Mina. He had learned in the short time with Mina that no man was capable of holding her. Money was her first priority and when the fun was gone and the honeymoon was over, so was she. Peter could never go back with Mina, he had nothing to go back to. He has to pick up the pieces and try to make some kind of life for his children. As he watched Ellen, he wondered what would become of her if Mina did not make it. He was determined to fight for Katie Lee, he did not know how but she had become like his own. He would have to find out now as much as he could from Ellen. Relatives, any family at all, anywhere that might be out there but the biggest questions on his mind was, what kind of people were they? Ellen touched his hand bringing his thoughts back to reality. A doctor was coming down the hall toward them with two other gentlemen dressed in surgical gear. He stood bracing for the worst, Ellen placed her hand in her stepfather's and held tight, Peter was shocked but didn't react, she needed his strength even if she wanted to play miss rough and tough girl, "Mr. Patterson, I am Dr. Chung, your wife is out of surgery but we had complication. She is in grave condition. We will not know the outcome for another forty-eight to seventy-two hours. She should be in recover within the next thirty to forty-five minutes." He was brief and to the point, Peter knew what the doctor was thinking. He understood the doctor's hostility toward him, for now anyway. "Is my mother going to live?" The doctor looked down at the young girl with such emotion and stress, composing himself for the young girl, he would answer but distant himself at this point in time until he had more facts. "We have done all we can. God willing and no infections set in, she has a fifty to fifty chance but I cannot promise anything under the circumstances." Looking at Peter he motioned for him to step to the side away from the young girl. His heart skipped a beat knowing it would not be good. But Ellen followed, she was not about to be left out of any news regarding her mother. "She is my mother, what you have to say to him, you can say to me too." Peter nodded at the physician as Ellen pulled her hand away from her stepfather. "Mrs. Patterson has lost a lot of blood." Ellen interrupted the doctor in a rude manner. "She is not Mrs. Patterson, her name is Mina Lowe," Peter was astonished. "Ellen," Peter blurted out. The young girl immediately coped an attitude. "No, you're not really married, you are so stupid." Ellen snapped at Peter. "Your mother and I are married, you insisted on being there with your mother in front of the judge. Ellen cut the crap this is not about you." The doctor seemed to be as confused as Peter, but he was not in the mood for drama. "Mr. Patterson, I do not know what is going on here, but you will have to talk to the authorities. We have to report any serious incidents especially with life-threading issues." Peter was between listening to the doctor and the words that Ellen had just blurted out of her mouth.

    The doctor continued but with some hesitation, he could see Peter was in a state of confusion and he did not like the rudeness nor attitude of this young adolescent. "She has forty-eight stitches from the middle of her forehead to the mid center of the top of her head, approximately six and a half to seven inches long and about a quarter of an inch width. We have to wait for the results from all the tests to see what kind of damage if any she may have, which could include neurological issues. When and if she regains consciousness, we will see how coherent she is. There are a lot of issues here Mr. Patterson, she has sustained a serious head injury, loss of blood which has not helped the situation. A head trauma like this can go in any direction, we just won't know until we get all the results. If you will please excuse me, I have one more surgery and I should be in my office in about two hours. I need to discuss some medical issues with you if you could meet with me there, lets say in three hours?" Peter only shook his head yes, but his mind was racing. Peter realized as the doctor was half way down the hall that he had not even asked if either could see her. "Dr. Chung, when can we see her?" The doctor turned for a few seconds looking at the young girl standing in a defiant stance. He could see the sincere look on Mr. Patterson's face but was not sure exactly what was going on in this matter. "We will talk in my office Mr. Patterson, we will decide then what is best for her." Peter's shoulders sunk in remorse of the whole situation, Ellen stood beside him knowing she had some explaining to do, she was acting as if this was something routine.. "How about some lunch, I am really hungry, in fact I am so hungry I could eat a horse." If that was meant to be a joke or break the ice between them, Peter was not amused.

Picking up her bag for her, he handed it to Ellen as he nodded towards the front entrance of the hospital. The charge nurse interrupted Peter before he was able to walk away. "Mr. Patterson, do you have somewhere we can reach you if needed?" Not even looking at her, Peter answered. "We will be right back, I need to get her something to ear and she does not want hospital food.." The nurse was more than insistent on the issue and Peter finally caught on, it was not so much for his wife but for the police who were probably on their way. "If you think I am not coming back, you are mistaken. That is my wife in there and I am will be back in less than thirty minutes. If your local detectives arrive before I return, I will be back." She looked embarrassed as she saw the young girl smile, she took it as a smug gesture. She would love to tell Mr. Patterson what she thought of his obnoxious daughter. "Thirty minutes, are you serious I cannot eat in thirty minutes." The nurse gazed at Peter as Ellen stomped out the front door, Peter just looked at the nurse without any expression or emotions.

The nursing staff was deep in their routine when two plain suits came to the station wanting to know the condition of Mrs. Patterson. The head nurse said she was still in recovery with no visitors. "The doctor in charge, who is it and where is he?" She knew the drill on this one, good cop bad cop, this was not their domain and she didn't have time to play games. "He is in surgery, Dr. Chung. If you take the elevator he has his office here at the hospital. I am sure his girls will have more knowledge of his schedule." They had ran into this nurse before and it was better not to rile her. They did know a "no visitors" meant it was not good, they usually let family in for a few minutes unless they suspected some kind of involvement also. Yep, there might be something to this case after all. "Where is the family, have they seen her?" The younger of the two continued to drill for information. The nurse turned not wanting to seem unfriendly but she herself was not sure of the situation, so she had to be careful not to give the wrong body language. "She is considered in grave condition, so no visitors. Dr. Chung will have to answer any questions you might have." She handed him a card from beneath the counter with the doctor's name, address and phone number. "Mr. Patterson and his daughter have gone to get something to eat, they should be back shortly." The two men stood for a few moments trying to decide to leave or stick around and wait. They studied the card and decided to leave the doctor their card, he could return their call. It would take only about fifteen minutes for them to return. Since the doctor's office was there on the sixth floor of the hospital, they did not have to go far to see the patient or the doctor. As for Mr. Patterson they would wait. The lead officer, Detective Cruz, was feeling as if there was more to this story than being said. His partner, on the other hand thought it was just another domestic situation that got out of hand. He kept telling his partner they would probably kiss and make up, no charges unless a slap on the hand or maybe some time. It was just routine get the report and be on their way. But Detective Cruz was not too keen on wife beating or harming a female. He was determined to nail this jerk. They had been to the house and had seen the blood everywhere. They had mixed feelings on the conversation with the kids, they seemed to say it was self defense but Cruz didn't buy it, too much blood. Maybe they were not talking out of fear of their father.

  The picture they had seen of the little girl was disturbing, In fact the detectives had tried the nice guy, bad guy to get the young boy to release the pictures he took of everything but he refused. It was personal property he said, he would turn the pictures over after he talked to his father. That was exactly what Cruz wanted to do, talk to Mr. Patterson. Detective Cruz was talking himself into believing the little girl's beating must have come from the stepfather, no woman could have done that. Checking the prior record they had found this was not the first time a domestic violent incident had occurred at the Patterson's home. All the police report stated it was after a night of drinking, to their amazement the only injuries written down were on Mr. Patterson. Some slap marks on her, but he usually looked the worst by the time the police arrived. There were reports of scratches and nail marks all over his face to his chest, torn shirt but never a word against his wife. The police had talked with many of the bar attendants but usually found out Mrs. Patterson was the problem, always dancing with other men in a seductive manner. Sometimes she would sneak out when he played pool, nothing but good things regarding Peter Patterson.

Sometimes her husband would leave rather than get into any confrontation, then come back finding her gone with some stranger, always a male companion. Peter was always praised as a nice guy except when it came to his wife. It seemed like the possession held over him was more than he could break away from. Sooner or later they figured, like in most cases, it would go too far. The difference was Peter was the suspect and would be treated so until proven wrong. It was hard to believe a woman would do that much damage to her own little girl. They were used to women and children fearing the father and in so many cases, a stepfather. Police did not take these cases lightly when a woman was hurt this bad. They took it personal and gave no mercy but when they had a story like Mina's, Detective Cruz knew if he was wrong, it was to become every cop's nightmare. Women were rarely convicted, especially women like this one. Peter was aware of this, but he was ready. Somehow he did not know how he was going to handle it, only to tell the truth and get the kids out of there, that is if they let him. He was sure Child Protective Services would be called in, he may even lose his own children over this. It was no one's fault but his own, he had to somehow get justice for his kids. His children were all he had except for Katie Lee, she did not have anyone, or did she?

As they sat and ate, Peter was quiet waiting for his stepdaughter to start the subject she had so quickly blurted out in front of the doctor. He did not feel like eating, he could not eat. He sat and drank more coffee knowing the caffeine would kick in pretty soon and make the day even worse with a headache. Ellen was acting as if nothing was wrong, she complained non stop about the hamburger, the fries were too soggy, the coke was watery. Peter could not believe he was sitting here listening to her nonsense. There was not one question about her mother, it was all about her. Finally, he could not stand it any longer. "Ellen, you need to explain yourself, I need to know what you think you know?" With her eyes rolling like a typical teenager with an arrogant attitude, she just wadded up her wrappers from her meal. As she rose from the table she acted as if he had not even spoken to her. Again Peter pressed her. "Young lady, your mother is near death, and I need some answers. In fact I need to know what you know about any family." The girl started to laugh as Peter became disgusted, he wanted to turn her over his knee and give her a good old fashioned spanking. One that she probably had never received in her total spoiled life. "Oh come on Peter, don't take it so seriously, Mom never took anyone serious. You should know that by now, she never divorced my dad, are you satisfied?" He was hurt, disgusted, confused, and total irritation sucked in. "Ellen, I need answers. If your mother does not make it, I need to know what will happen to you girls. There has to be family somewhere." Ellen drank her coke as if she had to think the matter over. Peter was just about at the end of his rope with her, her mother, and the whole emotional situation. He grabbed the coke out of her hands, placing it firmly in front of her with a look of total determination. "Okay, what do you want to know, my dad, aunt, uncles, cousins, What?" Peter shook his head in disgust, "For heavens sake girl, your mother is in serious condition, she may die. You say she is not my wife, I never know when to believe you Ellen. We are not on a shopping trip for God's sake." With her arrogant attitude she picked up her coke like not a care within her. "Well, she isn't you wife, Mom never got divorced that I know about. I know she had some sisters and brothers, I think. She doesn't like them, so we don't see them or talk about them. That is all I know, she had the information in her Bible, at least she used to have it but last time I looked, it was gone."

"Think Ellen, this is important, the police are going to be all over this and if I am right. Child Protective Services will be involved and probably take you girls, mine too maybe. I am sure they will take you and Katie Lee until this is figured out." With that Ellen became hysterical, now Peter had her full attention. "What do you mean? I am not going anywhere, I am staying right in the hospital with my mom. They cannot make me leave, she is my mother." Taking a big breath in, Peter needed to bring her into life outside Ellen's world. "Yes they can young lady, they can and they will unless you tell me some names that I can contact for backup." "Backup, what is that suppose to mean, let them take Katie Lee, you can keep her. I don't care, I am not going anywhere. I will run away they cannot make me leave my mom." Peter could see this was not getting him anywhere. She was stubborn and just as determined in her decision as her mother was with her secrets. "Ellen, give me a name, please?" The young girl just sat there not looking at him, just out the window as if he had not even spoken to her. The she got up as if nothing had transpired between them. "Can we go back to the hospital now?" Peter was exhausted with the whole ordeal. Now he believe he probably was not even married to the woman, he absolutely had no right to Katie Lee and he had no idea whom to get a hold of for help with either of the girls. He knew Ellen would make it in any situation, she had her mother in her and that attitude would not change.

Ellen was in the truck before Peter got through the door of the fast food place. The ride back was silent and uncomfortable for Peter, his stepdaughter could care less. He knew she was doing this on purpose. He almost felt sorry for her but there was no feeling sorry for this girl; she would survive just like her mother. He was trying to think of their friends or acquaintances. There had to be someone that would know something. He had never looked at any legal papers, maybe he needed to check and go from there. As they parked in the parking lot, Ellen did not even wait for Peter. Peter was not going to argue anymore, he was exhausted mentally and physically. He needed to see how his wife was, well or not his wife but he would still take responsibility. He still needed to talk with the doctor's and get back to the kids. He was sure they were worried and distraught. He had to take them some news and he did not want it to be negative. There was enough negative in their lives right now. His biggest worry increased now, Katie Lee as well as his son Charles David. He wondered if the police had been to the house yet, if so, he had a lot of answers to give and what other secrets were going to pop up that he was not aware of. Were the children even still at the house, had they been taken already? He was not sure if they could take Mary, Vera or Charles David but Katie Lee yes, they could and they would. As Peter was coming through some hedges that lined the sidewalk of the hospital entrance he saw Ellen coming back towards him in a run. Her face was pale and bland. Oh God he thought, Mina was dead! She was dead for sure. Ellen came quickly to Peter almost in a panic. "Peter the police are here, they are waiting for us." Peter really did not hear what she was saying, his mind was focused on the worse news and he was expecting her to say her mother was dead. "What, what did you say, what about your mother?" The girl became fearful to which Peter was amused. Ellen in fear of someone or something? Never! "The police, they are waiting for us." He took a deep breath and let it out slowly. "Ellen, they are going to want to talk to everyone. It is their job, just be honest, stay calm, tell them what they want to know." She actually started to get tears in her eyes, he started walking forward thinking she would keep in step. "What do you mean be honest, I cannot talk to them. I didn't really see anything." Appalled in her dishonestly, he should have seen that coming. This was not her normal reaction, but it was her normal way of thinking. "Ellen, clam down, they are not going to go away, just answer their questions the best you can. The sooner they get what they want, the sooner you can see your mom."

She looked at Peter as if she was going to collapse. "I want to see her now, I do not want to talk to them. Can't you stop them?" Reaching for her hand, she jerked away as she always did leaving him standing alone. "This is your fault, this is all your fault. Why didn't you just leave my mom alone and stay out of our lives?" The young girl could not believe her ears when Peter shot an answer back to her. "Believe me young lady, I wish I had." Peter no longer tried to comfort her, it was hopeless just like their whole life had been hopeless. It just took him a long time to wake up and smell the roses. He was the fool, yep he certainly had taken the cake on being stupid. He continued to walk through the door and immediately recognized the plain clothes detectives as they sat patiently waiting for him. As he looked toward the nurse's station at least the head nurse pointed toward them, trying to give him heads up. He was thankful for her kindness, as before she and the others in the staff all seemed to be judge and jury. He could not blame them, Mina was in there half dead with her head split open, and he had blood all over him. Who else was there to blame? So it was time to face the music, he did not feel his options were good in any case.

CHAPTER ELEVEN

As Peter approached the detectives, he watched Ellen deliberately pass them heading for her mother's unit. He didn't care, the nurses and detective could deal with her. The detectives were caught a little off guard when they saw Peter approaching them. He was not what they expected. His structure, the body language was not the normal wife beater or abusive husband. Peter did not bother to extend his hand to either of the men, he was sure they could care less about proper formalities at this point. "You are looking for me?" Detective Cruz was not sure how he was going to go about this, his whole plan just went out the window. His partner was even more taken back, they had figured they were going to nail this in less than record time. From seeing the patient's chart, viewing the injuries, she had a six and a half inch trauma to the head in length and about a quarter of an inch in width; they were sure he was aware of the same information they had acquired.

It was a shock from their point of view and past experiences that the woman was still alive but it was not over yet. With a head trauma like that, no one was going to walk out without some kind of permanent damage. The question was, what and how bad? Peter sat down in a chair close to the window so he could use that as a distraction if needed. "We just have a few questions Mr. Patterson. We have already been out to the house, quite a bloody mess." Peter was not going to walk into anything, he had to think of the outcome for the children, all of them, not just his son. There was Katie Lee to think about. What would happen to her if Mina did not make it? He had no idea of any family. Mina kept most of her prior life to herself and was adamant not to discuss it with anyone. He was beginning to wonder if all she ever told him were lies. He did not understand what had happened to her, possibly it was a buildup of past abuse. Peter could not excuse himself from any of his own actions, so matter what provoked him, his own past actions could never be justified. He had lost something when Mina came into his life, he lost his own pride in what a man was suppose to be.

"Mr. Patterson, your son showed us pictures he had taken of your stepdaughter and they all seemed to think you were defending them as well as yourself. Can you tell us what happened in your own words?" This was not a surprise to him, he knew it was coming. "I am not sure where to begin. The whole day was unpleasant, not just for me but also for the children. It was a day that seemed to come out of hell." Now they were really confused, it was not exactly what they thought he would say. He did not even defend himself, or say he didn't do it. He started going through as much as he could remember and when something was a blur he told them. It seemed to go on forever before he finally relaxed back in the chair and blew out his breath that was endless. Both detectives went back over the notes they took and shot questions at him, he answered as they came at him. Finally, he was not sure he heard either of them correctly. "Mr. Patterson, if we need anything else, we will get a hold of you."

Detective Cruz turned to Peter before he extended his hand to the man. "Maybe you need to think about rearranging your life in another direction, Mr. Patterson?" He watched the detectives walk down the hall toward the entrance of the hospital. This could not be all, it could not be the end of his interview with them. Everyone in the hospital thought the incident was intentional, he was expecting to be arrested. He sat there focusing on the outside activities, away from what he was thinking and feeling.

So many people coming and going, many just to visit friends and others family, he was not sure of his own feelings now. Yes he was responsible for Mina being here in may ways, it was his fault. He should have walked away a long time ago. All signs were there, he was in his own denial from a man's lust and desire when he should have been thankful for what he had; not what he thought he didn't have. What he would do to change that last couple of years. Well, he could not change the past, but he could control the future. He had to be careful, there was more at stake than his own children. There was a nine year old that had nowhere to go, no one that wanted her and no one but him to protect her. Peter saw Ellen coming down the hall with a bag of chips, being very cautious, he knew she was too curious about the police and if they were still there. "Did they leave already, did you tell them I did not want to talk to them?" Peter looked up at this young girl and all he could see was a younger Mina. God, how he wanted to run. "No, I didn't even mention your name and neither did they. They left said if they needed anything else, they would be back." He did not know if she was relieved or mad. "Well, they said they wanted to talk to me. What is up with that?" Waving his hand toward the girl, he really didn't care what her attitude was at that moment. "Ellen, do you want to go over to Dr. Chung's office with me to talk about your mother's results and what to expect?" You would have thought she was offended. "You cannot go without me, I told the nurses that I would be staying the night and every night?" Peter was not surprised she was marking her territory like a dog.

Not getting a response, she was irritated she could not get a reaction out of Peter. She had to throw in her negative response towards him. "Well, I just figured you wanted to go home and be with everyone. I am sure they don't want to be here, even Katie Lee if you ask me." Pulling his jeans over his boots making sure his shirt was tucked in even though it was bloody, he said. "Well, I am not asking you Ellen. Fine if you want to stay, but you will have to ask the doctor not dictate to the nurses and don't put words into anyone's mouth but your own." She had never heard Peter talk to her in that

Pacific Redwood Mystery: Do you believe in the little people yet?

manner and she was beginning to see that he had just about enough of everything. It would be just like all the others, he was growing tired and he would leave soon leaving her mother to move on to the next. It did not matter to her, that was why she refused to get attached to any of her mother's boyfriends. She was surprised that her mother married Peter even though it wasn't legal, it wasn't suppose to be part of the plan. But Peter did have a lot of money, beautiful cedar home, a very distinguished looking man. Maybe she had to make it look legal to get all the goodies. Too bad it wasn't legal, maybe she could come out with some goodies, but her mom had messed this one up. She knew another one would come along, always did and the money was a sure thing. Mina made sure of that.

As they reached the elevator, Peter just pushed the bottom looking down, it was as if he was all alone, that was the way he felt. He knew there was nothing he could do for Mina, but the children at home were still waiting to hear some news and now knowing that the police had been there, what were they thinking about? How was Katie Lee? Questions after questions were racing through his mind. "Are you going to let me listen to the doctor, or am I gong to have to wait in the waiting room to hear it second hand?" Her attitude had not changed much since her mother had come out of surgery. On the way to the hospital, she had been a different teen altogether. What must have these two girls really been through that made this one hate so badly, the other one feared life period. As the elevator opened, he was glad to see Dr. Chung's office right in front, as he opened the door for Ellen, he was seeing again the looks and expression on everyone's face as they saw the condition of them both. He was more uncomfortable than earlier, the bloodstained clothes must have been a sight.

The receptionist's greeting was friendly, she was already aware they were coming. She asked Peter to go ahead and enter the door to the right; he noticed a woman coming toward them dressed in a uniform, wearing a smile. "Mr. Patterson, Dr. Chung is just finishing surgery, he should be here in about twenty minutes. Would you and your daughter like to clean up some?" With her normal bad attitude and forceful mouth, Peter knew she had to make some kind of remark. "He is not my father, if you must know." Paying her no mind, she was not impressed in the young girl's attitude. She escorted them into a room where she handed him some towels and liquid soap. With Ellen complaining all the while, he wished he had left her with her mother, but he felt she had a right to be here. The nurse had returned a couple of times to make sure all was okay and if they needed anything else. Peter noticed that Ellen only rolled her eyes each time and on the nurses last visit Peter apologized for her behavior right in front of Ellen. "Don't worry Mr. Patterson, we all have had bad days." The intercom buzzed, Peter heard someone say the doctor was in. The nurse walked them to his office as they passed the doctor in the hall, he nodded to Peter while giving another nurse some instructions. Ellen did not wait to be asked to go in his office, she just walked in and sat down in the nearest chair. Looking around the room, she could not help but admire the beautiful art work. Wow, her mother would love this office. She heard the doctor outside the door again and picked up on his accent, something she had not noticed so much at the hospital. She had not really heard him talk until now. "Oh great, we probably won't be able to understand him." Peter stood blocking the door where he hoped the doctor had not heard. "That is enough, if you cannot behave you can go out in the waiting room and wait. I won't have you disrespect this doctor, or you can be taken home and left there." The roll of the eyes told Peter his words were a waste of time. "Whatever," She remarked at Peter.

 Dr. Chung came in walking around Peter wondering why he as standing in front of the door. It did not take any time for him to see why. Every time he tried to explain something she had a negative attitude and smart remark. The doctor was not impressed either as it began to answer a lot of questions. "Your wife has lost a lot of blood Mr. Patterson. The head trauma is very serious and her condition is grave. I cannot tell you how much now, the results that are in do not tell us much. Hopefully with some good changes in her condition, if she is a strong person we can hope for the best. I have a specialist coming in tomorrow. Let's just hope she starts to show signs of improvement. If she is a fighter. Mr. Patterson, she has a good chance, has she been in good health?" Before he could answer Ellen did, "Yes, she is. Are you kidding? She can withstand anything, she always does." Dr. Chung decided he needed to get the young girl to elaborate on that, with the little history in her file and no other family but Peter and two daughters. "Has your mother sustained other injuries? It would help with her care if you could shed some light on her medical history." Ellen immediately withdrew and Peter was at a loss for words. "We have only been married for a couple of years and her past is very much a secret as far as I know. In fact Dr. Chung her daughter here informed me we are not really married, guess a divorce slipped her mind with the last husband." He knew that remark hurt Ellen and he really didn't mean to, it normally was not his character but things changed now. "Ellen, what can you tell Dr. Chung, do you realize the seriousness of your mother's condition?" Becoming very angry, she turned to her stepfather.

"Well, you should know since you were the one frightening with her, you kept grabbing the gun from her." She had not even realized what came our of her mouth. "Why did your mother have the gun?" The doctor was writing but careful not to look at the girl or show any sudden alarm to the question, he needed to make her feel comfortable and at ease. She was angry, but that was a very explosive statement from a physicians point of view. He was hoping she would give some kind of explanation to clear a lot of questions up. Her anger got the best of her and she lashed out again toward Peter. "Why didn't you just stay away? All that family stuff and crap, we didn't need it." Peter tried to figure out where her anger was coming from, a place deep somewhere she would not let anyone in. Dr. Chung appreciated Peter not responding to her anger, it gave him the opportunity he needed. "Why did your mom want to gun?" This irritated Ellen more, "She just gets mad sometimes and my sister makes her crazy. She doesn't really want to kill her, she hasn't so far." It was certain to the doctor that this was not the first time but was it the first time for this husband?"

She did not like being put on the spot and felt Peter was not helping her, so she lashed out verbal on them both. "Why do you think she played as if she married you? It wasn't for love, Hello. Peter you are so stupid and you are playing doctor sitting behind your fancy desk you need to fix my mother so we can get the hell out of here," The doctor stopped writing placing his pen on the folder, he could see this teenager was hurting inside herself but was too angry to even see it. "Ellen, that is enough, I warned you he is trying to help," she broke his sentence by slamming the door behind her as she left them both sitting there.

"Welcome to my world," was Peter's only statement. Dr. Chung sat back in his chair watching Peter's facial expression. "What happened in your home Mr. Patterson, to place your wife in this critical condition?" Dr. Chung watched Peter intently as he went through the story again. He normally had lots of questions but he sat listening, not interrupting until he was sure Peter was finished. He certainly had a different outlook in the situation. "Have you spoken to the police yet?" Shaking his head yes, he expressed his concern, they were too nice and too quick to leave. He expressed he really thought he would be arrested. "Mr. Patterson, have you considered therapy for the family?" As Peter drew his attention back to the doctor in front of him, he answered that question. "I tried."

Peter was surprised he had talked so much, maybe it was something in the back of his mind that needed to be said. "How many times has she been married, is there family we can contact?" The doctor seemed a little anxious, he needed the information for there was a lot at stake. "I have no idea doctor, I just leaned I am not her husband. Ellen says there are sisters and brothers but swears she doesn't know anything." Dr. Chung considered if he should make a comment or spare his feelings. "Well, if you are going to consider staying together you do need to think about therapy. I cannot promise you she will return to you the way she was. I cannot promise you she will even make it." With that Peter's heart sunk, it was something he would have to bear. No one forced him to make any decisions and now he was having to pay the piper. "Her daughter wants to stay at the hospital, can that be arranged? I need to get home to the other children they need to know something." The doctor stood breathing several times, as if it was not something he wanted to discuss. "Yes, we will have to call them, she will have to stay in the waiting room area Mr. Patterson, I have to report all domestic violence incidents." He wanted Peter to know it was his office that reported the incident. Peter shook his head and thanked the doctor, at least Peter felt the doctor didn't have such a bad opinion of him. There was some dignity for his soul.

He knew it was too soon to really know anything but the doctor was good, he was a good man. The wound was life threatening, it was serious. She would wear a scar for the rest of her life if she came though this. Peter left the office feeling as empty as when he walked in. He knew there was nothing that really could be said or done that was not already in progress. Time would tell one way or the other. He found Ellen in the hall near the elevator when he came out, she barely looked at him. "He says you can stay in the waiting room area near the unit but not in your mother's room." Ellen grinned like she won the battle. "Fine, if you are coming back will you bring me some clothes? I have so much blood on me I am a spectacle for anyone to look at." He did not answer her, he would take her to some store but right now he wanted to see what the nurse would say when he got back to the unit. Then he would decide if he was coming back or not for the night. As he reached the main floor, Peter was surprised when Ellen walked ahead toward the unit. Peter just let her go on ahead as he passed the nurses station, he noticed the looks still suspicious. He only nodded, passing them with grief that none would ever understand. As he struggled with the gown he noticed Ellen did not have one but the nurse's were in deep discussion with her. As he entered the room the nurse moved away from the young girl and asked Peter if he had any questions. "No, I got my answers from Dr. Chung." She sensed his unfriendly tone, feeling a little guilty as she judged him as well as the other staff but since the police had come, rumors flew in a different direction. It was a situation when he was protecting the children and the mother had actually beaten her nine year old child. This was a good example of assuming before the facts were in.

Peter watched Mina as she lay there so still, no sign of life. He could see the head trauma and it was ugly as the doctor stated. The butt of the gun had done terrible damage. The force of the swing from Peter's weight had caused this, no way around it. As he watched the woman he thought was his wife, he was trying to figure out when it all began and when it all stopped. He honestly could not feel that deep lustful love he had for her, that desire he had. It was almost as if a light went off in his head, there was a vile feeling in his stomach as he really looked down at her. Not her injury, but her. Yes, she was beautiful even her features as she lay there could not be ignored. She could turn heads but under all that beauty was a venom, a poison that took hold until destruction was the only thing that stopped her. He did not want to be there, he wanted to be with the children but he needed to know how this was going to play out. Whichever way, he might need the advice of an attorney. Mina was so obsessed with money maybe he could buy her youngest daughter from her. He would sell everything he had if she agreed. He was sure the little girl would go willingly with him and his children and be happy.

They only had a fifteen minute time limit to visit in intensive care, Time went slow it seemed to Peter. Glad the time was up he torn the gown off and threw it in the hamper beside the door. As he left the room, the same nurse came to his side. "Mr. Patterson, I don't mean to insult you or your daughter but we have a change of clothes that will probably fit her if she would like to change." Peter found himself correcting the nurse before Ellen could complain, "She would appreciate it if you did not call her my daughter." She handed the clothes in Ellen's direction. "Did they belong to a person?" The ward clerk was standing near the station and heard the remark. "No honey, in fact they were purchased from the gift shop by some of the nurses." Her tone was about as friendly as Ellen and she was not going to apologize. Clearing her throat the nurse picked up Mina's chart.

"Will you be returning this evening? I understand your daughter will be staying?"

Peter took a pen that was lying near the phone and wrote down Davie's number. "If you need anything, don't hesitate to call, I will be back in the morning." He did not wait for Ellen to return, he walked away without a word. The nurse did not blame this man for his anger towards anyone; they had let their personal feeling interfere with their work ethics, something nurses are not suppose to do, it was a hard lesson for them all, One they would not forget anytime soon. All the way home Peter's thoughts raced, not really knowing what he was going to find, no phone to even call and check on them. They must have been scared when the police came but he had faith in his children, he knew they had handled it well. His biggest worry was protective custody, he had dealt with them when Carol Ann broke down, and he knew how they functioned. They could be pretty unfair and one sided if they chose to be. He needed to be the one to prepare them for what was coming, not some stranger. "Oh Lord, what am I going to do?" The drive seemed to take forever and he needed a shower, a good hot shower. It would be dark by the time he got home and it had been all day those kids had been by themselves, confused and horrified. Katie Lee had a broken nose, he knew that for sure and he had to leave her as he rushed out of the house with her mother. It was when he was in the ER that it dawned on him that the young girl was left in pain.

Peter had asked to leave to get back but the security had said he was not to leave the hospital or the doctor's office until they could speak to him. He knew they did not believe his story. He wasn't going to worry about them right now, he needed to take Katie Lee to the emergency room just as soon as he got everyone settled down. He knew she was in good hands with Mary especially, but his guilt was unforgiving to himself. As his truck began to climb the hill he was so ecstatic to see them all run to the porch, he was looking frantic for Katie Lee but he did not see her. He did not want to think they had came already taken her, he would never forgive himself, ever. As he exited his truck, his son was the first one to greet him, seeing the bandage on his son's eye he pulled his son toward him in an embrace. Then he asked. "Where is Katie Lee?" His son answered him as quickly as he asked "She is asleep dad, Mary taped her nose and gave her some aspirins. She fell asleep about an hour ago, we put her in my room." Mary was beside her father asking abut Mina, but you could tell the shock on her face when she noticed all the blood on her father's clothes. "Daddy, you need to clean up and change your clothes. Let me get some clean towels for you." His daughter was like an angel, always thinking about others and their comfort never her own.

First Peter gathered his children into the living room to give them the details of what he could tell them. They all sat not really knowing what to say because there was really nothing to say. The fear that fell through his children were on their faces. "The police were here and Charles David showed them the pictures of Katie Lee." As he looked over at his son, he was too exhausted to ask questions as how they had accomplished that. They were all together, they were safe. "Is she still in pain? Maybe I need to take her to the emergency room, you too Charles David." His daughter sat beside him as his son stood looking at his father. Peter seemed to sense their fears and concerns, he knew he needed to assure them this woman would never step into their lives again. "Daddy, Katie Lee is in less pain now that we taped her nose." Mary assured her as Charles David jumped in "She lost her two front teeth, I'm better dad, the patch helps." But Peter knew he had to still be uncomfortable as well. "She needs to rest, tomorrow is another day." Mary spoke softly smiling as she headed for the bathroom for fresh towels.

Peter praised his son, he praised them all, their braveness, their love. They had never seen their father so distraught; all they could do was just be there. "It's late you all need to turn in. I will sleep out here, come on lets go now." One by one they left their father's side watching as he rested his head back against the couch. As he heard their doors close he could see his bedroom with a sheet over the entrance, it could stay that way, he was glad he didn't have to cope with that laid behind that sheet. This night could stay trapped there forever.

Lifting his heavy body he went to check on Katie Lee, as she entered his son's room he saw her crumbled little body curled at the end of Charles Davids bed.. Her nose was swollen and looked ugly. Leaning over his son, he checked her breathing and temperature. She seemed a little warm, but he was not surprised in that, he just hoped that was all. Her little nose was already purple, almost black, and a lot of red around the eyes. Covering them both, he saw four little legs tucked under her arm. He did not have to look, he knew it was Penny, her own little security blanket. He headed for the shower where his daughter had placed not only towels but also a change of clothes for her father.

The water felt good, he just stood letting it spatter all over his body. It was hot and steaming, he placed his hands on the wall of the shower, stuck his head under the water and let his mind drift to another place.

CHAPTER TWELVE

Mary was the last to wake up the following morning, as she looked around the room she saw it was empty. To herself she was mad, if her sister had taken off in the middle of the night to be with Davie, she was not going to let it slide this time. She grabbed her robe and headed down the hall. She could smell fresh coffee, it smelled so good. Her father would either be standing on the porch drinking a cup or standing at the coffee pot waiting for it to brew. She peeked into the kitchen, not a sign, she did not knock on her brother's door she went right in. Also empty, in fact the whole house was silent. Going to the front porch everyone was sitting comfortable and at ease. Davie was already there. Was she surprised? No, she knew her father wasn't serious, he was just upset. He would try to control Vera and Davie but not separate them.

"Why am I the only one that slept like a log?" Peter tipped his baseball cap to his daughter, pointing towards the clock on the wall near the front door, 8:45am. Charles David was putting his shoes on to feed the animals as Katie Lee was resting in one of the lawn chairs with her puppy. Vera and Davie were sitting together on the steps, looking distant from everyone. Peter broke the silence as he watched his little pumpkin sat with her pup not saying a word in fact she had not talked all morning. "Everyone, get dressed. Charles David get the animals fed and turn the horses loose to graze. I am going to treat everyone to breakfast in town. Davie, I fixed the phone, get your father on the phone for me if you want to tag along?"

Pacific Redwood Mystery: Do you believe in the little people yet?

    Peter could not shake the thought that something might be more wrong with Katie Lee than just her nose, he needed to get her checked but he did not want to spend all day in the emergency room. He needed to check on Mina anyway, maybe he could ask Dr. Chung to take a look at her or recommend someone to take her to. Vera was carrying Katie Lee a set of clothes when she told her father that Davie's mother was on the line. "I don't want to talk to his mother." Peter remarked firmly. Davie swallowed as he held the phone receiver with both hands. "He is not there Mr. Patterson, he is already at the shop." Davie replied to him. Peter didn't look at the lad just passed him in the hall as Davie held the receive in his hand. "Fine, tell your mother I am taking you all to breakfast and I will stop and speak to your father." Vera shot Davie a look of "I have no idea, but I don't like it."

    Peter grabbed some blankets out of the hall closet, a lantern, some batteries, anything that he could see that they would use for camping. He found a box filled with old stuff that he just dumped on the closet floor and placed everything he had in the box and headed for his truck. He did not want anyone to see what he had, so he made sure the blankets on top covered everything. Entering the house, he picked up the phone, it still had a horrible sound but it was good enough to use for now. He dialed the hospital and asked for the intensive care unit. He got disconnected, so he dialed again, he could barely hear the operator but he needed to get through. "This is Mr. Patterson, how is Mrs. Patterson this morning." The nurse informed him that Dr. Chung was in the room with her already and asked if he wanted to leave a message. "Yes, yes please. I do need to speak to him right away. Could you tell him it is very important that he call me right back." She repeated the number as he hung up. Charles David was just coming in from outside. "Son take that bucket over there and fill it with water, take it to the tack room and put it in there. Make sure you show Penny where it is, put some extra good out for her but don't say anything to Katie Lee." He instructed Vera as she came around the corner with Davie to go make some sandwiches for everyone and put lots of chips and cookies in. Also, he instructed Davie to take the ice chest and put enough soda in for everyone for the day. He instructed Vera to make sure she put enough food in for the day, it would probably be late by the time they got back. As he was thinking what else he would need he heard the phone ring. "Hello, Patterson's residence, yes this is, one moment please." Peter was coming around to see if the doctor was returning his call, he saw the haunted look on Mary's face. "She says she is from Child Protection Services." Peter slowly placed the receiver to his ear, not knowing what was coming. God he thought, please don't let them demand Katie Lee this morning. "This is Mr. Patterson." The voice on the other end was a lot more friendly than he expected. "Mr. Patterson, this is Mrs. Emerson from Child Protective Services. I have been asked to investigate the case of Mina Patterson and her two daughters, Ellen and Katie Lee. I have most of Monday open, would morning or afternoon be better for you."

She had taken Peter totally off guard with her mention of Monday and not that very moment. "Yes, Mrs. Emerson Monday would be good. Your schedule is probably busier that mine, so you tell me." She did not pause with her answer, "Well Mr. Patterson will you be working Monday, like I said I have Monday pretty open. So I am giving you the option here." She was definitely trying to catch anything in Peter's voice that might make her rest easy through the weekend, trusting her last report from talking to the detectives and Dr. Chung. Peter was thinking fast, what would be best for the children to prepare, especially Katie Lee? "Afternoon, that way I have everything taken care of and be back from the hospital in time." She found his voice pleasant but nervous, something she had expected, if he had been too calm or avoided her, she would have taken the time to remove the youngest one today until she could put all the facts together. "That would be good Mr. Patterson, I look forward to our meeting Monday lets say 1:30pm and all the children will be there, correct including Ellen?" Now he was nervous. "Yes, of course." Peter's hands were sweating and then he heard her last words. "Have a pleasant day Mr. Patterson, I will see you Monday afternoon, Oh Mr. Patterson is your turn the first or second to the right after you turn off the main road?" He caught

Pacific Redwood Mystery: Do you believe in the little people yet?

himself picturing the road so he would not give her wrong directions. That was silly he drove that road every day, "The second, there is a mail box with an American Flag you cannot miss it." He heard the click from her end as the phone went dead.

Holding the receiver, Mary took it from him replacing it back in place. "So she is coming Monday, why not today?" Peter could not answer his daughter. He was not sure, he thought they would be knocking on his door last night. Maybe there was a God, after all that made his plan easier. Maybe God was giving him this idea with them all before the final curtain of his life came to an end. He would take whatever time he had, he was not going to tell himself this was a good sign it was just time, a little extra time "Daddy Peter, Charles David took Penny." As he looked down at her, he could see her two front teeth missing as she was dragging her left leg. Not wanting to alarm her he said, "I told him to show her where he was putting extra food and water. It is okay, pumpkin." Bending down, he saw several black and blue marks all over her little legs all the way past her knees. Her left knee was swollen pretty bad. As he tried to touch it she flinched back. He did not want to upset her any more than she was. He had to take her to be checked now, he couldn't wait any longer. No telling what else was wrong, he should have checked her last night when he got home, he should have taken her right away to the emergency room. He could replace her teeth, but maybe something more serious was wrong.

Picking her up he carried her to his pickup, as he walked through the house he yelled at everyone to hurry up and just get in the truck. Wrapping her in his jacket he placed her in the front seat beside him, he told her he would be right back, he would get the other kids and they would be off. He made the top of the porch in two huge steps Vera was coming almost in a run. "Dad, Dr. Chung is on the phone, the connection is real bad but he said you called him." He shot past his daughter and told her to get everyone in the truck right now, he needed to take Katie Lee to the hospital. Peter had the phone in his hand as Mary heard his remark to her sister, she knew something must be wrong. She hurried collecting everything he had asked her, she rushed Davie and Vera and Charles David to the truck. She was just closing the double cab of his truck when she heard her father call her. Jumping back out, she ran into the house. "Mary, get me a change of clothes for Ellen and a jacket, maybe grab some socks too. Dr. Chung is going to see Katie Lee and Charles David in his office in about an hour." He did not look so frustrated as before, maybe hearing from the doctor and knowing the two would be in good hands relaxed him some. As she came back down the hall, he was still standing in the same place she left him "Are you okay, dad?" He had his head against his arm leaning to the wall. "I didn't even ask about Mina, I didn't think." Mary couldn't imagine what was going through her father's mind or how much pressure he was under. "Come on, we need to go. Why are we taking all this stuff?" Placing his arm around her shoulder, they walked to the front door. Pulling his keys and locking the front door he turned the porch light on. "It is a surprise, something I have been promising you all for a long time." She did not question her father anymore, they just walked to the truck together and everyone settled down. He refused to answer any questions only told them the more they asked the less he would tell them. As he backed out of the driveway he began to explain to Katie Lee she was going to see Dr. Chung so he could check her nose and leg. She did not respond to him, which was not like her. She just sat with her hands folded in her lap, looking at the floorboard of the truck. Charles David tried to play with her, teasing that he had to see the doctor also, but he too looked at his father in concern, there was no response. Why should there be? She had been beaten pretty bad, her mother half dead, her sister hated her, and the only family she knew was probably going to leave her. Where was she going to end up and with whom? She may only be nine, but she was sure it was not a happy ending, it never was as long as she could remember.

Pacific Redwood Mystery: Do you believe in the little people yet?

It is said in the scriptures that he gives you no more than you can handle. I wonder if Peter and Katie Lee believed this?

It took no time all to get down the hill towards town, if anyone of the kids noticed, Peter was hitting seventy and above. Mary did not think her father even noticed how fast he was going. How could he even think straight? She told herself that when she got to town, she needed to suggest they call Allie. Her sister needed to hear from her father, and she needed to know about Mina regardless of her feelings. "After you take Katie Lee and Charles David to see the doctor, I will go with you to the hospital. Vera and Davie can stay with her until we come back." Peter only nodded at his daughter in approval. "Aren't we all going to see her, or is that a no no?" Sometimes Mary could not believe Davie's intelligence or his timing, this was no the time to ask such a question. "If you want to, I do not care who goes and see's her, but I do not want Katie Lee going in there." Peter could feel Katie Lee move closer to him as he talked. He patted her little hands, assuring her he was right there. Peter was pretty direct about that, no one bothered to question him. He could tell they were not sure what to do. He would leave it totally up to each of them, it was now emotional, no longer stepmother, stepchildren. That was all out the window and Mina had no one to blame but herself.

Feeling a soft touch on his arm, he looked down at his little pumpkin. "I am hungry daddy and my stomach is talking." Charles David took that as an instant sign to make her laugh and forget about all her pain. He shook in the seat as if electricity had hit him and leaned over and placed his ear on her stomach. "Hey dad, she is right I can hear it." Everyone started to laugh, this time Davie's remark was right on. "What is it saying, Charles David?" He again put his head close on her little stomach. "Feed me, feeeeeeeed me, I am hungry, pancakes, pancakes." Katie Lee started to giggle as Charles David continued to mock himself. "Look Mr. Patterson, there is Sambo's, they have great pancakes." Peter had never been in Sambo's but knew it was a pancake house, so he turned his turning signal on. Katie Lee stretched as far as her little body could, looking out the window to where Peter was turning, she smiled at him as she tried to sit up closer. Peter realized Katie Lee looked so small in the truck, but he was surprised when he first met her, she was extremely small for her age. She didn't look nine, she looked a lot younger. His mind began to questions her natural growth now that he had been awaken by this horrible ordeal and what Mina was capable of. As Peter looked over at her smiling face, he noticed the missing hair where Mary had tried to put her hair in a ponytail. He could not imagine in his mind how anyone could hurt a child, especially one's own child. Wanting to tear the steering wheel out of the steering column from anger he was so pissed off. He had to really compose his emotions. Finding a big enough space to park his Diesel truck took two turns into their parking lot. Helping Katie Lee down he really saw the black and blue marks all the way up her legs, he had to turn away letting Mary take her hand and move forward towards the door. He hesitated to get composure as Charles David waited for his father knowing exactly what he saw.

 They all got out excited and it seemed as if Katie Lee forgot all about her fear, that was until the waitress opened her mouth when she came to the table. "My goodness honey, happened to you?" Katie Lee immediately ducked behind Peter and hung on to the back of his shirt. Peter was ready to defend if he had to but Charles David's quick wit came in at the right time. "Man, those go-carts are a killer, but she rode it all the way." Charles David poked Davie in the ribs for help, he could see her starting to tremble. Davie was glad to jump in "yea, she is only nine years old and look at her brother. She whopped him good and the go-cart still runs." They all started to laugh, Peter was not sure it was a laughing matter but he had not thought of her little face when she said she was hungry, he just wanted to get them all some food. "Good heavens, I think maybe she needs to play with dolls." The waitress came back at the boy not thinking it was funny at all. Her face showed her irritation which the boys didn't like either.

She was looking at Peter as if he was the worlds worst dad. "I tried, you should see what she does with the lawn mower." Peter could feel Katie Lee giggle behind him as he looked back into the waitress face as he could tell she was not amused as she placed the water glasses down on the table except for Peter's, she put his right in front of him with a frown. "I don't think you are having a good morning mam, if you would like us to sit at another table, we will be happy to move." Vera started to stand as Davie asked if they were moving, the waitress immediately apologized but Peter nodded then asked for her to bring all the kids orange juice, please.

"We don't need menus, Dad. We already know what we want." Everyone agreed with Charles David, when the waitress returned, Peter asked her to bring everyone pancakes. "Also, bring those that want hot chocolate and please put some extra whip cream on this little one," Peter pointed towards Katie Lee. He nudged Katie Lee as he looked at the waitress, almost daring her to say another word. After she picked the menus back up, he got up from the table and went to the coffee machine. He poured his own cup of coffee as another waitress came by. "Your waitress will get that for you, sir." He just took his cup and went back to the table, he didn't care to have her do anything for them except bring the breakfast. They ate in silence but Katie Lee was having problems swallowing as Peter caught Mary trying to get him to see the problem. He watched her as she really struggled with each bite. Rubbing his unshaven face, he motioned for the waitress to come. As she approached, he asked her to please bring some cream of wheat in a small bowl. Katie Lee had not even noticed what was going on, she was drinking with each bite thinking it might help her get the food down her throat. It was hurting fiercely but she did not want to complain. When the waitress came back, she looked at Peter, he took the bowl as Davie's humor saved the little girl's embarrassment in front of them. "Hey, Charles David, you missed it. You said her stomach said pancakes, you never said cream of wheat." As he looked at his father then back at Katie Lee she made her own joke. "I get extra because I won the race, didn't I daddy?" It was the first time Katie

Lee had called him just daddy, rather than daddy Peter. It brought tears to his eyes. Charles David had no idea what the laughing was about neither did Vera. But Mary and Davie had been very disturbed by the young girls struggles just to eat a simple breakfast. As they all finished up Peter handed Charles David a fifty and the ticket the waitress left on the table without a word. He knew under her breath she was probably cussing him and thinking the worst. "Do I get the change?" "Of course, the whole amount." As Charles David looked at the ticket, he did not see any total, as he stood with his father at the cashier she only handed him a couple dollars and some change. Peter picked a tooth pick out of their little holder and opened the door for everyone knowing she was pissed he didn't give her any tip. Peter wanted her to be pissed.

The ride to the hospital was only about three blocks, as he turned into the parking lot, Katie Lee stiffened beside him. He parked to the far side of the lot, more to the back of the hospital making it an easier entrance to Dr. Chung's office. Going through the front door, they may run into Ellen, that was not a chance he wanted to take. Peter helped Katie Lee struggle out of the truck making sure she didn't loose her balance. Handing Mary the change of clothes for Ellen, Peter knew he did not want so say anything. What happened next took Peter back a few steps. He watched as Charles David asked if he could catch up with with his sister and Davie as they headed for the hospital entrance. "My eye really doesn't bother me that much dad, it hardly hurts." Making sure it was no longer red and irritated he hugged his son. He knew it was going to be hard for them to go, but he also knew they were doing it for him. He was proud of them but did not expect Charles David to go along.

Peter took Katie Lee's hand and escorted her through the back door of the hospital near the emergency room. The emergency room was packed, he was so glad he did not have to put her through that ordeal. As they turned one corner, there were two sets of elevators, one said Hospital Entrances, the other Doctor's Annex. Katie Lee seemed to be okay with everything until they reached the doctor's office. She

Pacific Redwood Mystery: Do you believe in the little people yet?

held Peter's hand tight as they walked out of the elevator toward the door. There was little light in the waiting room and Peter wondered if he was too early. Maybe there was no one there yet. It was a weekend and he was sure no patients were there. Thank God for that. As he tried the door, it opened and he could hear voices behind the receptionist area. "Hello," Peter softly called out through the little window that was barely open. He recognized the nurse from the day before, she came with the same warm smile and same colored uniform, except she wore a lab coat this time. She opened the door as Katie Lee held Peter's hand, when the nurse smiled down at her, she gasped at what she saw. "Well, you must be Katie Lee, how are you this morning?" "Dr. Chung just called, he is on his way. Let's take you back to X-ray and we will take a beautiful picture of you, young lady." She followed the nurse but did not let go of Peter's hand. The nurse could tell this child did not fear her stepfather, there was nothing between them but trust and love.

 She was placing Katie Lee on the X-ray when Dr. Chung came through the back entrance. Katie Lee looked a little scared but the doctor quickly won her over the moment he spoke to her with his charming wit. "Good morning, do you think I can get a tape job like that, then all my nurses will do my work for me." He made a funny face at her as he came closer. "Katie Lee, my name is Dr. Chung, may I take a couple pictures of your nose?" She paid attention to his every instruction, watching Peter to make sure he was still there. Peter would wink at her, nodding her through every step. He was proud of her. Dr. Chung could see the instant connection between the two, and his heart went out to them both as he knew this was not going to be an easy fix. He asked the nurse to develop the films and bring them to his first treatment room. As Peter helped her of the table he noticed Peter was helping as she favored one knee. "Now did that hurt?" Dr. Chung asked as Katie Lee shook her head no, she gracefully took the lollipop the doctor held out to her. She was not thinking of anything sad right then, she liked him and he was nice, the nurse too. As she smiled at him he noticed the missing teeth and he could tell it was not an even break. Dr. Chung wanted to watch her walk down the hall to the treatment room, he told Peter to go ahead and meet him in the first door past the bathroom. He began to write in a chart as he watched from afar.

She was trying to walk straight but he could tell she was in a lot of discomfort, it probably was coming from her hip area, but he needed to examine her to make sure. He also saw her many black and blue marks on her legs. When he finally arrived in the room, the nurse already had the X-ray up on the board and Katie Lee on the table with a large gown taped to fit her a little better. "Well, I guess I am going to have to hire you to teach my girls how to tape, or did my nurse do that?" she giggled "It was my daddy, I am a little cold." Dr. Chung smile at the nurse "Your daddy, well, do you think he would charge me to learn how to do that?" There it was again, daddy. Peter only smiled wishing with all his heart he was her real daddy. The doctor began to explain he was gong to look at her nose, but not touch it, she relaxed. He could also see missing hair from the left side of her head and nail marks on her neck. "How are you feeling Katie Lee, do you have a headache that I can help you with? If you tell me where all your hurts are, we can deal with them one at a time." Peter was impressed in the choice of words the doctor used towards her, she was relaxed and felt comfortable. "Yes sir, my head hurt at first but my stepsister gave me some aspirin and it went away but my nose hurts when I turn my head. This morning when I was getting dressed my knee was hurting and when I tried to walk it hurts when I take a step." He could see that her nose was already starting to turn purple and he knew it was broken; the problem was how bad. He made small talk with her while he examined her knee, trying not to bend it too quickly or turn it too fast. She was very sensitive for sure, she did not have any other broken bones except for the nose but she sure had some serious markings and bruising. He examined her mouth and expressed to Peter she needed to see a dentist as soon as the swelling went down. The doctor wheeled his stool over to the wall and turned off the overhead light and switched on the light where her X-rays hung. "How about those

Pacific Redwood Mystery: Do you believe in the little people yet?

pictures, can you see your nose from here?" Sitting up a little further, Peter came closer and helped her raise herself in a better angle. "I look funny, don't I daddy?" Peter winked at her, "Well I think it looks like Charles David said, you have a nose of a movie star."

Trying to laugh at her stepfather, Dr. Chung could tell she was in pain, a lot of pain both from the nose and the upper leg. He got angry just looking at this child's face and body, what she must have had to endure. For the first time, he felt some compassion for her stepfather. "Well Katie Lee, you do have a broken nose but the good news is whoever taped it did a good job and I think with the proper care and re taping it, making it secure, you will be as good as new before long. For your knee, it is more from the hip and the knee probably was twisted pretty bad. She should avoid bearing weight on it for a good week or two and hot baths would do wonders." Peter could tell he was mad by the strain in his voice but as a professional he was trying to control himself. "Will you let me fix your nose a little bit Katie Lee, and re tape it so it will look better than a movie star?" She nodded it was okay and took a hold of Peter's hand as if she knew it was not going to be pleasant. He explained to Peter he wanted to give her a small amount of sedative just to relax her so she would not feel the discomfort. Dr. Chung opened the top drawer just below where Katie Lee was lying. "Look here, I have all kinds of colored tape. Which color would you like?" The nurse came towards her and placed some of the tape on her fingers so she could see all the colors. She studied them all and the picked the bright pink. She got scared when she saw the nurse with a needle but she explained to her it was for the doctor. "Me, well If I have to get a shot then I think you father needs one too." Katie Lee laughed at Dr. Chung as he put a small tube under her nose, he told her to breath normally and just relax. It would make her a little drowsy but that was okay. She just needed to hold her daddy's hand, it would be over before she knew it. He asked her to count backwards, it didn't even take to number four Katie Lee was already out. Peter was so thankful, he knew it was going to hurt when he straightened it but she would not feel it. Dr. Chung watched as Peter's face felt pain for his stepchild. He let Peter stay during the whole procedure which was not normal but Dr. Chung felt this was an exception more for Katie Lee.

    Dr. Chung assured Peter it would take only about thirty minutes for her to come around after the procedure and she'd be fine; the nurse was going to give her something to fight an infection, that was when Peter realized that was what the shot was for and very thankful the nurse gave it to her while she was still out. He told Peter he needed to make sure for her to be very careful throughout the next week, he wanted to see her back in a week. He also instructed the nurse to use the portable X-ray machine get a couple views of her hip and knee. He wanted to make sure they was no hairline fracture hidden anywhere. "I see she had three bald spots, missing hair several nail marks along the front and left side of the neck." Peter stayed quiet as he watched the doctor continue to document in Katie Lee's chart. "How is her mother doing this morning doctor, any changes?" Dr. Chung was thankful he had miss judged this man, he was an amazing father with true compassion and care. "Mr. Patterson, let's not give up hope yet." He shook Peter's hand as he excused himself from the room as the nurse smiled at them both. Peter sat by his little pumpkin until she started to move, He immediately call the nurse. "Hello, little one did you have a nice sleep?" Katie Lee was not sure for a second where she was until she saw her stepfather. "What happened, I was counting?" He laughed with the nurse and showed her the pretty new tape job the doctor had done all in pink. The nurse gave Peter instructions again and handed him a card with the appointment times as reminder for the following week. She also handed him some samples of infection medication and some children's Tylenol. As Peter escorted her out of the office, the nurse gave her a sticker and another lollipop. She offered Peter one, he took it making a funny face to his stepdaughter. He never wanted to see her any other way except with a smile on her face. "What are we going to do now daddy? You said you had a surprise for us" He was swinging her hand when he noticed Vera and Davie coming out of the elevator. He was surprised to see them but he was more surprised to see Ellen. "They brought the wrong clothes now what am I suppose to do? They said you have a surprise, what's up?" Ellen was her bold self as she blurted her remarks out to Peter.

Katie Lee did not even acknowledge her sister and Ellen did not brother to speak to her little sister. "I am sorry about the clothes but they will have to do. I am sure you will make due with them for the day, Ellen." She was not happy with Peter while rolling her eyes as always, Katie Lee peeked out from behind her stepfather. "Oh my god, what the hell?" She had not seen her little sister since the incident, she had come to the hospital with Peter and refused to leave. "She just got her nose fixed by Dr. Chung, it is broken pretty bad but he managed to fix as good as new." Peter was trying to make Katie Lee feel good in spike of her sister's outburst. "Oh no, that did not happen she must have fallen. Right, you fell, didn't you? You little brat, you just want sympathy." Katie Lee immediately stepped behind Peter for protection but Peter backed Ellen off. "That is enough from you. No, she did not and you know it. Now let me know right now, are you going to stay here today or do you want to go with the other kids for awhile?" Ellen was still staring at her little sister, she did not know her mother had done that. Mina had hurt her before, but not this bad. "What do you mean get away, you need to be here with my mother, she has not moved at all and you guys are planning an outing." Peter could understand how it looked to the young girl, but she did not realize that maybe tomorrow they may not be here. He decided to pull her aside and inform her of a few facts, whether it would calm her attitude down or make it worse. He was not in the mood for her bad attitude. Vera and Davie took Katie Lee down the elevator Peter instructed. Peter took Ellen and sat on a bench by the water display. Ellen listened, which was something Peter was not used to. He could tell nothing was going to matter. "I don't care about any social services, they cannot make me leave my mother, let them have Katie Lee. It is all her fault anyway. I don't want to go anywhere and you all can just leave me and my mom alone." She got up and stomped towards the stairs. Peter let her go, there was no trying to reason with her.

When Peter reached the bottom of the stairs, Ellen was yelling at Vera ad pulling at Katie Lee. "What the hell are you trying to do? I have enough to worry about without you pulling your crap, Ellen." She looked Peter in the face and threw her clothes on the ground in front of him. He didn't even bother to pick them up he just motioned for everyone to go to the truck and wait for him there. Katie Lee was beginning to tremble but Peter told her to lock the doors. "Davie was not going to let anything happen to you, lock the door and don't let anyone in, I meant it Davie, Vera I need your help here." With out another word they watched as Peter walked off in a stern manner towards the hospital. As he approached the front entrance, he could see Ellen getting a soda from the machine. As he passed her, he did not know if she had enough money to care for herself and he was not going to ask. It would only give her an excuse to make another scene. He went straight to the nurse's station while asking for an envelope and a piece of paper. The ward clerk handed him some paper from the copy machine but said they did not have any envelopes. Peter took his wallet from his back pocket and placed a twenty dollar bill in the middle of the paper, folded it, wrote Ellen's name on the front then handed it to the nurse. "Please make sure Mrs. Patterson's daughter get this after I leave, thank you." He never looked at any of them, he just turned and went into Mina's unit. Then he realized why Ellen was coming back so soon, Mary and Charles David were standing there just staring at Mina. It was almost as shocking as seeing Katie Lee's face, now they realized she did not look like herself. She had lost a lot of blood, the wound was long and wide. Her unconscious body just lay there with hardly even a sound of breathing. It looked as if she had already died. Peter prayed for her to recover, he did not know why he just did not want her to die.

Mary came to her father and hugged him. "I am so sorry, I didn't realize, is she going to be okay?" Peter just looked at her as Mina lay there helpless and motionless. Charles David left the room without a word, the young boy could not handle what he saw. "Take care of your brother, I won't be but a minute, the other's are already in the truck." As Peter stood looking down at Mina, he could not help but remember some of the good times but in his heart that was not enough anymore. He took her hand in his and pressed her petite fingers to his lips. "I am sorry Mina, I truly am, whatever it's worth, I am so sorry." He held her hand for a time just staring into her swollen face, she was warm. He knew that was a good sign, there had been no fever. As he moved his eyes to the entire length of the wound, he could see the extent of the injury. How deep the wound was, how gruesome it was. A nurse came in to take her vials and noticed Peter just standing there. She moved around him silently as possible, not saying a word or disturbing him. She could tell this was a moment that no words were necessary. Before she left while she was replacing the wires closer to the monitor, she carefully ran her hand cross the back of Peter's shirt. It was cold in there, but he knew if had to be a certain temperature for medical purposes. In his heart he knew it was the end, he had to walk away, it was not worth her life and it certainly was not worth it to the children. Part of him wanted to protect her and make it all right, but the other part he'd seen could not be fixed. One had to be willing, again like the old phase says.

You can lead a horse to water but you cannot make them drink.

Smoothing the sides of her hair, he gently touched her cheek. She was a beautiful woman. God had blessed her with the ultimate glamour most women pay thousand of dollars to achieve. Then he remembered his grandmothers oldest lesson, which by the way he failed to learn.

Beauty is only skin deep and do not judge a book by its cover.

Peter could stand there all morning and remember phrase again and again but it would never change yesterday. He could only control himself from this day forward. Touching her face one more time, he whispered "Take care pretty lady, prove them wrong and come out fighting." Leaving the room, he noticed Ellen standing just outside the door, he knew she had heard him. As he passed her, he ran his hands through her ponytail. "Take care of her Ellen, I'll be back." She never turned to face him but in her heart she was glad it was over. Nothing good ever came out of her mother's relationships. She really liked Peter, but like all the rest, he was just another toy and sooner or later he would be thrown away.

As Peter walked back through the nurses station, he handed the clerk a paper with a number. "I can be reached at this number until tomorrow morning if needed." Keeping his pace he left heading for his truck and the children. He was glad to see everyone in a better mood playing around in the small grass area. As they saw him they ran to him wanting to know what the surprise was. Katie Lee seemed still a little slow to move, but that was to be expected for most of the afternoon. "Well, get in the truck and let's see." Mary seemed extra quiet as they drove, Peter knew seeing Mina the way they did brought things to reality than just saying she was in grave condition. Vera was busy with Davie in the back seat as Charles David struck up a game with Katie Lee on who would see the most blue cars in one minute. It was good to see them busy and content. Peter had one more stop to make and they were off. Peter whispered to his inner soul, "God please make her strong, if it be your will to take her, please don't take her today."

Letting them look out the window and play games, Peter made his way to Davie's father's shop. He asked Davie to stay in the truck with Vera. They all seemed anxious not knowing what he was up to, so they just sat and waited. Davie could see Peter and his father, then they shook hands and Peter got back in the truck. As Peter put the truck in gear, he suggested that they all settle down and find something to talk about, it would take about another hour before they arrived at the surprise. He could see immediately that Charles David and Davie were trying to figure out their destination. "I know we are going fishing," Charles David yelled. David squealed right after him until Vera gave him a look of saying, "Oh no, you don't agree." Vera hit Davie in the

Pacific Redwood Mystery: Do you believe in the little people yet?

ribs as she voiced her opinion to her father. "Dad, come on, he can't be right. We are not going fishing, are we? Katie Lee cannot be by the water, what if she falls?" Verna was non stop complaining. Katie Lee just wanted everyone to have fun, if was the first time she ever spoke up now that she was without her mother's control. "Daddy, are we going fishing? I won't mind if that is what you want to do." Peter was seeing where Mary was rubbing off on the her, but she had already a good start in being a very special girl. "Well, if anyone wants to fish, I guess they can but there will be lots to do and we have all day. It will be everyone for themselves today?"

CHAPTER THIRTEEN

It was getting close to noon and Peter wanted t get the BBQ set up before long, he wanted the whole day to be dedicated to the kids; everything had to be perfect. As he turned off the main road onto a logging road, which soon got everyone's attention, everyone began to laugh as they bounced and jerked inside the truck. Peter of course made it worse by hitting every hole he could, swearing into every bad spot the road had just to hear them laugh and go from side to side, pretending to slam into each other harder than they really did. He kept an eye on Katie Lee to make sure she was okay, but when it got too rough, she would huddle under Peter's side and hang on for dear life. She was having so much fun she completely forgot about her nose. Peter teased them about running into a logging truck on this narrow strip of road, where were they going to go? Davie was the only one in the truck that got all paranoid. He was easy to tease and easy to play tricks on.

"Its a weekend. No one works on weekends, Mr. Patterson." Davie was laughing just as hard as the rest when they heard Peter say. "Whoa, whoa, what do you mean no one words on weekends?" Coming down the hill and making good speed, Peter spotted a logger coming around the next bend. He pulled the pickup as far as he dare into the ditch at the side of the hill. "Dad, there is not enough room to go to the other side." Looking at his daughter through the rear mirror Peter replied. "Okay Vera, let's do that, that side has a cliff straight down to the road below." Mary knew her father had been through this a thousand times, knowing exactly what he was doing. They had ran those roads for years passing one another with just enough room to squeeze an ant through. As the logger got closer, everyone started to scream and duck in the pickup. Peter made noises like "Oh boy, here he comes, anyone got a measuring tape?" Charles David leaned clear out the window to see how much room he had to pass. The boys were temporary speechless, Peter leaned down to Katie Lee and told her. "Don't worry pumpkin, he is a friend of mine and there is plenty of room." Winking at her, he saw her face relax. "Dad, dad, do something." He watched Vera and Davie the most, Charles David did not know whether to jump or wet his pants. As the truck went whirling by, it felt as if they were not even sitting there; they all dunked as if something was going to fall from the sky. As the truck went down the hill, he honked his horn and waved at Peter. Peter honked back twice, acknowledging the driver. "Does anyone need to go to the bathroom or change their clothes?" Peter turned the big diesel pickup onto the road as if it was just as normal as driving into their driveway. He chuckled inside as he watched their faces, not daring to admit to one another they were scared. "I knew he would make it. Man, he had plenty of room." Davie motioned, his hands as if saying it was cool. "Yea, that was cool but I think I pissed my pants, dad." Usually Peter would have corrected his son but everyone laughed so hard Peter just raised his eyebrows at his son.

Peter turned a couple more turns, then took off on another dirt road that was worse than the first. Before anyone could complain too much he came upon an open space where the kids could see all kinds of equipment, buildings and cabins. "Hey, this is the logging camp we went to before, right?" Peter just grinned at Charles David as he pulled the pickup right up in front of the largest building. It was long and skinny, made of cedar and pine. "Oh man, this is so cool dad, this is the cookhouse, I remember and those are the cabins the loggers and cutters stayed in. Over there is the tool shed and over there is where they parked their trucks." Charles David was talking a mile a minute as they all got out of the pickup to inspect the area. "Each of you, get your own stuff and remember, you do have to clean up after yourselves. There is a big kitchen inside this building where you can put all the food. I know there is still a phone, it is in the tool shed. Mary, go make sure it is still working." As with all young people the excitement of a new adventure was mote then their patience could stand, they couldn't wait to take off. "Nope, no you don't. I don't care what you do after all the food is packed inside and your personal items are where you want them for the day." Peter was firm but smiled knowing they would take him serious.

Vera loved the little cabins, they were perfect. Also, in her mind she was beginning to think this was also a great hiding place for her and Davie, if needed. Mary felt as if she was home, it was good to see her old friends, the giant redwoods and ferns. Peter had never seen Charles David and Davie work so fast, he knew they wanted to go fishing and explore. Katie Lee was not saying much, she was overwhelmed in everything. When everything was done and Peter had the BBQ out and ready to go, he sat them all down. "Okay guys, there is fishing poles in the tool shed, you can shock worms if you want but make sure you shut the hose off before you take off and put the shockers away. You all have to promise that you will go no further than that hill right there, it has a great stream and you can fish there. No walking around without me any father than that. There are oodles of berries and what does that mean Davie?" It took him no time at all to answer Peter. "Bears, big brown, black and grizzly bears." That was not the answer Peter was looking for but is it scared them fine, the girls had not thought of that until Davie made it sound so spooky. "Yes, but also elk, deer, bobcats and some pumas have been seen up here, so don't go wondering off." Peter was serious, his tone and facial expression were straight forward.

"I brought plenty of batteries, you can play your music if you like, there is plenty of room to run right around here and if you want to go berry picking, I will go with you. Now, who wants to fish so I can get that out of the way and deal with the girly stuff." They all laughed

Pacific Redwood Mystery: Do you believe in the little people yet?

hard as Peter referred to the girls interest as girly things. Davie and Charles David were bent on fishing, so Peter got the poles out of the shed, helped them shock worms and sent them on their way. He told the girls to open a couple of the cabins and he would be right back.

Mary noticed Peter took a rifle out of the pickup, placing it over his shoulder. There was a box of shells in his hand as he took them in the building. She did not want to look at the gun, she knew this was for protection, but with what had happened was still too vivid in her mind, a mental scar to last a lifetime. She distracted herself by asking Katie Lee to help her find a good station on the radio and they could play it as loud as they wanted. Katie Lee noticed a little squirrel over by the trees, so Mary told her to go get some bread but be careful not to get too close. She kept an eye as she watched her try to get close, but the little fells was too quick. Vera was disgusted because Davie had gone fishing and left her. "Come on Vera, he asked you if you wanted to go. It is beautiful out, let the boys fish." Mary poked fun at Vera as she moaned and groaned but soon joined her sister at one of the picnic tables, getting involved in a game of hearts with Katie Lee.

It was a great day, they watched as Peter was busy fixing a feast and enjoying the music. They could hear birds singing, the winds whispering through the treetops. Katie Lee saw a small rabbit under some wild mushrooms. They were invading nature and animals territory but what a place to spend the day. There was just enough breeze to settle the dust from the old logging road, there was nothing life a breath of air. It was nature, beauty hard to describe. The redwoods were giants, some you could not even see the tops. The ferns were all over in large bundles, all green surrounded in moss. Mary loved the redwoods, she remembered her mother making their clothes and when she would run, her dresses would flow wildly through those endless paths among those giants. She wanted to teach her children when she got married what it was like. She wanted to run with them, play hide and seek, teach them what nature was all about. She had the best of both worlds in her life as a young girl. She loved the city and longed to live closer to the coast after she graduated but close enough not to lose this pleasure of freedom that surrounded her, She noticed Katie Lee was in her own little world, watching her look as high as she could trying to find the tops of those giants. "Won't do you any good, they go forever. They have a secret you know?"

Katie Lee came hobbling over to Mary as Vera was also intrigued with her sister's mystery. "A secret, what secret?" Vera was not going to fall for that, or her sisters sister's foolish games. "Yes Mary, what secret?" Mary smiled at them both but started to talk as if she was telling some great, mysterious secret. "Well, they say if you listen real closely on how they talk to you, they can tell you which way to go. There are little people that live here in the forest and the play in the redwoods all day. When night time comes, they fall asleep under those bundles of ferns. The ferns go forever, some hug the ground, others grow up on trees. They make a wonderful place for all the little people to sleep. When you hear the wind whistle at night, it is really the redwoods warning the little people where danger may be, those mighty redwoods won't allow no harm to come to them." Katie Lee was listening intensely, Vera was not sure what to think. "Oh come on Mary, where did you hear that?" She leaned over Katie Lee and pointed her finger at her sister. "They did, when I was Katie Lee's age and played among the redwoods, they made friends with me and I am still their friend. I can run among the redwoods forever and play. No one will ever know I am here, just me and my little friends." Katie Lee believed every word, one could tell by the way she looked at Mary. Vera was not convinced but it was a good story. "You wait Vera, when it gets close to dark you will hear the little people hustle under those beautiful ferns. If I died tomorrow, this is where I would want to be, here among the redwoods, playing forever."

Peter approached behind the three noticing Vera was in a mysterious daze with an uneasy look, maybe wanting to run somewhere. "What is going on girl, you all look as if you saw a ghost or something?" Mary began to hum, swinging her arms and dancing like a ballerina when her father used the word "ghost." "Dad, Mary is telling her story again about the little people in the redwoods. She is making Katie Lee believe her. She said if she died tomorrow, she wanted to play in the redwoods forever." Peter looked at Katie Lee, he could see she was completely spellbound by his daughter's story. "Well, I have heard about these little people but you have to be careful they are pretty small, they don't like to be seen. I have heard they play among the trees though." Vera was astonished that her father was joining in with Mary's silly nonsense. "Really daddy, have you ever seen the little people?" Katie Lee was so taken with the story she couldn't stop trying to see the tree tops which was impossible for a young child like her. Peter winked at Mary as she took Katie Lee by the hand and started to point under the ferns and up into the trees. It was a fairy tale she had created in her own mind as a child and now, she was sharing it with a small girl that needed something wonderful to believe in.

Peter checked the fire on the BBQ before going to call the hospital to make sure everything was okay. He was not going to bother anyone with the information but he just needed to make sure. He watched Vera play a few games of solitaire as Mary was making the fairy tale more realistic. She made everything seem so perfect anyway, that was one thing about her, her grace, belief and dreams. She could make a story come alive right in front of you. He knew that when they went home this day, Katie Lee would believe in the little people and have the same bond to the redwoods that Mary possessed. As the afternoon wore on the boys came back for more worms, they had only caught three fish. When Peter said it was getting late and they needed to eat and wind down in a couple of hours to head for home, he was outnumbered and attacked. "NO, please let's stay until the morning, really we can leave early." Peter was insistent on leaving within a couple hours, but they kept on and on; even Katie Lee was pleading for them to stay the night. He gave them a time limit to finish playing and enjoying the afternoon and for the boys to fish for one more hour. They all went off with their heads down as if he had taken the world from them. "Is there a reason whey we cannot spend one night dad?" As he looked around, it was Mary asking. He thought it would be more from Vera due to Davie being there. "It is so peaceful here and it has been awhile since I have been near the redwoods. I just hate to leave." Peter pointed his finger at her. "You just want to prove there are little people, I know you." Grinning at her father, she kind of danced away. "Well, they can hear you, so you better be careful. Don't you remember me playing with them all the time when I was Katie Lee's age?" Peter remembered too well many times he had gone to look for her and she would be running as if there was no tomorrow through those big trees, free as a bird and happy as a lark. Yes, he remembered those days and he wished he could turn back the time for her.

He waited until everyone came back to camp and he had several grand old fashioned hamburgers, hot dogs, beans, chips and potato salad. Peter smoked the three fish the boys had caught in the pit. It tasked so good they all ate until they felt they were going to bust. Charles David was lying flat on his back, looking up at the trees. Katie Lee now believed little people hid and slept. Vera was cleaning up the paper plates while Mary was watching Katie Lee with a smile that sparked the very stars at night. Davie was on the other side of Charles David just watching nature and all it's wonder. Peter took the grill out of the BBQ carrying the hot coals to a hole he had dug for that purpose.

Coming back, they all just watched their father, never wanting to move. "Well, Davie what do you think, do you like it out here?" Sitting up on one elbow, he just eyed the marveled around him. "What is there not to like? This is heaven right here on earth." Peter kind of kicked the bottom of his boot as he stood about the lad. "Well then, I guess you better go use the phone and tell your parents we will be staying out here tonight. I will bring you home first thing in the morning." When everyone heard that they were all over the place. Katie Lee and Mary were hugging him. "Are you serious, no way, you are serious, right?" Charles David was beside himself, he couldn't stand still, "Come on Davie let go call, hurry." Peter watched them run towards the tool shed then enjoyed his daughters astonished excitement. "Mary and Vera, help your little sister pick out her cabin for the night and you girls will stay there. The guys will stay next to whichever one you pick. I guess I better go look for some wood, might get cold tonight and I guess we better get the marshmallows out."

As he walked off, Mary tried to do a Michael Jackson moonwalk as Katie Lee giggled. It was bad, real bad. Katie Lee wanted to stay in the cabin right next to the path where the massive redwoods began. It was obvious it had been some time since anyone was here, the cabins were really dusty. "You started something girl, now she will probably be up all night listening and looking for the little people." Mary pulled Vera's hair gently from behind. "Good, then they will have another friend to play with besides me." "Oh Mary, I swear, you would probably be happy if you turned into a tree." Only a giant redwood she replied. Shaking her head at Mary she heard little Katie Lees question with so much seriousness. "Vera, do you think they know she is here?" Katie Lee was sure Mary was telling the truth and who was Vera to ruin it for her little stepsister. "Yep, I am sure, they will probably want her to come out and play." Vera watched Katie Lee's face as she stopped in her tracks as she stared towards all the mystery of the forest.

Davie and Charles David came back looking for their father more excited then before. Vera had never been in a situation where Davie did not give her all his attention. She was beginning to feel left out. As she placed her hand over her stomach, she wondered if that was going to make a difference. Of course it would, it would make everything complete. A family, a connection to a new start, something no one could take away from her. She started to sweep the cabin and dust the curtains as Mary took Katie Lee headed for the bigger building for supplies that Peter instructed her to bring back. When they had finished bringing what Peter asked Mary disappeared, Vera was in her own zone inside the cabin making it all cozy, Peter and the boys came back with arms loaded with wood for the night. He would have plenty of time to get them back in the morning. They would have to leave at the crack of dawn, but that was okay, especially if this would be their last night all together.

Vera ad Katie Lee took out the marshmallows. "Who decided to bring these, neat idea?" Katie Lee held up her hand, they all giggled. She could eat marshmallows all day long. Peter told the boys to go find some branches to whittle down so they could roast them. Looking around, , he yelled to the boys, "While you are out there, see if you can find your sister. She ran off to play with her little people." Peter gave Katie Lee his jacket as he laughed when he saw the sleeves hanging clear to the ground. She was comfortable and did not want to take it off. He didn't mind if it made her happy, that was important, flopping the sleeves if Peter's jacket Katie Lee twirled slowly as she stopped long enough to ask Peter a question. "Daddy how long will Mary stay away playing in the redwoods?"

Peter looked over his shoulder at his other daughter as she looked at her father, putting her lips into a fish shape, he remembered now how hard it was for her to learn that. He chuckled towards Vera as she remember so many wonderful memories of those days when they were young. "Well, she will be back soon, the little people don't really like to stay out at night, they are too small and the wolves and coyotes will eat them, so they disappear fast when it starts to get dark." As Peter and Vera looked at each other they knew there was no way Katie Lee would ever believe anything different. "Are you all talking about me, awe you miss me?" She was carrying a bucket filled with salmon berries and raspberries. "Look what the little people sent you for desert tonight. They wanted to thank us for coming and spending the day with them." Peter was shaking his head. This was unbelievable now she had little people bringing gifts. Mary washed the berries and passed the bucket around to everyone. As Charles David and Davie came running back, they were out of breath. "Hey dad we saw something, really we did?" Peter turned to see if the boys were teasing or being serious. He was not sure about Davie, but he could tell his son was serious. "What did you see Charles David, the little people?" Vera couldn't resist that remark to the boys. "See Vera, they are real." Katie Lee was more convinced now than ever. "What son, and where?" Charles David came right in front of his father "We were gathering more kindling like you asked

Pacific Redwood Mystery: Do you believe in the little people yet?

when we went on the other side of the river. I don't know, but it was coming through the thickets, honest. Dad is was." Peter did not want to alarm anyone it could be anything passing through. "Well, it is getting close to sundown, so maybe it is some deer heading for the river to drink, it is about time son." Charles David and Davie helped Peter set up the lanterns on the small tables, it would be darker than any of these children had ever witnessed before in these part of the woods. The girls got the operation game out, Peter had never seen so much laughing and carrying on before. No one was able to get it right, the little buzzer kept everyone on their toes in laughter for over an hour. As the mist of the night crept upon them, Peter was silent as he listened to the mysteries of what his world was all about. As the children kept playing near the fire, he took one of the lanterns off the old picnic heading towards the cabins to make sure the heaters were burning well without any safety issues through the night. It got pretty cold up in these camps, it got pretty cold and pretty creepy, if you let it get to you. As he was beginning to check the guy's cabin, he heard a prairie wolf cry not too far off. Before he could explain he saw Vera dashing towards the cabins, Davie was standing right beside Charles David, waiting to see what he was going to do. Vera was firmly telling Katie Lee and her sister to get inside. Again they heard the howl, it took the two boys three giant steps to make it past Peter as he stood in the doorway of the cabin. He noticed Mary was walking very slowly towards him as she spoke loud enough for everyone to hear. "Does this mean the game is over, guess so?" They all stood looking at back and forth to beach other waiting for Peter to do something. Peter laughed at his son, "Charles David, that is just a prairie wolf. He won't come into camp, he is just letting you know he is out there. Remember, you are in his backyard." Davie was standing behind Charles David "What is a prairie wolf, is he dangerous?" Even Vera started to laugh, she knew what a prairie wolf was. Looking at her boyfriend as if he really was dumb, she giggles as she raised her voice towards Davie in the next cabin. "Prairie wolf and coyotes are the same thing, Davie. You do know what a coyote is?" Looking at Charles David, he could care less, he wasn't taking any chances whatever it was. "Well, he can have it tomorrow morning. Can we play the game in here." Mary could not help laughing at her brother and Vera's boyfriend. "Lord help you all, especially if a bear comes into camp."

Mary helped her father pick up the rest of the camp putting everything away. Each time she threw something into her fathers large garbage bag, she would poke fun towards her father. He had gotten all the kids out of the two cabins to help pick everything up and lock it up in the cab of the truck to make sure it wouldn't draw little or big varmints. That was except Vera, she would not come out of the cabin and Katie Lee was not sure if she wanted to. Peter just smiled and winked at Katie Lee when she would peak out watching everything they were doing. Again they heard the cries of the wild. Katie Lee immediately got on top of her bed, with Vera right behind her. Mary came into the cabin turning on the little radio she had found in the closet trying to find a station. She was beginning to get some reception when the other two girls showed interest. They could hear several stations, but none clear enough to enjoy. Mary had left their bigger radio from home for the guys. Katie Lee peaked out the door again then back at Mary like she was a little scared, Mary grinned to herself as she assured he little girl all was well. "Dad and the boys are going to see how close the prairie wolves are and scare them off with the rifle." That seemed to ease Katie Lee as her body relaxed but Mary knew neither of them were going outside that cabin door. As she passed them both she patted Katie Lee on the arm as Vera stuck her tongue out at her sister knowing Mary was laughing at them inside. Mary went on the little half bathroom to make sure the water was working and the toilet flushed. As she came out of the bathroom, she found Vera and Katie Lee both laughing as Vera was dancing the twist and monkey. "Awe see you got a pretty clear station, be careful you two, we don't need any accidents up here, Katie Lee be careful of that left leg." Both girls didn't even look up at Mary, Katie Lee held on the Vera and she kept trying to do the twist. "I'm only twisting my upper half, see." Just smiling, Mary went back to making sure all the food was secure and put away. The girls were deep in their own fun and totally forgot about their little friends outside that door. Mary watched Katie Lee still dragging her left leg, she was not going to ruin her that young girls fun.

Mary was so pleased to see Katie Lee totally at ease, if she had to, she would give her pain medication the doctors gave her father but for now let her have be and forget her ordeal. Maybe that was what was missing, the fun of togetherness without the drama. That was something Mary siblings were well aware of, unfortunately Katie Lee was not. How sad it seemed and soon it would be over for her. Her father would have to return her in the morning either Protective Services or the detectives would be waiting. Mary thought of Allie and how much she would have enjoyed this day, it would have been so perfect if they all could have been here. She was sure Allie was fine and happier at home with their real mother. It would be good to see her real mother again, even with her deep depression. The anger would stir inside Mary as she remembered those wonderful days before her father got under Mina's spell. She blames them both, maybe she totally could forgive her father one day, but she would never forget. Somehow she would find a way to stay in touch with Katie lee. She wanted to make sure she had a good life. The story of the little people was a fairy tale, but it was one that made her youth magical in a positive way, she wanted Kate Lee to experience the same. It helped through her hard times to have imaginary friends.

The girls didn't even hear Peter and the boys walked into the cabin, Peter's face lit up as he nudged the boys to notice the girl's silliness. The boys joined the girls and began dancing everything from the fly, the stroll, jitterbug, ending with the Cotton Eyed Joe. Of course nothing was to the beat of the music but they all pulled Peter in until they all landed in the middle of the floor exhausted. Peter had accomplished the memories he so wanted to leave each of them. It has been along time since so much peace, warmth and comfort had been between them and never for Katie Lee. Peter continued to watch as they wrestled a little as the girls were whipping the boys butts, Katie Lee was trying to cheer Charles David on warning him when Vera or Mary were coming at him. Finally Peter laughing out loud in amusement with them all.

Katie Lee was like a baby in a candy store for the first time. They all finally took deep breaths laying on their backs in total pleasure. Peter's eyes became slant as he listened to scratching just a little too close from outside, Charles David immediately stood still "What was that?" Vera and Davie set up as Mary put her arm around Katie Lee. "Where is the gun, dad?" his son asked, Peter held his amusement as he noticed the tail of a small raccoon going under the cabin near the front entrance. "It is in the pickup son, you and Davie go out and get it? We need to have it inside for the night anyway." The boys looked at Peter like why don't you go, Vera leaned up and shut the screen door on the little cabin. As her father looked over at her she blurted out. "Well, we don't want to invite anything in, do we?" Peter unlocked his hands from behind his head as he rose from the floor telling the boys "Go on now boys, I'll get the flashlight." Obviously, he had forgotten his father already brought the gun into the cabin, in fact it was just above his head lying on top of the refrigerator. Davie was not sure if Peter was joking or expecting the boys to go out there. This time they all heard a rustling by the door just outside. Vera dropped Davie's hand like a hot potato heading behind her father. "Did you hear that? It's right outside the door," Vera whispered as if anything that was out there might hear her. Peter started for the door putting his hand on the doorknob. "What are you doing dad?" Charles David asked with his face white as a sheet. "I am going to see what is scaring you all and making that noise, that's all." Peter almost felt bad, he knew it was the raccoon he saw minutes before, he had seen signs of earlier when they first got there, she thought he saw her also crossing the road with a couple little ones knowing she would appear sometimes scourging up all the scraps for her little ones.

Peter jerked open the door but lunged forward with a big roaring sound, he scared everyone of them but in turn her jumped when they all screamed so loud they took him by surprise. Peter explained to them it was just a raccoon he had seen go under the porch, nothing to worry about. They all took their pillows and started hitting Peter as Peter acted like they were getting the full advantage of him in the

Pacific Redwood Mystery: Do you believe in the little people yet?

pillow fight. If he only had more time to keep this going, but what a day and evening for the children, his children, including Katie Lee. He was completely satisfied with his decision to come here. As he pretended to fall down, they all landed on top of him Davie making sure Katie Lee was on top having the most fun. As they all laughed Peter rose from the floor grabbing little Katie Lee putting her on his shoulders twirling her around as the other kids laughed and sang ring around the rosie two times and everyone fell back to the floor completely exhausted. "Well, I think it is time to call it a night. We have to leave early, you girls get your pj's on, we will be right next door." There was a sudden silence through the room. Peter realized the girls were uneasy with the dark night and strange surrounding, he needed to make sure they all felt safe for the night. "Charles David, I would leave you here to protect your sisters but I think we all need to be in the came place, so let's go next door and bring two cots over here." Immediately shaking his head, Charles David replied "Oh no, they can go carry them over, besides I hurt my foot when I ran from the creek, its hurting some." Peter knew that was not true, but his son wanted to have dad time. "Come on Davie, let's go get those cots." As Peter was turning to make sure Davie was behind him, he noticed Davie already had a large piece of wood in his hand. Peter reached over taking the wood from the boy throwing it back on the small pile of wood just outside the door. Mary reached for her sweater, "Come on everyone he needs help but you better not stand too close to Charles David. You might get trampled if he hears a noise." Peter patted Charles David gently as he gestured for him to follow Mary. Everyone but Charles David was humming as they carried the cots back to the girls cabin, the girls only smiled at each other with excitement, the boys never made one comment. Once everything was in place and room made for the extra cots, Peter took Charles David for a walk, Mary only smiled as everyone else didn't even notice they had left the cabin at all.

As they walked Peter wanted his son to know he didn't have to worry about anything, the worst that would happen was he would go back home to his mother, if that happened Mary was old enough to over see them all. How Charles David had to be strong and make sure his sister's were ok if things turned bad, he was depending on his to take the lead if he was not able to be around for some time. Peter stopped turning towards his son as he placed his hands on Charles David's shoulders, "Son, lets make this night one to remember no matter what happens. We all have each other, no one can take that from us, but little Katie Lee does not and it will never be the same for her again, she is not ours and never will be." Charles David bowed his head as his father actually saw tears coming from his son's eyes. "I wish I would have better to her, what will happen to her dad?" That Peter had no idea as he took a deep breath and slowly turned his son around to return to the others.

Settling everyone down for the night wasn't easy, they had a full day but no one wanted it to end. Tonight would probably be the first time any of them slept good. Trying to convince them there was no animals that could come through the smallest crack and eat them took some work. Their bodies physically exhausted but with minds at peace, the cabin was now silent. All Peter could hear was their restful breathing as the fireplace crackled keeping the cabin toasty and warm for his sleeping angels. As he stepped outside near the little walkway, he studied the stars, sky, God's nature all around him. The smell of those beautiful redwood beasts lurking through the forest was a delight one had to see with their own eyes. The cedars had been cut mostly for homes but the scent was still heavy and appealing. He thought about his conversation with Ellen, he had not told the kids he called earlier to the hospital, especially his talk with her. The conversation was cordial meaningless. There still was no change, the night was healing as he sat and soaked in the wonder of it all.

He would never forget this night, he knew his soul was doomed for hell for the mistake he had made. After all was said and done, he thought he might come back here with his son, if he was able to keep any of his children and let the healing process begin. Mary could visit, he knew anywhere she could be among those giant redwoods she would come running. As for Vera, he thought the break away

Pacific Redwood Mystery: Do you believe in the little people yet?

from Davie would be good before anything happened to ruin both their lives. She would fight him, but he would worry about that later. Davie could visit but under his rules, not theirs. Throwing a small mattress from the cot just outside the front door on the porch, he settled down himself, crossing his arms behind his head, exploring the little people's magnificent playground.

CHAPTER FOURTEEN

Vera was not pleased that they took Davie home first. She was squeezing his hand but did not get it. He thought it was just her being attached to him. When they arrived in front of Davie's home his father came out flagging Peter down. "Peter have you heard anything?" Rolling his window down the full length to give the man more respect, he acknowledge his concern. "No, I wanted to get all the kids home and settled. Go to the hospital then I have to be back home in time for a meeting with Protective Services." Davie's father looked and felt so helpless. "Oh my, I am sorry Peter, what can we do to help?" He liked Davie's father, he had worked hard for what he had. He was a decent, honest, hardworking man that prospered well. "Nothing really, it just has to take it's course." Nodding his head, he stepped back to let Peter be on his way, he could see his wife peeking out behind the kitchen curtains. "Tell your mother good morning, talk to you later Davie." Peter backed out of the driveway without another word. He watched Vera as she seemed to look more disturbed than usual. He knew she did not like being away from Davie, but he was going to make sure that distance increased very soon. He drove through town heading south towards their country road. It was quiet, only loggers and lumberjacks seemed to be around at these hours.

The ride to the house was probably the only time Peter could remember no one uttered a word. As he reached the turn, the climb up the hill seemed harder, the road had taken a beaten that winter.

Pacific Redwood Mystery: Do you believe in the little people yet?

Penny was barking, running back and forth when she saw Peter's pickup. She did not ride well, so Peter decided it was better they did not take her, if she got sick, Katie Lee would not be able to participate in anything. He was glad the pup was making such a fuss, in got Katie Lee attention. He made sure everyone helped unload everything and immediately take care of all chores. Mary was quick to head for the kitchen, knowing her father had to leave for the hospital. As Peter entered the house, it seemed different now. He doubted if he wold continue to live here after this, probably sell or lease it, whatever came first. He wanted this day to be over with so he could get everything cleaned out, especially the bedroom. He had hired a maid service before he left without telling anyone. He did not know if they would object to the bedroom, but he had given instructions. They knew the situation, he had paid them extremely well. The police had finished with that they needed. He did not want the kids coming back to the bloody mess, the memory was bad enough.

"Don't bother with breakfast for me young lady, I will grab coffee and something to eat on the way." Charles David was coming out of his room and Vera disappeared to her. "I need to fix something for everyone anyway, won't you eat something?" Mary pleaded. "No, I need to get over there, I am sure I am the talk of the place leaving like I did." Mary felt the same as her father, it was a good idea, no regrets. "You did the right thing dad, don't think abut anyone else, they don't matter anyway." He had such respect and love for Mary, she always knew what to say and when to say it. It was a trait she surely got from her mother, a true southern belle.

Katie Lee was coming in with Penny right on her heels. "Are you going to see my mommy?" He bent down in front of Katie Lee, hugging her tightly. "Yes, I am but I do not want you to worry, just stay close to the house and play with Penny until I get back." It was a solemn moment, they watched Peter pick up his gloves at the back door and leave. They could hear the diesel pickup back up and head down the hill. No one was really hungry, they just wanted to remember yesterday in their minds and not think about today. Mary scooted them all outside, she figured she could get more done without them. Suggesting from the back door she remarked after Katie Lee and Charles David. "Why don't you two go down to the barn and rearrange the small stacks of hay. Dad is going to be bringing more in, he needs the room and I think you can make it easier for him." Charles David put his coat back on and handed Katie Lee hers. "What about the princess in her room, is she going to help or sulk all day. Katie Lee's leg is still stiff." Mary shot him a dirty look as she walked down the hall to Vera's room thinking. Can't he do anything for himself? "Vera, I need you to go help your brother in the barn, come on right now." She did not have to wait long, her sister opened the door with her coat on. Vera stopped off towards the back door barking her comment at Mary. "Might as well keep busy, can't do anything else."

Mary watched as all three reluctantly went toward the barn. Waling back to the kitchen, the phone rang. "Hello Patterson residence." There was no noise or "hello" as Mary repeated herself several times but no voice on the other end. Mary hung up the wondering if it could have been Ellen checking to see if they were back or hopefully not worse news on Mina. Trying to shake that horrible feeling off the phone rang again. "Hello, who is this please?" She could hear like papers ruffling in the back ground then "Is Mr. Patterson there? This is Detective Cruz from the police department." Mary felt panic going from her head to her toes. Why was he calling so early? "No, he is not sir. He is on his way to the hospital, may I take a message?" There was a longer silence then she expected. She didn't like the long pause, it made her feel as if he had something to hide. "No, I will drive over and meet him there, thank you." Mary could not help thinking something must have gone wrong or had Mina died? Her mind was flying in all directions.

She decided to call the hospital, she could pretend to be calling to tell Ellen they were back and her father was on his way. She frantically dialed asking for intensive care then asking for Ellen. They only took her number, they could not hold call on that unit. As she cleared her throat and made sure they had the correct number, she watched and waited for the phone to ring. As she made her way down the hall she hesitated at the door way then stepped forward. She noticed immediately that the room was not a mess, nor was there anymore blood; it had been cleaned. She looked around feeling coldness pass through her entire body. The room looked as if nothing had happened but something had! Hearing the ring she jumped, then realized it was just the phone. Rushing through the sheet she ran to answer. It was her father "What is wrong, Mary?" He must have gotten the message or Ellen told him. "Nothing, really daddy, just one of the detectives called and said they were heading to the hospital and I was calling to see if everything was okay." Relieved, Peter let his body go limp. "She is still alive, she had moved her fingers early this morning, so they are excited about that. The doctor will be here around eight or eight thirty, so I will hang around to see what is up."

He heard his daughter sigh, he knew the feeling. "That is good, right daddy, that is a good sign." Peter was delighted yes but he did not want to give too much hope, he knew it was still serious and Mina was a long ways from being okay. "Don't say anything to the others just yet, I want to hear what the doctor has to say, I will talk to you when I get home, okay?" She assured her father she would obey his wishes but it gave her peace of mind for her father than for any other reason.

Peter watched as the nurses went about their morning shift change, they asked him if he could possibly give them just about thirty minutes. Ellen was still asleep in the waiting area, he was not aware if she knew about the change in her mother. He left no need to wake her just yet. He knew if the detectives were on their way, that meant one of two things, either they were not finished with him or they were informed of the update and were coming to see for themselves. Anything to see if they could talk to Mina, he knew the routine. He headed for the coffee shop, he was figuring that if they wanted him they could come look for him. As he passed through the hall he heard a priest giving the last rights to someone, his heart almost stopped That could still be the same scenario for him before this was over. The coffee smelled good as he entered, not seeing very many people he decided to see what they had to eat. As he passed the donuts chart, he noticed little biscuits, he reached over to put a couple on a small plate when he heard a voice behind him. "Mind if we join you?" He looked to see the two detectives. "No, sure don't smells just like mamma used to make." Taking his plate he went to the coffee machine, pouring himself a small cup. He would love to have a large but now he wanted to get out of there, the company was not exactly what he planned. He sat beside a window near the garden area, might as well have a good view while they ruined his breakfast.

He watched as they made their way around through the different food carts. He was amazed at how much food they piled on their plates, they were either hungry or had been up all night without anything to eat. Maybe that was the way they ate all the time, he doubted it. They both had pretty structured bodies. He knew their hours were pretty rough but he also knew they had quite a workout program. As they came to sit with Peter, he downplayed his emotions. "Hear you got a call from Protective Services, sorry about that." Detective Cruz commented. Now, was this guy for real? Sorry, what could this guy be sorry for? Detective Cruz took a long sip of his coffee before he continued, with Peter knowing all too well they were prolonging the purpose for their visit. "Hear the Mrs. Patterson moved some this morning, doctor got all the reports back. Unfortunately Mr. Patterson she is still in no condition to talk. Dr. Chung thinks it may have been self defense." He paused then added, "for now." Peter was not sure what they were telling him but he still could not rest, he felt they still has a card up their sleeves. Peter just drank his coffee and ate, not wanting to have any conversation with anyone. "Mr. Patterson, you maybe lucky this time, the whole family was lucky. Next time, it may play out different." Peter knew what he meant, he knew better than any detectives warning and he knew he could not afford a next time. "Detectives, there won't be a next time, I am staying here until I see the outcome, see what is going to take place with the kids then I am out of here." Peter did not want any surprises so he needed to let them know straight up what his plans were. "You have a good little

Pacific Redwood Mystery: Do you believe in the little people yet?

business here, Mr. Patterson. What, three logging trucks and your big rig? You mean you are just going to give up and leave it?" Peter wiped his face with a napkin. "I have my responsibilities to this woman and the children, but yes I see no other way. Unless she dies and I am sure you boys will." Peter didn't finish, he just looked both detectives in the eye as if saying "read my mind."

Peter heard the doctor's name over the intercom, the detectives eyed Peter as he gathered himself to leave. "Mr. Patterson, we need you to come to the station so we can get a written statement from you. Since there is an investigation on the children and their home situation, they require our statement as well, so if you don't mind." Peter shook his head, knowing what choice did he have. None. He nodded and left before they could come up with anything else. "Poor guy, had no idea what he is up against, does he?" Detective Cruz looked down at his coffee as he thought of his partner's question. "Nope, and it is just the beginning, it can still turn against him if she comes out telling a different story."

Peter knew exactly what they and everyone else was thinking, there was no idea how things would change especially if Mina recovered, she could say anything and Peter could be charged with a serious crime. They watched as Peter disappeared almost feeling sorry for him. Ellen was talking with the doctor when he arrived, when she saw Peter he was taken back when she smiled at him. The doctor turned and saw Peter, out of respect he waited until he reached them before continuing the report. "The nurse said mom moved her fingers, isn't that great?" Peter was trying to read the doctor's reactions before he mad his own comments. "Good morning Mr. Patterson, it is good news but we are not out of the woods yet. She had maintained this far without any fever which is a good sign. I have a neurologist coming again this afternoon for further testing. If she continued to show signs of movement, then we can move forward some." Peter wanted to ask him what he meant by "more forward some" when he noticed a nurse coming from another unit with a look that seemed to alarm the doctor. He excused himself and told Peter he would be while, his apologies.

Ellen was anxious to go to her mother's room and she wanted Peter to accompany her. "Let's go, let her know we are here. I bet it will make a difference, come on." He has so many questions for the doctor but Ellen was pulling him away. As they entered the room, a nurse was working on her tubes, he noticed they had added another bottle of something to the IV. As he placed his hand near her check, she felt clammy. They had wiped her down several time to keep her temperature under control, he could tell there was a difference in her color, she did not look as gray as before but the wound was still nasty and ugly. It was going to take a long time for that to heal. She was lucky it didn't split her head right in two. He wondered what damage she would have. Would she remember anything, would she be able to care for herself in time? There are so many things that he needed to know. "She looks better, don't you think Peter?" The nurse looked at Peter, smiling at them both. "You need to talk to her, we need to see if we can get her to wake up now." Ellen was exalted as she held her mother's hand. "I'm here mommy, it's me Ellen. You need to wake up so we can go shopping." Peter could not believe his ears, but then thinking about it, if she would wake up for anything, it would be money to shop. He didn't know what to say, he really did not have any words to say. It would probably be better if Ellen was the one talking to her anyway. There was no need to make her hysterical and go into any fit as she was just beginning to respond. Peter just stood his distance and watched. Ellen talk on and on as if there was no tomorrow. He looked at his watch he had four hours to go before he needed to get back home. "Ellen" He had to call her name twice before she acknowledged him, then he motioned her to the side. "You know about the social worker, she is going to be at the house today at 1:00pm, I have to be here and she will want to talk to you." The girls mouth became tight and Peter could see her attitude kicking in. "I am not leaving her. If she wants to talk to me, she can come here." Ellen just turned away from Peter. As he thought the worst thought in his mind he wasn't gong to share it with Ellen (they might be coming

Pacific Redwood Mystery: Do you believe in the little people yet?

for more than just a talk, young lady) Peter sat there the entire time while Ellen talked to her mother about all the things they were going to do and the things they were going to buy when she got well. It was as if he was not even in the room but he felt he needed to stay until the last minute. Not knowing if it could be a good thing or a bad thing, that remained to be seen when and if Mina recovered. He did not want to do anything to upset the situation but Ellen seemed to want him there. He did not have anywhere he needed to be at that particular time anyway, except the police department.

Ellen tried not to think about Protective Service, but in her mind she was scared. She knew with Dr. Chung's help and the police going to the house that they had pretty much figured out what had happened. It was a good chance they stick their noises in her mother's business. She was not going to let any strange woman cause them any trouble. Peter was going to have to fix it until her mother got well and they could get a new place, then everything would be okay. She did not want to tell Peter what she was thinking but if she could convince this woman that Katie Lee was the problem, it would be okay to place her in a foster home things would be just fine. She needed a good home anyway, Peter could not keep her and besides his kids would be going back to their nutty mother. No professional woman in her right mind wold let a nine year old live with someone that was not ever her stepfather. No, it would be best if she was placed in a foster care, then when her mother got better, they would start over and do just fine, They always did.

The ward clerk came to the door, not authorized to enter the room she motioned for Peter to come into the hall. "You have a call, I can transfer it to the waiting area sir." He figured it was Mary or Vera, he had not called them back to give them any news. It seemed as if things were just getting the best of him, he couldn't keep things straight in his mind, "Hello, this is Peter" Immediately a female voice came on the line but he didn't recognize it. "Peter, this is Sally, Mina's friend from the bar, I just heard." That was the last thing he needed one of her bar friends, he hoped her friends would have the dignity to stay away. "What can I do for you, Sally?" Maybe that was the wrong approach for him to take with her but he did not have much patience right now. "Well, I was calling to see how my friend is and let you know I will be right up. Where are the girls?" Peter guessed she was really concerned, they were drinking buddies and she had known Sally long before Peter came into her life. "Ellen is here, she won't leave. Katie Lee is at my house with the others." Sally jumped in almost before Peter finished his sentence. "Oh good, that is good Peter. Well I will be right there, just need to find someone to take my place at the bar tonight. Why didn't you call me?" Peter could not even think of an answer "I have not called anyone, Sally, it has been pretty tense." He heard disappointment in her voice but he was being honest. She was not his friend, she was Mina's and that was part of their problem, her drinking friends. "Well, that is okay but I will be there shortly, please tell Ellen I am on my way." With that she hung up. Peter went back to the unit to tell Ellen he was going to meet Mrs. Emerson and Sally was on her way.

Ellen's face began to show enthusiasm that Peter had not seen in awhile. That was okay, it would be okay for him to leave now. In fact, he probably would not be wanted around much now. He preferred his distance away until he figured out what the best way to handle everything. He reminded Ellen he needed to go meet with this lady, but she was so wrapped up in telling her mother Sally was on her way, she did not even hear Peter. As he went to leave, he started to move closer to Mina but Ellen blocked his way just enough to keep him from touching her mother. Peter felt bad but it was okay, he expected it and he knew it was for the best. He stopped at the nurses station advising them he had a meeting he could not miss and if the doctor looked for him to call right away to his home. The ward clerk took the information placing it on the front of Mina's chart. He headed for the parking lot knowing this lady would want to see the whole house, especially the bedroom where everything took place. He knew that when he went through the investigating with his ex-wife and her breakdown they didn't miss a trick. They looked everywhere, talked to everyone, turning every leaf.

As Mary and her sibling waited for their father to return, they were tense, little conversation was exchanged between them when the day prior was fill of love, fun and closeness. Peter stopped by the police station to let them know he had about an hour before he needed to be home for his other appointment. Both detectives were distant but helped him set up an appointment with the court recorder for his statement later that afternoon if he was able, if not the following morning for sure. As Peter was leaving Detective Cruz had to add, "Don't leave town any time soon." Peter just kept walking, those words haunted him the entire drive home. When he arrived at the house the kids except for Mary were outside. He was pleased his daughter had taken so much time getting the house to to look its best. It was a beautiful log home, the smell of cedar and pine when one first walked in gave that rustic aroma of any fantasy home one could imagine in the wilderness. Again he checked the bedroom that he and Mina had shared. Again he was pleased, the maid service had done an outstanding job on such a short notice. He had learned from the detective that the social worker had already done her homework on the incident, requesting pictures of the scene, so there was little this woman did not know. He found himself pacing as he saw Charles David heading for the house, he could hear Penny barking, so he knew someone was coming up the hill. He braced himself for the unknown. He decided it was better to meet her on the porch. What did he have to hide? She knew he was there, so be might as well greet her straight up. He was pleased to see she was an older woman, he didn't know why except he felt she had more experience and knowledge. She was a heavy well groomed lady with a blazer and tailored dark slacks. Her personality matched her smile and she seemed like a notable person. She wore low heels, modest makeup and shoulder length hairstyle almost in the old fashioned bob. She was the first to extent her hand toward Peter, it was firm and professional. "Well, Mr. Patterson we meet. Your directions were very good, thank you." He widely opened the screen door to make her comfortable to enter his home. "Would you like the kids to join us now or would you want to talk to me first?" She smiled in a pleasing manner as she passed in front of him, then waited for his further directions before continuing on down the hall.

Mary was usually the calmest of the clan but today she was a nervous wreck. She remembered the first go around with these people, when her father got custody of them from their mother. She had made ice tea just in case, as he father was coming down the hall with Mrs. Emerson she entered. As Mary introduced herself with true poise she offered them both ice tea and left before the lady could extend any concerns her way. Peter heard the back door open, so he knew the others were sneaking in to listen somewhere. "Charles David, is that you son?" As his son peeked around the corner of the hall Mrs. Emerson extended her hand towards the young boy. "Where is Katie Lee?" Charles David never took his eyes off the lady as his father did not know if he was trying to make a point with her or just scared. "She is with Vera in her room, listening to music and working on the picture album. Want me to call her?" Peter looked towards Mrs. Emerson for directions, he had already asked her but she had not given him any reply. "No, I don; t think that is necessary yet, you are Charles David and I understand you helped assist in the safety of your family. Is that correct?" The boy was so taken back not only by the questions but also of what she blurted our first thing. He could not seem to answer her and was relieved when his sister entered with more tea. Mrs. Emerson thanked Mary but when she started to leave the room she asked her to stay. "Well, I guess we need to get started so let's just get right down to everything, shall we.? Mr. Patterson, I have seen all the pictures and I really do not see putting the children through any more unpleasant issues than necessary. Why I am here today is for the purpose of Katie Lee Rossman and Ellen Wright. Before I get to those issues let me ask you a couple questions, then we can move on. I also want to discuss your children, Mr. Patterson. Can you explain what your plans are until Mrs. Patterson's condition is stable?" Peter liked this lady and he knew even though he needed to be careful, he could answer all her questions in one summary. He was no fool and he knew she was aware of his prior case. She could be his friend or she could be his worst enemy.

Peter cleared his throat as he began to talk to her about his responsibilities which he had no problem with. He was honest in his goal that he could no longer stay in the role of her husband. He expressed his fear that something worse could happen and he would not risk his children nor hers. His goal was getting Mary and Vera back to their mother where his other daughter already was prior to the incident with Mina. She had ran away to return with her mother. As Peter spoke, he noticed she opened a file and they could see his ex-wife's name at the top. "Carol Ann Patterson," so he knew she was comparing her notes to his statement. Peter deeply expressed his concern for his son to stay with him. He was not going to dispute any help or suggestions from her or the courts, he was just asking to be heard and the truth be known. He added without hesitation, especially Katie Lee. Breaking into Peter's explanation the social worker said, "Let's talk about Katie Lee, Mr. Patterson. She seems to be the major concern for everyone right now." To Peter's great astonishment Mary broke into the conversation and asked if she could please speak. Mrs. Emerson turned to the young girl but Mary did not wait for an answer. She began to express the young child's abuse from her sister, mother and the low self-esteem and fear Katie Lee carried. Mary went on refusing to be interrupted to explain just how close they had come to death and her father was the only stable person for Katie Lee in spite of the fact he was not her real stepfather. It became very emotional as Mary described that night of horror that no child should have to endure but she did and if it had not been for her stepbrother and stepfather they may all every well be dead right now. She felt her father would have been dead for sure. Mrs. Emerson noticed Charles David had his head down the entire time. She asked Charles David, "Do you have anything to add? It seems like you all are very protective of Katie Lee but I must say if there was such concern, why did you let it go on for so long." Peter was not prepared for that question, but he should have been. Charles David looked into his father's face. "It is more my fault, I was selfish. As long as Mina and Ellen were happy shopping, she didn't bother us, we didn't tell dad a lot. She let us pretty much do what we wanted when dad was not around." Being embarrassed by what he admitted to Mrs. Emerson and his father, she was not impressed one bit, in fact her stern look towards Charles David told him what she thought. "Is that why you are trying so hard to defend her now, you feel guilty?" Peter could see where she was going with this, she was trying to put him in a position to see if they were defending themselves and their father to make a good case in their favor.

Peter shifted in his chair, anticipating how to get his son out of this without looking as if it was anything but the truth, an accident. Yes, one that should never have happened but that was his mistake, not his children. This answer could decide his fate. "Daddy, can I come sit with you?" They all turned to see Katie Lee and Vera standing between the French Doors of the living room. Mrs. Emerson's eyes shifted back to Peter as she watched him swallow hard, then as the little girl came closer, she focused her first glance on her. Holding her breath, she asked God to please keep her emotions serene as she saw Katie Lee's face, watching her limp forward. Vera joined her brother and sister on the couch as they all watched Katie Lee struggle with Peter's help to settle her beside him with her puppy in her arms. Looking up at Peter, she held her puppy close with both hands. "Do I have to leave daddy? Is she gong to take me away?" Peter started to twist her long ponytail in a nervous way. "Hey, no one said anything about that. Mrs. Emerson is here to find out what is best for everyone. Now pumpkin, we talked about this and you have to trust me." Mrs. Emerson could see right away the bond between the two. Dr. Chung had been so correct in his observation. It was sad and would be making her decision every harder. His wife would most likely live but of what capacity was another question.

Peter was not her stepfather and there had been a life threatening situation with her mother. "Mr. Patterson, may I talk to Katie Lee alone for a few moments?" Peter got out of his chair, settling her carefully and motioned for his children to leave the room. Charles David hesitated but Peter gave him a firm look to get up and move. Katie Lee took hold of his hand not wanting to let go. Penny was licking him as if to also say "Please don't leave us alone." "It is okay." He patted Penny on her head, "Just answer her questions and I will be right in the kitchen, it will be okay." He gently tapped her on the nose out of habit, then moaned looking at her broken nose knowing how sore it still was. He apologized to her instantly and Mrs. Emerson could tell Peter was very sincere when it came to this child. She was still concerned why it had gone on so long and had to come to this tragic end.

Peter walked out of the room looking back at Katie Lee several times, more out of guilt for tapping her nose than concern about Mrs. Emerson. Mrs. Emerson watched her body language and her heart told her almost everything she needed to know but the law was the law. He was not her legal guardian and she did not think any judge would grant him even temporary custody of the child. Mrs. Emerson held out her hand towards Katie Lee, "Let's sit on the couch together with your puppy, so we will be comfortable." She helped her out of the chair and guided her towards the couch. Peter watched as she helped Katie Lee up, placing her a small pillow behind her to make her position more comfortable. Her fate was in this woman's hands as he closed the French doors, he didn't care if she saw his tears, Peter did not cry easily, but this was not easy!

CHAPTER FIFTEEN

Katie Lee wondered how her friends were doing and what they were doing right now. She was so hurt and drained. As she stayed cuddled in her aunt's arms, she could not believe the day, the most important day in her life was ruined. She could hear her aunt and uncle talking in a whisper, she did not care, they could talk out loud if they wanted. Nothing was going to change, she was not graduating with her friends and she was not doing anything except running. The only sound she heard was the ringing in her ears with the distant echoes of the traffic as they drove out of town farther and farther. She could hear her uncles and aunt that they did not have to run, that they had custody of Katie Lee.

She felt the car slowing down and turning. What was he doing? Why was he stopping? They needed to keep going, Katie Lee leaned forward towards her aunt. She just turned smiling at her niece with compassion while smoothing her hair away from her face. Without consulting his wife, Jack decided to take the next exit off the freeway pulling to the far side of a convenience store. When the car came to a complete stop, her uncle asked them to please listen to him for a moment. He too had so much grief as her aunt cried. But this was different, his was anger, intolerable anger. "Katie Lee, I know you are upset but we have custody and she cannot take her. Your mother can make all the accusations she wants but we have the paperwork proving you belong to us. We need to go back and face her, let the law handle this." Katie Lee's heart died inside, her uncle did not know her mother like she did. Why, after all this time had Mina surfaced again? No words could come out of her mouth, she just shook remembering when Mina took her from the Paddocks, a family she would never forget. Her uncle touched her head in a compassionate way but his heart was grief stricken for not being able to comfort her with any satisfaction. Looking at his wife, he sighed and began to turn the car around back towards the on-ramp. Suddenly a police car flashed his light to stop Jack motioning for him to pull over. Katie Lee grabbed her aunt's hands even tighter as Jack pulled a safe distance to the side of the road, rolling down his window. As the officer approached he asked for identification not only for her uncle but also for everyone in the car. After looking closely at each one, he asked her uncle to exit the vehicle. They were trying to see and hear what was going on but they could not. He had her uncle at the very back of the car and it seemed like a tense conversation. She nudged her aunt as another patrol car came with a male and unidentified woman in plainclothes approaching the first officer with her uncle. Then her uncle started to walk their way but the first officer stopped him. They could see her uncle was becoming very upset.

 The second officer and woman approached the passenger's side asking her aunt to exit the car. Loie asked why and said that her niece was extremely upset over a family matter and they wanted to get her home. The officer opened the car door firmly instructing her aunt to exit the car. She tried to let go of Katie Lee's hand but she would not let go. The woman with the second officer told Katie Lee she could come with her aunt, it would be okay. As Loie reached the back of the car with Katie Lee she didn't like the look on her husbands face. He put his arm around his wife as if he was shielding her. Then the second officer asked Katie Lee to step away from her aunt, she needed to ask her some questions. She looked so confused, but her aunt motioned it was okay. She did not think it would hurt to cooperate, she just wanted her niece back home and call a lawyer. As they separated Katie Lee from Jack and Loie the strange woman started escorting her towards the second police car with that officer directly behind. Katie Lee called back to her aunt trying to seek help but the officer put a firm hand on her, together the two authority figures guided Katie Lee further away. Her pleading and begging were useless. Katie Lee tried to get away but they only restrained her as well. Her uncle tried to come to her rescue but he was turned harshly on the hood of the police care and cuffed. Becoming alarmed Loie demanded. "What was happening?" But no one would offer any explanation. "If you do not release my husband right now and tell me what is going on, we will have charges on all of you." She was screaming without being heard. She could hear her niece sobbing and trying to escape with every strength she had.

They restrained Katie Lee in the second patrol car with the woman as her aunt and uncle watched them drive away with their niece looking desperately out the back window. The first officer stood with his head high telling Loie she could follow him to the police station without an incident or she would have to be restrained also accompany her husband in the police car, rather than following in their own vehicle. "What are the charges?" She lashed out at him. "Runaway with possible kidnapping." Both stood looking at each other in utter shock. "Kidnapping, we have full custody of that child." Her uncle was yelling at the officer. He decided to put Jack in the back of his patrol car while Loie stood and watched in disbelief, telling Loie she could meet them downtown at the station on Jackson street. She quickly ran to their car trying to get control of herself to calm down enough to drive. She started the car as the patrol car was still idle behind her. She got out of the car hurrying back to the patrol car knocking on the window of the officer, he had not rolled down the window, he exit the car. "May I ask my husband a question, please?" He nodded yes, opening the back door so she could talk to him. Making sure she stood a good distance Loie leaned towards her angry husband. "What do you want me to do, call a lawyer or one of the boys?" Jack was so angry his thoughts were so out of control he had to stop and think what to tell her, what was she suppose to do? "Do not call anyone, go

Pacific Redwood Mystery: Do you believe in the little people yet?

to the prison and talk to the warden. He is working late tonight. Tell him everything Loie, everything." You could tell the officer was tense at that statement Jack had made. "Go Loie, now go. He will know what to do and whom to call. There will be heads rolling tonight, I promise you that." She did not hesitate, she turned from her husband rushing again to the car.

Jack had been a guard at the prison for over sixteen years, well-known and well liked. He had been promoted several times by the warden and rightly so. He wore his captain shield proudly. He decided it was best he just remain as relaxed as possible until he could get help. These officers were not going to stop and find out facts or care what the facts were. He respect for law enforcement was high but he knew Mina. He had underestimated her and what she had used or whom she had used to get this accomplished. So until he knew, his mouth was shut for all their sake. The ride to the police station was quiet only because he refused to answer any questions. The young officer tried to make small talk and get what he could out of Jack. It was not going to work, he had enough years to know the drill. The officer asked him what he did for a living and how did he know the warden, those questions Jack could not resist answering in pride. "Have worked out there for over sixteen years, I work for him." He could tell from where he was sitting that he hit a nerve of "oh crap, something is not right here." Jack knew the officers mind was racing trying to figure out the facts before they reached the police station to possible save his own butt if needed, maybe! Jack just grinned so that the officer could see him in his rear view mirror. He again turned his head towards the window as if he could care less what the officer was saying. "Why didn't you tell us who you were when we stopped you?" Again he smiled, it was obvious they didn't look too closely at his ID when he handed it to them. What part of Law Enforcement on an ID didn't these jerks understand. Jack leaned sideways adjusting his position as the officer said he could release the handcuffs before they got to the station if he could control himself? "No, young man, I don't think you better do that, I think you just need to do your job. I will take care of all the answers to your questions when we get there." He turned his head again toward the window and ignored the officer the rest of the ride.

He could tell by the radio communication that the mother of the supposed runaway-kidnapped child had been notified. Yep, he was correct, Mina had some how gotten to someone. Why and who were what Jack wanted to know. He was praying that Loie made it to the warden before he left his office. He did not trust Mina, she could have phony papers stating Katie Lee was in her custody and being this late at night another negative, it was Friday, a weekend. He did not trust the system not after the way they handled this situation. As they drove into the station, the young officer had definitely changed his attitude. The second officer was just returning to his car when he walked over to the car Jack was sitting in. "Any trouble?" The young officer leaned into him and Jack new he was informing him of the needed details that he was not going to like. Watching the two officers just stand there and look at each other, he grinned to himself. Using his shoulder speaker, the older of the two spoke into his mike and walked away from the car. The younger officer opened the back door and gently guided Jack into the building.

As he looked back at the older officer,, he was shaking his head, them hit the top of a truck with his fist, both the officer escorted and Jack himself looked back, "Oh my, I hope that was his truck." Jack chucked at his remark as the officer beside him looked pretty uncomfortable. Jack guessed that the cat was out of the bag, they had not followed procedure and they has not taken time to get facts or check anything out. As they walked down the hall, there was silence all through the squad room as the young officer walked Jack pasted the front desk. The young officer released the cuffs and asked Jack if he would like some coffee. Jack took a small breath and looked at the other officers, nodded politely. "Nope" he cleared his throat, sitting down on a chair beside an empty desk. Two men came out of a glass framed office sitting more to the back from the desks side by side in the outer open space. Coldly they motioned for Jack to follow them, pointing to the glass framed office. Not knowing word had reached them of their grave mistake, he thought it was just a matter of time before Loie and the warden got there. She would also have to go home and produce proof of custody, which was fine with him. That would take more time, he decided to push the issue and make his point. He could not imagine the fear and terror his niece was going through right now. "No, I think I will sit here and wait for my wife, the warden and my lawyer if you don't mind. That is, unless I am charged with something I am not aware of?" Immediately the only man wearing a suit appeared in front of Jack, a little too close. "Why don't you and I wait in my office, we can have a little chat and you will be more comfortable there." Jack looked up at him and smiled. "Lieutenant Andrews it is Lieutenant Andrews, isn't it?" "Well, how more comfortable can I be with a room full of officers, just right here. I should be real safe and I am kind of talked out, so I will just wait here all the same to you, Lieutenant Andrews."

As the tense mood ran through the room Jack was holding firm. They could force him to go there but he did not think they were that stupid. He stretched his hands above his head and asked. "Where have you taken my niece?" The lieutenant immediately said she had been taken with a case worker from Social Services. "Good, that is good." Jack stayed grinning like a cat, he knew he was making them all feel like holy crap. Then suddenly he saw a young officer come to this lieutenant's side. "The warden is on line 2, the chief is on line 3 and the commissioners on his way down here, sir." Jack felt a twinge of satisfaction as he knew this smart lieutenant was about to learn the connection between his supervisors and Jack's boss. There was nothing like family ties. Jack's intentions were honest, he would not say the same for Mina. She lived by deception. Faces went white and breaths went cold. The lieutenant did not know which direction to turn. He stood looking at Jack with his hands feeble to his side. "Sir," the young officer said, "What do you want me to do?" Jack got out of his seat and pretended to stretch again and took a few steps towards the elevator as he turned to face the lieutenant head-on. He made him walk around him in order to get to his office. Shutting the door, Jack wished he was a fly on the wall for this conversation.

Viewing the room, he smiled at each officer. There was one older gentleman in the far corner, it seemed like he was enjoying every bit of what was going on. He held up his coffee cup to Jack as if he was toasting him, then went back to the paperwork piled over his desk. It did not take long for the lieutenant to return and ask Jack to accompany him upstairs. "What is upstairs?" Jack asked with another sigh. "The administration offices are up there, being the warden is on his way with your wife that would be a more reasonable place for us to meet. Your wife will be stopping by your home to obtain any necessary papers on your niece." Jack did not move, he sat back in the chair, crossing his legs. The lieutenant started to walk to the elevator when one of his officers motioned for him to look back. Turning, he rolled his eyes, his subdued personality took on a different tone with Jack. "We can do this the hard way or the easy way." He was swaying his hands as if saying "Let's go" he was daring Jack. "This is fine with me, I am not budging until I see my niece's face." The defiance was overwhelming to the lieutenant, something he would normally not tolerate, especially as a ranking officer.

Smiling back in Jack's direction the lieutenant said. "She has already been taken to a good home for the night. A good night's rest will be good for everyone. So you need to follow me upstairs and stop wasting my time." Folding his arms over his chest, Jack knew he had the upper hand, this was not going to be one of those "oops, I am sorry, quick fix, our way." He was arrogant and cocky something Jack did not tolerate in any officer. The badge did not give them the right to any superior attitude. Jack again did not move and the tense atmosphere in the room was getting bad. One could tell some of the officers were getting pretty upset, they did not like someone coming into their part of the world with an attitude. But then he did not like the way they had handled this, the exact reason people on the outside have no respect for law enforcement anymore. The lieutenant did not go back to where Jack was sitting he went to the phone on the nearest desk. Before he could finish the call, the double doors flew open with the commissioner plunging towards them. He had gotten there much quicker than Jack figured. Waking up to the lieutenant, he ran his fingers over his name tag, then flipped it hard, turning toward Jack.

Out of respect, he came to his feet offering his hand. They exchanged small talk and Jack asked how long it was going to take to find his niece. His wife was on her way to their home for the necessary papers, that along with the warden and attorney. The commissioner asked Jack to step into the lieutenant's office, Jack immediately complied, following the man. As the lieutenant went to step into the room, Jack blocked the lieutenant from the room, shutting the door right in his face, knowing that the commissioner did not even notice the man was not in the room with them. The Commissioner continued to ask Jack what had happened as Jack quickly gave him the rundown. As Jack talked, the commissioner would directly look out into the outer room at the lieutenant in charge. It was not a pleasant look, more like your job is on the line.

Many of the officers had gone back to what they were doing, but the two officers that had been at the scene where Jack had been escorted where still waiting. Then Jack noticed out of the corner of his eyes the woman that had taken Katie Lee walked into the room. You could tell she was upset and throwing remarks around by the way she was waving her arms and body language. After little cooperation from her so called buddies, she turned and noticed what was taking place in the office. She ran her hand through her shoulder length hair moving closer to the lieutenant. But all he did was throw up his hands and walk away from her. Pacing was about all he could do since Jack had denied his presence with them. Jack was appreciating the attention the commissioner was giving him and the fact that he came in person. He could have just made a phone call, Jack felt he had his full attention, and at one moment he asked Jack what mental state Katie Lee was in when they took her. Did they explain the charges and was it done in front of the girl? Jack answered all his questions as promptly as he presented them, that they had no idea what was going on. They were stopped, she was taken with no warning or reasoning, except being told it was a runaway-kidnapping charge, cuffed him and brought him in. His concern was for his niece and wife. "Did they ask you for ID Jack?" That was where it got even better. "Sure did, and I gave it to them." Jack pulled his ID out of his wallet so he could see exactly what the officer had seen. Yes sir, there it was right there, law enforcement ID. How was that missed?

The commissioner stood for a few moments without saying a word and then motioned for the lieutenant, almost running in, he offered his hand towards his superior. "Yes, sir!" All the commissioner did was hand him Jack's identification. They really screwed up, it is obvious they couldn't have looked at it. Favor for favor to speak had been done and he was not without fault. A call was made, not one question was asked, you fill in the blanks!! The commissioner was raising his left eyebrow. "Who is that young lady there lieutenant?" He was pointing towards the young woman standing near the two officers in question. The lieutenant was dropping his head as if saying, Oh man, you would have to ask. Before he could answer the commissioner went to the door and called her himself. Jack took that opportunity to ask the lieutenant. "May I have my ID back lieutenant, or were you going to use it as an example for your new identification class, you might want to consider?"

As she entered the room, she tried to make small talk, telling the commissioner what a pleasure it was to meet him. "How did you get involved in this case is all I want to know from you, young woman." Looking embarrassed but unshaken, she stated it was her case, when she learned the young girl had been found, she immediately secured the safety of the teenager. She had her removed and placed instantly in a foster home for the night until she could be returned to her mother, whom by the way was on her as they spoke. Frowning at the woman, the commissioner said. "I did not ask you how you handled the case, I asked you how you got the case. If you can't answer maybe we need to wake someone up and find out." The young woman immediately became defensive and informed him that she was very good at her job,

Pacific Redwood Mystery: Do you believe in the little people yet?

and she had spoken to the distraught mother personally that evening. That just because a teenager was throwing a fit and running away did not give family members the right to interfere. Now the lieutenant knew his ass was grass, this chick had played the wrong card. Was she out of her mind or did she really want to look for new employment. "I intend to get counseling for them, and other measures will be considered." She would look into it when she got the complete file on Monday. Also she would schedule a hearing before the judge after she had a change to view the care in more detail. Pleased with herself, she knew had impressed the man and put this rude jerk of an uncle in his place. She had bigger people to impress, she had immediately recognized the name Mina gave her of the supposed husband, deep pockets and big influence. She wasn't going to let this little no body stand in her way with this opportunity knocking at her door. The commissioner came closer, "Miss, what is your name, never mind. What made you think this was a runaway-kidnapping case, may I ask?" She placed her hand into her Ralph Lauren jacket, pulling her business card as she flipped it towards his face, "I have resources, sir."

Her superior attitude of "I am impressive" was about ready to be deflated. Jack seemed as shocked as the commissioner and he knew fireworks were coming, this was going to be better than the Fourth of July on main street. Wetting her lips she seduced the situation, she winked at the lieutenant. Wanting to throw up the lieutenant wanted to stuff the whole file down her throat. The commissioner stepped back, placed his hand on the glass door, he slid the card into his pocket of his shirt. "Lieutenant, why don't we ask the two officers to join us, those that helped this fine lady solve her case tonight." Walking in front of her to get to the door the lieutenant said. "You are a real piece of work Denise, hope you like McDonald's." With a sullen face, she couldn't even figure that remark out. When everyone was crammed into the small office Denise arched her back, extending her breasts as if saying "okay guys praise time" and I am the sexiest one in the room, look at me. "I have brains too." Someone forgot to tell her that the train already went by, her brains were aboard.

"How in the hell did you two officers get this call, who marked it as a runaway-kidnapping? Tell me right now or someone is going home on suspension." As the conversation continued, answers began to unfold. The veins in the commissioners neck were protruding, Jack stood quiet as the commissioner's intolerance of the situation increased, and his blood pressure shot through the roof. Before he could have eye contact with the woman, he saw the warden and his wife coming through the double doors. Quickly taking an exit from the profound one-sided conversation, Jack waited for Loie to get control of herself and asked for the paperwork. He walked back to join the happy group getting their behinds torn up. The commissioner walked to the side away from everyone as Jack noticed all eyes on him with mouths closed. Watching Jack hand the commissioner the paperwork, Jack was pleased to finally see Denise wiggle and twinge as she grouped closer to the lieutenant. He was going to have her job for this. He knew he was right, he knew she could not be wrong with this one, she had crossed the line. Was it money for favor? Worse yet, what did the lieutenant have to gain.

As the commissioner finished reading the paperwork out loud to irritate them all more, a sense of ignorance fell over the entire room as he intended. Looking to his wife, he decided to join her, the look on her face told him she needed him more than another satisfaction round that was about to take place. Quietly making an exit, he gently placed his hand on Loie's back, assuring her Katie Lee would be returned home that very evening. As they started in deep conversation, Jack expressed to his wife they needed to take a vacation, long overdue. It would be just what the doctor ordered and especially good for Katie Lee. Loie hugged her husband as a young clerk ask Jack to step back into the office where the meeting was taking place. "Can you take my wife and get her some coffee, I would appreciate that." He was a cute young man, no bigger than Katie Lee, he could not have been more than nineteen or twenty. "Sure, I just made a fresh pot and I think we have some cookies back there too." As Jack re-entered, the woman immediately attacked his unprofessional manner as she put

Pacific Redwood Mystery: Do you believe in the little people yet?

it, not to identify who he was to the officers, Jack only moved his head in her direction. "I am sorry miss, I thought they learned to read before they entered training." Denise was not going to back down, she knew her job was on the line and no help was coming from her majestic lieutenant.

As she used her vocabulary to her advantage, it made her feel superior and in control, to her Jack was no body. They were all unimportant except for the commissioner of course. She would play this old man. She would show these idiots just how it was done. After tonight, she was done with the lieutenant, it had been fun but he was only for introduction to a better society. She hated to break his heart, Oh well there was always his wife to run back to. As she paraded in front of her audience, she wanted to make sure the commissioner was watching. She turned her neck just the right way but she had no idea she was an amateur in this group. All she heard was as she lifted her head was a roar of the very man she thought she had seduced successfully. The commissioner yelled at the top of his lungs, he did not give a damn what she thought, or who she was. Tomorrow she would be flopping hamburgers if she was lucky. Twisting completely around at the desk, she was appalled at what she heard. "Now that we have that cleared up, give Lieutenant Andrews the address of the girl and get the hell out of here before I have you arrested for obstructing justice."

Nodding at Jack and the warden he exited the office and stepped briskly through the doors and was gone. Everyone stood completely still as if they would be walking on hot coals if they moved. The lieutenant swung the door open and yelled, "Officer Stanley!" Jack saw the older gentlemen, who had lifted his cup at Jack earlier, grabbing his jacket off the back of his chair and headed toward the lieutenant. Denise was still holding the folder the commissioner had shoved into her chest before he left with the most pathetic look. Grabbing the folder without asking for it, the lieutenant handed it to officer Stanley, "Go to this address and bring Katie Lee Rossman back here right now." Placing his coat through his arms and holding the file under his chin. Officer Stanley waved at his fellow officers. "Excuse me guys, I have to go undo you all's screw up." Laughing as he exited you can tell he was enjoying every minute.

There was good officers and Jack knew that, they were really upset with him right now because two of their buddies were on the line, but before this night was through they would know what was up and they would settle down. They were not going to like the outcome of how three of them had been played but he was sure they would take care of it among themselves, one way or the other. He could sense the restless feeling, it was time to make his exit to find his wife and wait for Katie Lee. He shook the warden's hand and offered his to the lieutenant for the first time all evening. He knew this man had lots to account for, he would be informed of how this played out. He knew one thing for sure, the young female was definitely the bigger player. He knew that the warden and the commissioner would make an example of her and she would not be employed within twenty four hours. Just because one had connections did not mean one did special favors at the expense of an innocent person. Jack also knew the commissioner was anxious to solve the situation it was election time. That meant publicity for the man. He would have to check all the McDonald's in the area within the next couple of months and see which one Denise worked at, he surely did not want her fixing any of his fast food. Going to find his wife, he gave a small salute to the lieutenant, his mind was frustrated as he thought of his niece. How was he going to make this up to her? He knew Mina would never show her face as any police station but he also knew whoever the money man was behind Denise was probably Miss. Mina's new beau. It has to be money or society for Mina to come back after all this time. To appear at his wife's employment and demand Katie Lee, he was certain. Shaking her out of his mind, he found his wife talking politics with the young man. "Welcome to my world!" And he kissed his wife on the cheek. "They have sent an officer to get her, she should be here soon and we can go home." Loie sighed with pleasant relief. "Praise God." The young clerk offered Jack some coffee and he accepted but he decided he would stay clear of their conversation, he would get

Pacific Redwood Mystery: Do you believe in the little people yet?

enough political talk with her at home. His thoughts went back to his niece again. Her sacrifice, her graduation, she had lost the evening of joy and happiness that could never be replaced. That walk across the stage to receive her reward for hour years of school and excellent grades, that must hurt. It could never be given back to her. He decided right then enough was enough. Katie Lee also needed to know she did not have to hide anymore. It was time to put an end to it all.

CHAPTER SIXTEEN

The ride from the police station was long, Katie Lee just wanted to go home and be in her own bed. She sat in the backseat of the car still shivering with fear. How many times had her mother made her life a living hell. How many times over the years had her mother taken everything and everyone away from her? Her stomach was still in knots as she watched the moving cars all around them on the freeway. She still carried inside the fear that her mother would reappear. It was not over, she felt it. Even though they had proved their point, Mina wanted something. She needed something, or she would not be coming around. Was it another chapter in Mina's life to ruin someone's glory? Especially at this time when it was the most important time of her life? Well, not anymore, she had not been with her friends, she had not walked across the stage to receive her diploma. Sadness filled within her heart. How could such happiness end so cruel? Was this going to be the story of her life? Maybe now that she was out of school, it would be best if she took what savings she had and went as far as it would take her. It surely would not take her far, but she could change her name. Thinking abut the doctor's office saddened her even more. All her dreams and goals were gone. She lay her head against the seat, just closing her eyes. She pictured all her classmates having a wonderful time and celebrating those years of hard work and friendship. Katie Lee had worked hard those four years. She wanted to be the top of her class, not just for herself to prove that she could

Pacific Redwood Mystery: Do you believe in the little people yet?

do it but also for the four people that meant everything to her, Peter, Mary, her aunt and uncle.

She watched as they exited off the highway toward their home, it truly was a home, not just a house you walked into. She watched as the car stopped just before turning onto their street. The music on the radio was soothing, a soft classic. It was dark outside and only the streetlights welcomed her as she felt that warm feeling when she saw the house. They all just seemed to sit very still as her uncle turned off the car. Jack leaned over and kissed his wife on the cheek. His smile was warm and sincere, his face with the gentleness of her hand, she looked back at Katie Lee. "You know we love you dear and we are not going to let her take you away from us!" Katie Lee smiled at her, trying to convince herself as well as her aunt. Katie Lee slid out of the car waiting for her aunt. She was glad she did, her uncle came around opening the door for his wife. He hugged them both as he closed the passenger door. "You are our girl now and you are going to stay our girl. Remember, we all promised Peter." Peter, she thought, how she missed him terribly.

That smile, the large figure of a man that had sacrificed so much for her those last few years. He had looked long and hard for some family members. She remembered Peter told her he would find a family member there had to be someone that was not like her mother. The search had been long but very rewarding especially after a long stay in foster care and Peter never gave up in spite of loosing Katie Lee to the system. She longed to remember what his voice sounded like and she wished he had lived long enough to see her graduate. Well, that would not matter now either. She walked slowly and quietly into the house, her aunt was already in the kitchen with the refrigerator door open. "I am starved, how about the two of you?" Without hesitation, her aunt brought life back into her. They all decided it was banana split time. That was what she loved about them, they were so crazy and wonderful. Who else would have thought of banana splits to put a smile on a young girls face who just had her heart torn out? Laughing and spreading whip cream, they heard a gentle knock on the back door. Katie Lee went stiff so did her aunt. As Jack put down his ice cream, he spread the little curtain covering the window on the back door. Looking back at them, he made a motion with his hand that it was all right. Opening the door, Katie Lee saw Mrs. Hanson, Nancy's mother standing there in her PJ's. Jack motioned for her to enter. "You are just in time, come on in. We'll make you a banana split, the best in town." Looking bewildered Mrs. Hanson came close to Katie Lee. "Sweetie, where were you? It was graduation, everyone was looking for you." Knowing that there was no easy answer, Katie Lee had no intentions of sharing her despair with anyone. "I know and you are about to get the prize of the night. My aunt and uncle make the best banana splits that are to die for." Seeing her aunt shake her head toward Mrs. Hanson, as to say, "Don't press the issue." they got the ice cream back out and started putting it together for their guest.

Mrs. Hanson was amazed at this but in her heart she wondered what on earth would make this child miss such an important evening, she knew these people had looked forward to this night for four years. They had talked about it numerous times. But this was not the night, she realize that, so she joined in the fun and laughter making everything more upbeat. Mrs. Hanson had never had so much fun that she could remember, she needed to make sure she did this with Nancy. Her daughter would probably think she was crazy but this was fun and such a family thing. "Where is Nancy?" Katie Lee tried to ask without too much strain in her voice. She knew that her friend was probably at some party enjoying the night of her life. Sadness and anger at the same time came into her mind. Without thinking Mrs. Hanson blurted out "Why she is with Jacob at the swimming party." Everyone became very still, worried to see what Katie Lee's reaction was going to be. Nervously, her aunt looked deep into her eyes hoping the mood would not change. Enough had happened to destroy this young girls evening, she could not tolerate anything else. It was her uncle that set his bowl down leaving the room. They all looked at one another as Mrs. Hanson fumbled through an apology. Jack came back into the kitchen with Katie Lee's jacket in his hand.

Pacific Redwood Mystery: Do you believe in the little people yet?

He was just placing his own jacket around him as he handed Katie Lee hers. "Well, lets go girls, time is wasting, Katie Lee has a party to get to." Mrs. Hanson knew immediately what her uncle was doing and she said, "Really, can we ride along, it is a beautiful night and I think it is just going to get better." Her aunt hugged Mrs. Hanson picking up her purse. "Katie Lee, you cannot swim, so I am not going to suggest you get your swimsuit, not on this night." Smiling as if her heart was bouncing right out of her chest, Katie Lee grabbed her jacket and headed for the door. "What about the ice cream," her aunt asked all three looked at their bowls still stacked high with the goodies all banana splits were made from. Jack gently took the bowls placing them in the freezer, "What is a freezer good for if you can't depend on it for a happier moment when tomorrow comes, Let's go."

All kinds of reactions were going through Katie Lee's mind. She may not have been able to walk across that stage, but thanks to her uncle his keen mind she was off to be where her friends were celebrating the most perfect night of their lives. She was going to be part of it after all. Excitement was beating within Katie Lee's chest as if there was a war going on. Mrs. Hanson held Katie Lee's hand throughout the whole way as they sat in the backseat together. The laughed and joked all the way. It did seem forever before they turned on the county road toward the park as the excitement grew. What was she going to say to her friends? She was tense about that, but she didn't want to ruin anything else. She just wanted to get there and have this one memory rather than a night of horror. "Wow, look at the cars." Her aunt was leaning forward in her seat as she started to count them "I didn't know there were so many kids in your school that had cars, dear." Katie Lee was so stunned with excitement she could not even answer her aunt. She hadn't even realized her uncle had stopped the car.

Mrs. Hanson puller her hand free. "Well, go get them girl and tell Nancy to use her common sense." She hugged Nancy's mother, then threw her arms abound her uncle from behind. Leaning over to kiss her aunt, Loie held her chin. "If you are asked any questions, just say, I am here and let's party." Her aunt always had the right answer for her in troubled times. Jumping out of the car, the first she saw was the Miller twins, she moved quickly toward them, calling their names. Even though they both toted a beer, she grabbed one of them by the neck and just hugged. "Where are Jacob and Nancy?" Looking so surprised at her forwardness, they mentioned she did not need to find them; she could hang with them. Laughing, she hugged them both squeezing their necks. She raced towards the pool area as the boys pointed in that direction. She almost lost her footing as she cornered the building where a hose was lying across the lawn. Seeing Jacob in the pool playing volleyball, she looked earnestly for Nancy. She was nowhere to be found, working her way to the pool without Jacob seeing her, she leaned over the edge of the water and thew a small tennis ball in his direction. Turning to swat the tennis ball out of his way, he noticed her squatting at the edge. Getting so excited to see her, he missed the ball completely. With his classmates yelling and slapping the water at him to serve, he totally ignored them as he swam in her direction leaving them without one player. Coming up out of the water with a confused looked, he grabbed one of the boys near and threw him into the pool. "Hey, take my place, will ya?" Looking back at Jacob, he saw Katie Lee. "Only if you ask nicely," his friend yelled back at him, Jacob turned toward his friend, "PLEASE." Smiling his friend gave him a wave as if to say, "It was cool."

Jacob started to throw questions at Katie Lee faster than she could answer. "You are making my head swim Jacob. I am here so let's party." Grabbing his hand she lead him away from the pool towards the table with all the food. "Where is Nancy? I have to see her." Jacob did not like the idea that she shrugged him off, he had been so devastated with her absence at the graduation, he wanted to know what could have caused her absence. "Did someone die or something like that?" She did not want to answer his questions nor did she want to think about that night before she was able to join her classmates. Spotting Nancy just coming from the rest rooms, she tapped Jacob on the arm and sprinted toward her friend. Nancy saw her hauling across the lawn, she too had the look of utter surprise as Nancy raced to meet her friend halfway. "What, why. What is going on." The words were coming out so quick and excited that Katie Lee just laughed.

She again remembered her aunts words. "Are you going to stand here and talk about something unimportant or are we going to celebrate our night to remember?" She took her friend's hand and started to walk back to where Jacob was holding something in his hands that was quite large. "What is it Jacob? Come on, let me see." Katie Lee tried to see what he had, but he turned to where she could not even get a glimpse of it. He smiled at Nancy and walked away from them both. Katie Lee looked at Nancy as if saying, "What's up with him?" Then she saw Jacob talking to the coach and pointing towards them. There became a huge smile on the coach's face as he patted Jacob on the back turning in the opposite direction. Jacob waved at the girls and motioned for Nancy to stay where they were. Nancy started to get excited and silly, she jumped up and down. "Oh, Kate Lee, you are going to be so surprised." Looking from Nancy to where Jacob was standing, she did not know what else could make her happier than to be here. She noticed everyone pointing at her, some started coming towards her but Nancy put up her hand "No, don't tell her, she doesn't know, please wait." Katie Lee was very confused, thinking what could she possibly be talking about. She knew it could not have anything to do with what she had just gone through, so why all the secrecy and why the demand to hold her back from her classmates? She wanted to talk to everyone, she began to hear the coach on the mike asking everyone to get out of the pool and gather near the food table. He again announced it, only this time he moved closer to the pool, asking for the ball to get everyone's attention. Jacob walked towards the two girls just grinning. "Smarty, have I got a surprise for you." She jerked Jacob back from taking her hand, but he took it again as the two of them escorted her towards the large group beside the coach. She noticed her senior counselor standing beside the coach with that looked like to be the same object that Jacob wouldn't show her.

When Jacob pulled her up front, the seniors began to applaud and shout her name. "Katie Lee, Katie Lee." She was so dumbfounded, she did not have any idea what was happening. She was sure this was not her reward for not attending her graduation ceremony. Maybe it was her diploma, she hadn't got her hands on it yet. The counselor was smiling and told Jacob to stand beside her and Nancy. The coach was trying to settle everyone down. "Senior, we won't spend a lot of time, in fact I will let you all take the time with this young lady and fill her in on all the awards at the graduation, but I will take the honor of presenting this award for outstanding student by her peers and all staff members for the senior class." As he held up the award for all to see again, they all shouted, the Miller twins jumped and started doing back flips. One fell in the pool accidentally, the other showing off and not paying attention to what he was close too hit the food table as cupcakes flew everywhere. Everyone busted out laughing when he raised his head covered with yellow, blue and red frosting and chocolate icing. Just grinning and licking the icing the other Miller twin yelled out, "Way to go Katie Lee, what happened to my brother?"

Katie Lee was so moved, the feeling inside her was something she could not describe. The warmth that came over her with the award in her hand and the looks and shouts from her fellow students made this her night forever. She looked at the Miller twin in the water, then handed the award back to the counselor as she ran for the pool. Just as she jumped screaming out loud, "I really cannot swim Ron Miller." Before she hit the water, the other twin dashed in behind her, alone with the other two classmates in the pool they grabbed her arms and legs. After dunking her good, they made sure she was safe and carried to the side of the pool right to the steps. Her clothes were soaked, she did not care and they did not care. The Millers twins help her the rest of the way up the steps then grabbed the coach taking him back into the pool with them. Nancy saw all the other chaperon's head in the opposite direction, knowing they might end up where the coach was.

Nancy grabbed her and explained that the coach had asked her and Jacob to accept the award for her. She was so nervous and Jacob was too. Everyone was talking at the same time, everyone trying to get to her, handing her towels laughing at what she had done. She was the happiest girl alive, as she looked upwards she felt there was a god, and deep inside she knew not only was Peter looking down with cherished approval but Mary also. Yes Mary, the one that had become her constant companion for almost six years after they took her away. The one that took her back to the redwoods more times than she could remember to refresh their last day as children together with Peter. She knew they must be standing together looking at her with pride as well as they should be.

CHAPTER SEVENTEEN

"Thank you for the safe ride home." Katie Lee turned as Jacob opened his truck door for her. She saw the humble look on his face as she took his arm while walking up the driveway. "Well, I still can't figure out why you missed the ceremony." Resting her head slightly towards his shoulder, she appreciated his friendship and respect, she was well aware of how he felt about her and she almost wished she could feel something back. "Jacob, please try to understand it was a family matte and I couldn't let it ruin the entire night for me." He felt so strongly for her, he wondered why she didn't care for him. Was he so different from the other boys in school? As they started up towards her steps, the were interrupted by a voice from hell, "Well, it is about time young lady. What does a mother have to do to see her daughter on her graduation night?"

Stumbling into Jacob, her eyes focused in the direction of the voice, seeing her mother within a few feet from her, she raced into the house in full terror. "Aunt Loie, Uncle Jack!" she was screaming, such fear in her voice. Hitting the side of the door with full force of her body she fell, collapsing in her aunt's arms. With tears rolling and coming down her cheeks, she was in such a stage that her aunt and uncle could not believe what could possibly have gone wrong. Then without warning they heard Mina say, "Well hello, how is my favorite sister? Oh sorry, "favorite" I guess is the wrong word. Loie's feet crumbling beneath her, Jack caught his wife as she almost went down beside her niece.

Pacific Redwood Mystery: Do you believe in the little people yet?

Jacob came rushing in behind, couldn't comprehend what on earth happened. His friend was on the floor where she fell, it was obvious that this was a family situation and a crisis. This woman said she was Katie Lee's mother, he didn't know she even had a mother, who was alive anyway.

Jack had hate in is eyes as he turned to Jacob, "Jacob help Katie Lee off the floor please." Jacob rushed towards his friend to assist but the look she gave him was utter fear. Jack immediately assured Jacob it was ok, just help his wife. Jack placed his arm around his niece so Mina could not even get a good look at her, Loie moved towards Katie Lee to put her between her uncle and Jacob. "Aren't you even going to give your mother a hug? Got you a gift." With that Loie saw her throw a present on the love seat as she threw her head back to laugh. "Too bad Peter could not have lived to see this day, I personally wouldn't have believed it, if I was a beating person, that is." Mina eyes danced as she spoke the cutting remarks to her daughter, Jack took Katie Lee by the arm, moving her closer to Jacob pointing to take Katie Lee towards the hallway out of Mina's sight. "Oh, don't leave on my account Katie Lee. We have so much to catch up on."

The ugliest feeling came over the young girl before she reached the hall to her room. Mrs. Hanson was running with Nancy on her heels through their front door. Nancy's eyes were wide, they had heard the solid screams moments before. "What is happening Jack?, what can we do?" Mrs. Hanson stood as firm as Charles David had that day in the bedroom when she was so young. Turning to Katie Lee Jack looked into her eyes. "The question is to you dear, do you want to stay or go over to Nancy's?" Fearing to be too far from them but her memory of her mother's terror was greater, she decided out of fear to go next door. "Jacob please escort the ladies next door, I would appreciate that, thank you."

Kissing his niece on the forehead, he deposited her in the arms of his neighbor and two friends. She staggered looking back, leaving her aunt and uncle to deal with her mother. Mina was older, she had not lost her love for style or beauty nor her intimidating ways. He only trace of age was the streak of gray in her hair that lined the scar from her widows peak on her forehead to the middle of her crown. The gentleman that accompanied her was younger. No doubt he had money, his clothes and jewelry cost more than their home. She knew she should stay and help with her mother but because of fear lurking from past experience, she knew her freedom was at stake. No, she had been there, done that, never again. Never would she live that nightmare. They had the papers, and the police would have to make her leave. As they entered Mrs. Hanson's home, she told Nancy and Jacob to stay with her as she ran for the phone. Jack had handed her a card with a Lieutenant Andrews name and emergency phone number instructing her to call him right away, he would know what to do. She told the male operator it was an emergency that the lieutenant would know, her neighbor worked for the prison and there was an emergency at his home. It was obvious they knew exactly what she was talking about and repeated the address of Jack and Loie, the officer on the line informed her he had dispatched a unit and notified his desk sergeant. Mrs. Hanson took Katie Lee into the area where Nancy's nice beautiful new piano was sitting You could tell Nancy had been playing a lot, there was song books all over the place.

Katie Lee was staring from Nancy to Jacob and then back to Mrs. Hanson, she began to apologize but Mrs. Hanson shook her head no, "Katie Lee, we do not pretend to know what is happening but your aunt and uncle are good people, you are a good girl, do not try to explain right now. Let's just settle down and wait for the officers or your aunt and uncle." Jacob, with his manners of politeness for the first time did not know what to do. Nancy was sitting beside her friend but could not help ask the question. "Was that really your mother?" Striking up and away from them as if they were going to do something bad to her, she braced herself against the wall. Mrs. Hanson right away saw the sign of a very badly abused girl. Nancy and Jacob heard Mrs. Hanson reply as she slowly moved in Katie Lee's direction. "Sweet Jesus, No one is going to hurt you here Katie Lee. Look where you are, you are in my home, I am Nancy's mother. Do you know where you are, honey?" Mrs. Hanson reached her hand out for the young girl, but her emotions were beyond what Mrs. Hanson dare push. She kept her eyes on Katie Lee and began to talk to her daughter and Jacob. "Jacob start talking to her, and Nancy go to the kitchen and get me a glass of cold water." Nancy moved quickly towards the kitchen with her eyes still on her friend, Jacob shrugged his shoulders as if he didn't know what to say. "Talk to her about the award Jacob, in fact ask her where it is." He went to move toward her and she almost climbed right up the wall. Mrs. Hanson motioned for him to stay put but talk slow and softly. Before that could occur, there came a fierce knock on the front door. Katie Lee took off into the kitchen as if she had been shot. Mrs. Hanson, hurrying to the door, spoke over her shoulder to Jacob. "Whatever you do, don't let her leave this house." Jacob sprung into action after Katie Lee, as Mrs. Hanson reached the door, two uniform officers stood. As they stepped into the hall entrance, she was glad to see one was female.

As Mrs. Hanson familiarized them with what little she knew, the female officer asked where Katie Lee was. "She is in the kitchen with my daughter and another friend. Won't you follow." Before she could finish they heard tired squeal and brakes burn, as they looked toward Katie Lee's house next door they saw a back sedan with two men. "Oh my, that is the warden but I don't recognize the gentleman in the suit. The female officer followed Mrs. Hanson but she instructed her partner to check what was going on next door. They found the three teens sitting at the kitchen table, their hands locked together. Jacob's face was tight and twitching, he looked so dispelled. Mrs. Hanson realized Katie Lee was reminiscing from somewhere back in her past, as she told the officer this was not normal for the young girl. They could hear Katie Lee's voice in almost a whisper as if she was speaking to someone.

Mrs. Hanson placed her hands on top of a kitchen chair without a sound, motioning for the officer to sit down as she pulled a pen and pad from her jacket and keeping a close eyes on the young girl. They all sat there just listening as the officer began to write. Katie Lee must have been remembering the most horrid time in her life. Something she had pushed so far back in her mind that she almost forgot those years of abuse and neglect. She was remembering all those nights, alone only to hear the loud music from within the walls of what was suppose to be a lovely home. The men, all those men, she kept muttering. The sounds, the noise, the laughter, the sounds of Mina entertaining men over and over again. 'I was so small, I was so little, but Daddy Peter loved me, but she ruined that too." There was so much coming out of her that they were all overwhelmed. The female officer knew it was important no one made any sudden movements. Jacob watched as the officer spoke into the shoulder mike but he could not hear what she was saying.

Nancy began to put the pieces together and feel sick to her stomach. No wonder her friend would never talk about her past. No wonder she would never let the conversation begin in any manner what so ever. Jacob began his own interpretation to realize his friends nightmare prior to coming here. How could Kate Lee, his friend ever think of any male in her life without disgust. He had no idea, none of them could have imagined. Nancy saw someone she didn't know, no one would ever believe such a horrid story. As they sat and tried to piece her going from one incident to another in her mind, they must have thought how in the world she lived through it. One thing for sure, that at some time in her life, she had a stepfather by the name of Peter that meant the world to her. That was the only time a softness came over her. Mrs. Hanson noticed when she mentioned Peter, there was this determination to keep him alive somehow. Mrs. Hanson wondered what had happened to him, what had happened to this young girl that was so beyond their help. Then Katie Lee suddenly collapsed off the chair, they were all on their feet as Mrs. Hanson was trying to make her way between Nancy and Jacob as the officer shoved the table out of their way for immediate access to the young girl. Mrs. Hanson pointed to Jacob to get next door and get her aunt, "Go Jacob, go."

"Mom, is she okay, what happened?" Mrs. Hanson was pulling her daughter down to the floor with her as she laid Katie Lee half

Pacific Redwood Mystery: Do you believe in the little people yet?

in her lap and arranging the rest of her limp body flat on the floor. She looked through her own tears at the officer for some kind of assurance. The female officer bent over Katie Lee, she felt her pulse. She looked up at Mrs. Hanson and smiled. "I think she is okay, just fainted from all the emotions but the paramedics are coming just in case." Still on the floor when Loie came running, she bent over her niece looking bewildered. It was so quiet all of a sudden, not a sound, not a move. It was something as if no one dared to speak for fear of what else could happen. Then the male officer came in, seeing the sight, he only looked at his partner in the eyes placing his hands on his hips. Jacob was behind him but he would not let the lad enter the room. Sirens, they heard the sirens, it was like a sudden relief they were coming closer and closer. Jacob sprinted toward the front, he was waiting when they arrived to hurry them into the house. Everyone was escorted out of the way as routine procedures were performed on her, Loie wanted to take her home but a voice from behind spoke up. "No Loie, we are taking her to the hospital if only for a twenty four hour observation. That way, we know she will be safe." Everyone turned seeing a fairly tall man with a suit standing beside Jack. As he came forward, he introduced himself, "I am Jeff Moorehead, I am the attorney representing this young lady, so we will be transporting her right now." Jacob asked if he could come along behind, but Jack suggested that she was going to need rest and he had done so much. He looked helpless as they rolled her out, he took his keys out of his pocket as Loie hugged him. "You can see her in the morning Jacob. Maybe Nancy would like to come with you?" Mrs. Hanson held her hand out to her neighbor and squeezed her. "Absolutely and I will drive them personally. I bet she won't want hospital food, we can smuggle some donuts, something more exciting." The officers were outside talking to Jack now while they placed Katie Lee in the ambulance, Jacob no longer saw the woman that said she was Katie Lee's mother, he hoped they had seen the last of her. Mrs. Hanson put her arms around Loie one last time and whispered that if she needed anything, no matter the time or situation, they were there.

Nancy held back in disbelief as she watched them place her friend through those back double doors. It was like watching a movie that she could not figure out the ending. Jacob walked to his truck, waving at Nancy as he was just sitting until the ambulance driven off. He too then slowly turned the corner and headed for home. The things he had heard were going like whirlwinds in his mind. He did not know how, but he was going to help, he understood so much now. Jack sent his wife off to the hospital to be with Katie Lee that night but he walked back into their home, closing the door behind him with the lawyer and his boss, the warden. Jack stood inside his home with his hand on the door as if he was trying to make sure it stayed shut. The lawyer and warden waited for him to get his composure. They entered the kitchen where Jack fixed them all a drink, well deserved. As he took his drink, he swallowed it all in one gulp. He poured another one but just looked at it. "I cannot believe she came. What for, why?" Jack sunk into one of the chairs sinking as if he had just ran a marathon. Looking at Jack and the warden Mr. Moorehead knew it was time to inform them what he knew. "I think I can shed some light on the situation Jack." Looking over at the lawyer and his boss, how could he know more than they did? "I made some phone calls earlier this evening and guess what? Katie Lee is the heir to a lot of money, providing she graduated from high school." Stunned, Jack asked, "What do you mean, a lot of money? How accurate is your information?" Beginning to talk with his hand like most lawyers Jack listened. "Well, it seems like this Peter Patterson left her quite a bit of money, one hundred and fifty thousand dollars to be exact, but not knowing for sure what the outcome in her life would be, he left her mother as beneficiary, if something happened to you or your wife before she turned eighteen. How old is Katie Lee?"

 The warden stood, then started to pace. He could see Jack was letting the information sink in, he wanted to make sure he understood what Mr. Moorehead was really saying. "So, let's see if I have this correct, this Mr. Patterson left Jack's niece this money, but not knowing who would still be alive when she graduated and if she graduated she got one-fourth of the inheritance. When she reached twenty-five, she gets the rest." The lawyer nodded head. "Yep, but I guess this man figured that if Jack and Loie were not still alive, she probably would not graduate, so he assured no money until she was twenty-five." Jack stood rubbing his chin with his right hand, "Exactly, she wants the money, that is all. She knows Katie Lee will give it to her to make her go away. Why did Peter even tell her?" The lawyer looked at Jack as if he did not want to reveal this part. "What, what did she do Mr. Moorehead?" Taking a pretty big breath he looked Jack right in the eyes, "Well she didn't do anything really, she just happened to be at the right place at the right time. The insurance company was trying to get in touch with your niece. Mr. Patterson's middle daughter was the contact person since a previous daughter name Mary was deceased. She still lives in the same town as Katie Lee's mother. She has been out of the country with her husband so the bank hadn't gotten in touch with her yet to notify Katie Lee. Its a small town Jack, and that is a lot of money so rumors can spread fast, real fat in a little town like that." In desperation Jack's mind raced. "Is there any way we can bring charges against her?"

The lawyer stretched his hands into his pockets, "I am afraid she had not done anything wrong, except like she told the officers, she was just trying to bring her daughter a present, and it will be Monday before we can really activate the restraining order." Jack was furious, sometimes it didn't matter who you were. Paperwork had to take it course. "Present, yea right. If I believed that, I need a drink." Jack was not going to have his wife or niece be put through Mina's games. "Can she get her hands on the money, does she have any rights to it?" Jack was trying to figure out if they could stop Mina from getting what the girl deserved and what Peter wanted her to have. "Well, I don't think so but I do need to see the paperwork, evaluate what he actually did for her., but if she is not her legal guardian, then no. She had no right unless the girl gives it to her. We can file our own wrongful lawsuit against her if you like Jack. That will give the judge something to work with. Your niece will have to testify. It could get real sticky. That really set him off, "What do you mean real sticky?" Mr. Moorehead knew he had to be careful but Jack needed to know everything right up front. "We have full custody of her, you saw the papers." The lawyer saw that Jack did not understand. "I mean, she may have to answer questions about the past that you and Loie have tried to keep buried. Is she up to it Jack, can she do it without crumbling?" He was right and Jack also had to protect his wife. They were not as young as they used to be, they had taken Katie Lee at a late age. He could understand why Peter had make those arrangements; there was a lot of age difference between this young girl and them. "A fourth was a smart move on Mr. Patterson's end. Either way your niece will have the last say."

He had to think of something, they had to arrange something. He just did not know what. "We have to talk to my wife and Katie Lee. Mina will not stop at just someone telling her no. She will keep coming, she is not afraid of the law. In fact she challenges it." The lawyer was intrigued to think this woman felt she could beat the system. Who the hell was she anyway, he needed to do some further homework. After what he saw tonight, they needed his services; Katie Lee needed him. Jack had the law on his side, he always did but this woman was a snake, she knew how to bite at the heels and strike until you were weakened. He was going to call in every favor he had. No wonder Peter had been so adamant about Katie Lee getting an education. If only he had lived to see this day, well maybe that was not such a great thought, if Peter was alive, Jack knew for sure he would probably put a stop to Mina once and for all. She had become a thorn in Peter's side from the day she left the hospital, until the day they laid him in the grave. Jack remembered the words that Katie Lee spoke at his funeral. "He can rests in peace now." He could hear Mina laugh just like it was yesterday. "Ha, are you serious Katie Lee, he will never rest from me, I will haunt his soul until mine is sent to hell." Jack shivered as he thought of the power of her words. He would never forget the look on Katie Lee's face when Mina walked away from her that day. Was it going to take sending her to hell to protect his family?

CHAPTER EIGHTEEN

"Do you believe in the little people? Have you been to the giant redwoods where they play, have you ever looked under those beautiful flared ferns where they sleep or up high in the branches of the treetops where the wind whistles, reaching the stars?" They hide there, you know, that is why you cannot see them, unless you believe.

She was a tall woman, maybe close to five eleven. Heavy accent, somewhere like Romania or Hungary perhaps. Most men were intimidated by her, which caused her private practice some side effects, like getting referrals from them, but she didn't care. She felt most physicians in her field over medicated anyway and never got to the root of the problem. As she read the police report, she felt this was a vibrant young lady with a lot of anger subdued somewhere in her mind refusing to deal with the problem. There was not a lot of information except a mother that seemed to appear when convenient and unannounced. She needed more information before she made any opinions, it was a favor anyway looking into this case. She had spent most of her time in forensic science but lately had been asked to assist at the prison. It was not her cup of tea but a service greatly in need.

Throwing the folder on her desk, she needed more, much more. She decided to see what could be found on the net, she was most interested in this teenager's mother. This was an awesome generous gift to leave a stepchild and not even that. The report said there had not been any legal marriage. There were a lot of holes in the report, she felt there was something real serious happening but she just couldn't put her finger on it. She found several Peter Patterson's death records, she needed his date of birth, she found some information on a Peter Patterson that owned some logging trucks in the same area but what she did find next disturbed her. There was also an article on this Patterson and was attached with investigation information. It was in the blotter of the Tribune but no follow-up. Bringing up her password to secure files, she typed in "Mina Patterson" she sat waiting for the secure files to load. Or other records on Katie Lee Rossman and her family, especially the so called stepfather. She checked her schedule for the following day, the request was marked "urgent" but they all were.

Her secretary knocked on her door as she stuck her head in. "The warden say he has noting but to give him a call, he wanted to give you heads-up on some issues he witnessed." Just grinning, she knew how difficult it was to be put in the middle of employee-and boss situation. She was aware this was a family matter of the supervising guards but how did the warden get so involved? "I am so glad Stacy you have your life in order, I don't have to worry about some mysterious employee's secret to fix."

They both just smiled and agreed it was very difficult to sometimes solve or work with favor situations. Most times they turned out pretty bad and you were always the bad person for your advice. She was not used to teenagers either so this was a case with a big negative marked on it from the get-go.

"Oh shit," she heard her secretary say, "Oh Dr. Badea I am so sorry I just glanced at your screen, it took me by surprise." As the doctor turned towards her computer, she too was taken back for a second. "Oh heavens, that woman lived." Stacy gasped as she turned her face away. She handed her secretary some papers and asked her to shut the door on the way out. She started to surf pages and speed-read through the articles. She could not believe her eyes, the wound was unbelievable and the woman lived. She brought up the hospital records to see what the doctor's name was, then protective services had a report attached to the hospitals. Seeing the children involved, she compared the date of birth to this Katie Lee Rossman and the one listed on this report. Same and another child, an older girl. No comments had been made on the older sister except a runaway report. But the youngest had been placed in foster care until she was placed some years later with relatives. That must be the prison worker as she compared the names, again the same.

It was amazing to her that the police had drastically change their minds in the midair of with this case. They came on strong with a case against the stepfather then turned tail and went the other direction. As she sat studying what she was readying she became intrigued with the case. What was the story here?? What about the money, and what had happened to the first daughter? It was obvious this Peter Patterson was dead, What happened to him, matching records he was the same Patterson that disappeared from his successful logging business? Well, maybe tomorrow or the next day would be pushing it. Picking up the phone, she called the nurse's station at the hospital where Katie Lee was taken. "Hello, this is Dr. Badea, I have a request to see patient Katie Lee Rossman. Is her family with her?" A welcome voice on the phone made it easier for the doctor "Oh hello, Dr. Badea, this is Stevenson. Well her aunt is here, the lawyer and her uncle were earlier but I have not seen them in about an hour." The word "lawyer" went through her thoughts as "oops" that could mean good or bad. "Lawyer, why is there a lawyer?" she asked the nurse, Stevenson knew she was not suppose to give information, there was no order on the chart for the consultation, it was a favor to favor and the patient could decline. "I am not sure, something about her mother, the girl doesn't talk much. In fact she seems real withdrawn." Dr. Badea wondered if she should go in this evening but didn't want to go without maybe talking to the warden. "Okay thank you Stevenson, I think I'll do a little QA and call you back." The nurse was so grateful for that, she knew the QA mean questions and answer research before attempt to approach the patient. This took the nurse off the hook and the conversation did not need to be documented.

Turning to her computer she decided to print everything on the secured site. She would like to have a copy of this to study as she questioned the warden. Maybe she should not have been so quick to judge the warden as to the importance of talking to his employee. Well, this would be the first if this turned out to be a real case and one that needed her expert knowledge. "Dr. Badea, you have a call on line 3, it is the hospital asking if you are going to make the staff dinner at seven?" She hated those functions, they didn't want her there anyway. She didn't know why she went other than she needed to stay in good standings with the hospital. She decided to call the other female doctor in town that her colleagues also gave their arrogant attitude towards. Dr. Regina Trevino was a more pleasant female doctor but she too was having a hard time. The other OBGYN's on staff wanted to make sure she stayed low on the totem pole. What was with this attitude she asked herself a thousand times in her mind? Never had she seen such ego and macho attitudes among doctor's, she buzzes her secretary "Get me Dr. Trevino, try her office first."

Printing all the reports, she placed them in a new file writing Katie Lee Rossman on the top. Looking for the form to be signed to treat someone underage, she figured it would be better to be safe than sorry, a month before legal age was still under age. She was not taking any chances. "Dr. Trevino on line 3, doctor." Placing all the files from her lap back on her desk, she was glad the good doctor had returned her call. "Hello Regina, how are you?" Laughing, the doctor gave similar details of any fasted-paced physician's office with a lot of pregnant women. "Well I tell you what, you come here one day and I will go there, but not to check any heartbeats or personal issues, just talk." Both laughing Dr. Badea like this doctor, she was fresh and compassionate like herself. "How about riding with me to the staff dinner tonight, might as well walk in together so they can talk about us at one time." Knowing that was a true statement, Dr. Trevino told her she had to check one of her patients she had admitted anyway so why didn't she just meet her at the hospital. "That will work, see you around seven in the lounge, then we can walk over to the dinning hall, see you later Regina." Relieved that she had agreed, it would make the evening more enjoyable and less stressful.

Leaving her office she went to the front office to collect paperwork from the rest she had printed from this teenagers close-out report. If that was going to be the case, she would have to pull back on their medication refills until she got to the bottom of their problem. She was not the kind of doctor that would just write a script and refill it numerous of times before finding out what happened to the patient. No, you had to see her on a regular basis until you were stable enough to function on your own. If future treatment was not needed she just maintained your treatment as needed, she adjusted but never without some communication.

Bidding her staff a good evening, she locked the doors behind them. Usually her staff took care of all that but she wold be working until she left for the meeting so it wouldn't hurt her to lock up letting her staff off early. She wanted to talk to the warden anyway but she didn't need anyone over hearing their conversation. It was not that she did not trust her staff but she was also aware people talked. In this case something told her this was a special case and one that maybe she needed to keep to herself for awhile.

Turning off all the lights, she went back to her office and dialed the prison hoping he had not left yet. He answered right away, "Well that was fast, it hardly rang." Excited with her call, he reminded her he had caller ID. "Oh yes, well I guess that would be appropriate for out there. I called to discuss some issues on this Rossman case." The warden was a patient man but for some reason this case gave him a case of anxiety. "Oh yes, have you seen her yet? She is a sweet child, but I am afraid this is going to be disastrous if we don't get her help. Her uncle is a good man." He was talking as if he needed to convince her how important this case was. "Hold on there warden, I am going to see her but I haven't yet. When I called the hospital they said she had a lawyer. What is up with that?" His voice was speaking more rapidly, "No. no. Don't worry about that, the lawyer is one of my friends that I called. He is there to protect her money rights and make sure the restraining order is carried out." Now that was something they had not bothered to tell her. "Restraining order, you failed to mention that warden. Knowing this was probably better, he didn't even look at his schedule. He would clear it for her, he could come in a little early and that would give them more time. "How early can you be here Dr. Badea?" There was a hesitation in her voice as she realized that to him this was one of those "must" cases that needed attention immediately. "I can be there by eight." Before she could add anything the warden replied. "Perfect Dr. Badea, I will be here by seven if you can make it earlier." Now that was a man determined to work a case. Thanking her for the call, he did not want to give her any other information to make her think it could go another day. He rushed out of his office to catch his secretary before she left.

"Mrs. Bradshaw, I have Dr. Badea coming first thing in the morning, she will be here before eight and I do not want to be disturbed." Looking at him as if he was acting awful hurriedly, she asked if there was something wrong or something she needed to be aware of. "No, no it is about Jack's niece." His secretary sighed with relief. "That is wonderful, but will the girl talk to her.?" He didn't want to think about that, he just patted her on the shoulder as he returned to his office. The warden made a quick call to Jack and Mr. Moorehead, he was pleased to announce Dr. Badea had agreed to see Katie Lee. Mr. Moorehead was delighted, not just for the girl but also because he knew it would look good if this case went before a judge. Jack was happy but worried that his niece would refuse. He agreed to talk to his wife and Katie Lee personally when he went back to the hospital. He dressed so he would have time to sneak his niece something special like ice cream, Katie Lee loved ice cream. He grabbed his wife another change of clothes knowing she would not leave the hospital. Loie was watching a movie with her niece by the time Jack go there. In fact it was one of his favorites. "Fried Green Tomatoes" he could hear them laughing from the hall. That was a good sign. Putting the butterscotch sundae's behind his back, he walked into the room. 'Hey, how are my ladies tonight?" Before he could get an answer, making sure no negative came from anyone, he whipped out the butterscotch sundae. "Hey, you remembered." Katie Lee was excited, the look on her face gave them both great relief even if for a short time.

"Jack, you better not get caught and get us into trouble." He waved his hand. "Oh, fuddle duddle what can they do? Look at her, she almost has it all eaten" Laughing, Katie Lee was eating it fast, in fact she was beginning to get a brain freeze, so she slowed down. "You are crazy Jack, but that is why I love you so much." Kissing his wife on the cheek, he handed her the fresh clothes and went to sit in the other chair opposite side of Katie Lee. "Thank you, but I don't now if I will need them, Katie Lee wants to go home, so the doctor said he will talk to her when he makes his rounds around 8:30 tonight." His heart skipped a beat, that would not work. If she went home it would be harder to get her the help he knew she needed; she could not find any excuse and would not take this opportunity. "Well, not so quick, let her rest. I think she should stay at least one more night and maybe tomorrow." Katie Lee almost chocked on her ice cream. "No way, another night and day, I don't think so. It is not like I broke anything, I rested all day. In fact, Nancy her mother and Jacob came today. We had a great time." He was glad of that, now how was he going to deal with this? "Okay honey, how about some coffee Loie, want to walk down to the coffee shop with me dear?" Loie knew her husband well enough to know something was up.

He needed to get his wife to help him talk her into staying at least one more night for this doctor to see her. She was too anxious to get Katie Lee home, where she could protect her and move forward. "Will you be okay while us old folks go get some java?" Katie Lee giggled as her uncle referred to them as old folks. For their age they were so active and full of life but she knew they both drank far too much coffee. "Of course, I will just watch this movie. It is about to my favorite part anyway." They smiled as they joined hands walking out into the hall. Jack reminded the nurses "NO" one was to enter the room except the nursing staff and doctor. "We know, you go get your java and we will take good care of her. Dr. Longoria is on the floor but we will have him wait to visit with her." When Jack heard that, he changed his mind about the coffee and asked if there was a way he could speak with the doctor before he saw his niece, Jack was glad to see his wife shake her head in agreement. "Oh please, can we just take a moment of his time, it is really important?" Jack looked at his wife as the pleas in her eyes told it all.

A little nervous about what Katie Lee might think but they were willing to risk disapproval. As they sat talking among themselves agreeing with each other, a knock came on the door then a tall man, fairly average looking gentleman wearing glasses. He did not look Hispanic but they noticed he spoke in Spanish to the nurse as he entered the room. Greeting them in a very friendly manner, they were impressed immediately. "What can I do for you and how can I help your niece?" That opened the discussion easily for them as Loie felt that this doctor was going to understand and not just label their niece as a nutcase.

As they went over some facts, he was most interested and asked several questions. Making notes as they talked, he went over all her tests that came out negative and everything looked great. Katie Lee had suffered anxiety attack. Given more facts and current information, he understood why. Then Jack suggested the warden's idea of Dr. Badea, the doctor did not look up. "Dr. Badea, has she been notified?" Both shook their heads and told the doctor that the warden had touched base with her by phone only. "Well, we are having a staff dinner this evening, I will put an order in Katie Lee's chart and talk to Dr. Badea myself. How do you think Katie Lee is going to take this?" That was the problem and he could tell by the way they looked at each other this was something that had not been discussed with the young girl. "Would you like me to discuss it with her and see how that goes? You can jump in at any time if you think she may listen to you better?" With a plan in place, he told them he had a couple more patient to see but would be in her room shortly.

Pacific Redwood Mystery: Do you believe in the little people yet?

Feeling better but anxious themselves, they were hoping it went well. Loie couldn't help thinking that maybe she should have approached Katie Lee first. Well, it was too late now, so they would have to just hope for the best. As they entered their nieces room, she was in good spirits laughing with the movie. "I love this movie, I need to be Towanda." She had eaten all her ice cream and hidden the plastic carrier in her garage pail. Her uncle laughed as he shook his head, Loie sat on the end of Katie Lee's bed rubbing her niece's knee as Jack watched their closeness admiring what they had so special. She had brought a lot of love and happiness into their life, he wished Peter was alive so he could shake his hand and express his thankfulness for searching so long for them. Peter never gave up the search.

As the movie was coming to an end, Katie Lee had tears n her eyes as she watched the last part with sadness, knowing it was going to turn out great but this part always made her cry. "I hope those tears are because of the movie and not because of me." They turned to see the doctor enter the room, Katie Lee did not brace herself back against the head of her bed as she had done prior but she kind of laughed at his remark. "No, unless you are not gong to let me go home." "He was impressed with her quick wit and cute personality." Winking at her aunt and uncle so she could see he replied to her comment in as much wit that came towards him with her "Gosh, then you have to write me a ticket to be released." He grinned at her and took her arm, taking her pulse. She knew that was unusual for the doctor to do what the nurse had already done, her vitals but if that made him happy so she could go home. Then she sat perfectly still for him, he looked into her eyes and listened to her chest.

As he wrote in her chart, he was very quiet, she looked from her aunt to her uncle and they only grinned as if saying, "be patient." He could sense she was anxious for his answer and he intended for her to be carious, that was the approach he wanted for himself to start the conversation with her. Putting her chart down pushed his glasses back upon his nose. "Well, I cannot find anything wrong with you, I think you suffered an anxiety attack. Do you know what an anxiety attack is?" She was surprised he asked and she was not sure whey he asked other than he needed to know if she would have another one. "Yep, I think they are brought on by stress and pressure." He knew she would have the answer, the trick was to work around that information to convince her she needed to talk with Dr. Badea. "You are correct but some people do not take them serious enough and it can lead to other serious things, even for a young lady like yourself?" She knew she could get around this, it was a piece of cake "Well, It was graduation and all the excitement and parties, deadlines final grades, it was pretty tense." He nodded his head and Loie realized he had lost her. Jack was not so sure, he felt he was making a point.

"Graduation, how did you fell when you walked across the stage and received your diploma?" There it was, Jack was pleased. Loie's heart fluttered, Katie Lee looked at her aunt as she took her hand. "It is okay honey, no shame in it." Leaning against the door he smiled down at the young girl. "I understand you got the award of all awards, outstanding student voted by school administration. That is nothing to take lightly young lady. I would give my eye tooth if one of my kids came home with a good report card." That made her smile but he could tell she was still uncomfortable. "You are a very vibrant young lady with a lot ahead of you. I see no reason why you cannot look forward to a great life, but as a physician we like to make sure our patients get the best opportunity to achieve just that. I would like you to promise me if I let you go home in the morning you will see one of my colleagues." She squeezed her aunt's hand, "Why cant I go tonight?" Just starting at her, she was doing exactly what he wanted, he needed her to play by his rules with complete confidence. "Please, I am sure someone else needs this bed more than I do."

Picking up her chart again, the doctor wrote the order for Dr. Badea on a follow-up and signed then signed her release. "If you really want to go home then I need your promise you will follow up with Dr. Badea for an appointment tomorrow or the next day at the latest., you will like her, is that a deal?" She wanted to get out of there so bad but she hesitated, thinking why was she going to another doctor rather than him. Maybe he did not see patients other than in the hospital? "Why do I need to see her?" He was ready for that question but he could see her aunt and uncle were not. "Well I will repeat myself, I think you are a very bright young lady and I want to make sure these anxiety attacks do not re-occur, so I want you to see her and I want you to cooperate with her. She is a good doctor and I know you will like her." With that he offered his handshake to her uncle first the her aunt but as he stood and looked at Katie Lee, he shook the chart at her. He nodded toward them and left the room. Katie Lee was quiet as she played with the sheet on her bed. "I don't like going to another doctor and I don't want to." Her uncle handled it with ease. "Well, what will it hurt? If we have to go to court Katie Lee it will let the judge see you followed the doctor's orders." Katie Lee looked at her uncle with a shock look. "Court, are we going to court?" She was becoming anxious as her aunt tried to calm her down before she didn't get to go home, "See the doctor dear as requested and get on with our lives." Jack explained Mr. Moorehead had a lot of answers for her but she would have to work hard keeping control of herself. "I know why your mother found you but before I let you know, you have to promise me here in front of your aunt you will see this doctor. I need you to be well Katie Lee, I do not need your mother destroying all you have worked for." Jack could tell she was not buying it, she was going to be stubborn and fight them, she might run if the fear of Mina coming back was a possibility. "If you won"t do it for yourself dear, do it for Peter." Jack looked over to his wife as those words came out o her her mouth but he knew she too was trying to think of whatever means she could to convince this girl. She needed to help, not just because of the anxiety attack but also for all the anger and hate she still held within herself. "Peter left you a gift dear, for your graduation night, we just found out about it ourselves. Let's go home and talked about everything." Her aunt was hoping her niece would settle down some, it seemed to work just the idea of Peter made Katie Lee's whole mood change. If was as if God knew what he was doing when he brought Peter into her niece's life.

As the nurse walked in with her paperwork it didn't take her long to get out of bed and head for the bathroom to get dressed. Being just a few distance from her aunt and uncle was a relief from her mind for a second, everything was overwhelming but she had made a promise, she remembered what a promise meant. Peter had taught her the importance of keeping her word. What did her aunt mean that he left her a gift? But that would be so like him, a golden touch from the grave, a whisper through her mind, he was still there. He was keeping his promise never to leave her. She did not care what it was, maybe some pictures, a letter – yes a letter. She couldn't wait to get home and read it and she could place it in her journal where all her other special things were. She would paste the picture she had of him to the letter, it was a small photo but it was hers.

When she entered from the bathroom her uncle had already left to compete the paperwork downstairs, her aunt was handing her a sweater. Thanking the nurses at the station she wanted to walk out, but as with all hospitals rules. One had to take that ride for the safety on ones life, their wheelchair express. Her uncle was waiting right in front when they came around the business office exit, he honked his horn getting their attention. Katie Lee didn't waste time getting into the car, but the nurse leaned in handing her aunt her discharge papers. "The appointment time in on the discharge papers and the doctors card is staples there as well, don't forget your promise sweetie." Just grinning at her the nurse waved and was gone. Katie Lee had not let that really sink into her mind yet, but if they already made her an appointment then she knew he guessed well. She probably would not have made the appointment on her own.

Not saying much on the way home, Katie Lee was not surprised to see her friend and her mother come across the lawn to greet her home. Mrs. Hanson had a single carnation in her hand as she kissed Katie Lee on the cheek then turning to hug her aunt. It smelled so good, right out of her own garden. It was a perfect gesture. "Hey friend, how are you feeling?" Nancy did not want to say much, she did not want to trigger anything else. "Good, I am good and I am so glad I am home." Mrs. Hanson declined to enter the house with them, she knew they had plenty to discuss and needed some alone time. She reminded them she was just next door and would see them tomorrow. Taking Nancy by the elbow, she escorted her daughter back across the lawn.

Katie Lee went to take a shower, change her clothes, she could hear her aunt's little footsteps behind headed for her room as well. Handing Katie Lee a nice warm towel "You take your time and when you are settled, we will talk." "Is it bad?" Her aunt was not surprised with that question. Nothing had been good, so why would she think any different. "No, sweetie, it is not. It is good and Peter loved you so." With that remark, she left her room leaving her niece alone to ponder what Peter would have said. She was anxious to see but she was also not sure if she was ready. She was nervous and not trusting at all. She left her bedroom door open and the bathroom a jar just to make sure someone could hear her if she needed to call for help. Making sure all the curtains were closed, her closet door shut tight, she knew she was being paranoid but she didn't care. With her mother around, she was not taking any chances. At first she tried to convince herself out of taking a shower when she heard the phone ring. Moving to the edge of her door, she heard her uncle talking to Mr. Moorehead. He was coming over, she knew then whatever it was they needed to tell her and it probably had to do with her mother, that could not be good. Leaving the door ajar, she went to the bathroom and showered. It felt so good as she just stood there letting the water run down her face and body. She was still tired, but mentally in her mind she wondered what she was going to hear and have to do. She had made up her mind she would call Mrs. Owens tomorrow and accept her job offer. Save enough money to just disappear. She wondered how much it would be to change her name and how far she could go. Whatever, it didn't matter she needed to take her first step in accomplishing this.

By the time she walked into the living room she was surprised Mr. Moorehead had already arrived. "Why, you got here fast. What kind of a car do you have?" They all chucked at Katie lee as she cuddled up in one of the chairs beside the couch. She chose not to sit on couch where Mr. Moorehead was with her aunt, she wanted some space between her and the lawyer. "Well, when I am going to work, I drive my sedan but when I am away from the office and have the opportunity I drive my vet." Katie Lee's eyes twinkled. "I am impressed. Mr. Moorehead, any time you want to let me borrow it, I promise to let my aunt drive." Loie's face was flabbergasted at her nieces remark "Oh my, I don't think that would be a good idea. We may never come back?" Jack thought it was a good ice breaker and he just waited for his niece to feel comfortable enough to hear what Mr. Moorehead had to say. "It is a lot of fun ladies. But the gas will kill you, doesn't get very good gas mileage and there is only one extra seat." Loie asked if anyone wanted anything, Katie Lee thought of some nice hot cocoa. Out of the chair she bounced and said, "I think I would like some hot cocoa, anyone else want any?" Her aunt immediately offered to get it for everyone but Mr. Moorehead declined as well as her uncle. Katie Lee sensed they wanted to get right down to business, so she offered to let her aunt go off to the kitchen alone.

As she sat back down, Mr. Moorehead settled on the couch in an upright position with some files. "Well, I guess you did not come all the way over here to drink cocoa with me, so what is the bad news?" Both men looked at each other as they felt a little guilty about her feeling so negative. The attorney spoke first making it clear she didn't need to worry so. "It is not all bad, let me start with the good news and then we will talk about your money and what we need to do to stop her." Katie Lee moved forward as her aunt entered the room taking the cup she handed her, it tasted great. "Okay, I'm ready but I want the bad news first, I am sure if it has anything to do with my mother, none of it is good." Mr. Moorehead handed her the first file on his lap and just watched as she wondered why without any explanation. As she opened the file it read as, "Last Will and Testament of Peter Patterson." Her heart sank "You don't have to read it all Katie Lee, in short there is a policy attached where Peter left you a college fund." Her heart pounding, she lifted the papers very carefully to the back

Pacific Redwood Mystery: Do you believe in the little people yet?

page. She read, "Mutual Of Omaha" at the bottom she read the total and then saw Peter signature at the bottom right above a notary seal and signature. Looking just above Peter's signature was the total but she blinked her eyes and brought the paper close to her face to make sure she was reading it correctly.

They all sat in silence waiting for her to respond, seeing she couldn't think of anything to say, Mr. Moorehead knew questions was were more likely going off in her head faster than she could respond. "Your stepfather was very cautious." He went on to explain to Katie Lee all the details of the will as well as the policy. "So that is why she has come around, the money?" Letting her digest what Peter had done, she just fumbled with the papers. When her aunt started to speak, Mr. Moorehead gently reached placing his hand over hers, he knew silence right now was more important than anyone trying to put their comments in. It took her awhile to settle into the thought but as she ran the explanation back through her mind, she could picture Peter taking great lengths to make sure everything was carried out. It was so like him and it was so appreciated. Finally she asked, "Can my mother get her hands on his money?" Her uncle moved forward in his chair, wanting her to know they were willing to fight if that was what she wanted. "It isn't her money, sweetie. He left it for you, your education and to have a good start in life, but yes that is why she is here. We all know that." She got out of the chair carrying the file with her, moving to the window she moved the curtains aside to look at the beautiful night. It was a quiet peaceful night, the stars were exceptionally bright while the darkness around them gave birth to a new meaning for her. She remembered Mary, as she closed her eyes she heard her words as if she was standing beside her. "Twinkle, twinkle little star, how I wonder what you are, up above the world so high like a diamond in the sky, I wish I may, I wish I might, I wish my wish would come tonight." She believed at that moment Mary was standing right beside her and together they would make a wish while holding hands. Then Mary would squeeze her shoulders and tell her, "Remember not to look at the star again and your wish will come true, but if you look at it, well, it is just a wish."

It was so quiet Katie Lee almost forgot she was not alone. "But it is my decision, right?" He didn't leave it to her, it is for my education." Her aunt and uncle were not sure what to make of her reaction, it was not what they expected. "That is correct, he only put her on there in case your aunt and uncle had passed on, but I don't think any judge will let her have a cent since they are alive and very good health. It is entirely up to you but as your aunt and uncle pointed out to me, she will probably come on strong and if you decided to give her the fourth then it is up to you." One could tell they were a little concerned that Mr. Moorehead did not push the issue that she did not have to, if she wanted to he could help her transfer the monies without her being involved. "If I do that then when the time comes for me to receive the rest, she will be back, I know her." That was exactly what Loie and Jack were thinking she would never go away. Again everyone sat in silence, waiting for Katie Lee to either break down, get angry, they were not sure she was going to do. "Does anyone know where she is?" Katie Lee asked.

It was obvious to them she was fearful but Mr. Moorehead seemed to be in the control of the conversation, looking back at Loie and Jack he had not revealed to them that he did not know exactly where she was. She had rented a motel room for a week with her gentleman friend. He seemed to have strong connections with someone in Social Security and in the police department but he was guessing the police department connection was the lieutenant that got himself in a world of trouble with the commissioner. If that was the case that could be rectified. "I do know that she rented that room for over a week and if my guess is right, she is here to try and get money out of you. To everyone's surprise, Katie Lee handed her uncle the file looking him straight in the face as she replied. "Well, I guess hell will freeze over before she gets it." "I know you are all shocked but she robbed me for the last time, this is something Peter left me. I just cannot believe it, I would never have guessed he would do something like this but it is so like him and from him. He would have died for nothing if she gets this, so if she thinks she is going to get one cent of something from him after what she put him through, no way. I will fight her if it cost me every cent he left." Mr. Moorehead smiled at the young girl, it was music to his ears. "Well, she can't win, as long as you are here under your aunt and uncle's legal care. Your determination will prevail. In fact, you don't even have to see her. If she persists after I meet with her and give her your answer, then we will go before a judge." Katie Lee became irritated, "No, I want to be there what you tell her myself. Then she will believe I mean it."

Her aunt and uncle were alarmed, "Are you sure you want to do that dear, she is pretty domineering." Jack was trying to focus on her newfound bravery while Loie was doing everything she could to discourage her. Mr. Moorehead looked at her then smiled as he took the file from Jack. "That can be arranged but I am not so sure that is a good thing, but it is up to you." Katie Lee looked from one to the other, seeing they were afraid thinking she could not do it. "Mr. Moorehead, you go to the courthouse a lot, right?" Nodding his head yes, he was not sure where this was going. "Well then I would think that you would have advantage to borrowing a room there, wouldn't you?" Her uncle began to see where his niece was going. "I am trying to beat her at her own game and make her realize she is not going to win and if she doesn't go away and leave me alone she will wish she had. If I met with her inside the courthouse and let her know she is not going to get a dime, I can also tell here I am ready to walk right into a judge's office and have her arrested for harassing me. She is on a restraining order, correct?" Mr. Moorehead was impressed with this young lady. Well, if it were me, I think I would think twice, but then we are dealing with someone that doesn't take no for an answer very well but it is up to you, I can set something like that up."

Jack's mind was ahead of them both, he knew that if this was played correctly, Mina might even end up arrested. "What about getting the lieutenant that she made such as ass out of in the room with the two of you to enforce the restraining order if needed. I think, under the circumstances he would be more than happy to assist." Mr. Moorehead was tapping his fingers on the coffee table as he thought of all suggestions. "We ca do that, but we have to be careful. If something should happen inside the courthouse using one of the rooms for that purpose could create some problems for us. It is deceitful, my butt could be on the line and they will ask me why my office was not used for the first meeting." Katie Lee knew it could probably be done but she also realized he was an attorney and did have to be professional. Looking Katie Lee in the eye he was studying her. "I want to talk to you about Dr. Badea, when is your appointment." Loie got the discharge papers out of her purse and handed them to him, giving the answer as she handed everything to him "Tomorrow at 1: 45 pm." Mr. Moorehead was insistent that she go to the appointment, if it went bad then he would reconsider her request but give the doctor a try. He would meet with Mina and tell her Katie Lee had no intentions of giving her a dime. If she proceeded in coming on strong, then they had the doctor to put a legal stop to it. He strongly disagreed with Katie Lee meeting with her mother. Loie shot a not-so-pleased look at her husband knowing he would rather have the conflict just to put Mina in her place but nothing was going to be solved by that, only more agony. Katie Lee finally agreed with disappointment and excused herself as she went back in the kitchen to make another cup of cocoa. She wanted so bad for her mother to hear from her there was no way she would let her have one thing from Peter. She had cost her many years of being away from Peter and living in foster care, Peter did not have to leave her a dime but he did; she owed him that much. In fact, she owned him much more. Realizing Mr. Moorehead was probably correct if something did go wrong, it may make matters worse and she didn't want to end up back in the hospital.

Taking her drink back into the living room they were just making small talk, but not about her; she was glad they had waited for her before "Okay I agree, you can meet with her and I will go see the doctor. You have to promise to tell her it was my decision and not anyone else. He agreed, in fact he told her he would be happy to tell her she wanted to come but as her legal representative, he advised her against it." Katie Lee bid the attorney a good night, she hugged her aunt and uncle heading for bed. It did not take her long to drift off into a deep sleep, she did not want to think of anything that night that would remind her of her mother.

She placed her mind back in years when Peter had taken them to a logging camp, when she was first introduced to those giant redwoods. She felt as if the room was warm and pleasant, as if she was not alone. It was a peaceful feeling almost serene. She knew it was silly but she didn't care. "Good night Peter and thank you. Good night, Mary." As she pulled the quilt over her shoulders closing her eyes, she was feeling safe and totally in control.

CHAPTER NINETEEN

The waiting room was unique in color as well as the décor. The dominating Victorian style was very becoming but a taste of European made her wonder where some of the artwork came from. The drawings were very different but pacific. She arrived a little early to make sure she found the place okay, she wanted to come by herself. Her aunt and uncle had been through enough and she knew they needed a break, especially some time for themselves. They had both worked hard, she needed to get a grip on her own life and stop hiding behind them. As she looked around the waiting room, no one seemed to be out of the ordinary; they all looked just like her. No one was acting any different from normal people. She was so caught up in her own thoughts she didn't hear her own name called the first time. As the receptionist came out further into the waiting room and called her name the second time, she was embarrassed. "I'm sorry, guess I was day dreaming." Escorting her down the hall she noticed many employees, it was a lot larger than what one would think. There were probably more than one doctor as they walked down a very long hall to another waiting room. "Just have a seat here and Dr. Badea's nurse will be right with you." That was strange, well she was here and she had promised, so she might as well just put the thoughts on hold and go through the motions.

It didn't take long for a very thin Oriental girl to call her name, she had that small petite structure with long black hair and one of

Pacific Redwood Mystery: Do you believe in the little people yet?

those pearly smiles. Her coy personality made her likable at first sight. "Dr. Badea will be right in, may I get you something to drink?" She was offered something to drink, two waiting rooms, very classy. "No, thank you. I would have to go to the bathroom. I am already nervous, but thank you." There it was again, that pearly smile that made you feel as if she was your best friend. "Well, If you change your mind, I will be right out here, just let me know." They were all dressed alike, she didn't know who picked their uniforms but they were not cheap. Very colorful and professional looking, the pullover sports tops looked real good on everyone. She could actually smell a pleasant smell like a very faint candle scent. Maybe that was part of the treatment, whatever it was, it made the wait pleasant.

Finally the door opened, it was not what she expected, not at all. The woman was tall, she had to be close to her uncle height, but she was tall. Dressed in a plain black dress just even with her knees, her jewelry was eye-catching. Her necklace and bracelet matched as well as the earrings. She either made a lot of money or had money. Her printed shoes were not something she was used to seeing but the pattern was very attractive. Her hair was tinted, not out of control but slightly uncombed. She thought for a woman with such a beautiful office like this and attire, she could get a better hairdresser. Maybe she was between appointments. Her eyes were medium brown with soft eyebrows but heavy eye makeup, lots of deep colors. For most woman this would look pretty made-up but her features were different, maybe European because it looked really good on her. Her fingers were long but only one ring on her right hand, she did not wear a wedding band or set. Katie Lee thought maybe she was not married, why was she thinking this, it didn't matter. Getting irritated wit herself she twisted her brain back to what that doctor was saying like she was suppose to be doing. She did notice a photo of a young girl possibly her own age sitting on her desk, possibly a daughter, their features were the same. "Hello, my name is Dr. Badea and I have been asked to visit with you, do you like to be call Katie or Katie Lee?" She asked at least before calling her Katie which she hated. "Katie Lee, please."

Her hands began to sweat, she didn't know why, she had nothing to worry about and she didn't have to talk unless she wanted to. It was just a visit, that was all. It was not going to destroy her or lock her away somewhere.

Like Mr. Moorehead said, she would be good for them if they had to go to court. "You were discharged yesterday, tell me a little about yourself." That was not what she thought would happen, of course it was not like a cold or cramps. She had to remember what kind of a doctor this was. "What would you like to know? I am pretty simple really." Dr. Badea had already received all the records from her Internet search; she was well aware of what she ha gone through with her mother, Peter and her siblings. The foster care, the years to find some relatives. No, this was anything but simple. "Well, lets see, you had an anxiety attack. Do you want to start there?" She didn't but felt she would not be able to get out of that question, that was what led her here in the first place. "Well, my mother came to find me and we don't have a good relationship, it really upset me." Seeing from her body language, it was clear she was more than a little upset with the issue; it was fear and control. This girl was hiding her past and wanting to run into the future without closure. Dr. Badea knew that it never turned out good for anyone.

"Katie Lee, let's just cut through the chase here. You know why they sent you and I have to be honest with you. I agreed to see you as a favor but after I researched your past, I am glad I agreed. I honestly think you have either subdued part of your past and want to run forward without some closure, or you just refuse to talk about it because of the pain it brings you." Wow, Katie Lee thought, it didn't take her long to figure things out. "It looks like you already know everything and I really don't know what is expected of me." Dr. Badea was good at noticing body language and guessing better atmospheres, that was why she decorated with that in mind. She felt the office scene was too informal for her. She wished she had put her the garden area, she felt that would have helped a lot better. "Well, I think your anxiety attacks will continue until you let go, that is not a bad think, but since your mother has surfaced; I think maybe you need to bury some issues." that was an understatement Katie Lee thought. "And how am I suppose to do that, doctor? You have no idea what she has done to me and others for that matter." Dr. Badea saw a twitch in Katie Lee's face that made her see just how deep her scares were. "Mr. Moorehead has been able to keep your mother away from you so far." He had, but Katie Lee didn't think he really would be able to stop her. She began to tell the doctor what the conversation in their living room was after she was discharged, her request and his advice. She was very surprised in the information she gave this doctor but she seemed sincere while asking the right questions.

Dr. Badea was very careful to make sure Katie Lee was comfortable, she felt a lot of her abilities were being held back. There were some issues she needed to work through and she needed to learn how to cope with her mother rather than a negative codependent. "Katie Lee I would like to help you, how would you like to handle things if you had a choice?" If she had choice, she wished she would have had those choices when she was young. Her whole life had never been what she wanted or needed; decisions were always made for her. "I don't know, to be honest with you, I never had that opportunity. If I had, I wouldn't have the nightmares I do." That opened a whole new conversation for Dr. Badea and a good one. "You still have nightmares from your past or things pertaining to now?" This was the beginning to go in a direction that she had not wanted but again she felt at ease in her mind; there was something about this doctor that made her feel comfortable and secure. "Mostly the past and my mom always seems to surface ruining everything. She never seems to go away."

Dr. Badea watched as Katie Lee went into a little of her past and memories. Katie Lee made sure she didn't go into detail and the good doctor figured that was because she was afraid she couldn't handle her own fears. "Let's go back a bit if we can here, tell me about the first things you remember as a child and the last thing." Not knowing if she was going to get an answer on that one, she waited patiently to see how Katie Lee was going to react. It seemed to be more difficult than the young girl wanted to remember. "Would it make it easier on you if I asked you, were they good experiences or bad?" Now that was a question she could handle. "Bad." Dr. Badea didn't feel as if there was going to be any more input than that. It had taken almost forty-five minutes just to this point where they were. She didn't want to cut the young girl off but she had other patients. "This is still very difficult for you today, isn't it? Why did this doctor want to dig into her past? It was painful for her, especially Peter and Mary; that made it hard. She could push the rest in the back of her mind but not those two, losing them was unfair and too much to accept." "I don't miss my mom or sister, we weren't that close anyway but I miss my dad and other sister. Well, he wasn't really my dad and Mary was his daughter. Not, really my sister either but I still make pretend they were, we made a promise to believe we were."

Making a few notes Dr. Badea didn't think a long-term was going to work with this girl, she would run if things got out of control or she could break the anger she had for Peter and Mary. She express that to Katie Lee as she voiced seriously, "You need closure and I don't think you have ever had it." Katie Lee got very upset with Dr. Badea that she even suggested it. "I know you mean well Dr. Badea but I don't think you really care about my feelings or you wouldn't make such a cold remark about the people that mean the world to me." That remark took the doctor by surprise, she had no idea what was going through this girls mind. "Katie Lee, if I hurt your feelings, I surely did not mean to. What makes you feel as I don't even care? Because I really do!" Katie Lee decided she did not want to be there anymore, and she stood up. Dr. Badea felt she might be losing her and was not sure how to correct it. "Was it something you think I said, because it was not intended, please tell me straight out." Katie Lee really didn't want to have anything else to do with her, but she would be kind enough to let her know that it was terrible when you love someone and those lives were over before they even got a chance to live. "Well, you think that just by talking about my sister and remembering it will bring closure, what about the murderer running around out there free and not caring what a precious life was taken? My dad, it broke his heart, it killed him. Mina killed him, Mary's murder killed him. They took him away from me. They took her away from me." Before Dr. Badea could make out the realization of Katie Lee's anger, she knew to just listen rather than advice now was best.

With her hand on the door to leave, Dr. Badea came around her desk. "Do you mean to tell me her case was ever solved? Do you know who killed her, Katie Lee?" She was not going to wait to answer her questions; they were gone, both of them, gone, taken away before they should have been. She watched Peter die slowly with Mina's help, she watched him fade into death with believing he had nothing to live for. She couldn't get down the hall fast enough and out the front door. It was as if she needed fresh air, she couldn't breath. The Oriental nurse came after her asking if she was okay, did she need water or did she want to go back to the hospital. "No." She pulled away from her. "Go tell your boss no and she cannot make me." Katie Lee puller herself farther away from her towards a small mall across the street. She wanted to call her aunt, she didn't want to even be near this place. If this doctor thought she was doing her a favor, she wasn't. She was cold heated, daring to ask her to close her thoughts on the ones she loved so dearly. Finding a phone outside a small store, she dialed her aunt. "Just come get me, okay. Can you come now?" Without asking any questions and knowing something went wrong, her aunt panicked inside. "I am on my way, wait right these, dear."

All through dinner she didn't talk, she didn't say anything about the visit and just wanted that day to be over, but when the phone rang she knew when she heard her uncle say Mr. Moorehead's name that it was going to be a late night. He was on his way over to talk to Katie Lee. He really didn't have to tell her anything, she knew her mother probably laughed in his face. She went to her room and wrote in her journal until her aunt asked her to come in the living room, Mr. Moorehead was there. Following her aunt downstairs, she felt sad and empty. "Didn't go too well today, I am sorry. Anything I can do to help?" He was always nice and seemed to ask abut her first, maybe he was a good lawyer trying to fix things. "No, it is okay, just really don't want to talk abut it. Did you talk to my mother?" She didn't have to guess, his facial expression told her what she needed to know.

"Well, she says that before Peter died he told her about the policy and it was written the way it was because he really wanted her to be as secure as his stepdaughter. She is seeking a lawyer to ask for full beneficially or at least half of the full amount." "What, can she do that Mr. Moorehead?" Jack was getting madder as information continued to surface. "She can hire all the people she wants and she can delay everything, but in the end I really don't think with all the evidence we have that she will win but it could take time. Do you want to go through it young lady? She is a bear, I will tell you that." A bear, that was a funny way to describe her, more like snake. "I don't care, I really don't. Well I do but right now I can't think straight. Dr. Badea really upset me today." Her aunt and uncle had not had the privilege of knowing what happened on her appointment; they were anxious to find out. "What happened that upset you so or what went wrong? Can you tell me that much?" She really didn't want to answer him in front of her aunt or uncle but he probably would find out from the doctor anyway and tell them. "She was so cold when it came to Mary and Peter for that matter. It was as if she was saying I needed to forget them and what happened, I needed closure. I don't want to forget Mary or Peter." Mr. Moorehead could understand how she felt. "Katie Lee did Dr. Badea know how Mary lost her life? Does she know the full story? Is it possible she doesn't know? Closure does not mean to forget, it means to cope with what happened and you being able to move on."

Katie Lee sit there listening to his words, maybe he was right but what about her not knowing? She knew the doctor knew, she told her she researched and had all the information. "Of course, she knows. She told me she researched and had everything." Mr. Moorehead could tell she was very angry, her aunt and uncle just sat there not wanting to say the wrong thing. With little prompting, she decided to return the next morning to Dr. Badea's office and try again; she felt bad she had misjudged the comment. As she listened to the attorney, she knew the next few days were going to be worse before they got better. Feeling defeat, she asked to be excused, she was so mentally tired. Her aunt was unsure but Mr. Moorehead suggested they could talk again later, get some rest and try to let the doctor help her. Slowly walking up the stairs she didn't even notice they watched, not knowing how to comfort her.

She sat on her bed trying to write in her journal but words wouldn't come. She was all talked out and her mind just wouldn't work anymore. She has no idea what or where her life was going to unfold. She has no idea what conversed between her aunt and uncle the rest of the evening; she was not even sure if what Peter had done was worth the effort. Where had her confidence gone? Maybe she wasn't ready to take her mother on. It seemed that even in death, Mina controlled Peter's soul. How sad and disappointed he must be with the outcome of such a good gesture. Taking a deep breath, she wished she could just see him one more time, tell him thank-you and see his smile. Closing her journal, she was upset with herself, she lost her self-confidence.

The next morning she learned Mr. Moorehead would be picking her up and taking her to her appointment with the doctor. Her aunt explained Mr. Moorehead got a call before he left their home but did not discuss it with them. That, to her meant Mina was somewhere close and ready to leap into action again in spite of the order. She dressed slowly, feeling even more defeated than the night before. When she came downstairs, Mr. Moorehead was waiting for her by the front door, his good humor didn't faze her but she managed a fake smile as she passed him going out their front door. He nodded toward her aunt, signaling that it was okay. Walking to catch up with her to open her side of the car door. Keeping her head down, she didn't have a thought in her mind except an emptiness that was far too familiar to her. She had not felt like this since she was very young. It was a scary feeling, one she learned to live with. The ride was silent mostly at her lack of conversation. Mr. Moorehead gave her the respect, he felt she needed the silence. His observation was appreciated and she knew he didn't take it personally.

Sitting again in the waiting room was something Katie Lee didn't believe she would be doing but it was something she felt she needed to do and apologizing was not easy for her but when she was wrong she was wrong. She wondered how the doctor was going to react with Mr. Moorehead being with her. Well, whatever the outcome, she was at least going to admit her emotions got the better of her on the last visit and apologize but only for her misjudging her, not for anything else. She had to wait a lot longer than the first time and it must have been an off day, the patients today were a lot different than on her first visit. Some talked to themselves while others twitched and seemed agitated with imaginary friends. There was one particular woman in the corner that seemed in a state of confusion or deeply depressed. She never looked up just sat there and rolled her thumbs over and over. Once in awhile she would clear her throat and push her hair back. Katie Lee noticed that as she did her hands were shaking beyond control. She felt out of place and wondered what was taking so long. The waiting room door opened with a huge fore as she noticed a make figure coming through like he was in a race or something. Behind him were two officers trying to slow him down. He was cuffed and shackled; she couldn't believe he could even walk that fast. They sat him as far away from everyone else as possible, even asking one patient to move to the other side of the room. He started banging his head against the wall and spitting obscenities at the officers, they completely ignored him, then just as quickly as he arrived they escorted him to the back. Katie Lee had a feeling this was going to be a very long afternoon.

She was glad she was sitting in the waiting room when she heard all the commotion coming from the back. Then two officers other offices arrived going straight to the little window but no one opened it for them, Katie Lee only heard a buzzer go off and the door opened as the officer's went straight to the back. She had never been in an office where a buzzer was needed to enter the back where the staff and doctor's were, but after today she realized it was probably a good thing. Some of the patient's were rescheduled and when it came to Katie Lee's time for the option, they did not offer it to her. They asked her to please be a little more patient, Dr. Badea would see her shortly. Now she knew she was in for a bad visit, the doctor could not wait to let her know she did not appreciate the rude exit yesterday. She tried reading several magazines, nope it was hot going to work, she could not concentrate. She walked around a little, she was amazed at how Mr. Moorehead buried himself in paperwork. He patiently grinned at her from time to time. They were the only two in the waiting area since they cleared it out due to whatever the commotion was about. She decided to go outside and walk around the nice atrium. She told the girl behind the glass she would be outside waling around but was asked not to leave the waiting room. No way she thought, they cannot tell me whether I can walk around or not. She went to the glass and gently tapped the second time. "I really need to walk, I will be just right outside."

Turning from the window, she picked up her purse and headed for the door, they must have really thought she was going to leave. "Katie Lee, won't you come on back." Laughing to herself, she wished she would have thought about that earlier, maybe she wouldn't have waited so long. It was close to noon and she had been there since 10:45am. Mr. Moorehead closed his briefcase, walked close behind her and taking pride in her insistence, he was also tired of the wait. They were taken straight to Dr. Badea's office. Mr. Moorehead was in a pleasant but firm humor, which was fine with her. It was starting to rain, that was a good thing. She always felt that when it rained, it was like cleaning, starting fresh. She didn't feel like sitting, she moved to the window watching the little birds flop around and flutter their little wings. They seemed to be enjoying the fresh rain. She didn't hear the door open, she was too deep in thought. It was not until the doctor spoke to Mr. Moorehead did she turn, watching the doctor sat down at her desk. "Do you two know the rain s good for therapy? Makes some people calm and refine." Katie Lee was surprised with her information, but glad to hear she felt that way. "I was enjoying the little birds, guess they are enjoying the soft rain." They only smiled at each other and Katie Lee decided it was better if she sat down for a moment to get her thoughts before speaking her mind. She was not sure where to start when the doctor opened her file and began to write. "I am sure you are a little ticked off at me. I guess I misunderstood you yesterday. I thought you wanted me to forget Peter and Mary., I cannot do that." Before she could finish, the good doctor put her pen down and looked across at the young girl. Mr. Moorehead took that as a cue to jump in. "I am here today to represent this girl. I think you can help her even though she thinks otherwise. I just need to make sure we are all on the same page and see if we can move past this miscommunication." You could tell Katie Lee was grateful for his word but she was till a little uncomfortable, that would soon change. "Mr. Moorehead, I commend you for your interest in her. She will need your emotional support and legal advice. My job will hopefully be to help her. Your job will be to protect her." Her words were gentle and sincere. Mr. Moorehead looked at Katie Lee with satisfaction to her answers. He looked at his watch and said he would be back in about forty-five minutes. 'Do you feel comfortable to continue?" Katie Lee smiled, "Yes sir, thank you." Extending his had toward the doctor he winked at Katie Lee as he left.

"Well, now that is out of the way, let's get started okay?" Her smile was warm and caring. Katie Lee began to relax, she needed to stop jumping to conclusions when it came to people trying to help her. "I feel you have some issued that are going to continue to control you if we don't help you learn how to handle yourself." Learn how to handle herself, she was glad she used the word we. The doctor came from around her desk sitting in the chair beside the young girl. "I have been giving your case a lot of thought this weekend and learned a lot from yesterday's session. Let's start a new slate today and see how we can move forward." "What do you mean I need to learn to handle myself? I wish I could." The doctor took a pad and drew Katie Lee a picture to explain where and why her thoughts and nightmares were happening. It seemed to interest her, but she could tell the girl was still confused. "I feel there are deep, very deep feelings, you have pushed so far back in your mind. That may be the reason for your nightmares.

Pacific Redwood Mystery: Do you believe in the little people yet?

I know you don't like to talk about things but I think I can help you. You have to be willing." There was a long pause and then the doctor placed her hand over Katie Lee's. "I think it might bring you the peace your Peter wants you to have and maybe you can let him and your sister rest. I understand the murder is still unsolved." The doctor was correct, she could not find an answer. There was none, it still was painful even after all these years when she thought of Peter and Mary.

It was like yesterday and it all flashed in front of her eyes, especially the brutal murder. "I can't talk about it, I have tried. It doesn't work and then I think of my mother and it makes it worse." They sat in silence for a few moments when the doctor stood and leaned over her desk to retrieve her file placing it on her lap. She handed Katie Lee some pictures she had downloaded, waiting to see the young girls reaction. As Katie Lee stared at the pictures she realized the hate and disgust she felt, the anger and fear that it aroused within her. She felt she was going to faint or have a heart attack. Dr Badea told her to place her head down in her lap as she buzzed her assistant for some water. It has been a long time since she had seen those pictures, a long time since she had to remember the horror of it all. The doctor could tell this was the heart of her misery, her nightmares. She wanted to help this girl, especially get her to a stage where she could deal with her mother. "Katie Lee, there is a way to deal with this. It is harmless and painless, but I need your cooperation. We can use hypnosis and I think under the circumstances, it would be a benefit for you." Katie Lee was not sure what she thought about it and it scared her. Dr. Badea could see the concern in her face and her body language, so she asked her to go with her assistant and view a video that might help her. "Can I see the pictures you didn't show me?" This girl was very observant. "I don't think you are ready for that. We'll talk about that later." She felt she better take those pictures and put them under lock and key, they were crime-scene photos and Katie Lee did not need to view them.

Dr. Badea decided against better odds to go ahead and call her aunt and uncle to see if they would consider meeting with her along with Katie Lee, maybe therapy would be good for them all. She wanted them to know before she arrived home the options she gave the girl. It would be something for them to think about and move forward. She found her aunt to be extremely protective, even with her suggestions of her joining her niece in the therapy, her husband she could not speak for, bu she would ask. This case was a challenge to her profession and something she needed to do, she needed to find a way to help this family before there was another "after the fact" issue. She joined her assistant in the viewing room and found Katie Lee leaning forward on her knees, most intrigues with the video. Whispering to her assistant, she was anxious to know how it was going. "She has not said a word since it started, she sat for a while, then after about seven minutes into the video, she leaned forward and has been glued to it." Dr. Badea sat very quietly not wanting to disturb the girl or make her feel uncomfortable and leave. She motioned for her assistant to join her quietly.

The video was about forty-five minutes long with several different cases and real stories. When it finished, Katie Lee just seemed to be idle in her seat, neither the doctor or her assistant disturbed her. They just sat in silence, waiting for her to decide what to do. Katie Lee turned and saw the doctor. "What are the chances that his can be negative to you after it all comes out." She was pleased she had paid attention. "Well, it can go many different way. In some cases as what you saw, they come out okay and move on. In other cases, it takes some sessions to adjust and mend." Katie Lee was not sure what she thought, she was scared but she was also tired of the nightmares and fear of her mother always popping up. She didn't really want to run away, she didn't want to leave her aunt and uncle but she was really scared. "Can I talk to my aunt and uncle? How much is it? Feeling for the first time, Dr. Badea thought there was a chance this vibrant young girl could move forward in a small way.

"You insurance covers it, it goes under your co-pay." Both the doctor and Katie Lee looked at the assistant, Dr. Badea knew this girl better know what she was talking about, Katie Lee didn't like surprised nor be tricked. "Are you sure?" The assistant told her they would call

Pacific Redwood Mystery: Do you believe in the little people yet?

the insurance in the morning and make sure about it if that would make her feel more comfortable. The doctor assured her it was good, it would give her a chance to talk it over at home. Nodding her head, she hesitated to stay put and decided she didn't want to ask any more questions, she needed to go home and see what she felt after really digesting this video. Neither the doctor nor her assistance followed her, they both knew it was best to stay put and let Katie Lee exit on her own. Dr. Badea looked at her assistant and made a cross with her index and middle finger. Her assistant just smiled, "I hope so doctor, I like her but I think she had some deep issues." The doctor only nodded while waking back to her office.

All the way home, Katie Lee thought about the people on the video, there were several different cases. She was impressed most by the gentleman whose wife was so deceitful and abusive to him and her children. He had an issue with the children becoming abusive because of his anger and hatred that he couldn't let go. Then there was the young boy who buried both his parents from an accident on his graduation night. How his nightmares triggered his drinking problems and then into drugs. She had not done any of that, which she was thankful, but she wondered when she got on her own, what would happen. To cope with her biggest fear and never say anything to anyone, her fear of being alone. She didn't have anyone but her aunt and uncle, all the other relatives distanced themselves from her from the very beginning due to Mina. She had no one to run back to and that was thanks to Mina. So she had no one except her aunt, uncle, Peter, Mary and the nightmares. What would the doctor do if she admitted to her that she still pretended Peter and Mary were still alive? She even pretended she visit them and the fun they had. She used the experience of the woods at the logging camp as an example. Then she would pretend she was with Peter taking care of him in his older years. Mary would come to visit with her children and the would go off and have a wonderful picnic near the redwoods and the ocean. It was wonderful until she woke up or felt defeat; her mind was cracking, she had to stop her stories to herself. It was only make believe. She even caught herself sometimes wishing Nancy and her mother was Mary and her daughter, that Peter was just off on a job. How long could she keep pretending before it created a serious problem for her? The video said it could cause long-term illness, unless it was addressed. That scared her more, maybe she would go crazy and end up in a mental hospital never to live a life at all. It that what happened to Peter's first wife? Oh Lord, she thought, how horrible.

This was depressing and she was scaring herself, she needed to get home. Mr. Moorehead was extremely patient and kind, very caring to her. She thanked him for being there to make sure it went well. After sharing the doctor's request, he had her agree, what could it hurt? She needed to be sure and discuss everything with her aunt and uncle, he would call later. They turned the corner toward her street and she was happy to be home. Was she ready? Was she able to face her fears and see what the outcome would be? Maybe Mr. Moorehead was correct, if she did maybe she could give her all the money, that would make her go away. How could a thought like that go through her mind? Peter didn't have to leave her that for her mother to have the final glory. The money was such a surprise and it would help her so much, she planed a good life and pay her aunt and uncle back for the unselfish life they gave her. What would Peter think if he knew she was thinking about letting Mina have it all? It was something she didn't want to imagine.

"Hello, I'm home." placing her belongings on the small table in the entrance way she headed straight for the dinning room. "Hi, Mr. Moorehead will call later. What's up." Her aunt had a pen in her hand and there were papers on the table that Katie Lee was far too familiar with. "Is that Peter's will and the insurance policy?" Her aunt shook her head yes looking at Katie Lee with sincerity. "Yes, it is and Mr. Moorehead's secretary found out that Mina cannot be awarded any monies unless you agree to do so, you are close enough to legal age; she cannot touch it, if needed they will use a stall method for a month. Then you will be legal age which solves the underage problem." Her aunt was restless and Katie Lee knew something else was bothering

Pacific Redwood Mystery: Do you believe in the little people yet?

her. She was trying to avoid whatever it was. "Okay, what is it you are not telling me?" "Well dear, your uncle went to answer the door right after he came home, there is a certified letter for you. It if from your mother." As her aunt handed it to her, she went cold. "Actually honey, we got one from her." That got Katie Lee's attention more than the one she was holding. "What does she want?" Frowning her aunt had to remind her, "I think we all know what she wants Katie Lee and I am sure you agree with me and your uncle. She is not going to get a dime."

As she held her letter, she saw the hurt look on her aunt's face. "What did she say? I really want to know." There was no getting out of this, she had to tell her. She suggested a trip and some traveling to get reacquainted and then decisions could be made later, etc. etc. "It is just repetitious, dear." She could tell she was very irritated by Mina's attempt, she didn't fool her. Katie Lee kept thinking abut the video and how brave some were and how many were pushed into further problems. Then she felt that feeling again that she felt in the car. It was almost a pain of loosing her breath and someone holding her. Jacob's words echoed in her mind, he had told her he thought Peter was trying to tell her he didn't leave her this for her mother to get. If she gave it to her, Peter might as well turn over in his grave. Throwing the letter on the bar, she asked her aunt. "Do I have to read her letter?" "No, you don't. It is not a bill. It is a letter from you mother. She is just making sure you get it, but if you choose not to read it, it is entirely up to you." Katie Lee started to tear the envelope with the letter inside when her aunt stopped her. "Wait, I think that is not a good decision. Let's not tear it up in case she tried to play the court card. We can prove you got it but at your own decision chose not to read it."

"Now tell me what you think what Dr. Badea wants to do. Do you think you can do it, Ms. Under Control." She knew that with her aunt's way of telling her she was not only proud of her but she was making wise decisions and standing up against Mina. They talked abut all the negative and positive results, but they all left the decision to her. She wanted to sleep on it and her aunt knew that was the way she made decisions. She did not know in her heart if it was the best for her niece. She too was afraid but it was in God's hands, she had to believe in her niece and Mr. Moorehead seemed to have things going in a positive direction.

CHAPTER TWENTY

Does the rain really mean clean, refresh, a new start? What would Mary say? She would be running through those redwoods looking for the little people and playing near the ocean. Katie Lee could almost see her, she could see her thick hair as she ran on the beach, she could smell her tanning lotion as they made castles in the sand. She could even see herself and Peter looking far up, trying to figure out how high those giants went. She believed in the little people, they had to be real and that was the only way she could cope with Mary's death. Katie Lee believed she was taking care of them now all the time. Helping to protect those giants to keep growing bigger and higher.

    She lingered in her room longer than usual but she wanted to feel that closeness she felt right now from both of them. She felt if she could close her eyes and open them again, they might be standing there. Then she was afraid to close her eyes and open in case it would happen. She knew breakfast was stewing downstairs, she could smell her aunt's java all the way to her room. She hoped she was making fresh toast, her favorite and her uncle's too; he had taken the day off. Katie Lee knew he was sure she had made the right decision for hypnosis. Mr. Moorehead had been the one to call Dr. Badea's office to make the arrangements right away. He didn't want to delay for many reasons and Katie Lee knew he wanted to make sure it was done quickly for her benefits. Was she up for this? Yes, she was she was up for it because she believed Peter and Mary were somewhere trying to help her. She felt so good inside to have the assurance that Peter really love her like a daughter. She left that with her strength, she could do anything just like when he was alive. She had to keep this confidence, she couldn't get weak again.

As Katie Lee bounced downstairs she was struck by something disturbing. The TV was on, the smell of coffee was in the air, but there was no sound anywhere and the house seemed empty. As she called out before entering the kitchen she felt a twinge in her gut, as if when she knew something was wrong, It was as if she felt she shouldn't go beyond the door. What was wrong with her? This was her home and she was letting things get to her, she needed to get a grip. As she placed her hand on the door into the kitchen she heard a voice that put her almost into a trance. "What do you mean she didn't read it? And don't tell me I am not suppose to be here. Go ahead call the cops, I want to see that little brat now Loie, right now!" That voice, how did she get in there, where was her uncle? Katie Lee did not know what to do, she was terrified. There she was again right back in their lives when she thought she had it all decided. "Mina, you need to leave my home now, Jack will be right back. He will call the police. Mina please, you can go to jail." Hearing her mother laugh made Katie Lee sick to her stomach. Her uncle was not there, he must have went to the corner store.

She slowly moved away from door walking backwards towards the phone. She was scared but not too scared to call 911 herself to get Mina out of there. Maybe now she would go to jail and never come out. She carefully pick up the receiver and dialed 911. She could hear Mina's voice becoming louder as the operator came on the line. She was whispering the best she could. She gave the case number asking the operator to get help quickly then she hung up. She was making her way back towards the kitchen door when Mina came barreling through with Loie right behind her. "Well, are you eavesdropping Katie Lee, not brave enough to face me, your own mother? I want to talk to you right now, and I don't need my sister interfering. Do you

Pacific Redwood Mystery: Do you believe in the little people yet?

mind Loie, I want to talk to Katie Lee alone." Mina started to reach for her daughter arm as Katie Lee pulled away.

That's irritated her mother more, Mina knew she did not have much time before Jack returned and she needed to make her point getting her daughter's signature even if it was out of fear. "I don't have anything to say to you and my aunt does not have to leave the room. You need to leave Mina." Rage that Katie Lee had long pushed to the back of her mind instilled on Mina's face. Seeing that look after so many years, Katie Lee's knees began to wobble and her hands started to shake. "What do you mean calling me Mina, I am your mother and you will respect me? Who do you think you are?" Katie Lee prayed she would hear the police coming. "Maybe so but you don't deserve respect, just leave; I have already called 911." She could tell Mina could hardly compose herself. "Well fine, if that is the way you feel, good riddance. But I need you to sign this paper and I will be out of your life." She shoved some papers in Katie Lee's face with a pen. "What is it?" Loie started to come forward to assist her niece in seeing what her mother was shoving in her face. "Loie, I told you to say out of it. Katie Lee just sign the stupid papers and I will be on my way, out of your life forever." She started to sign when Loie standing behind her sister couldn't stay quiet. "Katie Lee what are you signing? Did you even look?"

Mina was losing patience, she knew if she kept the pressure up her daughter would sign just to get rid of her. Loie's pleading with her nice to read before signing and Mina's interruptions was giving Katie Lee a headache. As she put the pen on the line to sign to shut Mina up he glanced to the top and there it was, her mind snapped. Blinking here eyes to make sure she was reading correctly, "Transfer Funds Agreement," Katie Lee back away dropping the pen she was holding as her heart sunk. It was almost a whisper as Katie Lee slowly looked towards Mina. "Is this part of Peter's money you are transferring?" Smiling and easing into a more relaxed position Mina reached down picking up the pen handing it back to her daughter. Mina's voice became soft and compassionate as she came closer to her daughter "Yes dear you know I deserve it. You of course get the bulk of it, but that's okay. I deserve something from him, so sign it and let me leave Katie Lee." Loie had her hand over her mouth as Katie Lee looked from the paper towards to her aunt. She was shaking her head no to her niece as she prayed with everything breath had hoping any minute her husband would walk through the door. Mina was smiling so gently as she touched Katie Lee's arm softy. The touch of Mina put her in a tail spin, she turned back towards her mother standing firm "What do you mean you deserve it? He only said if I was with you but I'm not, he didn't want you to have anything. No, I won't sign it, get out of here." Loie was watching as Katie Lee swung her hand in the air towards her mother to leave. Mina stayed under control, she acted so soft as she reached again for her daughter. "Katie Lee, stop being silly now, Peter was not even your father. If it was not for me, he would not have even been in your life." Katie Lee felt strength coming from everywhere within her. "He was my father, he proved it by what he did for me and you are not going to ruin it. I am not giving you anything, get out of here now. You may be my mother but you don't deserve respect." Before Katie Lee could say another word, Mina's hand came quickly across her cheek. Stunned, Loie grabbed Mina's hand as she was about to slap her daughter again. "Mina, that is enough, get out of my home."

Readjusting her purse on her shoulder Mina's stare never left Katie Lee. As Mina went to pass, she pulled her purse off her shoulder swinging with force towards Katie Lee. Loie ducked as she saw the candle holder fly off the table, she yelled for her niece to be careful as Mina turned her vengeance on her sister, Mina grabbed Loie by the hair flinging her own sister to the floor. Katie Lee saw her aunt hit the floor with a cry of pain, Mina was ready to swing one of the candle holders down upon Loie when Katie Lee came forward lunging to stop Mina from hurting her aunt more, she caught Mina completely off guard.

Pacific Redwood Mystery: Do you believe in the little people yet?

As they tumbled to the floor, Loie could hear her niece screaming, "You don't touch my aunt, you witch. You should have left you should have ran, I am going to make you feel every pain you created here today." Loie was struggling to keep out of the way, her eyes were stuck to the commotion going on before her. Mina was plunging and trying to overpower Katie Lee as the young girl kept fighting to keep Mina's hands off her throat. She was younger and stronger fear came whirling back into Katie Lee's mind as Mina continued to chock her. Her aunt in a panic tried to pull Mina off her niece as Mina turned her legs in Loie's direction to kick her further from them. That gave Katie Lee just enough to get her knees under her mother to throw her mother off.

She was like a raging bull struggling to come right back at her daughter, Katie Lee saw one of the candle holders stretching her hand as far as she could to grab it. When she finally had it in her hands, she brought her hand towards Mina's head when she heard her aunt scream. "No, Katie Lee, don't, Jesus please don't." Those words echoed through her mind as she looked Mina in the face, her mother was smiling and enjoying the challenge. Katie Lee worked the candle holder under Mina's forcing her head backwards. She thought she was going to break her mother's neck before Mina gave up. It was just like with Peter, she enjoyed the abuse. Watching her mother roll over onto the floor Katie Lee couldn't believe her ears. "Well, that was a good fight Katie Lee. I am proud of you. Now sign the damn paper and let me leave, or your aunt and uncle will pay."

Those words were more like a thunderstorm inside her head. She thought of Peter and Mary, as she came off the floor she grabbed her mother by the front of her blouse and started pulling her towards the front door. Mina was laughing as she grabbed at Katie Lee's long hair and pulled backwards as Katie Lee was pinned against the wall when Mina struck her in the middle of the stomach knocking Katie Lee's breath out of her. She doubled over trying to breath as Mina leaned against the wall to catch her own breath. Hearing the door bell ring, Loie screams from the hall over and over as the door came open with a force that startled Mina. Seeing Katie Lee position and Loie yelling from the floor to please help them, make her sister leave. The officer came forward as Mina tried to run but taking the time to retrieve the paper. The officer ended up wrestled Mina to the floor. She was screaming that Katie Lee had attacked her and she was trying to get out of the house away from them. The officer had to use force to get her outside. Mina fought the entire way, he placed her in the back of his patrol car as she continued yelling her threatening abuse. Another officer arrived on the scene and Nancy and her mother came running. The other officer noticed a car parked down the block with a gentleman just sitting. He motioned for his partner to block him off if he tried to drive off. Katie Lee was still trying to get her breath, the blow had been hard. Loie was hysterical and wanted everyone to leave, just leave. Nancy and her mother were helpless and couldn't do anything except to stay outside. The officer was keeping everyone away. Loie was so hysterical she couldn't get herself off the floor. Her head hurt, she had a huge bruise on her face just above her lip, her hair was a mess and where her sister kicked her it looked like her shoulder was injured.

The officer asked if they wanted to press further charges besides Mina violating her order to stay away from their residence. Loie couldn't answer but Katie Lee breathlessly yelled, "Yes, Mrs. Hanson do you still have Mr. Mooreheads number? Can you please call him?" They could hear Mina hitting the rear window of the patrol car and then they saw the man exit the car down the street and walk toward them One of the officers met him halfway and insisted he stay right where he was. He tried twice to pass the officer and finally realized he was not getting anywhere and left. The officer came back with his information, but no one knew who he was. He said he was Mina's husband and Katie Lee had called her mother to come over so why was she being arrested. As Katie Lee looked at the officer, she started to throw up rushing towards the bathroom. They could hear Loie inside asking for Mrs. Hanson, so she was let in to be with Katie Lee's aunt, but Nancy had to stay on the lawn for now. Mrs. Hanson used

Pacific Redwood Mystery: Do you believe in the little people yet?

Loie's phone to make the call Katie Lee wanted her to. It took only five minutes for Mrs. Hanson to return to the front door telling both officer one of them was needed on the phone, looking at each other the first one on the scene went inside and took the call. All you could hear was, "Yes sir, absolutely sir, right now." As he turned Loie asked him to please help her off the floor before her husband returned. He was hesitant as Katie Lee came around the corner from the bath room coming to her aunt immediately rising her up into a comfortable chair. Turing to the officer all three were informed Mina was finally in serious trouble. "Is she going to stay in jail or will she get out? You all need to keep her, she is a horrible woman. Look at this girl and her aunt." The officer stood firm and assuring Mrs. Hansen she was going to jail where she would be booked.

The officer informed them the gentleman down the street was given the stern information if he too returned he would go to jail as well. They could not take him in because he had not done anything, he was not on their property. Katie Lee was beside herself and she knew her mother would want to press charges on her as well. She was thankful that Mina was in the police car but she was livid that she had attached her aunt. She knew when Mina got out, this was not the end. She was yelling her lungs out at what she was going to do, she even told her what she did to her when she was nine would be nothing to what she would do when she got her hands on her this next time. Loie was pacing anxious rocking wringing her hands and watching every car throw the front door go by hoping it was her husband. After all the reports were taken and additional information to the officers were given they left assuring them not to worry. They would put a watch on the house but Mina was going to jail and have to appear before a judge before she could even get bail if she even got it. If she got out Katie Lee was not sure she believed them, she didn't have much luck when it came to her mother.

It was almost an hour before Jack came back with flowers in hand for his wife and a box of gummy bears for Katie Lee, her favorite candy. It was the only candy she really liked enjoyed. No one liked them because they were gummy and cinnamon, a little too hot for her aunt and uncle but she loved them. When he entered the house, they were still sweeping and picking things up. Katie Lee didn't realize there was more than the candle holders that went flying. Loie had not bothered to comb her hair and Katie Lee still looked like the battle she had been in. Jack took one look around and saw Mr. Moorehead coming up the driveway behind him talking very forceful to someone on the phone. "What the hell is going on?" His wife just started to cry as Katie Lee started to fill her uncle in. He was so furious the flowered ended up all over the hall way that Mrs. Hansen had just sweep. "How did she get in, did you open the door to her?" His wife was shaking her head that she did not know, one minute she was pouring coffee, she turned and there she was. Katie Lee was upstairs. Katie Lee asked her uncle to stop yelling her aunt was hurt and scared enough. Mr. Moorehead just motioned for him to settle down some, he would be off the phone momentarily. Jack saw the bruise on his wife's face and her hair; he looked at Katie Lee and his hands tightened as his mouth turned almost blue from the pressure he was putting on his lips. Loie told him how Katie Lee had defended her but got hurt in the process, but Jack was so beside himself he didn't even hear her. The papers she had tried to retrieve were in Mr. Moorehead's hands and he was reading some of it to whoever he had on the phone. "Who is he talking to?" Neither knew, they just said those were the papers Mina had brought for Katie Lee to sign, when she wouldn't it became violent. Mr. Moorehead came directly to Loie and Katie Lee, he leaned forward to them both as he said "Got ya now Mina. You will serve time for forgery and assault." He motioned for them to pull up chairs by Loie and he would go over it all. Sitting quiet Jack pulled up a chair right beside his wife as he brought Katie Lee over to join them. Mr. Moorehead made small talk to thank Mrs. Hansen and asked her to please document everything she saw and heard, he was delighted to do so. Motioning for Nancy to come to her, she hugged her own daughter and patted her shoulder letting

Pacific Redwood Mystery: Do you believe in the little people yet?

her know all was ok. Mrs. Hansen kissed her neighbor on the forehead taking her daughter back across the lawn again home to pray and hope this may be the end of their nightmare.

Moorehead sat very quiet as Jack was still trying to compose himself, he asked Jack to walk around, get a drink, a glass of water, what ever it took so they could move forward fast in decision making, he wanted to make sure Mina didn't make parole or get out of jail before a hearing was scheduled. They could all tell that this was not the kind soft spoken Mr. Mooorehead, it was a firm, pissed off attorney ready for blood. Katie Lee was feeling pretty confident with his manner and she was ready, she was really ready to stop Mina once and for all. "I need some water or something to drink, I am going to get my aunt some water who else would like something so we can get to what Mr. Moorehead is wanting to talk about." Mr. Moorehead suggested she bring everyone something to settle nerves and just relax. As Katie Lee was in the kitchen putting filled water glasses on a serving tray, she heard the phone ring. She jumped then closed her eyes not wanting to answer. She immediately saw Mr. Moorehead come from the living room picking up the receiver asking directly who was calling and who did she want to talk to. Humm she thought, she had never seen this side of him but she was fine with it. You could see by the look on his face he was embarrassed. "Oh, so sorry. No we did not forget, we had family emergency I guess you could say. Can she reschedule?" Katie Lee realized it was the doctor's office "Oh, shoot, we were suppose to be at Dr. Badea's office thirty minutes ago," When Mr. Moorehead heard that he asked them to please hold on for one moment, he motioned for Jack to join him and they whispered for a moment then Mr. Moorehead got back on the phone. In Mr. Moorehead's professional swaying voice he let the girl know who he was and he asked to speak to Dr. Badea.. It was an emergency. They were not sure what he was doing, Katie Lee knew her uncle Jack still couldn't get control of his emotions. She knew he probably wanted to get in his car and go to the jail, he would be able to get in, but he was not sure if he trusted his own emotions.

Hanging up the phone Mr. Moorehead stated Dr. Badea stated it would be an excellent time for them all to meet with her. Loie did not want to go and neither did Katie Lee, Jack was smart enough to know what Mr. Moorehead was thinking, this would put Mina in jail for more than just one night. He showed Jack the papers and explained to them all that they the papers were something she must have had someone prepare for her and there was a nice legal issues to make sure Mina stayed in jail until he as Katie Lee's attorney could set a hearing which he was going to do on his time frame to make sure Mina stayed put in jail for awhile to think about she was not in control. The legal transfer forms to transfer the funds into the bank account she had just opened for that purpose taking funds from Katie Lee insurance settlement was without an amount. This was a huge problem, the amount not filled in told him Mina knew what she was doing and it was preplanned. Mina had left that blank to be filled out after Katie Lee signed. She was cleaver and Katie Lee almost signed just to get her out of the house. It was even notarized before Katie Lee's signature was acquired, how did that happen, wow not legal number two. Yes, Mr. Moorehead could really use this as evidence with the assault and disobeying the restraining order she had crossed the line. He was sure he could get her some time, Katie Lee didn't care, she just wanted her to go away.

Mr. Moorehead realized this was not the time to discuss too much, he wanted to get them to keep their appointment with Dr. Badea. With hesitation from Loie and her niece, Jack's insistence putting them all in the car and leaving immediately, Jack was no more than ever prepared to keep Mina in jail. The ride was quiet as Loie continued to cry from time to time, which made Katie Lee more angry. "Uncle Jack, you need to leave one of your guns where we can get to it if needed." He looked at her through the mirror, knowing exactly where she was going with this. "Oh heavens, no Katie Lee. If we had a gun, she could have killed us both, Jack tell her that is not a good idea." Katie Lee looked directly back in the mirror at her uncle. "Not unless I kill her first." They both just stared at each other, her uncle was not sure is she was capable of doing that to her own mother, but since she had attacked her aunt, a possibility. She probably could have. He was going to make sue his guns stayed locked up but he wished he would have been there. He could have shot her and no one would have cared. He would have been justified. As they got to the parking lot, Loie asked her husband one last time for them to reschedule; she was too upset. Her husband told her that was the reason why it was better to see the doctor today.

As they walked into the office, there was no one there. Katie Lee knew it was a regular day for the doctor. He hope they had not had to clear the office again. The wait would be long and she knew her aunt would not stay. When she went to check in, she was surprised at the new face at the window. When she wrote her name down the girl asked her what time she had an appointment, Katie Lee she said it was at that time. She had missed it earlier but Mr. Moorehead had talked to the doctor and she was told to come right in. The girl did not seem to understand what she was talking about, she called the other girl up front and asked if she knew about any appointment. Jack was irritated as he asked them to go ask the doctor; they had already had a pretty bad morning. The girl asked what the problem was, upper or lower. As they all looked at each other, Jack picked up a business card and handed it to his niece heading towards the door. As Katie Lee looked at the card, she did not recognize the name and then noticed the words "dentist." She looked around then felt so silly, she had walked into the wrong office. "Oh, I am so sorry, I am so sorry I am in the wrong office. I need Dr. Badea's office." Both girls smiled raising their eyebrows. Katie Lee knew what they were thinking. The whole family was nuts. They kind of laughed and Katie Lee chuckled in an odd way. "See Jack, it is not meant for us to be here, let's just go back home and we'll make an appointment for another day." Jack did not even look at his wife or niece, he just walked across the hall opened Dr. Badea's door and motioned for them to enter. He went to the window and told them both to just take a seat. He didn't set down, he said they were suppose to go right back. It was the second time Katie Lee did not hear the buzzer go off, the door opened right away.

Dr. Badea was walking towards them as they walked forward. She extended her hand toward Jack and greeted Loie and Katie Lee. Neither said a word, but Jack smiled and suggested they talk. She took them into a different room, not in her office. Katie Lee noticed it was almost like a waiting room, everything soft and pleasant. She heard very soft mellow music in the background and water running in a beautiful miniature waterfall in the back by a garden scene. How unique and soothing, Dr. Badea said that Mr. Moorehead had told her just about everything but she would like to hear from Loie. She knew she needed to calm the lady down, she could tell Loie was in a state of emotional trauma. Loie did not want to talk, so she did not press her. She did make a comment to her that impressed Jack and he hoped his wife was listening. "It is okay to be angry even at your sister. It is okay to feel bitterness you are experiencing right now, but don't let it eat you up." Turning to Katie Lee, the doctor said "Well, I am pleased to see you return. I am sorry it had to be after such an ordeal but maybe that is a good thing Katie Lee." How could that be a good thing she wondered? Dr. Badea was learning to read her well, her face was not good at hiding her emotions. "By a good thing, I mean you protected your aunt and knew you had no other option. Now maybe you can realize your mother is human and not some monster to run from. Those ghost you are hiding can be dealt with." Maybe she was right, maybe she was so mad now she could let go. If not, well the next time she saw her mother, she was not going to run. She knew she would probably have to defend herself again. That was okay she had hurt her aunt and Katie Lee was not going to forget that.

Dr. Badea went on to tell them she was going to put Katie Lee under hypnosis by just talking to her, she wanted to see why she was so afraid to deal with her ghost and know what she had hidden so deep. Katie Lee was not as nervous as she thought she would be. Maybe it was because she was still so pumped up from the incident with her mother. She looked over at her aunt and knew that at her age, she shouldn't have been knocked down and maybe she should have gone to the ER like the officer wanted. But knowing her aunt that was a definite no. Her aunt reached over and took her hand, she smiled that loving smile at her niece. Loie kissed her hand gently with a tear finding it way down her cheek. "Do what the doctor wants you to, dear. Let's get her out of our lives for good. Do you think you can?" The doctor began to talk to Katie Lee and then started to instruct her on counting backwards, to relax and remember her aunt and uncle were there in the room with her. Loie watched her niece closely as she saw her relax and close her eyes. She couldn't tell if she was under hypnosis or not yet. The doctor was so calm and just taking her time. Jack sat very quiet and held his wife's hand. He knew he should be concentrating on his niece but all he could think of was his wife and what Mina had done to her.

He lost his own thoughts as he let his mind wonder what could be done. He knew he had to keep his cool, but there were laws and she had entered his home without permission and it was against the court order. Assault, damage of property, threats, forgery, false documentations-he still needed Mr. Moorehead to explain these to him. If that was not enough to stop her once and for all, them maybe there was another way. She had crossed the line just like Peter had warned him years ago. Peter knew her well, too well. God forgive him but why didn't he take Mina instead and leave Peter here. Was he listening, maybe not? Those were Peter's last words to Jack, he didn't know if God was listening anymore.

CHAPTER TWENTY-ONE

Katie Lee did not know what to expect, she was counting while thinking this was kind of silly. Nothing was happening and she was wasting valuable time. As she thought of her aunt and how angry she was at her mother, it put her in a stage that would help Dr. Badea more than she realized. When the doctor asked her a series of questions, Loie and Jack realized the doctor was having a hard time putting her under hypnosis. They held their breath, hoping this would work, it had to. They watched as the doctor reached over and turned on the mini waterfall. She kept things simple until she saw Katie Lee close her eyes without reopening them for about two minutes. She motioned for her assistant to turn the sound down a little but put the video recorder closer to the young girl. Dr. Badea began very slowly simply by asking Katie Lee what she remembered most, some happy moments from her youth. They could see the smile on her face as she mentioned Penny, it took them a moment to find out it was her puppy. There were all aware of Mary as the good memories were far and few between and she could see the young girl was having problems. It was time to try and enter her worse hidden secrets. "Katie Lee, can you tell me what you are afraid to remember? What scares you?" Her answer was no surprise to her aunt and uncle. "Everything, everyone, Ellen, mom, mom, especially my mom." She noticed the young girl's body began to shake some. She motioned for her assistant to cover her with a light blanket. "Are you cold, Katie Lee, is it cold?" She answered, "Yes, it

Pacific Redwood Mystery: Do you believe in the little people yet?

is cold very cold. I can smell the medicine from the hall. Mom is lying there, they think she is going to die. Dr. Badea pulled a sheet of paper from her folder and moved in a more comfortable position. "I hear the ocean, Mary loved the ocean and the little people. I hope she is playing with them now." Tears started to flood down the girl's face as the doctor moved closer. "Katie Lee, why are you crying? You love Mary so why are you so sad?" Her body began to shake and her mouth quivered, it was as if the words would not come. The doctor just waited patiently to see if she would be able to go on. "Where is Mary, can you tell me what happened to her?" Loie's heart was broken as she saw her niece sake uncontrollably. It was sad, they knew Mary was murdered but no details. It had never been talked about with them. Dr. Badea realized it was too hard especially for her first visit, she did not want to press the issue and make it worse on the young girl. She had enough to worry about with her mother in town and their battle today. Taking the conversation back to Charles David, they focused on his relationship with Katie Lee. She learned a lot from her and knew this was enough for the day. With this, she could ease into a darker side, one that Katie Lee kept hidden for so long. Dr. Badea bought her back as she instructed her to just lay there a while and breath slowly. Loie and Jack were understanding as they let her rest until she was ready to set up. The doctor instructed her not to focus on her session or what she heard, that would come just be patient and relax.

Finally, the doctor spoke very softly, "Katie Lee, I think you have been through enough. Get a good night's rest and call me tomorrow just before noon. I'll leave instructions for your call." As Katie Lee sat up, Dr. Badea knew this was going to be a lot harder than she anticipated, whatever she had hidden in the far back corners of her mind was buried deep. She wondered if Katie Lee witnessed the murder, did she know the murderer? Whatever it was, she could not stop now and the sooner she could get her back, the better. "How about Wednesday give you a days' rest and if that is not good, we'll work around our uncle's schedule."

As Jack sat and watched his niece and wife he realized this was not good for him to witness, he knew he would not be able to hold his temper. It would be better if he gave his support at home and listened as Katie Lee wanted to tell him. He held his thoughts for now but would discuss them with his wife later. It was most interesting and he was impressed with the gentleness of this doctor but she was going to h ave to dig deep. Jack was not so sure he could handle it, he hope his niece could. As they drove home, Loie kept pulling at her lip, every time Jack saw her, he got madder. Loie did not complain but Katie Lee knew she was hurting more than she was saying. She hurt herself and her throat was sore. When they arrived home, Katie Lee went to her room as her aunt and uncle went into the kitchen. She was getting ready to get in the shower when she heard a knock, she was surprised to see it was her uncle, not her aunt. He asked her to please go into the kitchen and to be with her aunt. He was going to the jail but did not want her leave until Katie Lee got downstairs. Katie Lee was not comfortable with it and tried to talk him out of it but she also was glad he was going to make sure she would not get out. She made him promise not to do anything to get in trouble. He left ahead of her as she went in the kitchen where her aunt was making her favorite coffee. "Hey, smells good. I wish I like coffee more. Auntie, uncle asked me to come and tell you he went to the jail. He promised to be back soon." Her aunt just stood with her back to Katie Lee, she did not know what she felt. "Do you think he will do anything? He is pretty upset, should I call anyone?" Katie Lee did not know what to tell her aunt, but her job was to assure her aunt that she had nothing to worry about.

They sat quiet, Katie Lee was beginning to feel her pains from her struggle she had with her mother. Her stomach was still soft to the touch from her struggle with her mother, she didn't want to talk about it even though a negative remark came out of her mouth from time to time regularly. She finally got the nerve to ask her aunt what she said while she was under hypnosis. Loie was honest with her niece and explained she showed more body language than talking.

Pacific Redwood Mystery: Do you believe in the little people yet?

She listened to her aunt as she started to talk about when they were young girls. Mina never was fair, she was always violent and selfish. She said how they tried everything for the family to be happy but Mina was only interested in money, shopping, fancy clothes, and the intimate life with no holes barred. She never seemed to care whom she hurt and what she had to do to get what she wanted. Katie Lee asked the question that had been riding on her mind for years. "Did you know my real father Auntie?" Her aunt felt hopeless looking at her niece. "No sweetie, I really don't know, no one really did. We didn't even know about you for a long time." She was not surprised, she only hoped her aunt would have known. "Do you know if he was the same man as Ellen's father? Mom said he died because of me, he sacrificed his life because of me and that was why she was so miserable." Her aunt looked astonished, they had never talked about the subject before. No one dared bring it up. "Oh heavens, that is not true. She had your sister from her first boyfriend. That is one of the reason's she left and never returned. So I know that is not true. Ellen's father was no more than fifteen years old and she was already nineteen. Why, I doubt if he even knew she was ever expecting a child. Just more lies." Katie Lee wasn't surprised anymore of anything she learned about her past life. Now Ellen was not her full-blood sister either or even half. She didn't have anyone for sure now, just her aunt and uncle. She was glad she had not kept in touch with Ellen. She felt that Ellen probably knew all along, maybe that was why she made her life miserable all the time, she wasn't anything and Mina made her lie as well. "Why did she keep me if she didn't want me? That makes no sense at all. She could have given me up." Loie looked at her niece, "That was not her style, honey. How would she get sympathy if she didn't have you and Ellen to use as bait for some poor sucker to give her everything she wanted. I would have taken you long before if I would have known." Katie Lee felt worse, "So I was a convenience for her and when she had want she wanted she kept me on hold in case things didn't work. She could move on to the next one?" Her aunt could not imagine her hurt. "Well, that was except Peter, he loved you Katie Lee, you must remember that. He loved you as if you were his own. Don't dishonor his love for you."

Those were strange words for her aunt to use, that haunted her most of the evening. "Don't dishonor his love for you." She would never dishonor Peter, how could she dishonor him? It was not the time to discuss it, she was very tired and wishing her uncle would hurry up and get home. She didn't want to talk anymore, she wanted to take a hot shower and fall into bed. "Why is it so quiet in here? Have you two gone to sleep or wishing you were already in bed?" They signed with relief, but Katie Lee did not waste time once her uncle told them Mina would be behind bars for a few days. As she left her aunt and uncle in the kitchen she was pleased to see them embrace. She wondered if she would ever have such a life. Could she ever care for a man in the same way her aunt did for her uncle? Would her past let her? Time would tell she felt.

She climbed the stairs feeling as if she was so heavy. She opened the door and looked out the window. Usually they would leave her window open to see the stars and enjoy the beauty of it all. But tonight she did not want to, she just wanted to soak and fall into a deep sleep. She closed her curtains and noticed all the lights were still on at Nancy's house. She wondered how she felt about not having her father? Did it hurt her to be only with the mother, did she feel alone sometimes and wonder what it would be like to have a father? Those were questions she would never ask her friend, but she did wonder if she was the only one that left so alone. Would she ever be privileged to have children, or should she stay single? She never wanted to bring a child into this world and risk any kind of hardship, but when she watched her aunt and uncle, she longed for that feeling. She sure didn't want to take the chance of producing another Mina through any genes. It saddened her to think about it, but it was something she did not dare to wish or think about those thoughts so she pushed it further back then her hidden ghosts. The water felt like heaven, just lying and soaking her whole body. She hoped to sleep good tonight, she needed it. She only had one day's rest before she had to go back to Dr. Badea.

Pacific Redwood Mystery: Do you believe in the little people yet?

She found herself so tired, as she lay across the bottom of her bed drifting off. She had not even put her towels away or taken the time to shut her TV off. This was unusual for her, she was so tidy and always wanted her room to be neat. She was too exhausted to care tonight. Her night was the worst nightmare ever, she tossed and turned walking several times. She remembered the doctor told her that might happen and to call her if needed. She had too much pride to do that. She went into the bathroom more times than needed, finally she crawled in between the covers and tried to settle down. She did as Mary used to tell her, "Put yourself somewhere else, somewhere you really want to be that will make you happy. Then imagine it in your mind and your dreams will be peaceful." She thought of the many things but the one thing that kept creeping into her mind was the times she spent with Peter on his truck. Those were priceless memories, they all were when it came to Peter. If Peter and Charles David had not been in her life, she might had done what so many disturbed teens did – take their life. It wasn't until the worst of things started coming to an end that she got close to Charles David. But she did adore him and she wondered how he was doing. He didn't keep in touch like they promised, they meant to but maybe it was all the bad memories and the loss of Mary and Peter that kept them apart. She knew he was always thinking of her as she was of him. He was married now with his own family and she cherished the pictures his wife kept her up to date with. Charles David had turned into a fine-looking successful young man.

Very much like his father in structure but more like his real mother in later years as far as his facial features went. She wondered what Allie looked like, she never asked. She felt if Allie wanted to know, she wold get a hold of her. Allie was like that, very private and don't mess in her business. Katie Lee had learned she too made her career in the military like Charles David with success in rank. Allie had gone a good distance around the world in travel, good education and married to a three-star general. Vera had married Davie as everyone knew, they had their first child before Davie finished business school but she knew he took over his father's business and they were happy now with five children.

She was happy for her, she was happy for them all. There was good memories, she continued to picture those memories. She could see it as if it was there in the room, that little emblem on the front of Peter's truck, the bull dog. He loved to have those shine like when one would wear it around the neck. Then those logs hitting the back of the truck while being loaded. The fist time she sat in the cab of the truck, she had no idea it would feel like an earthquake when the logs laded from the cat loader. She loved the ride down the logging roads, especially when they would meet other trucks. She enjoyed watching the funny things they did, yelling back and forth as they passed, honking and just being guys. She didn't like going in the mills, they made her stay at the office, and wouldn't let here watch as the logs were taken off. She wanted to because some went into the water and it made huge splashes but she wasn't allowed to watch. She could hear but that was not like watching. Sometimes Charles David would sneak out and get in his father's cab of the truck, but no one ever said anything. Yes, Mary was right, she felt good inside. She left real good, it was the first time in so long that she felt good about looking back. She smiled and that was the last she remembered.

CHAPTER TWENTY-TWO

It seemed as if the days went so fast and it was time for her to face her fears again. Katie Lee had gotten a call from Dr. Badea, thank heavens her aunt and uncle's were helpful; both had so many hours in at their jobs they could take the time off needed for Katie Lee. She said a little prayer to herself to get through this session and maybe start some healing. She was anxious to research some ideas she had about her future and anxious to see what her uncle and Mr. Moorehead thought about it. Her aunt seemed more nervous than she was, she kept telling Katie Lee it was ok but it was Loie that was was scared. Katie Lee was beginning to remember a lot of things Mary had told her. Like the way she felt at Mary rosary, yes she really felt Mary was there standing right behind her, maybe she was.

The office was in a rush, Katie Lee didn't like the feeling but it soon passed when she saw the assistant. "Man, everyone seems as if they are running with nowhere to go." The young assistant laughed, "You are funny Katie Lee, you always have a unique way to put things and yes, they are and no they don't know where they are running to." They get all excited when Dr. Badea is in a rush, they panic, she is very strict." Katie Lee was not surprised with that comment, she looked like one of those German officers you see in the movies. The again she had that soft side you could almost plea your case to her. "She is going out to the prison later?" The assistant just smiled. "Yes, she is call out there all time time, then she also does forensic science, always viewing a case for some attorney or physicians somewhere. The doctor lives a very active life." Katie Lee was not aware she did so much but she would bet the doctor was extremely good at anything she did. As the assistant pointed to the garden room, Katie Lee smiled at her aunt, she liked that room. Katie Lee felt good about it, this time she would be able to appreciate the surrounding sounds, especially the tinkling of the water behind her. She was trying to figure out where the bird sounds were coming from. "Do you have birds somewhere." the assistant pointed at the small round box beside the little waterfall. "See that little box? It is a sound system, it has all kinds of noises. You can hear birds, ocean, wind, music-whatever you want." She was impressed, "What does the ocean sound like?" The assistant shrugged her shoulders, "I am not sure, in fact no one has ever asked for it. In fact I stopped asking what anyone wanted to listen to because everyone always say they don't care. So I just push a different button each day between the birds and the music." Katie Lee thought for a moment and then looked over towards her aunt. She could tell by the look on her face it was as if she was saying, "If that is what you want?" Katie Lee waited for the doctor to enter before she asked, she wanted to ask a question first that she had heard somewhere. The bird sounds were a little too much for Katie Lee and she could tell her aunt was beginning to raise her eyebrows as if saying, "I think the birds have got to go."

    The doctor was dressed in Ralph Lauren fashion today, very becoming to the doctor's large structure frame. The skirt was just below the knees and the jacket cut just right. The bright gold blouse matched the emblem on the Ralph Lauren jacket. The earrings were large and old with blue circles hanging just past her chin area, but very fit for the outfit. The necklace, of course matched the earrings, she noticed she had additional rings on, but still no wedding ring. "Good morning, how are you ladies this bright morning?" "I want to thank you for coming early, I did not want to cancel." She studied the doctor to see if she was distracted by maybe where she needed to be, if she felt uncomfortable, she was not going to stay. The last time had been very hard on her and she didn't want to feel this time had been very hard on her, she didn't want to feel this meeting was rushed. "Are you sure you don't want to reschedule? I will understand, I guess what I am saying is, I don't want to feel rushed, sorry." The doctor was impressed with her concern as well as her frankness. "I agree, but what I have to do cannot be done until all the authorities have done their part. I will probably be out there for a couple of days. So I did not want you to wait that long and please don't say you are sorry, you have nothing to be sorry for." The doctor grinned sitting back in her chair as Katie Lee cleared her throat leaning forward to ask the doctor a serious question. "Would it be okay if I stayed here in the chair this time and one more favor, can we change the bird sounds?" The doctor clapped her hands as she stood to adjust Katie Lee's chair back, just enough to relax. Katie Lee and her aunt both jumped a little, not expecting such a loud response. "Oh, bless you sweet girl, I swear those bird sounds make me crazy. I think I even walk cross-eyed after listening to them so long. Let's see what do you think would be good for you?" Katie Lee decided she had asked enough so she just shrugged her shoulders as if so say "whatever" her aunt likewise seemed to have no preferences. She was upset with herself for being a chicken to ask.

The doctor was turning the knob when she stopped and stared at the young girl. "You love the ocean, don't you? Isn't that where you had your best memories of Peter and his children?" She was pleased the doctor remembered. "Yes it was, why?" She didn't bother to look back up at her. "Well, there is an old saying, what you love best soothes the soul and maybe just maybe the ocean sounds may help you with your therapy. Want to give it a try?" It was scary, that was what she wanted to ask the doctor. She had read that somewhere and she really wanted to listen to the ocean music. Before the doctor came back to sit near she felt her aunt's hand softly caress her forehead, that was all she needed plus the new sound of the ocean. She began to see the redwoods and the ocean just like when she played with Mary and hid from Charles David. She could smell the salt in the air, then the ferns all fresh and wet. She barely heard what the doctor said but she did try to count. She could feel her aunt's finger's running down the sides of her temples; it felt so good just having her close and knowing she was there. Dr. Badea expressed to Loie that she was not surprised she was going under hypnosis so fast, she was sorry she had failed to recognized how important that little significant sounds could make. She felt Katie Lee would place herself in a safe place with either Peter or Mary, making it easier to bring out some deep issues.

She had explained she was going to approach her questions differently in this session but said nothing else to Katie Lee. The questions would lead her to knowing if she may or may not have witnessed a murder. Loie was very nervous but prayed the good doctor was right; knowing her niece, she would not tolerate a lot of sessions especially digging into the past with her mother. As the doctor began to ask normal questions to relax the mind, Loie watched her niece closely. She had never known a lot of her past but could guess the misery by just having Mina as her sister and remembering her own childhood with her. She was glad to see Katie Lee was not sweating like before and her body was not shaking. She seemed calm but she wondered how long that was going to continue when the next question came.

"Katie Lee, I am going to ask you a series of questions. I want you to try and answer without thinking just try to listen to the ocean sounds behind you." Still, she lay calm and serene. "When was the last time you spoke to Mary." "Easter, we were hiding eggs for Cassidy and William." Loie noticed a smile across her face, the doctor just patted Loie's hand and motioned for her to continue to gently rubbing Katie Lee's temples. "What did you talk about Loie's heart stopped a beat, the smile turned to a frown." "She was sad, Brain was still overseas, she missed him." The doctor looked at Loie confused, Loie wrote on a paper that Brain was Mary's husband and he was in the marines at the time. "What else did you talk about?" Again a smile appeared but she didn't answer, it was as if she was in deep thought. Dr. Badea nodded to Loie, it was okay and she repeated the question. "What else did you talk about?" Katie Lee answered, "Charles David had a girlfriend, it was a secret." "Can you tell me where Peter was?" Again there was a big smile "In the kitchen drinking coffee and laughing"

Pacific Redwood Mystery: Do you believe in the little people yet?

Loie was tense but felt they were making progress. "What was Peter laughing about?" The doctor noticed Katie Lee's hands were calm and steady, a great sign. "Me, making my aunt fly with me." Her aunt wrote again on the paper she had flown with Katie Lee to see them on that Easter. "Are you afraid to fly, Katie Lee." Still calm the girl kept answering "No, I was afraid of my mom, she might find out I was there." Loie was shaking her head yes and then gave her niece a look of sadness. "When was the last time you talk to Mary after that?" As tense emotion went through the air as Dr. Badea even picked the feeling up from her aunt. "Never, ever, never again." The doctor did not want to take her concentration from Katie Lee but the tears were beginning to stream down Loie's face. She tried to reach the tissues but they were too far out of reach. The doctor leaned backwards motioning for her assistant to enter, she only pointed at the tissue box to be given to Loie.

It was as if a haze came over the room, Katie Lee shifted in the chair as she made a fist with her hands. "The funeral, dead, she is dead." Dr. Badea was pleased she was not shaking and some anger was coming through, maybe they could make some progress. "Why are you angry, what are you feeling?" The young girl's fist tightened even more, they were almost stiff at her side. "Murder, why was she murdered? Why?" This stage of the therapy was tense, she would have to pick her questions carefully. "Where are the children, where are Cassidy and William?" There was a slight release of her fists but very little. "Here with me and Peter, here crying." There was silence, but before the doctor could ask another question, she continued, "They are so sad. Cassidy is wearing the pretty dress Mary made for her. It was for her father's homecoming. They didn't understand, they want her to wake up, I want her to wake up."

Dr. Badea just sat very quiet, if she guessed right, Katie Lee might be able to go on with little help. She winked at Loie, giving her some comfort. "Go back Katie Lee, tell me where is Peter?" When she asked that question, Katie Lee's fists completely relaxed, they came across her chest as if she was holding herself. "He is crying, he never cries, he is crying, everyone is crying, we found all the eggs. It was a good Easter, the last Easter." She was holding herself almost as if her arms were around someone, maybe someone small. "What happened after you found all the Ester eggs?" "Auntie and I went home but Peter said I was always home in his heart. He liked auntie, "Be good, Katie Lee, be my Katie Lee. Your birthday is coming next and remember you are my daughter always just like the rest." Katie Lee gasped for a breath then spoke so softly "I was going back on my birthday." She paused but they just sat waiting to see if she could continue or needed prompting. By the sound of her voice, the doctor could tell it was very stressful. Some of the sentences took longer to bring out, others, due to anger came quickly. "The phone, auntie said it was Peter, Peter was crying. He just kept crying. She is dead, murdered. Mom called, but she said it was her own fault, it was Mary's own fault. Peter was crying. Why would my mother say it was her own fault? Peter was crying. Why would my mother sat that?" Loie noticed tears coming from the sides of Katie Lee's eyes she softly and slowly wiped them away. She couldn't help but run her hands over Katie Lee's hair. "I saw her, went to see her, Charles David and I went to see her. Blood, there was lots of blood." Dr. Badea looked at Loie but she was as surprised as the doctor. She shook her head no, that could not be right. They instantly saw Katie Lee start to rock back and forth very slowly. "Katie Lee, where did you see so much blood?" The tears were constant now, the doctor stretched her hand to Loie as if to say it was okay to let the tears fall. "Blood everywhere, Charles David saw, she was cold, wet. Her hair was wet, blood coming from all the holes."

Dr. Badea sat back to get a better sense of what she might be talking about, her mind seemed to be in shock. "Rest, Katie Lee just rest now. Listen to the ocean behind you and rest." She motioned for Loie to come out of hearing distance, not to disturb the therapy, but she needed some more answers and real quick. "Do you know how she saw all this and what is she referring to? Did Katie Lee and Charles David see pictures, the crime scene?" Loie was beside herself, "I don't know, this is the first I have heard about it. We flew that very morning but her body had already been taken away. Peter didn't even make the arrangements. Mary's husband and Allie did, all I remember is she has several stab wounds and I believe her throat was cut. Oh dear, what is she talking about?" Just rubbing Katie Lee's aunts shoulder, she told the assistant to take her for a break to get something to drink but Loie refused, she wanted to stay. As she returned Katie Lee was kind of mumbling. "What are you feeling Katie Lee, do you feel better?" Then the fist came up again as Dr. Badea stopped mid way to ask another question, she could tell by the look on Katie Lee's face, she was trying to say something. The hand motions alerted Loie as the doctor wanted her prepared for what might be coming. "We have to leave, we are not suppose to be here. Why, why can't we? She belongs to us. Charles David wants to know" Dr. Badea did not want Loie to see she was putting the pieces together, she felt this was going to be real hard on her aunt as well. "Where are the holes, where was the blood Katie Lee, where were you and Charles David?" The the fists really extended tight and Dr. Badea was horrified that she and Charles David had put themselves in some kind of trauma. "In the morgue, when is she alone? Blood all over, holes all over her."

Dr. Badea realized that somehow Katie Lee and Charles David had managed to get into the morgue and saw Mary before the funeral people had a chance to make her presentable. The holes were the forty-seven stab wounds the poor girl suffered along with her throat being cut. Dr. Badea began to understand a lot more and was overwhelmed that Katie Lee had survived through it all. She kept thinking about her mother's phone call. "Why did your mother say it was her own fault?" There was no answer and that was expected, it was an issue of protection for Katie Lee. "Where is Peter?" It took Katie Lee a very long time to answer, the doctor could see her aunt was getting scared, she patted her hand nodding it was okay. "Home crying, everyone is crying." Katie Lee screamed with such force Dr. Badea held her breath as Loie grabbed the side of her chair. "Make her stop calling, make her stop talking to daddy Peter, make my mother stop, please, please." Dr. Badea was breathing heavy herself, but she needed to get it out of her, Katie Lee needed to release. "Why is Mina calling Katie Lee, who is she talking to?" Katie Lee's body began to shake but only with exhaustion, Dr. Badea needed to get her calm and relaxed. "It's ok, she cannot hurt any of you Katie Lee, I will stop her, I will stop her." That seemed to put Katie Lee is a different place, she raised her hand like she was looking or reaching for something. Dr. Badea took her hand and started rubbing it softly. "Mina keeps calling and telling everyone to get a grip, why did she come when told NO, no, she was told no." Loie scribbled on a paper Mina had come to the house when asked not to and started an argument with Peter. Dr. Badea told Katie Lee to think of the last thing she remembered when she was her happiest with her aunt and uncle.

Dr. Badea had to get some information from her aunt if she could help she was praying she could. Guiding Loie closer to the waterfall to not be heard she asked her what did she know about Mina and the argument. "She showed up unannounced and didn't even knock, she upset the whole family and kids. She spoke real loud telling them Mary probably was screwing someone behind he husband's back and it was a lover's revenge." Dr. Badea was exhausted herself but she now realized the depth of this woman's destruction. Mina needed help, lots of help. As Dr. Badea was consoling Loie they heard Katie Lee starting to talk again, they both rushed back to where she was. "She is at peace now, the little people under the ferns are taking care of her." Dr. Badea was fixing to release her and bring her back. It had been a hard session and they all needed rest after this. Just as she began to tell Katie Lee to count back wards and remember her clue, the girl escalated, her voice even changed. "No, she is not. Who killed her, why can't they find out, my daddy is broken, my daddy can't take it, holes so many holes." Dr. Badea felt it was enough, she couldn't let her go on. "Katie Lee, when I tell you to wake up, remember you are fine, you have been under sedation and I want you to remember what you told me. Now on two, open our eyes and listen to the ocean sound behind you for a second." The doctor paused then counted, "One -two - open your eyes and relax."

Pacific Redwood Mystery: Do you believe in the little people yet?

Loie was waiting to see how her niece was going to react, but she just sat staring at the mini waterfall. That was exactly what the doctor wanted her to do until she could calmly go over each issue with her. "Are you okay? Would you like something to drink?" Katie Lee turned to see her aunt's wet face. "I'm sorry we were mad, we wanted to see what he did to her. Charles David was so angry, I don't think we knew what we were going to see. I wanted to go home but Charles David was froze and it took him forever to let go." Dr. Badea closed the file and learned forward. "You have a lot to absorb Katie Lee and I know it won't be easy. As the evening and next couple of days come and go, you will remember a lot more. I do not want you to disappear on me. I want you back here tomorrow at 12:30 sharp but not for you to go under hypnosis but to just put thing in order for you and begin some healing." She was already out of the chair and had her jacket on, "I thought you were going to be gone tomorrow?" She smiled down at young girl with so much compassion, she wished she could hug her but she knew it was not the time. "Well, I think you are pretty important and that is my lunch break. We will meet here at 12:30. Do you think your uncle would like to join us?" Loie quickly answered "Absolutely, he will be here." Katie Lee didn't answer, she opened the door and walked out. Loie turned to the doctor. "Its all right, take her home but do not leave her alone. If she wants to talk, it is okay, but if not, do not press her. She has a lot to digest. I will see you all tomorrow." Loie just nodded and turned to catch up with her niece who was already at the elevator.

Katie Lee stayed with her knees to her chest the entire way home but she kept telling her aunt she was fine, just fine. She wanted to go home and make sure Mina was still in jail. She wanted her aunt to call her uncle and make sure her mother was still in there, she needed to know. She was scaring her aunt she didn't mean to but she really had to know. The traffic was not bad, Loie was very thankful for that. She was very nervous and needed to get off the road. She knew her husband had probably called a dozen times to see how his niece was, it was going to be another lone evening, especially for Katie Lee. She hoped she did not have to tell her husband everything, she was not sure she could. Katie Lee spend most of the afternoon on the couch dozing off and on with the medication Dr. Badea had given her aunt to make her sleep rather than dwelling on the situation. She didn't really go into what the medication was for, she knew her niece hated medication but she needed this. She tiptoed around her niece as much as she could checking on her from time to time. It was only when she went to the bathroom that she could hear Katie Lee cry. Loie was trying to do what Dr. Badea suggested and let her niece say or do at her own pace but it was hard – especially the crying. She wanted to comfort her, she could tell the crying was coming from deep inside. Katie Lee would come out of the bathroom then pretend she was fine, go back on the couch cover up and stay very quiet. Loie was counting each minute until her husband walked thorough the door, the little conversation she was able to converse was little information. But Jack was smart and he figured out things were tense for Katie Lee after today's session.

    Jack greeted them both like any ordinary day, just hugged them and went to read his paper waiting for supper. He watched Katie Lee closely and noticed she was very stressed but trying to hold it together. When she would catch him looking he would only make a funny face or smile just to let her know he was near and was not pressuring her. She seemed really affected by the medication and Jack may not be able to get any information out of her, he might have to rely on his wife. That may not be such a good idea if it was really bad. Something must have affected his niece if she was willing to take medication, he knew that for sure.. The dinner was quiet, Katie Lee chose not to eat, she was more drowsy than hungry. As Jack and Loie ate, they would gaze back into the living room making sure she was okay and continued to eat as if nothing was wrong. When the phone rang, she jumped as is she had been shot, Jack grabbed the phone before it woke Katie Lee. "Hello Mr. Moorehead, yes but that is okay. What news do you have for me?" He was quiet as he listened to the answer on the other end of the phone. Katie Lee was trying to stay alert and listen, she couldn't hear anything. Loie was pretending as if she was busy but she couldn't hear either and very nervous hoping it was not bad news. "Thank you, oh sure, she is right here." He took the long cord handing the receiver to Katie lee. "He wants to speak to you."

The conversation was faint, so he knew Mr. Morrehead was probably doing most of the talking. He took the opportunity to inform his wife that Mina was still in jail and outraged with everyone. She definitely was not a happy camper and her bail was denied for the second time. As Katie Lee hung up the phone, she smiled at them both. "She is still there. He said she will stay there until she is charged with everything. She has felony hanging over her head, so it doesn't look good for her." Jack took the receiver as he also took his nieces elbow. "How do you feel about that? Your mother may do some time. She may not get just a slap on the wrist." As she looked at her uncle, she pulled back her shoulders. "Well, she is alive, she is still here better people are not." With that she leaned back on the couch and covered up. She wasn't really watching TV but her aunt and uncle just let it be. When Jack felt that Katie Lee had drifted off far enough he would talk to his wife, he motioned for her to join him in the kitchen in case she woke up, thinking they were talking behind her back. He was patient with his wife, but the unbelief of her story was more than Jack could believe. "She and Charles David did what?" He place his hands over his eyes shaking his head in disbelief. As she continued he was at the point of telling her to stop but he wanted to hear what he needed before tomorrow. "How in God's name did they all make it through all those years of abuse and end with such a tragedy? Why didn't Peter tell me? He never said a word." Loie looked at her husband as if she had not been listening. "He did not know Jack. It was something they did out of anger because of the murder. They were teenagers not knowing what they walked into. I just praise God that Peter found us when he did."

The sound from the TV didn't seem to disturb any of them, it was as if Jack was trying to picture what would possess two teenagers to go as far as they went. He tried to picture that if he was in Charles David's shoes, would he have done that. He was not sure, he had never lost anyone in that manner, he was only on the receiving end of prisoners coming into his house that had committed these crimes. He thought of many of the men he had watched over, the ones that were there for that very thing, murder. It was a slap in the face right now, something he didn't anticipate having to face. He told his wife just to put a blanket over Katie Lee and let her sleep on the couch all evening unless she woke up on her own and went to her room. Loie did not want to do that, of course she wanted her niece to sleep more comfortably in her room, but her husband over ruled her and said. "Leave her Loie, she is resting just let her rest. I will stay down here with her if she wakes. I will come upstairs." She never had disagreements with her husband and she didn't like to be in that situation this was different for her. The only thing she could do was abide by her husband and accept it.

The might was long for Jack. Katie Lee only opened her eyes a couple of times and went to the bathroom once. He was not sure if she even noticed he was there in the recliner. That was okay, the important thing was she was sleeping well and not crying. He had noticed his wife come halfway down the stairs several times during the night but he stayed firm. Tomorrow was another day and if it was anything like today, they all needed their rest.

CHAPTER TWENTY-THREE

By the time Jack came out of the shower and joined his wife in the kitchen, the back door was open and he could see his niece out by the bird feeder. "How is she this morning?" Loie kind of turned her head toward the open back door. "I am not sure, she is smiling but so quiet. She only took some orange juice and went straight outside." Jack picked up a piece of bacon from the little plate on the stove and went to join his niece. Loie watched intensely, wondering if she should stay put or join them. She noticed Katie Lee putting her arm around his husband's waist and burying her head in his chest. It was time for her to let them have their space together, she needed to dress anyway.

On the way Katie Lee asked her uncle to stop one time, when he looked at her, he knew she was about to throw up. He came around the corner as soon as the light turned while Loie jumped out to help hold her hair. He could tell it was nerves, she had nothing but dry heaven but they were strong and heavy. He felt so sorry for her, her stomach was contracting to the point they knew it was painful. They wanted for her to settle down before even trying to continue. It would have been easy for them to say to cancel the appointment, but her uncle felt it was like falling off a bike, if you fall you need to get back on. He needed to get her to the doctor even if it meant sedation. They seemed to be close for the first time in getting her to believe life was good and he knew his niece could handle it, maybe it would take time;

but he had faith in her. Besides he promised Peter she would make it all the way, no matter what.

The look on Katie Le's face startled the receptionist when they entered the waiting room, she left her desk and went right to the back. Katie Lee let her uncle sign her in as she sat down beside her aunt. She was kind of shaking and unstable on her feet from the dry heaves that were so bad. It was the doctor herself that opened the door. "Katie Lee, come on back, what is going on with you." For the first time she showed affection toward the young girl. She placed her arm around her shoulder and guider her back to the back. She wrote something on a piece of paper and handed it to her assistant. It was not the therapy room she had been placed in before, so she thought the doctor was going to call off the session. "I was feeling a little sick to my stomach, maybe something I ate." Looking more into her eyes, the doctor asked. "What did you eat after you got home?" Her aunt was not going to let this pass. "She didn't eat a thing, in fact she fell asleep on the couch and didn't move much until this morning." The assistant returned with a small tablet that the doctor handed to Katie Lee with some juice. "This will help with the nausea, I promise and you won't fall asleep. Between yesterday's session and all you had to deal with, I am surprised you made it."

Dr. Badea went over the session with Katie Lee, taking it step by step in case she had any questions or tied to retreat back into her shell. Katie Lee was not sure what to say, things that she didn't want to think about were coming to surface, the mental pain was horrible. "Katie Lee, I got a copy of yous sister's newspaper article and I would like to go over things with you but in order to help, I need to know what you remember and then we can get some goals to move forward. You don't have to look or read the articles unless you feel you are ready and want to," Her uncle s shifted in his chair as Loie was twisting the strap on her purse. "I remember everything, there are days I can't forget, especially when my mother comes on the scene." That was a normal reaction, Dr. Bade began to explain to the three of them.

"I remember the call, Peter was never the same. She was cleaning her apartment for Brian, her husband. He was coming home from overseas. She wanted everything perfect. Her little kids were with us for the night, but no one knows what happened. She didn't show up at the airport, So Brain took a cab to the apartment and found her. Charles David and I went to the apartment to get the children some more cloths. We saw all the blood. That was when Charles David got real upset and he wanted some answers, so we went to find out what the Medical Examiner said. Charles David said he knew Peter real well, so she would talk to us, she wasn't there so we went through the back hall and got in." All three sat listening to her comments, trying to figure out how horrible this must have been. "Katie Lee, did you enter the apartment before it was cleaned and permission given?" Dr. Badea immediately asked. "No man, When we got there, the yellow tape was still up and some detective was there. We told him who we were and why were were there and he said just not to take too long and don't touch anything in the living room or kitchen. We didn't know it was such a mess and all the blood was still there." Dr. Badea sat back in her chair totally frustrated. She could not comprehend why anyone would let a family member's at this age enter a crime scene, especially after such a brutal murder. She had read the report and newspaper, she was terribly disgusted with such a lack of compassion in law enforcement.

Dr. Badea excused herself for a moment and ask any of them if they needed anything, a soda, snack – anything. "No, I am sorry I don't, but I need something. I have diet drinks and juice." but Katie Lee and her aunt shook their heads no. Jack said, "He could use a drink but doubted if she had anything strong enough." "No, sorry I don't, but I need something, I have diet drinks and juice, which would you prefer?" Katie Lee did not know what to make of the doctor having to leave the room. She wished they could move on. "May I see the newspaper, please?" Katie Lee got a little irritated when she asked to read the newspaper and the doctor asked her to please wait. "Wait for what? How can it be more disturbing than what I saw with my one eyes?" She had a point and left the doctor with little option. As the doctor opened her file she handed her the article, she noticed Jack took his glasses out of his front shirt pocket and moved his chair closer to Katie Lee. Her aunt just bowed her head and looked the other way. Dr. Badea left the room asking her assistant to get the refreshments and take them in, she went to her office to catch her breath.

Dr. Badea was very upset, but there was little she could do. It was something she just found so unprofessional. She was concerned the case had never been solved and was sure this one of Katie Lee's nightmares; who ever killed her sister was still out there, free. A family completely disturbed, small children left without a mother, a husband home from the conflict from who knows what over seas. Finds his wife not only dead but also with forty-seven stab wounds, a slit throat and no answers. Good heavens, and Peter; she needed to find out what happened to Peter. She was not surprised with Mina's coldness, that woman should have been locked up years ago. She knew from years of experience that woman needed help, lots of professional help. She was going to put in a request that she get a psychiatric evaluation while she was in jail.

This woman needed to be off the streets and should be given proper care before something terrible happened to this young girl or someone else in Mina's path. The doctor rested her head for a moment on the back of her chair closing her eyes to get that extra bouts to get going again. She felt she needed to work with Katie Lee on a longer therapy session, but she was not sure she could get her to come back too many times. She guessed she would just play it by ear and see how it played out. She had to agree with the young girl on one thing, nothing could be worse than what she personally experienced at such a young age.

"Thanks you for your patience, I guess it has been a very long day already and to be honest I am having a very hard time with them letting you into the apartment before necessary arrangements were made." Katie Lee just shrugged and looked at the doctor. "Some of the information in this paper is not correct. It really isn't. Why did they print things that they don't know anything about?" That was always an ongoing problem with the press, they printed what makes money to sell, sad but true. "Katie Lee, don't dwell on that. The press is in it to sell newspapers. If they printed something incorrectly, there is little you can do. Too many years have lapsed but you know the truth. Did you ever see this article before?" Shaking her head along with her aunt and uncle. "No, not this one. I only saw the first one they did. Why do they use ugly picture, she was pretty, so pretty. Look, they made her look horrible in this one." Dr. Badea could only sympathize with the young girl and knew this emotion and release was what she needed. It had all been hidden far too long. "I have no answers, they usually ask the family for pictures or get them where ever they can. She was a parole officer, it looks like it may have been one they took somewhere when she was working."

Jack was still reading as the doctor kept talking to Katie Lee, he seemed very involved and it was obvious none of them had seen this article. "Katie Lee, what happened to Peter, can we talk about that." She noticed her fists clenched which she seemed to do when she was very angry or stressed. Katie Lee was trying to keep control and knew she needed to. "What do you want to know?" Dr. Badea didn't want to push her so she gentle move towards her "Well, I am sure it was hard on him after what happened to Mary. You seem to blame your mother a lot for his death. How did he die and why do you blame her?" Looking at her aunt, she looked sadder than any other time Dr. Badea had seen her. She was almost like a little lost puppy. "He never was the same, he never got over it. They arrested the wrong man. Peter told them but they wouldn't listen. Then after the trial and they cleared that man, they never pursued anyone else in spite of what the family tried to tell them. Peter tried every day before he died but they would not listen to him, so they never did proceed. They just kept saying that they believed they had the right man, and it just fell through the cracks and not enough evidence so he walked.

"Well, Katie Lee, I am sure it looks very bad and sometimes we don't see everything they do behind closed doors, which does not make it right, I will say most sincerely they must have a reason they felt so strongly." Those words no sooner came out of her mouth when Jack spoke up. "Excuse me, I know I am her uncle and very protective but let me give you a little enlightenment please. I spoke several times with authorities and even to Peter. I had some friends of mine here go over the case and they didn't believe they had the right man either. We tried everything and believe me doctor, they did not pursue anyone else no matter what any of us did and we tired. I tired, It went cold, still cold today." Jack realized he had just mentioned something he had not bothered to even discuss with either of them. Oh well, it was time for honestly, he didn't need to protect Katie lee anymore, not after he learned what her and Charles David had done. "Nothing fell through the cracks doctor, It was a lack of doing a thorough job. With all due respect, I am an office of the law and they did not do their job Mam." She was surprised by his firm statement he was very serious and seemed to know what he was talking about. "Well, I apologize, I did not mean to upset anyone, and I am so sorry. It looks as if a lot of things went wrong with this case." They could tell Katie Lee was dumbfounded. Katie Lee didn't know if she should continue or not, it became quiet and someone needed to say something. The doctor softly asked her. "Would you like, to continue or do we need to take a break for another day?" Katie Lee was not going for that. "No, I don't want to keep coming back. Peter died of a heart attack but he didn't have heart problems. Allie said the doctors told her he just wore himself out. He died of a broken heart. He never gave up, but everyone gave up on him. Mina called all the time and bug him. When she was between men, she drove him crazy for money. She said it was because of him hitting her in the head she couldn't hold a job, so he would give her money. When he refused, she would tell him he was a loser, a bad father, his daughter was probably a prostitute and got murdered by one of her johns. She never gave up. She pushed him and pushed him until she broke him. He gave up and died." She waited a moment before she went on, she was getting very upset and beginning to raise her voice. "When she gets out of jail, she will come back. She want his money – that is all she wanted. She never stops. Look at my aunt's

Pacific Redwood Mystery: Do you believe in the little people yet?

face, look what she did. She was not suppose to come near us. No one stops her, no one. She won't stop until she had his money or when she is dead herself." Those were some powerful words, there was no more guessing exactly how much hate this girl carried. "Do you wish she was dead Katie Lee?" The young girl looked the doctor straight in the eyes, "I wish she would have died rather than Peter. He didn't deserve to die, people needed him, I needed him." My mother never did anything but hurt people. All my life she made it miserable. Even when Peter was trying to find my aunt and uncle, she made his life miserable. I had to live with foster parents, do you know what that is like Dr. Badea? I was in three homes before I found a family that was interested in me and not just the money. And Peter was giving them more money to keep me safe, I knew he was, they would ask me to get more from him. It was horrible, he didn't have to. Do you know what it is like to listen to your mother bring men at night bring men home and entertain them? What it's like to love someone and you have to leave them, to live in a home and have to ask for a drink of water. To sleep on the floor in their kids room, promises that never come, counselors that never ask you anything. They don't care how you are being treated. They just care that you are placed in someone else home. "I'll leave if I have to, she won't hurt my aunt again, I swear I will leave and no one will find me."

The anger was spilling out of her, she was mad and flapping her hands all over. Her aunt and uncle had never seen her so angry, they had never experienced Katie Lee in this state of mind. "Oh Lord Jack, please stop this now, lets' take her home." She didn't even hear her aunt, she was so angry she just went on and on. The abuse from Mina, the abuse from her sister, how Mina had told her when she got older she would have to learn to please men, that was the way she would get anywhere in life. The foster care, the doing without Peter, who was sneaking her things and a little extra money for her when he could without anyone knowing. The foster brothers that tried to abuse her, Peter always seemed to find out and get the truth out of her so he could fix it saving her from a worse nightmare.

The trouble she got into rather that them really investigating. How thankful she was Peter knew her and got her out of those homes but always leading to another one down the line. Her aunt and uncle had never known; Peter had only told them Katie Lee had been through more than any girl her age should have to experience. She needed tender care and family, she needed to be trusted, there was nothing wrong with her and she was a good girl. Jack and Loie had never had any problems with her, it took her a long time to adjust but from day one, she had been an angel. Jack was silent and just looked at Katie Lee and his wife. Finally, she put her hands over her face. " I don't want to talk any more. Are you satisfied now? Is Mr. Moorehead satisfied, Is everyone satisfied? Okay, it's out, can I go home now?"

Her uncle got out of his chair and wrapped his arms around her. "Katie Lee it is okay, look at your old uncle." She wouldn't, in her heart she was afraid now that they knew the truth, they would be upset, she was embarrassed. "Katie Lee listen to me, you don't have to be afraid anymore but you need to face your ghosts, it is okay to be angry but don't worry about your aunt or me." Her aunt sat is disarray, they had never kept secrets their entire married life. He had never shared his knowledge with Loie. She did not know how she felt, she wasn't angry especially with her husband. She wasn't shocked about a lot concerning her sister she just wanted to take her niece home and make sure she was okay. Dr. Badea took the young girl's hand. "I think we need to stop here Katie Lee, but I am so pleased and proud of you. I am so sorry for all you have been through. It is appalling to me that some of the issues here were the fault of authorities that should have been role models but I cannot do anything about it. What I can do is work with you through your own issues to make it a better place for you. As for your mother, I am going to look into her case and see what I can do. She needs help Katie Lee. She needs help real bad. Your lawyer is handling the insurance case, you need to listen to him. I would like you to come back again. Katie Lee, I know you don't want to but a couple more visits and let's see if we can do some mending. I would like to hear your long-term goals and see if I can help you going in that direction. Will you work with me on that?"

Katie Lee looked at her uncle smiling "I feel like a hundred pounds went off my back, I can breath." There was a softness throughout the room almost tearful. "We will call you Dr. Badea, thank you so much for your time and all you have done for her." Dr. Badea looked softly at Katie Lee while answering that comment. "Well, I am going to make her an appointment and I would like her to write down on a piece of paper all the things she likes and all the things she doesn't like." She could tell Katie Lee was mentally exhausted as she learned against her aunt. Wanting her to fell as if it was still all about her, she continued her instructions toward her. "Then I want you to write down what you would like to do with our life?" Hugging her patient the doctor was pleased. "The worst is over, I promise." As they left, Jack lingered, "I do hope you can do something about her mother." She looked Jack in the face and relaxed her shoulders. "I do intend to do something, I promise you that."

As she watched them walk out with a different look at life, she felt this young girl was going to be all right. She had great support and a determination to achieve more than the opportunity she had been given from her past. Her assistant looked at her with the same expression. "I think she did good, that must have been hell doctor?" Handing Dr. Badea some charts, she couldn't agree with her assistant more. "Count your blessing Tina, count your blessings." Walking to her office carrying Katie Lee's chart on top of the stack she wanted to make her notes while they were still fresh in her mind. She would like to share this story with some of her colleagues but knew better; it would be great but she respected this girl's privacy. Maybe later down the road it certainly would be a benefit for those less fortunate than this girl. Peter certainly was an example of what a father and stepfather could be.

Searching inside her little ice chest, she made herself a small sandwich and picked a non diet drink. She needed some caffeine! She decided to dictate her notes on Katie Lee, she wanted to make sure she got it all and make sure the documentation was accurate. Looking for her cordless recorder, she ate quietly and relaxed. She dimmed her lamp to a softer light, setting the mood and her mind. She didn't want to miss anything, she needed her own memory to be sharp. The sandwich wasn't all that bad, she buzzed her assistant and told her to make sure the girl's checked out and locked up she would be dictating. The doctor further added, "Tell the staff good night and thank you."

Placing Katie Lee's file in front of her, she began as she turned each page of her research as she spoke slowly. She knew the rest of the day at the prison would be testy, so it would be better to dictate it all now. She felt the summary and outcome was more beneficial than she earlier anticipated. This young girl had come to her at the request of a colleague. Upon research, she found this pleasant young girl to be in a mental distress due to years of torment, abuse and neglect. Witnessing the scene of a murder crime with the victim sustaining nearly forty-seven stab wounds, tied with an electrical cord to the springs of an old mattress, the finally cut at the throat. This was overwhelming for her to witness herself, so she couldn't imagine the trauma for this young girl and Peter's son. The physical and mental abuse from her mother and some of her siblings were also subdued for a number of years. She felt this was her way of coping and maintaining her sanity.

She felt very strong that if it had not been for example and bonded emotional love Katie Lee had for her assumed stepfather she may have ended her life prior to living with her aunt and uncle. The environment they provided for her had been stable and rewarding, something that began a healing process but no closure. Dr. Badea was amazed that this girl was sane enough to talk about it with no therapy through the years. She felt her imagination to keep Peter and Mary alive was her lifeline. She was a strong girl but her dreams to have a happy married life with children may become a long-term problem. She felt she could function well among her peers and probably do extremely well in any field she chose. She was anxious to see what her plans and goals would be. The approach of a relationship may prove to be another problem but in time and therapy, she should be able to live a productive life.

She was tired it had been very emotional and she still had a very long day to go. As she closed her file, she was looking forward to her meeting tomorrow with Katie Lee. She hoped she followed her instructions, it would be interesting to see what she wrote. As she placed the file in her locked cabinet, she felt better if she kept it in her office for the time being. As she gathered her files for the prison trip, she gulped the rest of her sandwich, grabbing her drink and heading out the door. It was later than she anticipated but she knew by the time she arrived they would have things ready for her. She hoped anyway, Her car was hot and she had forgotten her coffee in the holder near the passenger glove box that morning. It still had the pumpkin spice smell that she loved. Disappointment that she had forgotten her favorite drink, she decided to drink this one anyway. The price of java these days would pay for this drink.

The drive to the prison was relaxing to her surprise, she had expected to have a rougher morning with Katie Lee. She was satisfied with the session and extremely proud of the young girl. She was a little hesitant about her aunt, the protection was overwhelming but that was to be expected. She like this family, she like this girl. She decided she was going to make this her priority making Katie Lee a success. It made her visit to such a depressed facility more tolerable.

CHAPTER TWENTY-FOUR

The birds were singing and enjoying the bird feeders as the breeze seemed to mold across the backyard even with the soft blue clouds. Katie Lee watched those clouds move across the sky forming different shapes. Some were blue while others were darker in color, dominating from the gray hiding behind. She noticed some of her aunt's flowers were beginning to have little buds, it would not be long and everything would be in full bloom and beautiful. She loved the backyard, it was one you could sit out all day taking in the sweet smell and defined décor.

The gardener was so particular in his arrangements that it made the atmosphere a little bit of heaven right there on earth. She stretched her legs across the little brick steps that followed the path to the gazebo. That was the first thing she noticed when she came to live here. All white lattice material with hanging pots and chimes. The decorative bench that was just inside was painted black and emerald green; it made everything come alive. She had seen her aunt more times than she could count sitting out there just enjoying her little haven. Over the years, they had great picnics and BBQ's there. There were also the long nights in the winter to swing on her uncle's hammock, watching the stars twinkle into the night. It was great just watching the first snow sprinkle down. As she walked down over the tiny path, peace surrounded her. She had loved these years and for the first time, she felt at total peace. It was going to be a good summer; she thought she might like to go berry picking. It was something she hadn't done

Pacific Redwood Mystery: Do you believe in the little people yet?

sine she went with Charles David and Mary. Again, she told herself how lucky she was that Peter had found them, how lucky she was that they wanted her in spike of her mother. She even felt sorry for her mother for the first time. Sh wondered if Dr. Badea would get her help. Would she ever be a good person and feel sorry for what she had done? She didn't want repentance for herself, she wanted it for Peter and his children. For Peter's first wife, she felt it was Mina's fault that Carol Ann had committed suicide shortly after Peter's death. She couldn't blame Allie for her distance, she had lost so much and Charles David. She prayed one day they would find just a fourth of peace she felt at this moment.

Taking what she had wrote into her kitchen, she noticed Nancy taking the garbage out. She didn't know why she had the urge to go see Nancy and her mother but she did. Leaving her writing on the kitchen table, she wrote her aunt a note. She wrote she needed to go next door for a moment, she would be right back to dress. There was music coming from Nancy's home, she hoped she wasn't too early. But when Mrs. Hanson answered the door she could tell it was more like spring cleaning. She had a handkerchief wrapped around her head and a dust cloth in her hand. "Hey, pretty girl come on it. Nancy is upstairs going through her clothes, trying to decided what she needs and what she can live without. How are you sweetie?" She couldn't help but like this woman, she was always so pleasant and happy. "Mrs. Hanson, I just wanted to come over and tell you I really appreciated your friendship with my aunt. You are such a great person and if you are what a mother is suppose to be, then you should go straight to heaven." She had really surprised Mrs. Hanson, she almost couldn't speak. The look on Katie Lee's face told her it was hard for her to say those words, but it was truly from the heart. "Thank you dear, why don't you go say hi to Nancy. She has missed you." Watching Katie Lee go down the hall, she was pleased that things were looking up for her. She had brought a lot of love to her neighbors and she believed this young teenager was a good person. She needed all the breaks she could get.

The visit was short but nice, Nancy felt humble towards her friend but still worried about her. They deciding to go to the movies that evening and maybe the ice cream parlor, Katie Lee asked Nancy to call Jacob and see if he wanted to join them. Nancy was thrilled and glad they made plans, she had missed Katie Lee and she knew Jacob would be beside himself. Katie Lee had to cut her visit short, she was anxious to see Dr. Badea and see what she thought about her list and answers. They had come earlier than she though, in fact she was able to do it quite quickly. Things she still did not want to remember but she had less anger now and no more fear. It was something she would never forget but she didn't feel like Mina was in control anymore. She was going to insist her aunt and uncle get some of Peter's money; she didn't care what they said. Maybe a trip or something but they were going to have something as a reward after all these years of taking care of her; they had suffered too. Her aunt and uncle were in the backyard when she came back, enjoying the very same she had enjoyed earlier. "Good morning sunshine, come join your aunt and I." The could see the smile on her face was different, it was peaceful, almost like a twinkle. They didn't want to say anything to heck her mind. "Well, I would love to but I better get dressed, we are suppose to be there and I remember she said it would be her lunch hour." It was good to see Katie Lee anxious to see Dr. Bahea, it was not expected at all. Agreeing, her aunt kissed her forehead and rested back on her favorite bench in the gazebo. It was a lovely garden in a very cottage-style home. Now Katie Lee could really enjoy her surroundings rather than feel that a dark cloud was hanging over her.

She dressed then spent time catching up in her journal. Her aunt was ready to go by the time her uncle had the car started and honking. It irritated her aunt that he would do that, but she knew it was just because she made such a fuss about it. It was much more pleasant ride to the doctor's office than any prior appointment. The parking lot was pretty empty except that Loie noticed Lieutenant Andrews first things as he exited his car when they pulled in front of the building. "Jack" Katie Lee was busy reading her notes and didn't notice until her aunt spoke. "I see him, don't panic. It doesn't have to be bad." "Katie Lee was a little disturbed and couldn't imagine why he was there. Getting out of his car before her aunt and uncle, she herself questioned him. "Good morning, are you looking for us?" He was glad to see this girl not so hostile, their last meeting had not been a pleasant one. She was a pretty girl with a beautiful smile, one of those sweet sincere aura. "Well, I was requested to be here at 12:30p, sharp, but not sure myself why. Now that I see you fine folks, I think we are here to see the same doctor." Jack was not impressed with this gentleman's personality, he had not forgotten his attitude and involvement with Mina that cause his family unnecessary hardship. "I cannot imagine why she has you here, but I will be anxious to ind out." The officer shifted in place not offering his hand towards Jack. "Well, it is good to see you too Jack." He nodded his head towards Loie but she quickly headed for the front door to the office, not wanting to have any kind of conversation with this man.

As they all entered the office, they noticed all the doors were open and there was little activity coming from the back.. "Do I hear people in my waiting room? Come on back." Katie Lee was surprised to see the good doctor in jeans and a cute T-shirt. The little sly smile on her face told Dr. Badea she was surprised in her dress. "We do like to dress down sometimes not always suites and spike heels." They all laughed as she described her professional attire. "I see you have noticed I asked the lieutenant to join us and I have ordered lunch from the corner deli, hope it suits everyone. "They had not expected lunch, they had not even thought about it. "I would like to know what possessed you to ask this officer of the law to join us? If you would mind to enlighten me." She sensed Jack's dislike for him, and she understood but she needed this man and they would soon realize the benefit of his presence.

"I understand there are some bad feelings here but lets see what we can do to justify this and move in a direction on Katie Lee's behalf." Jack as well and his wife could not understand how this man would be of any benefit to their niece. She had their attention which she needed and she appreciated their cooperation. "Katie Lee, were you able to do your homework?" She was hesitant to give the doctor anything she wrote with this man in the room. "While you ponder on our thoughts, I want to bring the lieutenant up to date so to speak. But first let me tell you why I have asked him here. I understand that you are on suspension for the episode with Mina Waterman. Katie Lee was alarmed when she called her mother by this name. Where did she get that name?" The doctor could tell Katie Lee was not aware her mother had again taken a false name through marriage but of course she had found out the marriage was not legal. "It seems like Mina married for the fifth time Katie Lee, but of course it is not legal. That is what her drivers license reads so until she comes before the judge and they get this all sorted out. We will refer to her with that name she is charge under."

Loie was shaking her head, her sister was on her fifth false marriage and how many in between, Loie lost count long ago. What had her parents done to make this sibling turn out so negative and the opposite of goals and a productive life. "Lieutenant, I think you and I need to work together here to make sure that Katie Lee's mother does not fall through the cracks again so let me give you some homework. I like to call it homework, it makes me feel important." He laughed along with the others but he was not sure where the doctor was going. "I have her file, her past history that I need you to go through and especially focus where I have highlighted certain activity. I have already put in my request for an evaluation, which by the way will be carried out by Mr. Munger Tuesday for next week. I want to make sure when she gets to court there will be no way she will walk. I know the attorney her estranged husband took her case, but the prosecutor's office is ready for her. Katie Lee will of course be called but I will handle that. I need you to be honest and especially make sure your little friend from Social Services is called for her part in this."

As the lieutenant shifted in his seat. Dr. Badea looked deep into his face, there were not going to be any secrets anymore. "I do not care what the two of you were doing or why. If you got caught with your pants down, well pay the piper. If you want to get back to work and make this go away, then I need you on our team and I need the truth – all of it." As the doctor leaned back in her seat she saw his head come up in his arrogant attitude. "Well, I have given a deposition already, why can't you use that? I think I have paid enough for this mess." Before Jack could speak his opinion of this officer and how he had offended them by inconvenience, the doctor put her elbow on the desk. "I think we can all be on the same page here. If you think about it, this is your chance to make a wrong right I understand the young lady is already no longer employed by the state and I am sure you would like to get back to your comfortable office as soon as you can? I have done my homework lieutenant, I am well aware of who Mina is telling everyone she is married to. Just how long do you thing he will stay around when the truth comes out? How long do you think Daddy will keep putting money in pockets when a scandal is threatened. Mina is depending on his reputation to get away and walk."

The room was silent, she could see everyone was in the dark except her good lieutenant friend. She handed Jack an article from a newspaper that reads, "Chicago Times" at the top. Katie Lee wondered what that had to do with her. Jack's eyes widened as he looked at his wife. Handing her the paper he was not sure if she would get it, but she did. 'Katie Lee, it seems like your mother is living with one of the biggest bad boys in Chicago or I should say she is involved with the son, not daddy. Unfortunately for her, he thinks they are married, "Will there be any chance that there could be a kickback to my niece?"

The lieutenant rose from his seat. "No Jack, they don't even know about her. They have no idea other than he brought her home one day and he won't listen to anyone when it comes to her. We have downplayed it waiting to see what the judge is going to do. He has some heavy hitters in his corner, Doc" She was not amused with him calling her doc but she would let it go for now. "I understand that, but if Daddy became aware of some very interesting facts, I don't think his son could afford his heavy hitters, do you?" He had to give her credit, she had done her research well. It would probably be disastrous for

Katie Lee's mother but he didn't care, he just wanted his badge back and he didn't care how he got it.

As they sat there and listened to the lieutenant and the doctor Katie Lee was appalled, she could not comprehend how her mother was living with and whom. How could see go from such a great person as Peter to such a thug dressed in fancy clothes. A drug dealer, son of some big flouting connection with family ties of nothing but dirty business. She didn't know why she was surprised, it was the money she followed. "What happened to Ellen?" She saw the look on her aunt's face as Katie Lee asked but she couldn't help it. She wondered what really happened to her. The lieutenant looked at her but didn't show too much emotion. "She actually left her mother about a couple of years ago. In fact, I spoke with her right after you were returned to your aunt and uncle. She asked about you she seemed sincere. She worked for while in the Seattle area went back to school and became a paralegal for an attorney up there. She is willing to testify, Doctor, if you need her." The shocked look on Katie Lee's face was impressive, she couldn't believe it. Left her mother and did something with her life. Wow, that was too much to digest in one afternoon. "What are you thinking?" She knew the doctor was taking to her, but she was still trying to picture this one.

"I am not sure, whey did she ask about me." The lieutenant only shrugged his shoulders as if he didn't have a clue. "I will tell you she didn't want any money from you, she will come to her own if needed." He continued but Katie Lee didn't appreciate his input. "Well, maybe she had remorse, maybe she lives a different life now. The important things is she got away from your mother and did something with her life." Since Jack and Loie did not know her, they felt it was something good, like what had happened to Katie Lee to them. "Don't be too quick to judge, maybe she has changed and feels remorse." That was so like her aunt to find something good out of something bad. "Is she coming?" Both Dr. Badea and the lieutenant shook their head yes at the same time. "We will talk about that later but your mother

Pacific Redwood Mystery: Do you believe in the little people yet?

does not know we have contracted her. We may not need her if Mina's estranged husband's family gets certain information, she will be helpless and placed where she can get the help she needs and pay for a few of those assaults she had gotten away with so far."

Katie Lee didn't even notice the lieutenant had left the room and had been escorted into another room until her aunt refocused her attention to the doctor speaking to her. "Can I see what you wrote?" She was scared, had she written the correct thing. Would they think she was silly and wishing too far out? Well, it was show-and-tell time. As she handed the papers to the doctor, she didn't know if her aunt or uncle had seen her note or not. Maybe they hadn't read it yet. Everyone was very quiet. She could tell by the smile on the doctor's face she must have written something that was right. Her aunt and uncle just sat still. "I am impressed, how do you feel?" She sighed folding her arms across her chest and then back to her side, kind of holding the sides of her chair. "Good, I slept very good. Don't remember anything, I didn't dream either. Nothing, I felt real comfortable this morning, especially when I was in the backyard. I really feel good. I an angry that the murder is still unsolved and I miss people but I think they are okay now." The doctor was pleased but knew not to be too confident, they had more work to do.

"Tell me about this house you want to open. I am interested in your details." Katie Lee grinned as if she was thrilled she asked. Her uncle put his head up in pride; her aunt patted her hand in approval. "I want to take some classes and see about opening a home for lost teenagers. Ones that don't have anyone or have been abused. I want to staff it well, not just people pulling a paycheck but people that are serious and sincere. I want to oversee everything, I want it different but I don't want to interfere."

She looked shy all of a sudden and knew she was going to be judged harsh for her next remark but she had to get it out. She had to make sure it was done her way. "Did you ever see the movie, Billy Jack or the Trial of Billy Jack, Dr. Badea?" "As a matter of fact yes I have. I had a patient a few years back that was Native American from the north. She had a sister that was in that school which led her to me." Katie Lee was really surprised. "What did you think about it or did you take it like most people. Just a myth and out of place for this time?" She was impressed with her choice of words. "I have to say that I agree with the concept of the movie, I just didn't like the reality. Is this the kind of home you are talking about?" Katie Lee had not thought of that, she didn't put the two together. "Not really, well kind of. I didn't agree with some of the ladies rules, but yes I guess when I think about it, I have to say yes."

Dr. Badea was now really impressed with this young girl and inside she felt she would accomplish her task. She just might pull this off. "I am proud of you and believe you can do this. I could not think of a better person to take on such an accomplishment. I can help you get started with some classes you would need and I would like to be involved with your progress. I think that if you look at your list every morning, you will stay focused. You have put some great goals down here. Take one day at a time Katie Lee. You will be fine!" She was happy with herself but she still was scared there were a lot of issues she needed to deal with. "If I bring you the class list from the college, would you help me, really help me. I want to work at the clinic part time. I don't want to rely just on Peter's money. I think I will need it later." Katie lee felt as if she had a direction, a purpose. She felt as if Peter was in approval, she knew if it had not been for him she would not have her sanity.

They spend about thirty minutes going over her goals and putting them in priority for her, they set her up with some therapy sessions. Dr. Badea was thankful she agreed to extra help. Katie Lee had asked to have a couple weeks before she started her therapy, but she would have to call her later and explain why. She was anxious to know the outcome of her mother's situation and how soon she would come before a judge or what actually was going to happen. "I think with all the help and favors I can call in, we can stall until you are of legal age. That is our goal unless her so called husband doesn't back off.

Pacific Redwood Mystery: Do you believe in the little people yet?

We will play by our rules not Mina's, she will be in jail for about a good three weeks and maybe longer if luck shines on us. I don't want you to dwell on it Katie Lee, it will be okay." She wasn't dwelling on it, she was but she had something else in mind, but she wasn't saying right now anyway.

She was not hungry when they left the office. She had not eaten that much but the lunch was good. She had never eaten from a deli before. She like the chips, they were different than those one bought in a store. The ride home was pleasant, she couldn't take too much credit, it was a remark that let her to the idea. She hoped with all her heart the same person was able to accomplish their little project. Turning into the driveway, she felt safe really safe. Mrs. Hanson was sweeping off her porch but just waved and threw her a kiss. Nancy was nowhere in sight but she would talk to her later. As she entered their home she noticed the answering machine's light was on. She immediately ran to see who had called. "Katie Lee this is Mr. Moorehead, a good morning to you. I hope all goes well with the good doctor, call me when you get this." Her heart was pounding as her aunt and uncle entered the room. "Is everything okay? Was that Mr. Moorehead?" Her aunt was nervous at the least little thing lately. Katie Lee didn't blame her, that was why it was so important to her this worked. "Fine, I asked him to do something for me, that is all." She didn't want to give anything away either, so she disappeared upstairs to her room to return his call. He wasn't there, darn she thought. His secretary said he had tried to reach her at the doctor office but she had already left. He left the office and would not be returning until the morning. She was asked if she wanted to leave a message. She had his cell, but she didn't want to bother him, it could wait until morning.

She didn't have to, he was in her living room when she walked back downstairs. He had a copy of her goals in hand. She should have guessed the doctor faxed him a copy. He had a huge smile on his face, so he must be pleased. "Hey, I like this idea of yours and I think you will be a great success but why don't you go about it a little differently? You don't have to use Peter's money to do this." She was confused, how was she going to do it without Peter's money?" He laughed at her and set his briefcase down but handed her an envelope with papers sticking out. She held her breath as she looked into his face to see if she could read positive signs. Her aunt and uncle were just as anxious to see what he handed her. "Well, it took about fifteen minutes to get a release from the judge, but we have to wait for the rest until the hearing but you got your wish. Congratulation young lady, enjoy!" She was overjoyed as she held the envelope to her chest.

"Can we know what the good news is? Looks like our niece has some good news Loie. Look at her smile." She looked at Mr. Moorehead, then back at her aunt and uncle. She handed them the envelope and giggled. Mr. Moorehead rested against the china cabinet grinning at Katie Lee giving her a wink. As Jack opened the envelope, Loie was trying to see over his shoulder but there were too many papers. "What is it?" Loie was nudging him to tell her. Jack just held the papers for a moment and looked as if he was going to faint for a moment. "And you can't change it either uncle, Mr. Moorehead fixed it for me, so there." Her aunt was trying to figure out what was the meaning of everything; her husband for once in his life didn't have a comment. She could see papers with a bunch of writing but didn't understand. "To make a long story short Loie, Katie Lee asked me to go to the judge and ask for a fourth of the inheritance now. We would fight Mina in court to make sure gets nothing. The other fourth, she asked me to place in your name to do as you all see fit." Loie was dumbfounded. "No, she doesn't have to do that. We don't want her money." Mr. Moorehead looked at the sweet lady. "She knows that and she knows you wouldn't accept it any other way. Besides she wants to make sure you have your own money to spend in Alaska." Katie Lee and Mr. Moorehead started to laugh as they looked at her aunt and uncle. Loie looked at Jack as he handed her a schedule for their trip. The trip they had always talked about, always dreamed about.

Both had wanted to go to Alaska since they had been married but had never been able to do it for more than one reason. "That is why I can't start school for two weeks and I cannot see Dr. Badea until we

Pacific Redwood Mystery: Do you believe in the little people yet?

get back, we are sailing out of San Francisco day after tomorrow. It was her uncle that was wiping his eyes, her aunt was too much in a stupor to think." "Oh, by the way, your niece thought of everything. Your employer's are taking you all to dinner before your flight, enjoy and I expect a call the minute you return. Don't worry about the home front, your doctor and I have that under control."

Leaning down from his tall frame, he gave Katie Lee the best hug any awkward person could under the circumstances. "Well, I have got to run, I think you all have lots to talk about and some serious packing to do. The funds are already in the account. Again, enjoy." He was out the door and had driven halfway around the block before Jack and his wife could get a hold of themselves. Jack looked at his niece with compassion. "I need one favor, please." As Katie Lee looked at them both they were compelled with her calmness. Her uncle continued "What could we possibly do for you? You know anything within our power we would be pleased to make it happen for you." She grinned but stayed back a little knowing emotions were high. "I am going upstairs and I don't want anyone to say a word, no regrets. You shouldn't have done anything except accept me as myself as you both always have. Let's just be a family and have a wonderful time. I am looking forward to it and I know you two have dreamed about it for years." Loie was holding her husbands as she tried to wipe the tears but Jack was just as emotional. They couldn't think of enough words to say how they felt, no one had ever done for them as much as this or had given them the love this girl had. She was theirs and always would be. Jack felt as if they could see the light at the end of the tunnel, after all this time. She leaned in and kissed them both as she handed them each a pamphlet of the trip and all that was expected. "You do have passports, don't you?" Loie started to laugh as Jack looked at his niece. "Mine is at the bank in the safety-deposit box. Where is yours?" As he turned to his wife. "The same place, you know that?" As the both looked at Katie Lee she smiled pulling hers from her back pocket. "Complements of special deliver, thanks to Mr. Moorehead and the post office."

CHAPTER TWENTY-FIVE

The morning was brisk as Katie Lee bounced downstairs with her suitcase in hand. She had been told by the lady in Mr. Moorehead's office to save room in her suitcase for souvenirs. Take very few clothes, like lots of shorts, sweats and a good sweater. A couple good outfits for dinner, tennis shoes, flops and only one pair of good shoes. Some goodies, scarves and for sure good gloves and warm socks for the night. She was so excited she had started to come downstairs last night to ask her aunt and uncle some questions but when she descended halfway she heard music. In fact, it sounds like an old Glenn Miller song. As she peaked around the corner at the bottom of the stars, she saw her aunt and uncle dancing. She had never seen that before, she was not going to disturb such a tender moment. They looked good together, they were happy and looked so much in love. She had done good, she had been able to give them something memorable. It would never be enough but a start.

There was no smell of java coming from the kitchen, maybe her aunt decided not to make breakfast this morning. As she rounded into the dinning room area, she noticed Mrs. Hanson and Nancy at the table in full enjoyment picturing the trip. The hadn't even noticed her when she walked up. "Cool, don't you think?" As they turned, Mrs. Hanson jumped swinging around in excitement. "Do you know how many years your aunt and I have talked about this dream trip of hers?" Katie Lee felt so good inside, but when she looked at Nancy, she had

Pacific Redwood Mystery: Do you believe in the little people yet?

her lip stuck out further than her chin. "What is wrong with you?" Nancy smiled and shook her finger in her face. "You were suppose to meet Jacob and me at the movies last night." Katie Lee threw her head back. "Oh man, I totally forgot, with all the excitement, I really forgot, is he mad?" Nancy was looking at her as if saying, "Well, maybe? He is really worried about you Katie Lee, You haven't exactly given Jacob the time of day lately and he did a lot for you." Mrs. Hanson was appalled that her daughter would talk to her friend like that.

"Nancy Lee Hanson, shame on you." Katie Lee immediately came to her defense. "No, she is right, I haven't and to think about it, Jacob was always there. It was me, I need to call him." She went into the living room where her uncle was already on the phone, talking to the warden with a big smile on his face. He winked at his niece as she walked back into the kitchen. "Can I borrow the car, auntie? I need to go see Jacob, please." Mrs. Hanson was still upset with her daughter and Katie Lee could tell she must have said something to her, she was looking down. "Nancy, get the keys out of my purse and you two girls go right now. That is, if its okay with Loie?" Raising her hand, she signaled she had no problem. "I think you two better hurry up. We all have a lot to do, Nancy remember you are leaving tomorrow, so get it done girls and get back here." Rushing out the back door, Nancy was ahead of Katie Lee. It was not often her mother let her have the privilege of driving by herself. "I think he has probably already gone to work, want to try his work?" Katie Lee was pulling the seat belt over when she noticed a little dog waddling by.

"Oh, Nancy look, look at that dog. He looks exactly like the one I had. Penny, she looks exactly like Penny, the one Peter gave me." Her friend smiled backing out the driveway. "Well, that must be a good omen, I think things are about to turn around for you, my friend." Katie Lee didn't hear much of what Nancy was rattling about, she was watching to see where the little dog was going. Nancy kept going straight, then turned at the end of the road. Katie Lee watched until the pup was completely out of sight. Yes, a good omen she thought. A very good sign. "Did you say Jacob was at work, I didn't even know he was working." Nancy looked over at her friend with a crushed look. "Well, maybe if you would call him once in a while, you would know."

She didn't have to make her feel any worse than she did but she wasn't going to explain herself to Nancy. She felt she was making her feel bad on purpose, so she would tell her nothing. As they approached the ice cream parlor, she noticed Jacob's truck on the side. Looking through the front door as Nancy drove up, she could see him. He looked real cute with his hat and fancy shirt. There weren't very many people there but it was a little early for ice cream. She slowly got out, giving Nancy a look as if saying "cut your crap." They walked together but soon heard voices behind that made Katie Lee laugh. "Hey, pretty girl want to take a swim?" Turning, she saw both Miller twins heading towards them. "What are you two up to? I bet it isn't good." Laughing they all hugged and Jacob came out on the sidewalk beside Nancy. As Katie Lee turned he was just standing there. "Hi Jacob, don't want to bother you at work but I guess an apology is in order." The twins were standing there as if waiting to see the outcome. Nancy pulled on both their arms and drug them away, so Jacob and Katie Lee could at least talk without them breathing down their necks.

"Hey, what is up with that? Have they got a thing goin?" Nancy wasn't sure what to say, she wished she could say yes but Katie Lee wouldn't get involved with anyone. "No, she just forgot to meet us at the theater last night and she feels real bad. Looking to see if they were okay or arguing, the Miller twins were not used to sad issues; they lived to party." "Bummer man, Hey Nancy, we are going up to Smith Park tonight and take the boats out, want to come along? Katie Lee and Jacob can come too?" It sounded good but Nancy knew if there was trouble it would definitely be the Miller twins. "I would love to but I am leaving tomorrow on a trip and Katie Lee is leaving for San Francisco." They both kind of threw their heads down. "San Francisco, for what?" She laughed, it would take longer than she had to explain that to them. "Come on, I will buy you an ice cream and we can take a rain check on the boat ride." From the look on their faces, Nancy was not sure if they understood what she meant by a rain

Pacific Redwood Mystery: Do you believe in the little people yet?

check for the boat ride. It looked as if Katie Lee and Jacob were fine, they were laughing and Katie Lee was doing most of the talking, so maybe it was okay. They had all finished their ice cream by the time Jacob walked back in. "Where is Katie Lee?" He just gave the Miller twins a high five and went around the counter. "She will wait for you in the car, thanks for bringing her." It was obvious she wasn't going to get any information out of either one of them. She bid the boys good-bye and told them to be careful and try to stay out of trouble. That was a joke, the Miller twins invented the word trouble.

Katie Lee was sitting and smiling as Nancy wondered what she was so happy about. It was as if she was a different person. The same Katie Lee, but something was different, something brighter and more content. "Is everything okay?" She just smiled nodding her head, "Yes, he will come over after work. I invited him for dinner, want to come join us?" She wanted to but she had not done a thing to get ready and she wanted to spend more time with her mother. "Sounds good but I need to pack myself and I would like to spent time with my mom, know what I mean?" Katie Lee knew exactly what she meant, if she wasn't going with her aunt and uncle, she would not have invited Jacob over. It seemed as if the house was even brighter to her when they drove in Nancy's driveway. Mrs. Hanson was already home looking out from the living room window. She just waved at Katie Lee, then disappeared. "Thanks, I do appreciate it. Listen Nancy, you have a really good time and when you come back, we will go off and have one of those girls nights."

To Nancy that was heaven, she always wanted to be close to Katie Lee. She always wanted a best friend. "Are you serious, Really Katie Lee? That would be the bomb." Hugging her neighbor, she again told her to have a good time and forget everything but good things. The TV was a little louder than usual when she walked in, she soon saw why, the fights. Her uncle was usually at work but today was his day off and would be off until they returned. Her aunt was off getting the last little things she felt she had to have for the trip. Jack had made arrangements with the neighbors across the street and Mrs. Hanson to watch the house. Katie Lee went to her room to pack, she wanted to get it out of the way before dinner. She had some explaining to do for Jacob. She felt now she could, knowing he would hold her with respect. She didn't have to worry about becoming the talk of the town of their graduation class.

She listened to music and it seemed as if some words were new to her, having new meaning. As she took each fresh breath, she even felt sorry for her mother locket up not being able to smell that fresh air and cool breeze that whistled through the window. Well, she had more opportunities than Katie Lee ever did. She wondered how Ellen would look; Mr. Moorehead had made the call for her. It was at Ellen's request they have their layover in Seattle to see Katie Lee, she would not say why it was so important for Ellen to see and talk with her. She was older now and wasn't afraid of her anymore. Ellen had really hurt her physically and verbal. Those words still cut deep. She had to admit she was curious to know whey she was not with her mother or why she had cut all ties from her mother. She hoped it was a good thing.

Her uncle's favorite person must have won, she heard a lot of yelling coming from the living room. Smiling, she was glad to hear some laughter after all the weeks of despair they had been living. She didn't know her aunt had returned until she went downstairs to tell them she had invited Jacob for dinner. She knew they wouldn't mind, they really liked Jacob and they encouraged her on more than one occasion to bring her friends home. Looking out the back window she saw Mrs. Hanson hanging some sheets on the line with Nancy standing beside her. She had to chuckle as she watched Nancy holding several clothes pins in her mouth. She had gotten closer to Nancy but still she was a chatterbox and didn't think before she opened her mouth. So most of her past would have to stay where it was as far as Nancy was concerned. She did want to talk to Nancy about her idea to open a home for abused children. She felt that if Nancy was going to get a social service degree, she might put some interest in her project.

"Daydreaming dear?" A little startled but pleased she and her aunt were alone, she turned telling her Jacob would be coming for dinner.

With delight, not only in her voice but also in her face. Loie tugged at her ponytail. "Well, it is about time we see some young faces here in the house. What do you think he will like?" Laughing out loud, Katie Lee answered, "Jacob eats pizza 24/7." Her aunt stood just holding a skillet in a little daze at what she said. "Pizza, oh my, I don't know how to make pizza. What else does he like?" Jack, clearing his throat stuck his head through the kitchen door. "Pizza, that sounds good and I like pizza. If Jacob is coming, why don't we order. It can be delivered, give us more time to visit and last minute details." They both broke out in laughter as if Jack had been so involved in the getting ready issue. "What, what is so funny, pizza is good." Katie Lee just picked up the phone book laughing as her aunt made funny faces at her uncle, not understanding what the laughter was all about.

They didn't have to wait as long as usual for the delivery, so she called Jacob asking him to come early, he was delighted. They spend most of their time in the backyard. Jacob was sitting and listening to Katie Lee go through each detail right up to the psychiatrist visit. She tried to see what expression would come across his face, but he just sat very quiet listening to every word. Sometimes he would put his head down and she knew he didn't know what to think. She was as honest as she could be but it took her some time to go back and go over everything, plus she wanted him to know about some good things. Especially those of Peter and Mary. She talked about Charles David and how their relationship changed but it was difficult for them, after their mother took her life. She knew they didn't blame her but it brought back bad memories, so she didn't blame Allie.

It was long after the pizza man left and her aunt and uncle were the ones left to enjoy the meal. Katie Lee and Jacob spent most of the whole evening just talking. Jack was glad she chose to confide in him, he was a good young man. Her aunt was not so sure, her protectiveness kicked in worrying about whom he might tell. Jack only ignored thinking that it would be fine. It was a good evening one that was long overdue. She had her friend back, her confidence, her peace of sanity. She hadn't felt that in a long time, she couldn't remember if she ever had sanity, really. As she bid Jacob good night, she promised to bring him something special from Alaska, he was pleased. He didn't want this moment to end but he knew in his heart this was a good beginning. He was happy for her, delighted she had a goal. The home she wanted to open was fantastic in his mind. He could see her doing this and being very successful. Maybe in time she would trust him a little more, let him in to her life a little more. Good things come to those that wait. That was one thing Jacob had, a lot of time especially if it was for Katie Lee.

Many wonderful things happened on that trip to Alaska. Katie Lee, her aunt and her uncle met a writer. Adding to her therapy, she was able to tell her story and live a positive life. She visited seven different cities and six different Native American villages. If time can bring you any close to someone, this trip brought her a bond with the two people that took a chance on her, closer than most people have the privilege of knowing. She converses with Ellen on a regular basis carefully, Unfortunately, Mary's murder to this day still remains unsolved. Katie Lee continues to pray that one day they will find it in their hearts to acknowledge their mistake, put their pride aside and reopen this case. The only other sadness she suffered was never knowing what happened to the Paddocks; all she can remember was the white house, the pastures, the creek and two adorable elderly people. She spends a lot of time on the phone with Vera and Davie. She made plans to visit at Easter the next year. She was humble to know Allie had requested she come for Mary's Mass each year she can make it.

Katie Lee went on to college and opened her home. Her aunt and uncle were there for the grand opening as well as Mr. Moorehead, Dr. Badea, Nancy and her mother. Many of her classmates came to support her project, especially Jacob who completed his business management degree. Her success has been awesome still today, as well as Jacob who now owns three hardware stores and the ice cream shop. She lives for her students, she lives for their lives to prosper. She is known as mom, grandmother, aunt and sometimes a saint. Whichever they chose to call her is a special gift she cherishes. She is humble and gentle. She

Pacific Redwood Mystery: Do you believe in the little people yet?

thinks of Peter each evening when she stands on her patio facing the open beach. As the waves whip in around the bottom of her landing, she send him messages through the wings of the doves as they come to her bird bath she made for them. She knows he hears her, she can tell. Often she visits the giant redwoods, she knows Mary is near.

She can hear the ruffle of the ferns as the mist softly falls upon their beautiful larger leafs. She hears the little people as they hustled to the very top of those giant redwoods. The best of all, she knows happiness, the happiness Peter worked so hard to see she achieved. She is blessed, she is complete. As she tucks her precious boys to bed each night, she is more thankful for her life. If one listened close, once can always hear her say good night to her babies, Litter Peter and Jacob Jr. Together walking down her own stairs hand in hand with her beloved husband, the man who believed in fairy tales, the boy who believed in her from having a life time crush from long ago and running down the halls of Westland Redwood High School. Jacob sighs as he whispers to himself. "My Katie Lee and I am hers forever." Always friend, now lovers and mates until life passed them through to eternity. So far now join Katie Lee in the greatest belief of fantasy.

The little people know you are there, but remain in silence. Just remember it is okay to believe in them. Mary did and then Katie Lee. Katie Lee smiles to herself knowing her stepsister is playing somewhere deep in the forest or near the ocean in the wet sand. Whether it is the whistles from the giant redwoods or those white caps hurling in around the sand. Mary left her small prints to whisper her message through time.

"DO YOU BELIEVE IN THE LITTLE PEOPLE YET?"

www.ingramcontent.com/pod-product-compliance
Lightning Source LLC
LaVergne TN
LVHW091532060526
838200LV00036B/582